BUR
DEEP

SUSAN WILKINS
BURIED DEEP

bookouture

Published by Bookouture in 2020

An imprint of Storyfire Ltd.
Carmelite House
50 Victoria Embankment
London EC4Y 0DZ

www.bookouture.com

Copyright © Susan Wilkins, 2020

Susan Wilkins has asserted her right to be identified
as the author of this work.

All rights reserved. No part of this publication may be reproduced,
stored in any retrieval system, or transmitted, in any form or by
any means, electronic, mechanical, photocopying, recording or
otherwise, without the prior written permission of the publishers.

ISBN: 978-1-83888-518-2
eBook ISBN: 978-1-83888-517-5

This book is a work of fiction. Names, characters, businesses,
organizations, places and events other than those clearly in the
public domain, are either the product of the author's imagination
or are used fictitiously. Any resemblance to actual persons, living or
dead, events or locales is entirely coincidental.

For Sue Kenyon, who makes it all possible.

PROLOGUE

She knows she'll die here. She knew it early on. Alone. In the dark. In a damp London cellar with a century and a half of coal dust weeping from every brick. How long does it take to realise the truth, to accept it? Bound tightly, round and round, the heavy-duty plastic tape biting into the flesh of her calves, her thighs, her arms, pinching her face.

Hours slide into days. She loses track.

He didn't blindfold her and she knows why. He wants her to see the rats. They come and go. Always scurrying, the scratch of their claws as they scamper along the beams above her head. Moving ever closer, whiskers twitching. She kicks them away. She knows they're biding their time. Waiting for her to lose consciousness. To become meat.

She always knew a time would come when she'd be waiting for death but didn't expect it to be so soon. She's stopped being thirsty. Dying from dehydration can take ten days or more. It might not be so bad – or is she fooling herself?

She waits. There's no choice. Random memories float into her head. Jumping out of a taxi and trying to run in stupid shoes when she was late for her sister's wedding. That one little teddy bear with a torn ear she had as a child.

He won't come back, she's sure of that. So the grate of the door bolt startles her. He comes thumping down the wooden stairs, which creak under his weight. The coal cellar is narrow and low-ceilinged, forcing him to stoop. Her eyes are adjusted to the gloom; the brightness exploding from the open door above is blinding. He squats in front of her. She hears his breath, feels the warmth of his body.

'I still can't get my head round it,' he says. 'Was it always just a pack of lies?'

Her mouth is sealed shut, there's no way of replying.

The light from the hallway above falls across his face. He seems more sorrowful than angry.

'I've got to kill you, you know that, don't you? I got no choice. You left me no choice.'

Her jaw is tightly taped. The only sound she can manage is a low pleading growl in her throat.

He shakes his head. 'Nah, the gag stays on. I know you. You're not going to fool me again with your she-devil stuff.'

In his hand he has a small kitchen knife. The blade will be razor sharp. Men like him don't go in for zombie knives or machetes. It's a question of professional pride.

Her arms are pinioned at her side, the tape goes round her elbows and torso. He grabs her hand, twists it round to expose the wrist. So that's his plan: slash her wrists, let her bleed out. There's a kindness in that.

But he lays the steel tip on her forearm in the soft flesh above the wrist. He's toying with her, teasing. Perhaps he thinks she deserves no better.

The blade is as keen as she predicted. There's a small sting as it breaks the skin. She imagines the blood bubbling up although she can't see it. He lifts the knife and makes a second cut at right angles. He's carved a cross on her forearm.

With a sour chuckle, he says, 'X marks the spot.'

Maybe it's his idea of humour. Or torture. He wants to ramp up the fear. But she's curiously calm.

As he raises the knife, light from the hallway above glints on the metal. Now she knows she'll never be returning to the world above, to the light.

She feels the honed point against the side of her neck just below the ear. If he slashes her carotid artery it will be quick.

'You broke my heart, you bitch. You know that, don't you?' His voice cracks.

Yes, she knows. He's right. She broke her own heart too. If only she could tell him that.

CHAPTER ONE

Monday, 7.15am

Grey dawn light seeps through the veil of mist over the bay. There's an offshore breeze which sends a ripple back across the crest of each small wave. The gulls are roosting in gaggles on a shoulder of hard sand. The adults, heads and beaks nestled in their folded wings, hardly stir as Megan passes. The season's babies, now gangly teenagers, as large as their parents but with mottled brown feathers, strut and squawk in hope of food.

As she reaches the edge of the lapping water her bare feet sink into the sand. The first touch of the sea is icy as she wades in. The green seaweed tickles her ankles but she doesn't care. She'd resisted at first – it seemed a crazy idea – but now this is her essential morning ritual. Her skin gooses up as she ploughs in and, thigh deep, she throws herself forward in a gentle splash and starts to swim.

The shock of it is the thrill. She's so far ignored the advice to get a wetsuit, although she does wear a cap to protect her hair. Swimming an easy breaststroke, she heads out into the bay. The tide is ebbing, exposing browny-green seaweed-encrusted rocks to her left below the imposing red cliffs.

Some mornings the tide is high, leaving only the narrowest ribbon of beach. These are the days she prefers. If it's not rough, the fullness of the bay, the shimmering depth of water, creates an eerie serenity. She rarely sees another soul – the odd dog-walker, but she's usually too early even for them.

As her body glides along, her mind empties. Her face dips in and out of the water. She tastes brine and glimpses the mysterious world below, then the vast sky, looming cliffs and tree-lined shore above. The sea cradles her, reminding some ancient part of her brain that this is where we all began.

She rolls on to her back to gaze up at the whited-out sky. Rain is forecast but that doesn't bother her. She slides into a relaxed sidestroke and slips along without too much effort.

Suddenly, bobbing in the water ahead of her, she sees a large object. A plastic bin bag? My God, a floating corpse? The front portion of it rises and she finds herself staring into two mournful black eyes. A huge Atlantic grey bull seal. He leans his head back to consider her. His nostrils flare, whiskers twitching. He seems to be wondering if she's a competitor for his breakfast, decides she's not and sinks away out of sight.

Her heart soars with sheer joy. She swims back to shore, wades out of the water and runs up the beach.

Detective Sergeant Megan Thomas sits in the low-slung armchair, arms folded, legs crossed. She's well aware the posture is defensive but she doesn't care. In the opposite chair Doctor Diane Moretti smooths her checked jersey pencil skirt with both palms and smiles.

'Well then,' she says, 'how's it all been going?'

Megan considers the stupidity of the question. Moretti has a slew of qualifications and whatever she charges for exactly fifty-five minutes of her time is not going to be cheap. But at least Megan isn't paying. Devon and Cornwall Police are footing the bill. And Moretti is definitely not a run-of-the-mill therapist dispensing a few cognitive behavioural tricks to burnt-out cops. She's a full-blown shrink, or consultant psychiatrist, as it says on the door. Megan doesn't know whether to be flattered or worried. Her new boss, Detective Superintendent Rob Barker, has made it a condition of her transfer from the Met that she 'sees someone'.

So she returns Moretti's smile and says, 'Fine.'

The doctor tilts her head. 'And how's the swimming going?'

'Yeah, it's okay.'

Okay. When Moretti had suggested to her that she take up swimming as a way to manage her moods, she'd thought it was a joke. Wild swimming, a pastime for weirdos, she'd read about it in the Sunday supplements. The shrink had thrown some statistics at her; its efficacy in the treatment of depression is well-documented. But Megan didn't think she was depressed.

She'd started in the summer when she first arrived in Devon, which made it easier. Now she was a total addict but she wasn't about to admit it to Moretti.

'And how are you sleeping? Any better?'

'Bloody seagulls still keep me awake.'

'They take some getting used to. Your sister's place is in Berrycombe?'

Megan nods. 'Overlooks the harbour. Nice view.'

Moretti grins. 'And lots of gulls.'

Polite foreplay. The first ten minutes of every session are like this. Then they lapse into silence.

Megan scans Moretti's expression. If she encountered it in an interview room she'd say the woman was over-confident bordering on smug. Aged around fifty. Expensive haircut but no attempt to eradicate the grey. Her clothes are the usual professional woman's kit in fifty shades of beige. Sensible shoes.

'Where do you live?' Megan asks.

'As I've said before, Megan, this is not about me.'

'Yeah, yeah, you ask the questions.'

'If that's all right.'

'Do I have a choice?'

Moretti laces her fingers, this time her head tilts the other way.

'Post-traumatic stress disorder is a serious diagnosis,' she says.

'Tell me about it. Isn't that why you've got me up at the crack of dawn every day freezing my arse off in the sea?'

'If you don't want to take medication it's a good alternative.'

'*You* don't have to do it.'

The doctor smiles. 'The notes I have from your London doctor suggest that you don't accept PTSD is an accurate diagnosis in your case.'

'No, I accept it. I just don't see the point of labels. I don't think they help.'

Moretti keeps on smiling. She has the kind of fey, one-sided lip curl that could become really annoying really quickly. Megan reminds herself that she wasn't going to let this get to her. Show up, sit there, go through the motions, box ticked. And swim. That was the plan. She takes a deep breath to calm herself.

'Well, in your view, what would help?' Moretti asks.

'Who the hell knows?' It comes out with a huff which is not Megan's intention. 'You get on with it, don't you? What doesn't kill you makes you stronger and all that crap.'

'That's not necessarily crap. A sense that you've survived against the odds can be life-enhancing.'

'Good. I'll take that.'

'I get the impression that you resent having to come here, Megan. You regard it as an imposition.'

'That's because it is. I told you, my old London boss and Superintendent Barker are mates. And they made a deal. Barker would take a chance on me if I agreed to continue seeing a shrink. It was that or retirement on medical grounds. And I'm forty-two. I've been a police officer since I was nineteen. I don't know what the hell else I'd do.'

'Is he taking a chance?'

Megan shrugs. 'Okay, look, I'm not very good at spilling my guts to order. But I'm not stupid. And I'm not a child. I know it's your job to help me. And I'm taking your advice, doing the swimming. I don't know what else you expect.' She heaves a sigh, uncrosses and recrosses her legs. Spiteful thoughts niggle at her. *'This is not about me.' Patronising cow.*

'I do understand,' says Moretti. 'You think that to need this kind of help is weak. But if you'd broken your leg, say, would you have objected to a surgeon fixing it?'

'Well, yeah, that would be easier. And it doesn't make sense. I get it. But head stuff is different, isn't it?'

'I don't think body and mind are separate. Trauma affects the whole person. I've treated combat veterans and I can tell you that the guy who gets his leg blown off often copes better than the one without a scratch on him.'

Megan inhales. 'Yeah, but it's obvious what's happened to him.'

'Do you feel a fraud because there's no visible proof of your injury?'

Unfolding her arms, Megan considers this. What she feels she can't describe. Shame? The shame of failure? The embarrassment of success. The secret fear of being found out. These conflicting emotions writhe in her brain like snakes.

Moretti seems to read her mind. 'You were awarded the Queen's Police Medal. That's pretty impressive.'

'A gong is a gong. I just did my job. It's no big deal.'

Megan breaks eye contact and stares out of the window. There's not much to see. Brick wall, grey sky, a ragged buddleia. The ceremony was a big deal. Togged up in a brand new dress uniform, she received her medal from the Commissioner in person. It felt uncomfortable and surreal; out of the whole team she was singled out. She hated that. She wanted to crawl into a hole and hide. Afterwards they all went out and got roaring drunk.

CHAPTER TWO

Monday, 9.30am

The A38 Devon Expressway down to Plymouth scoots round the southern flank of Dartmoor. As a Londoner born and bred, Megan's still getting used to the landscape. She's also getting used to driving a hybrid car. It's small and bright blue – not her choice – and cruises along like an electric lawnmower. The petrolhead in Megan hates it. The last car she owned before this was a growler, an old Subaru with a top speed that was totally illegal. She loved it, the risk, the rush. But this is her new, healthier, country life. It's better for the planet. *And it's better for me*, she tells herself, even though she doesn't believe it.

The moors rise up and disappear into a curtain of mist. The autumn fields are a patchwork of muted greens and ochres with occasional farm tracks, tramlines of raw red earth wandering over the hillside. Sheep and trees haven't really featured that much in Megan's life, now they're everywhere. Holidays are one thing, but actually living in a place where nature seems more in charge is unnerving. It's hard to take it all in. Her eyes flick from the road ahead to the sweep of hills. She knows it's going to take some getting used to. But that's the least of it.

The office is still in the temporary accommodation that the CID detectives moved into five years ago in response to the cuts. Police stations in prime locations had to be sold off to balance the budget. The Major Crime Team for South Devon operates from an upstairs suite in a small industrial park on the outskirts of Plymouth. Megan weaves her way round lorries unloading pallets and double-parked delivery vans to find a tiny slot in the pocked concrete car park assigned to the MCT. It's about the only advantage of having a toy car, as far as she can see.

As she walks in, the morning briefing is already in progress. Detective Chief Inspector Laura Slater pauses mid-sentence, registers her new sergeant's late arrival, and continues. 'And that means I'll need all outstanding documents for the file which will go to the Crown Prosecution Service on Friday.'

Megan has met Laura Slater twice, at the interview and during her three-day induction the previous week. Quiet but expensive clothes, blonde hair pulled back in a neat coil, Slater looks more like a lawyer than a cop and rumour has it she thinks like one.

The briefing room is too small for its purpose and contains a random selection of chairs and spare desks. Eight officers are variously sitting and perching in a semi-circle around the DCI at the front.

Vish Prasad, one of two detective constables recently promoted from uniform, jumps up and offers Megan his chair. Tall, with his jet-black hair shaved at the back and sides and a neat Van Dyke beard, he looks like a prince in a Bollywood movie. He smiles at Megan, she smiles back and accepts the seat. He's so young and unscathed and beautiful; she feels a pang of envy.

'Next up,' says Slater, 'everyone's favourite. A body has been discovered in a septic tank.'

A collective groan rolls round the room.

'For the benefit of our new colleague Megan,' – Slater gives her a nod – 'I should explain that in the more rural parts of our patch, mains drainage is rare and septic tanks are common. Bodies found in them are—'

'Covered in shit, yeah I get it, boss.' Megan folds her arms and gives Slater a tepid smile.

Slater turns to the other DS on the squad. Ted Jennings is munching his way through a large squidgy apricot Danish. 'Ted,' she says. 'Are you with us?'

Dusting pastry flakes and glaze from his chin, he beams. 'Yes, ma'am. Of course.'

Ted looks like a clone of all the paunchy, balding, middle-aged white blokes who have occupied every squad room Megan has entered in the course of her career. Some turn out to be ultra-smart geniuses behind the façade of a badly pressed suit. Others are just lazy sods sitting it out for their pension. Megan knows that the answer to the DCI's next question will clarify which species Ted belongs to.

'Could you go and take a look.'

'I would, boss,' he replies. 'But my tooth's been playing up again and I've finally got an appointment for a root canal this morning. Pain's been awful.'

'Luckily it doesn't stop you eating,' says the DCI drily.

'I try and chew on the other side,' he replies.

Megan scans the room. Vish and the other new DC, Brittney Saric, are alert and waiting for action like two puppies. A civilian analyst is checking her phone under the desk. Three uniforms on secondment are trying to look interested and another middle-aged, balding DC, sitting at the back, is taking copious notes. Or doodling. Hard to tell.

The team is missing its DI, who is on long term sick leave, Slater explained during Megan's induction. No one has been brought in to cover.

The DCI turns to Megan and sighs. 'Well,' she says, 'in at the deep end, I suppose. Hope you don't mind.'

The DCs smirk. The boss is a little too buttoned-up to do humour but Megan realises this is her attempt at a joke.

Megan smiles. 'Yeah, no problem. You want me to look first then call CSI or give them a heads-up now?'

'Probably make them aware,' Slater replies. 'People rarely end up in septic tanks by accident.'

'Okay.' Megan stands up and heads for the door.

'Vish or Brittney can go with you.'

This stops Megan in her tracks. Yet another thing she's not used to any more, working with a team.

The two DCs scramble to their feet. Brittney grabs her bag, Vish drops his phone. The new DS is from the Met and therefore they are in total awe.

Slater gives them a sardonic look, sighs and turns to Megan. 'Which one do you want?'

The pool car is a new Škoda. Vish drives, Megan sits beside him. Brittney is crammed in the back. Choosing between the two eager beavers proved impossible. Megan simply shrugged, it was Slater who decided that both the rookie DCs would benefit from the experience. Megan isn't sure she will. She prefers to work alone.

Vish drives like many twenty-somethings, foot hard on the gas pedal, braking sharply, then back on the gas as he taps out some interior tune on the steering wheel.

Megan glances at him, she finds his pent-up energy wearing. 'You're not on response now,' she says. 'Let's get there in one piece.'

'Sorry, skip,' he replies.

'Skip? What am I, your dog?'

'Isn't that what you call a sergeant in the Met? Skipper?'

'Not any time in the last fifty years.'

'Sorry, boss.'

'The DCI's the boss, I'm Megan. Okay?'

In the back, Brittney appears to be enjoying the exchange. She's a tubby girl with glasses that make her look like an owl. She's older than him, around thirty; she clearly assumes this gives her seniority.

'His actual name's Vishwajeet,' she says.

Megan smiles. 'Bet that was fun at school.'

He shrugs. 'Nah, mostly they just called me "Paki". They found it easier.'

'Better than "Miss Piggy",' says Brittney with some feeling.

They turn off the main road up a narrow lane and a steep hill running on to the moor. The hedgerows are set on high banks, known as Devon banks, which turn the road almost into a tunnel. It's mainly single track with passing places and the hedges make it impossible to see anything of the surrounding countryside.

A soft haze of rain is falling and as they emerge from the tunnel and on to the open moor the hillside disappears in a blanket of white. The car clanks over a cattle grid.

'Do you know where you're going?' Megan asks.

'Not really,' Vish replies. 'I just put the postcode in the satnav.'

'Postcodes are crap round here,' says Brittney. 'Same one can cover miles.'

'That's encouraging,' says Megan. She clicks her phone on and stares at it. 'I don't appear to have a signal.'

'You won't. Not up here.' Brittney seems to enjoy being the prophet of doom.

Megan sighs. 'Do either one of you actually know the patch?'

Vish shakes his head. 'I'm from Bristol. Only been down here two weeks.'

'I grew up in Bournemouth,' says Brittney. 'Had a spell in uniform in Exeter but that's different.' She chuckles. 'Bit of a change from London, eh, Megan?'

'Somewhat.'

A complete change from life as she's known it, Megan reflects. But is that a bad thing? The jury's still out. She spent the last five years in a netherworld of lies and pretence. That's what it means to be an undercover officer. And that's one thing she won't miss. She wants to return to normality, that's what she said at the interview. But what that even looks like, she's not sure she knows.

They drive on for half a mile into the veil of misty rain.

'It should be round here somewhere,' Vish announces. He points to the map on the satnav.

Suddenly two Greyface Dartmoor sheep skip out of the murk and make a dash for it across the road.

'I think we're lost,' says Brittney.

Megan sighs again. 'What's this place called?'

'Winterbrook Farm,' Vish replies. 'Maybe there'll be a track and a sign.'

'What if there isn't?' says Brittney.

'Okay,' says Megan. 'Next person or house, stop.'

They continue in silence until an off-road car park looms into sight. The neat square of stone chippings is surrounded by large boulders with a National Park information board at the entrance.

Vish pulls in. There are several cars, a small cluster of Dartmoor ponies browsing the nearby grass and a lonely ice cream van.

Megan gets out. She pulls her hood up. The jacket is new, waterproof and outdoorsy. She can't remember ever having owned such a garment before.

As she strolls over to the ice cream van, the driver gets up and opens the hatch. 'Nice day for a walk,' he says with a grin.

'Not really,' Megan replies.

'Oh it'll pick up. Sunny by lunchtime.'

'I'm looking for Winterbrook Farm.'

'You a fan then? Not sure I should say. She gets a lot of hassle.'

Megan gives him a quizzical look. 'I beg your pardon?'

'Georgia likes her privacy. Even though it's a while since she was on the telly, people still come.'

Megan pulls out her warrant card and holds it up. 'She's expecting me.'

He raises his eyebrows. 'Oh, I see. Well, there's no sign. But there's a track on your left. About a hundred yards down the road.' He points back in the direction they've come. 'Is it a stalker then?'

'Something like that. Who on earth buys ice cream on a day like this?'

'Loads of people. Walkers. Cyclists especially. Just had a minibus of Germans. Do you want one?'

CHAPTER THREE

Monday, 11.23am

The small dormer window is set into the sloping slate roof. Shirin has been staring out of it for most of the morning. The rain hasn't let up and the hillside opposite remains shrouded in a pall of cloud.

Her eyes float back to the computer screen. Getting on with work seems the best distraction but it's not going well. She stands up, interlocks her fingers behind her head and stretches.

The attic room is carpeted and cosy. It's kitted out as an office but it's also become her sanctuary. Being at the top of a narrow winding stairway gives her the privacy she craves. Mostly.

She looks out of the window again. Across the yard and down the hill the workmen are sheltering from the weather under a makeshift tarpaulin and sharing mugs of coffee from a flask. She wonders what she should do and concludes, for about the twentieth time that morning, the best thing is to do nothing. Until she can figure out what's going on.

The farmhouse is old, with thick walls of stone like a castle. When Shirin first arrived it had felt a strange and alien place. But now it's a second home, as far removed from the tower block in South London where she grew up as she could get.

As she's about to go back to work she hears a footfall on the stairs. She feels her irritation rising. *Now what?*

The door is flung open and Georgia O'Brien appears on the threshold in full Valkyrie mode. She's a large woman with a crinkly grey mane and an opera singer's bust. She's also Shirin's employer.

'This is bloody, bloody, *bloody* ridiculous!' she says in a booming contralto. 'Why is this happening? Why did we need anyone to look at the tank?'

Shirin shrugs her shoulders. 'I had to call them. The tank's fractured. It had to be dug out. There was no alternative.'

'It's been fine until now.'

'Well, now it's not fine. It's leaking. Badly. Polluting the stream.'

'You've done this deliberately, haven't you? And you deliberately didn't tell me. Yet another cunning little plan of yours to put the screws on me.' The spiteful comment surprises Shirin.

'Georgia, that is ridiculous and you know it. I just didn't want to bother you. I had no idea about this. Obviously I didn't. Calm down. Take a Xanax.'

The older woman stares at her, nostrils flaring, looking, Shirin thinks, remarkably like a horse. Or perhaps an angry donkey. She's learnt from experience that reading too much into Georgia's overblown manner is a mistake. It's all a performance. Usually. But today she seems genuinely rattled.

The delicacy of the situation was obvious to Shirin as soon as the workman came knocking on the door early this morning and said they'd found a body. It would be easy to panic.

Georgia flops down in Shirin's desk chair, bracelets jangling against the arm rest. 'Well, what are we going to do?' she says.

'Nothing.'

'When they arrive, what are we going to say to them?'

'Nothing.'

Georgia puffs out her cheeks in an exaggerated sigh. When she's upset, she morphs into an overgrown teenager.

Shirin scans her.

'Georgia' she says. 'Do you know something I don't? Like the identity of this corpse?'

'No,' Georgia replies. 'Course not. It could've been there for years. In fact, that's the most likely explanation.'

Georgia fidgets and looks away. *Is she lying?* wonders Shirin. It's impossible to tell.

There was a time when her employer's imperious manner intimidated her. But those days are long gone. The thirty-year age gap doesn't matter any more. They're both well aware who's really in charge. Shirin stands by the window, hands neatly folded in front of her. Somehow she has to get off the back foot and get ahead of this.

Georgia twizzles in the chair. 'You called the contractors. This is your mess, Shirin, you deal with it. I shall stay in my room.'

'Okay,' she says. *Probably best if Georgia does stay out of it.*

Shirin sees a car driving into the yard. She reminds herself that it's only necessary to keep her nerve. She has her own private fear: that this is a ploy to put the screws on *her*. But she's not going to think about that now.

'Looks like they're here,' she says calmly.

Georgia is on her feet immediately. She peers over Shirin's shoulder, she can't resist.

An anonymous-looking hatchback stops in the yard. No flashing lights or police sirens. The passenger door opens and a woman gets out. She has mousy hair and is tall and slim but with a defensive stoop to the shoulders. The driver and backseat passenger join her. They seem younger: a fit Asian guy and a fat girl.

'They're a bunch,' says Georgia. 'Don't look much like proper police to me. Do you think they know what they're doing?'

Shirin watches. The woman is looking up at the house, taking her time. Her gaze is steady and unnerving.

'Let's hope not,' says Shirin.

CHAPTER FOUR

Monday, 11.26am

Megan scans the front of the building. It was probably once a working farm but the yard is now set with pristine cobbles, the walls are brightly whitewashed and tubs of mauve winter pansies sit along the front wall. Even in the rain there's little in the way of mud. The main house is low and long, and behind it, the hillside rises steeply up to the moor. The land in front of the property falls away as sharply down to a small stream. A mechanical digger is precariously perched several hundred metres away down the hill, a mound of earth beside it; this is obviously the location of the tank.

'Posh gaff,' says Vish with an appreciative nod. 'Bet there's a hell of a view on a nice day.'

'Creepy, living in the middle of nowhere though,' says Brittney.

'Who reported this?' Megan asks.

Vish opens his notebook. 'Tony Wilson. Runs a local plumbing firm that specialises in septic tanks.'

'Not the owner of the property then? Let's see if anyone's home.' Stepping up to the front door, Megan lifts the brass knocker and raps. The heavy oak door shudders. 'Vish, go and see if you can find Mr Wilson.'

In her head Megan counts to twenty-five before the door opens. She holds up her warrant card and smiles. 'Detective Sergeant Thomas. Are you the owner of the property?'

The young woman in front of her is slight and dark. Her glossy hair is pulled back into a ponytail. It would be easy to mistake her for a teenager. She shakes her head, her voice soft and deferential. 'Oh no, I'm Shirin Khan. I just work for Miss O'Brien.'

'Is your employer at home?'

'I'm afraid she's gone to London on business.'

'May we come in?'

The young woman dips her head and steps back for them to enter. The hallway has a flagstone floor covered with several multi-coloured rugs. It smells of cleaning fluid. Is Shirin the skivvy? She's giving that impression. Megan notes her avoidance of eye contact.

Shirin opens the door to an adjacent room and stands aside for them to go through. The ceiling isn't high but the room is spacious. The furniture is either antique or passable reproductions. Expensive, but not to Megan's taste.

She turns to face the girl. 'Has Mr Wilson told you of his discovery?'

Shirin nods. 'The body, yes. Really awful.'

'Has Miss O'Brien been made aware—'

Megan doesn't get a chance to finish. The door swings open and Georgia sweeps into the room. 'I am so, so sorry,' she says. 'The truth is, I was so shocked I couldn't face anyone. Poor Shirin—'

Shirin is giving her a murderous look. *The mouse just roared*, Megan notes with interest.

'I told her to make an excuse. Not a deliberate lie, really. Only a tiny one. I do hope you can forgive me, Sergeant.'

'I'll try,' says Megan equably.

Brittney is gazing at Georgia, saucer-eyed. 'Wow! It really is you,' she says. 'My nan is absolutely your biggest fan. She's got all the box sets of *One Fine Day*. When I was a kid we were glued to it every Sunday night.'

'That is gratifying,' says Georgia. 'Thank you so much.'

To Megan's ear it sounds completely insincere but Brittney seems pleased.

'Well,' says Megan emphatically. 'In the course of the excavation of your septic tank, a body has been discovered. That's why we're here. We will need to look into the matter further. So, obviously, your contractors will have to stop work and we may need to bring in additional officers.'

'Will it take long?' Georgia asks with an earnest frown.

'At this point I couldn't say. How long have you lived here, Miss O'Brien?'

'Only five years. But I have to say that I bought the place from a very strange fellow. Rumours about him were rife.'

'Rumours of what?'

'Well, quite unpleasant things.'

Megan is increasingly aware of the tension pulsing off Shirin. The girl shifts from foot to foot.

But Georgia is in full flood. She strolls around the room as she speaks, using it as a stage. 'I had the house redone when I moved in. He had dogs. It's not a dog, is it? Well, anyway, the surveyor did say the tank was all right.'

'Do you know if he examined it?'

Georgia huffs. 'Who knows? Probably not.' Her face relaxes into a regal smile. 'But anything we can do to help, Sergeant. Absolutely anything, just ask. Can Shirin make you and your colleagues some tea?'

Megan and Brittney walk away from the house across the cobbled yard. Once they're out of earshot Megan says, 'What do you make of that?'

'She's awesome,' says Brittney. 'My nan'll go mental when she hears I've actually met Georgia O'Brien.'

Megan gives her a side-eyed glance. 'That's your analysis?'

'Not exactly,' says the DC defensively. 'She was just like her character. The voice, the manner.'

'Her character?'

'In *One Fine Day*. She played Mrs Tweedie, who's sort of the lady of the manor, but she helps people and she has magic powers.'

'You're saying she was acting?'

'Yeah. Completely. And the girl, Shirin, was really pissed off that Georgia was doing her number. Loads of tension between them. Definitely covering something up.'

Megan gives her a nod. 'Okay. Good. Let's see what the body can tell us.'

The contractor's vehicles have created a track across the grass and down the hill. But it's steep and slippery.

Megan strides down it. She's out on Dartmoor, in the rain, on her first case. But she's back to being an ordinary copper again. Through many sleepless nights she's worried about this moment and whether she could still hack it. In the event, she thinks, it's really not that complicated. Investigation is a process, you go through the stages, ask the questions, gather the evidence. She's starting to believe that she can do this. Her new jacket is keeping her dry and she feels almost cheerful in spite of the weather.

There's a thud behind her.

'Aww, shit!' Brittney has slipped and landed on her bottom.

Megan turns. 'You all right?' She offers a hand and hauls the DC to her feet.

'I just bought these bloody shoes,' says Brittney peevishly, 'to smarten myself up. But they're total crap. No grip.'

Megan chuckles and shakes her head. 'You're not hurt?'

'No. Just my pride.'

They continue down the hill at a more sedate pace.

Her morning swim, now this. Megan can't think of another time recently when she's felt such lightness in her life. Is this how normal people feel? It's hard to remember. But it feels like a gift.

CHAPTER FIVE

Monday, 11.40am

At the bottom of the hill near the stream the contractor's men have slung a tarpaulin between two trees to create a shelter. Vish is under it and he's squatting down to talk to a small boy. The child has an unruly mop of curly black hair, a yellow waterproof and matching duck wellies. He looks to be around four years old and his attention is focused on the biscuit he's eating.

As Megan and Brittney approach, Vish stands up. 'Meet my new friend, Noah,' he says. The child stares up at them.

'Where's he come from?' says Megan.

'Apparently he lives in the house. But according to Tony Wilson, he's left pretty much to his own devices. Wanders around the place on his own all day. The lads have been giving him biscuits.' Vish pats the boy's head. 'What's your favourite biscuit, Noah?'

Noah scans the circle of adults that surround him as he considers the question. Finally he says, 'Chocolate.'

'Me too, mate,' says Vish. 'No contest.'

'My daddy brings me Haribos,' says the boy.

'Does he?' says Vish. 'When does he do that?'

Noah ponders for a moment then shrugs.

'When was the last time?'

'Dunno.'

'Daddy doesn't live here then?' says Vish.

The child shakes his head.

'But he comes to visit?'

'He brings me Haribos.'

A figure appears at the top of the hill. It's Shirin.

She bellows, 'Noah!'

'Is that your mummy?' says Brittney.

Ignoring her, the boy turns and runs up the hill.

'This gets more and more interesting,' says Megan. 'Okay. Have you looked at the body yet?'

Vish shakes his head. 'Apparently it's down in the tank, sort of wedged or something. They've pumped some of the stuff out into the tanker over there, trying to get a proper look at it.'

'Stuff? Is that a technical term, Vish?' Brittney smirks at him.

'I dunno. Effluent? Shit? Whatever?'

'Okay, don't squabble,' says Megan. 'Whatever they're doing they need to stop so CSI can take over.'

'We're treating the death as suspicious, then?' says Vish.

Megan nods. 'I need to look but yeah.'

They walk down to where the tank is buried in the hillside.

Tony Wilson, in a beanie hat and high-viz jacket, is standing with hands on hips, staring down into a rectangular cavity a couple of feet across. A flexible hose, about six inches in diameter, disappears down into the hole. The other end snakes through the grass to a small tanker lorry. A second workman leans on the lorry, manning the suction lever. A third man, wearing a hard hat and face mask, is lying on his stomach across the concrete apron that surrounds the hatch to the tank and shining a torch down into it.

'Morning,' says Megan. 'I'm DS Thomas.'

Wilson grins. He's large and barrel-chested with the wrinkled, tanned face of a man who works outdoors. 'Tony Wilson,' he says. 'Probably best if I don't shake your hand.'

'You're convinced this is a body? A human corpse?'

He puffs out his chest as if this is a challenge. 'I been in this game thirty years, love, and it's not the first time. Soon as we got the hatch off you could tell there was a different smell.'

'How much can you see? Is it a skeleton?'

'We think maybe there's still a bit of flesh on it. We've just been trying to get a better look. Trouble is, we're all a bit big to get our heads right down the hole. And I don't wanna get my digger and take the top off and mess up your nice crime scene for you, do I?'

Megan smiles politely. 'That's very considerate.'

'Not a nice job for your crime scene forensic bods. You called them, have you? Cause if they need help we could come to an arrangement. We're a lot cheaper than some of these specialist outfits. Save the public purse a few quid, everyone wins.'

Megan looks at him. He has a smug grin as if he knows something she doesn't. Shutting the job down will certainly cost him money, so is he just hoping to mitigate his loss? Or is this a scam? They've found something in the tank and he hopes to double his money maybe, working for the police, who'll have to identify it, as well as replacing the tank.

The job has been flagged to CSI but they're still waiting for confirmation from Megan. Slater will hardly thank her if on her first outing she rolls out the whole circus and it turns out to be an expensive false alarm. On the other side of the coin, there's the suspicious behaviour of the women in the house. But they could just be innocent weirdos freaked out by a visit from the police.

There's only one answer. Megan takes a deep breath. 'Right, well, I'm probably narrow enough across the shoulders to take a look.'

'Oh, I wouldn't recommend it, love,' says Wilson. 'Not a job for a lady.'

She meets his gaze. How many times in her life has some patronising bloke fed her that line? Now her mind's made up.

'I've got a strong stomach,' she says. 'Have you got another face mask?'

'I could give it a go,' says Vish.

Megan looks at him. Well over six foot and broad shoulders. 'You're too big.'

She takes off her new jacket and passes it to Brittney. Wilson pulls a blue surgical mask from his pocket and hands it over. Kneeling down on the muddy concrete beside the hatch, Megan puts the mask on and takes the flashlight. The keyed-up feeling in her gut is familiar. She always used to get that before a big op. If she's honest, she's missed it. That buzz of adrenaline.

With the flashlight in one hand, she lowers her upper body down the hole. Vish hangs on to the back of her legs.

The stench makes her gag slightly but she holds her breath and swings the light in an arc. That's when she sees it. The body – and it is unmistakably a human corpse – is hooked round a side beam. Threads of muscle and sinew still hang on the bones. But what causes her to gasp and her whole body to convulse are the rats feasting on it.

Rats! Of course there are rats!

Pure terror seizes her.

'Get me out! Now!' she screams.

Vish grabs her round the waist and lifts her up and out of the hole. She rips the mask off, collapses on her knees in the wet grass and pukes. Her whole body is shaking. She can't control it. He offers her a tissue to wipe her mouth.

But her head's in a spin, a vice-like grip squeezing her rib cage and forcing the air from her lungs as her chest explodes with pain.

She's going to black out. She gasps. 'My heart—' Is she about to die?

But suddenly Brittney is beside her, gripping her hand. 'Breathe, Megan. Deep breaths!'

It's impossible. The pain rips through her chest. She's having a heart attack.

'You're having a panic attack. Just concentrate on breathing. In and out.'

'It's my heart—' Her voice is a croak.

'No, Megan. You're okay. It's a panic attack. I was a paramedic before I joined the police. I've seen loads. Trust me, just focus on breathing in and out.'

In and out. The air is helping. The pain recedes. She opens her eyes. She's drenched in sweat. But alive. And not back there. Not in that cellar, trussed up, rats scurrying around her. She's lying on wet grass on a hillside in Devon. Fresh rain bathes her face.

CHAPTER SIX

Monday, 11.05pm

Megan sits with a blanket round her shoulders, staring into the darkness. She's on a terrace perched on a hillside overlooking the port of Berrycombe. The sky is black, heavy with cloud and starless. Down below in the harbour lights wink on the rigging of trawlers, on motor cruisers and yachts. In the damp breeze there's the continual clanking of halyards against masts and a sharp smell of seaweed and mud.

The house belongs to Megan's sister, Debbie, and her brother-in-law, Mark. Megan is their lodger. It's part of a long Victorian terrace that traces the contour of the hill, a narrow lane at the front and a vertiginous drop at the back.

The glass door in the lighted room behind her is nudged open and the family dog, Scout, slips out. He nuzzles Megan's hand. She strokes his nose. He's a cross between a Border collie and a Labrador, and is a soft-natured mutt. The kids love him. In the sitting room Debbie can be heard remonstrating with her teenage daughter.

'Amber, just listen to me, will you? It's after eleven and tomorrow's a school day—'

The argument hardly penetrates Megan's consciousness. Her body is cold but it's her mind that's numb. Under the cover of the blanket the index finger of her right hand obsessively traces and retraces the scar on her left forearm. *X marks the spot.*

Scout rests his muzzle on her knee.

Debbie comes through the door carrying a mug of tea. 'Bloody kids! Why will they never be told? She wants everything her way. I know she's fourteen but I don't think we were that bad, were we?'

'Worse,' says Megan.

'You staying out here all night? At least let me get you something to eat.'

Megan looks at her sister and marvels. After all the vicissitudes of their childhood, how did she turn into such a calm and competent person? Three kids, two jobs, nothing seems to faze her.

'Not hungry,' Megan replies. The thought of food makes her feel sick.

Debbie puts the mug down beside her sister and sits on the other plastic chair. 'Meg, lots of people have panic attacks. Okay, it was a shock but—'

'The first job I go on I completely lose my shit. How's this ever going to work? It's not, is it?'

'As I say, it's unnerving. You need to talk to Dr Moretti. She can give you something.'

'I'm not taking pills.'

'Yeah, I know. You don't want antidepressants but this is different.'

'No, it's not.' Megan sighs and shakes her head. 'I can't do this. Today proves it. I'm trying to turn back the clock. But I'm not the same person. Going back to being what I was is impossible. I'm a mess. Look at me.'

'You give up too easily.'

'Oh fuck you, Deb!'

'Swear at me all you like, but it's true.'

Megan catches the look of sorrow in her baby sister's eye and it cuts to the quick. It always has.

She exhales. 'Sorry. You don't deserve that. I'm being a bitch.'

Debbie shrugs. 'This was never going to be the easy option.'

'I know. I just didn't expect to crash and burn on the first day.'

'Well, give yourself a chance to recover. Do you know what triggered it?'

Oh, she knows. A large brown rat, its tail swishing as it slid between the bones. Megan tries to shake the image out of her brain.

'Nothing in particular,' she says. 'I just flipped.'

'I wouldn't want to stick my head in a septic tank. Why did your stupid boss start you off on something like this anyway?'

'No one expected it to be complicated. It's me, I handled it all wrong.'

'I'm sure you didn't.'

'I think I should go and see Barker and say I've made a mistake. It's like a whole new job. They assume I know what I'm doing but I don't.'

Debbie grabs her hand. 'Listen to me, don't do anything in a rush. Wait. See how you feel in a couple of days.'

In the half light Megan notices a tear on her sister's cheek. She reaches across and skims it away with her thumb. 'Oh, Deb, I don't want to cause you any grief.'

'Your grief is my grief and vice versa. Always has been. Neither of us can help that.'

'No.'

Debbie gets up. 'Drink that bloody tea before it gets cold and don't sit out here all night.'

'I'll be okay. Don't worry about me. Scout'll keep me company.'

Debbie kisses the top of her head then goes back into the house.

Megan looks at the scar, the cross he carved on her forearm. The memories of that rat-infested cellar haunt all her dreams. She'd expected to die there. But, against the odds, she'd walked away. Did he suspect she might, is that why he marked her? So she could never forget? He got a life sentence for multiple homicides and drug trafficking with the recommendation he serve a minimum of twenty-seven years. The intelligence she'd gathered and her testimony, given anonymously from behind a screen, helped send him down. She did her job. But it was a totally different job to this.

Where does that leave her now? Ambushed by a panic attack? Will it happen again? There is no way of knowing. Probably.

She runs her fingers through the dog's soft fur. It soothes them both. He shuts his eyes, head resting in her lap.

Picking up the mug of tea, she takes a mouthful. Simple actions in a normal life. That's all she wants now. But if she can't hack it as a detective, she must let go. Today she was a liability, her colleagues had to rescue her. Barker would probably give her a backroom job doing analysis if she asked. But that would involve sitting at a computer all day and she hates being cooped up.

Gazing out across the harbour, she can see light dancing on the ripples of the incoming tide. When she was a child they went to the seaside possibly once. They lived on benefits, had no money for trips. Yet she finds being near the sea compelling. Debbie agrees with her, thinks that back in the gene pool they have Viking blood. And Debbie married a fisherman.

Now that autumn has come, half the cafes and chippies and ice cream shops that fringe the harbour have shut up shop. It's getting late and there are few people about.

The quayside below curves out towards the breakwater. Each of the street lights along the edge creates its own halo of light. Megan can pick out two figures walking along. They move in and out of the pools of light. One, much taller, tugs at the other's arm. He – it's probably a man – is pulling. She, the smaller figure with long hair, keeps moving away. Is it playful? They're too far away for any sound to reach her. They continue walking side by side along the quay. A couple mucking about, teasing each other? Lovers who've had a tiff? At this distance, looking down on them like ants, it's impossible to tell. Yet Megan's curiosity is piqued. Something about it isn't right.

She watches until they disappear. The sharpening chill in the air, the smell of rain, the black, moonless sky all conspire to give her an eerie feeling. Where is it coming from? Is it some vibe from the two passing strangers or is it something inside herself? The dog raises his head and pricks up his ears. Can he feel it too? She's consumed by a sense of dread.

CHAPTER SEVEN

Monday, 11.20pm

Kerry Waycott glances surreptitiously at her phone. She wishes she could video this and put it on Snapchat. Then those bitches at school would be jealous. But he's already told her no. She looks up at him. He's definitely fit but what's the point in hanging out with him in the freezing cold if no one else sees it? She wonders if she could sneak a quick pic without him noticing. But the camera would flash.

They stop at the end of the quay. He slots his hands in his pockets, looks her up and down and smiles.

'So what you wanna do now?' he says.

'Dunno. It's cold.' She has on her shortest skirt, the one her mum really hates.

'Don't be a wuss.'

She giggles. Flicks her blonde hair out of her eyes, tilts her head back and gives him what she hopes is a seductive look.

'Could go on somewhere else for a drink,' she says. 'Maybe a club.' Being seen out with him properly, that would be a coup. If someone else snapped them and posted it he couldn't blame her.

He chuckles. 'A club? On a Monday? You don't wanna drink at your age. Stunts your growth. Bad for your voice too.'

'Alcohol doesn't affect me.'

'Are you sure?' he says. She can feel his eyes on her. Part of her loves being admired but she also feels awkward.

'Fancy going on the beach?' he says.

'What, in these shoes?'

'Take them off.' Something in his tone of voice makes it impossible to refuse. And she doesn't want to upset him.

It's not even that much of a heel but she slips them off and carries them in her right hand. It's a pity, they're cool and cost enough. She used her birthday money from her gran.

The cove is small and stony, set between the outer wall of the breakwater and the rocks. There's less lighting and in her bare feet some of the stones are really sharp. He strides ahead of her, sliding down a shingle bank with a whoop. He lands on his back and laughs.

'Hey, c'mon,' he shouts.

She catches up. Away from the promenade and lights it's quite dark. She doesn't like the dark, still has a nightlight in her bedroom at home, but no one knows about that. Not even her best friend, Paige, who she tells all her secrets.

She sits down beside him, clutches her hands round her knees. It's important to be ladylike.

'Well,' he says, 'you gonna give me a kiss?'

'Are we going out then?' *They're all going to be so jealous.*

He laughs. 'Come on, Kerry. Don't be a tease. I bet you've kissed loads of lads.'

She hasn't. But she doesn't want him to know that. He'll think she's just a stupid kid.

'Maybe I'm picky,' she says.

'Yeah, right.'

He reaches over and drags her towards him. He's surprisingly strong. Strong as her dad was. But she can't think about all that now.

His kiss is hard, his tongue intrusive. It's not that nice. But when a really fit guy like him kisses you it's supposed to be amazing. She wants to enjoy it. She should enjoy it.

But, without warning, his hand is up her skirt, tugging at her underwear. She tries to pull away.

'C'mon,' he says. 'You know you want to.'

'I'd rather go for a drink,' she says.

'We'll do that after.'

After what?

He pushes her back down. She feels panic and confusion rising inside. If she upsets him he won't want to go out with her. But she's not ready for this.

'No,' she says. 'I'm cold. I wanna go for a drink now.'

'I've told you, I'll buy you a drink after. I thought we had a deal.'

Holding her shoulders down, he rolls on top of her. His weight pinions her. The stones are sharp, biting into her legs and back.

She turns her head away and tries to push him off.

'No,' she says. 'Stop it. You're hurting me.'

'It needn't hurt,' he says. 'You just have to relax and enjoy it.'

'I'm not enjoying it.'

'That's cause you're not trying, Kerry. Come on, give me a proper kiss. Then you'll get into it.'

'I don't want to.'

'Yeah you do. You know you do.'

'I don't wanna have sex.' She blurts it out. She starts to struggle.

He holds her down. 'Course you do. Trust me, you'll like it.'

'You said we were going for walk.' She's crying now.

'Yeah, but you knew this was going to happen. And you want it as much as me. So don't pretend.'

'I didn't know. Please, just let me go. I wanna go home.'

His reply is to kiss her again, harder still, his forearm across her windpipe. She can't breathe. She's choking. Panic seizes her. It feels as if she's going to die.

After that it all happens quickly. She can't fight him, he's too strong. All she wants is for it to be over. She thinks about what her gran would say, the lectures, the warnings. Only stupid girls get raped, that's what Paige says. Stupid is the least of it. Inside she's howling but she doesn't utter a sound.

When he finally stands up and zips his jeans, she rolls onto her side. She feels sick.

'Didn't have to be like this,' he says. 'This is your fault. You been trying to get my attention for ages, you know you wanted it.'

She can't speak. She puts her fingers to her lips. They're sore. Her whole body feels bruised; her rib cage, her pelvis, everything is thrumming with pain.

He stands over her, hands on hips, and sighs. 'I hope you're not going to be a silly girl about this.'

She says nothing.

He prods her with his toe. 'Answer me.'

'No,' she whispers.

'You go spreading lies about me, telling anyone I hurt you, anyone at all, I will come for you. I will come for your whole family. And I'll slice that pretty face of yours. Then I'll kill you. Don't make the mistake of thinking this is an empty threat. It's a promise. And I'm a man who keeps my promises. You don't though, do you, you stupid bitch. That's why you've ended up like this. You got no one but yourself to blame.'

She's curled herself into a foetal ball, her back towards him.

'You listening? You understand?' He prods her again.

'Yes,' she says. 'I understand.'

He starts to walk away up the beach. She can hear his trainers crunching on the shingle.

Finally she's alone with the lapping waves and she can cry properly. She doesn't want to move but she knows she must. The tide is coming in.

She tries to stand up. Her whole body is trembling and her legs won't support her. She takes a single step and tumbles. The sharp stones tear her palms. She can't find her shoes; the lovely shoes she bought with her birthday money. They're silver slingbacks with a kitten heel and so cool. He told her to take them off, she must've dropped them.

She starts to crawl up the beach on her hands and knees. How will she get home without anyone seeing her? No one can see her like this. It would be awful. And what if they find out at school? She can't bear to think about that.

Forget the shoes. Once she gets back on the promenade she must keep out of the light. Half way up the beach she manages to stand. Struggling to keep her balance, she picks her way across the pebbles. In her mouth she tastes blood; she's bitten her own lip. She did try and resist him, she put up a fight. But her gran is never going to believe that.

She has to stop crying. She has to stop shaking. Wiping a hand across her face, she finds it's wet with tears and snot and blood.

CHAPTER EIGHT

Tuesday, 9.57am

For the second day Megan arrives at the office late. A sleepless night hasn't brought her any resolution. A pervasive headache lurks behind her eyes. The morning swim was brief. It failed to work its usual magic.

Brittney looks up from her computer screen and smiles.

Megan walks over to her desk, folds her arms and says, 'Thanks for yesterday.'

Brittney shrugs. 'No problem. I've been doing some research on Georgia O'Brien. She and her second husband have split up. I do remember reading about it. Quite a big deal. Accusations flying in the tabloids and the gossip mags. His name's Damian Conrad.'

'Sounds promising,' says Megan. She hesitates but she has to ask. 'What did you say to Slater?'

After the panic attack Megan had been in no fit state to return to the office. The two DCs had driven her home.

'Well,' says Brittney, 'we explained about the septic tank and how it'd made you throw up so you had to go home. She sent CSI straight down there yesterday afternoon to sort it out.'

'You didn't say I'd had a panic attack?'

Brittney shrugs again. 'Not really relevant, is it?'

Megan looks at her, the big glasses, her round face, the dimples when she smiles. Any effusive expressions of gratitude would probably embarrass her. But it seems Brittney and Vish covered for her. They've given her the opportunity to take her sister Debbie's advice and see how she feels after a couple of days.

Settling for a small pat on the shoulder Megan says, 'Thanks, mate. Can I get you a coffee?'

'Oh, cheers, yeah. White, two sugars.' Brittney beams.

As Megan walks over to the coffee station she sees Vish talking to the DCI in her office. Noticing her, Slater beckons.

Laura Slater occupies a small corner room created out of opaque glass partitions, separate but hardly private unless she closes the blinds.

'Morning, boss.' Megan hovers in the doorway.

'You all right?' Slater asks. 'Sticking your head down a septic tank, that's crazy. You should leave that sort of thing to CSI, they've got the protective gear.'

Megan catches Vish's eye. She smiles. He says nothing.

'I thought the contractor might be lying, trying to pull a fast one,' she says. 'Didn't want to get a whole crew down there for nothing.'

Slater nods. 'Well, I appreciate the thought. That's a cost we can do without.'

'Brittney says CSI went down.'

'Yeah, Hilary Kumar's the Crime Scene Manager. She's very experienced. But they had to call in the underwater search team to help them get it out.'

'The hatch to the tank was quite small.'

Slater shrugs. 'I don't know the details. I think they had to do some excavation. But I do know it took them until nearly midnight to get it out and bag it up. It's gone to the mortuary. I'm waiting to hear about the post mortem.'

Megan swallows hard. 'From what I saw, boss, it must be quite recent. It still had rats feeding on it.' She manages to say the word but there's a lightness in her head. Fear bubbling below the surface.

Slater nods and scans her face. 'Grim. Rather you than me. In the meantime, Vish has been talking to the Sexual Offences Liaison Officer on the phone. They've got a fourteen-year-old kid, brought in by her grandmother in the early hours. Stranger rape, so they're passing it over to us.' She glances across the office at Ted Jennings, quietly consuming his morning Danish. 'I was going to give it to Ted, but I think I'd prefer you to do it, if that's okay.'

Megan nods. It's the line of least resistance.

Slater smiles. 'Vish has got the details.'

As they walk across the car park towards the Škoda, Megan says, 'I'm feeling a bit ropey this morning, mind if I drive? I find it easier.' *Ropey. Stupid word. Get a grip.*

Vish nods. 'Go for it.'

'And thanks, by the way.'

'Would've freaked me out too. CSI, I couldn't do that stuff.' He clicks his phone on. 'Do you want to take a look at this rape victim's video interview before we go?'

Megan sighs. She knows she should. 'I'll watch it later. Can you give me the main points?'

'I don't know why they've lumbered us with it, because the officer that interviewed her wasn't convinced.'

'In what way?' She unlocks the car and they get in.

'Kid clearly didn't want to be there.'

'That's understandable.'

'Not much in the way of forensics. She'd had a shower.'

'Okay.'

'Plus it was all coming from the grandmother. Sexual Offences thought she'd dragged the kid down there against her will.'

'So when and where did this happen?'

'Last night, elevenish. Your neck of the woods. On the beach next to the breakwater in Berrycombe.'

Megan feels the hairs rise on the back of her neck. The couple she saw? It couldn't be, could it? Fourteen years old! She saw it and did nothing. If she needed any further proof this is it. Her judgement is shot. She shouldn't be here. She can't do it. The panic attack was a warning. Her subconscious is sending her a message. And the message is: stop. If she ignores it, who knows what'll happen?

CHAPTER NINE

Tuesday, 10.45am

Megan has lived in Berrycombe for a couple of months but she doesn't know it well. The town is ancient, a thriving fishing port since the Middle Ages. Built on terraced hillsides above the busy harbour, the pastel-painted houses – pink, blue, yellow, green – line the slopes. She still gets lost in the maze of narrow, winding lanes and steep stone stairways that knit the place together.

They park at the back of the main street. Megan sends Vish for takeaway coffees while she watches the interview on her phone. It gives her time to pull herself together. She focuses on the screen. He's right; it's clear the girl is there under duress from her family. But is this the girl Megan saw? It's impossible to tell.

Vish returns with the drinks.

'She's so evasive. We should probably do this by the book, get her back in and re-interview her,' says Megan.

'Slater's gonna love that.'

Megan sighs, she's well aware that the DCI's priority is to cross it off her list.

'Okay,' she says. 'Let's just go and talk to them.'

Sheila Waycott lives in a bay-fronted thirties semi on the higher ground at the back of the town. She opens the door to the police before they even ring the doorbell.

'DS Thomas.' Megan holds up her ID. 'And this is DC Prasad.'

'I'm glad they sent a woman,' Sheila says, ignoring Vish.

They follow her into the house. The hallway leads to a lounge and dining room, knocked through. It's neat and clean. Megan notices the sideboard at the end of the dining room is arranged with an array of framed photographs. Mostly they're of one man; it gives the impression of being a shrine.

Kerry Waycott is curled up on the sofa cuddling a cushion. In ripped jeans and a t-shirt, with her hair pulled back in a ponytail, she looks about twelve.

'This is my granddaughter, Kerry,' Sheila says.

'Hello, Kerry. I'm Megan. This is Vish. We're here to find out about what's happened to you.'

Another woman appears in the kitchen doorway. She's much younger than Sheila but her hair is straggly and she has the zoned-out stare of someone on strong medication. 'And this is my daughter-in-law, Heather.'

Megan smiles at her. 'Kerry's mum?'

There's a second's pause, then the woman nods. Her eyes are glassy, her hand shakes.

Megan sits down on an armchair opposite Kerry. Vish remains in the background taking notes.

'I've watched a video of the interview you did when your grandmother brought you to see us. But listening to it, I'm wondering if there's more you want to tell us. So we have a clear picture of what happened.'

'Some bloke set upon her, that's what happened,' says her grandmother.

Turning to look at Sheila, Megan says, 'Mrs Waycott, I know you've already been through this, but I'd like to understand it from Kerry's point of view.'

Kerry clutches the cushion. Megan has a feeling it's a stand-in for her favourite cuddly toy. 'I was just coming home from my mate's house,' she says. 'And he jumped out.'

'Was this someone you knew?'

Kerry buries her chin in the cushion. 'No. Never seen him before.'

Megan tilts her head. Kerry Waycott is not a very good liar.

'In the interview you said this was in town. Is that right?' Megan asks.

Kerry nods.

'A particular street?'

'Can't remember.'

'Then what happened?'

'He dragged me down the beach.'

'Can you remember which way you went?'

'I'm not sure, it was all a bit confusing.'

'Poor child was frightened out of her wits,' says Sheila. 'You can't expect her to remember which way they went.'

'Anything she can tell us about the route would help,' says Megan, 'because we can check the CCTV.'

'Fair enough,' Sheila replies. She looks to Megan to be in her middle sixties, solid but not fat. The kind of woman you'd want on your side in a bar room brawl.

Kerry glances at her grandmother nervously. Her mother is staring out of the window. Megan wonders about them. The tension in the room is palpable. A family being held together by a feisty grandmother?

She returns her gaze to the teenager. 'What did you do afterwards, Kerry?'

'Ran home. Mum was asleep. Didn't want to wake her. I felt like, I dunno, it just hurt so much.' The tears in the child's eyes are definitely genuine.

'Then what did you do?'

'Just wanted to get clean, so I took all my clothes off and got in the shower.' She shoots a coy look at Vish. She seems to have flipped. Now she's more interested in attracting his attention.

Is this a game? Megan wonders.

'Do you think you'd recognise him again?' she says.

'Dunno. Maybe. It all happened too quick.'

'But you said he grabbed you in the street, in the town, and then dragged you to the beach. That's quite a long way. Didn't you get a look at his face?'

'He blindfolded me.' Megan scans her. The lies are piling up. Kerry presses her face into the cushion and starts to cry.

Megan waits. But Sheila steps forward and addresses her grand-daughter. 'Now stop all this grizzling and answer the officer's question. They can't catch him if they don't know what he looks like, can they?'

'But I don't know,' wails Kerry.

Megan wishes the grandmother would back off but that seems unlikely. She decides to take a punt. 'You know, Kerry, I can see how hurt you are. Being attacked is really horrible. And it's important we catch him. But I'm wondering if you're just too frightened to say who it is?'

'Is that it?' says Sheila. 'Cause now's the time to tell the truth, girl.'

'I am telling the truth.'

'Mrs Waycott,' Megan says. 'Maybe you could—'

But Sheila isn't listening. She wags her finger at the girl. 'All we been through. Look at the state of your poor mother. I won't have any more nonsense from you, Kerry.'

Kerry jumps up. 'It ain't nonsense. I'm telling the truth. This bloke raped me. He set upon me, dragged me down the beach by the breakwater and raped me. I don't know who he was.'

She runs out of the room, sobbing.

Sheila sighs and turns to Megan. 'What now?' The look on her face is blank and weary, and Megan suspects she's close to desperate.

'We'll look into it, Mrs Waycott.'

'She's not lying, y'know. Turned up here in the middle of the night. She does that quite often. I knew something was wrong straight away. She's ashamed, that's why she don't wanna talk about it. But you're a woman, you know that.'

'Perhaps she does know who it is and doesn't feel able to say? Do you think that's possible?'

'She'll tell me the whole truth eventually. But, for Chrissake, she's fourteen. She's still a child.'

'Yes, I know.' Megan meets the other woman's eye and holds her gaze. It's a long time since she's had to play the reassuring cop. It feels odd.

The Škoda winds its way round the narrow streets and up a hill out of the town. Megan drives, Vish is checking his phone.

Having spent the last five years dealing with vicious organised criminals, Megan finds herself at a loss when faced with the raw distress of an ordinary family. The grandmother is angry – understandably. The mother is absent and the kid is doing what? Lying. But what else is going on?

It feels to Megan as if she's the wrong person to be doing this. How can she help the Waycotts? She can barely help herself. She seems to be watching the world from inside a goldfish bowl. She has to focus on the facts.

She glances across at Vish. 'So what d'you reckon?'

'She had some kind of bust-up with her boyfriend. But most of all this is about getting her gran off her back.'

'That's a bit harsh.'

'She's all tears and cushion-cuddling today. But my guess is it's an act.'

'Girls get raped, Vish. Happens all the time.'

'I know. But did you see her nails?'

'Her nails?'

'Little stars on her nails. That's not easy. Nail bar job. Goes with full make-up and a kid who may be fourteen but who's not some innocent child, whatever her gran wants to believe.'

'You're making a lot of assumptions. My niece is fourteen. She's got this little kit for decorating her nails. Comes with all sorts of glitter and stick-ons.'

Vish sighs. 'Okay, maybe I'm totally wrong. Just feels to me like it's a fourteen-year-old girl and fifteen or sixteen-year-old lad. They're starting to have sex, not communicating that well, basically just learning. Maybe he fumbled the condom. She's thinking, shit, what if I'm pregnant. She needs a cover story.'

'That's quite devious and complicated.'

'When I was sixteen I was having sex with a girl of fourteen and a half.'

'She was your girlfriend?'

Vish looks at her and hesitates.

Megan shrugs. 'Too personal? You started it.'

'Okay. She wasn't exactly my girlfriend. It was more casual than that. We were in the school choir together. When we started I was the virgin, not her. We were trying it out. She knew more than me and had more confidence. Quite often girls do.'

Megan thinks about the couple on the quay. If it was them, it fits Vish's theory. As a childless, middle-aged woman she can hardly claim much understanding of the rising generation of teenagers.

She smiles to disguise her discomfort. 'You're making me feel old.'

'Nah, come on. What are you, thirty-two, thirty-three?'

Now she chuckles. 'You, Detective Constable, are a shameless flatterer.'

He grins. 'It's why everyone likes me. Actually I saw her again recently, the girl who popped my cherry, at a mate's wedding.'

'Don't tell me, she's put on thirty pounds and she's married with three kids?'

'No. She's stunning. She speaks four languages and she's working for an international law firm in Brussels.' A wistful look comes into his eye. 'I asked her out, but she's with someone.'

*

As they return to the office, Megan is still wondering if she should even be there. Whatever she'd expected or hoped to feel with this new job, this sense of niggling anxiety and doubt in her own competence certainly isn't what she wants.

Slater is on the phone, but waves her over. Megan waits for her to hang up.

'Right,' says Slater briskly. 'The mortuary's backed up today, so they're bringing in a locum and we've got a post mortem scheduled for tomorrow morning.'

'Okay.'

'Get down there. See what the pathologist has to say. If it is murder then there'll be press interest, so I want to get ahead of that.'

'Present owner's been in the house five years.'

'We certainly need to know if they're suspects. And what about this rape?' She starts to put her jacket on. Like everything else about Slater, it's pitch perfect, the colour, the cut. Megan feels scruffy.

'I've told Vish to try and dig up some CCTV to see if we can corroborate the story.'

'Any evidence?'

'Swabs were taken, there's underwear. The initial medical examination found some bruising on her throat. But her account of being grabbed by a stranger isn't very convincing.'

Slater checks her watch. 'I've got a budget meeting at one. Unless we think we've got a predatory paedophile stalking the streets of Berrycombe don't waste any time on it.'

'The family's quite distressed. Clearly there's stuff going on. I thought I might visit the school.'

'To what end?' Slater picks up her bag.

'I'm not sure. I don't think she was lying about the attack. It's more who the attacker was.'

'No. Waste of resources. Tell Sexual Offences to hang fire on sending the swabs to the lab. I'm not paying for a DNA profile unless we have to. Just get hold of her phone and get it checked. If you find a string of texts to some boy or naked pictures she's been sending then forget it, this is not going to fly. CPS have been going nuts about all that kind of stuff.'

'It could be a boyfriend and she's protecting him. But what if it's an older man exploiting a fourteen-year-old? And she's too frightened to say.'

'Speculation is good. I always welcome it in my officers. Lateral thinking. But there are two things you should bear in mind: we need robust evidence that will get a conviction and we're not social workers.'

'I get it, boss.'

'I know you do,' says Slater, fixing her with a penetrating stare. 'And I know I can rely on you.' It sounds like a threat.

Megan watches her leave, clipping down the corridor on her neat kitten heels. It's easy to imagine that in ten years, probably less, Laura Slater could be chief constable.

CHAPTER TEN

Tuesday, 6.10pm

After a frustrating afternoon trawling CCTV and going over Kerry's video interview Megan throws in the towel and heads home early. She feels emotionally drained and it's only her second day back on the job.

She leaves Brittney hard at it. The DC is a terrier. It's proving extremely difficult to track down Damian Conrad, Georgia's husband. It remains to be seen if this means anything. People disappear off the grid for all kinds of reasons. But, in a case like this, starting with the property owner is standard practice. Identifying the body is likely to be a long and tedious process. They have to start somewhere. Until they have the results of the post mortem the task is to gather information.

Megan gets home in time to share the family meal. Debbie's lasagne is legendary. As she lifts it from the oven, sizzling hot, the aroma draws everyone to the table. Cooking, Megan reflects, is another thing Debbie can do that she can't.

Seated next to her nephew Kyle, Megan says, 'How was your day?'

'Yeah, awesome,' says the boy without looking up from his phone.

'Phones off, now!' says Debbie.

Kyle and Amber look at their mother, affronted, although they hear her say this every day. Little Ruby, the baby of the family, fondles Scout's ears. His nose twitches too at the deliciously meaty smell.

Mark places a jug of iced water on the table and starts to pass out glasses.

'Aww, Dad, can't we have Coke?' says Kyle.

'You know your mother's rules and she's in charge,' Mark replies.

'Yeah, Kyle,' says Amber. 'You don't wanna turn into a blob.'

'You're the blob,' says her brother.

'All right, you two,' says Debbie. 'Let's all show Megan how nice we can be.'

Megan smiles. She's been their lodger for nearly two months but it still feels as if she's a guest. The plan was that it'd be temporary until she started the new job, then she'd get her own place. She wonders if it's becoming an imposition. The house isn't large, four bedrooms; the two girls are currently sharing to accommodate their aunt.

Amber gives Megan a speculative glance and says, 'So what's the latest on Kerry Waycott? Do you know who raped her?'

Megan is taken aback. 'How on earth do you know about that?'

'Snapchat. Paige Tucker's been posting updates. Some gorgeous policeman interrogated Kerry.'

'Well, that wouldn't be me. I did ask her some questions and my DC, who is handsome, took notes. I wouldn't say she was interrogated. Who's Paige Tucker?'

'Kerry's best friend.'

Debbie is serving steaming plates of lasagne. 'I hope you're not wasting time on Snapchat when you should be doing homework,' she says.

'I'm not,' says Amber.

Megan frowns and says, 'Has Kerry posted anything herself?'

'She's too upset apparently. So Paige is keeping everyone updated. And there's a Facebook page where people can check in every night and mark themselves safe.'

'Safe from what?' says Megan.

'The Berrycombe rapist.'

'Good God,' says Debbie. 'Is there a Berrycombe rapist? Should we be worried?'

'No,' says Megan.

'Wouldn't surprise me if Kerry's just made the whole thing up,' says Amber. 'She's a complete slut.'

'Amber, that's enough,' says her father. 'After what that poor girl's been through.'

'Dad, she's always posting something about her mental health problems and how emotionally upset she is by this or that. In between make-up tips. She just uses it all to get attention. Thinks she's gonna be some online star.'

'You used to like Kerry when you were at primary school,' says Debbie.

Amber adopts an imperious tone. 'Well I don't any more. Trust me, Mother. You would not want me hanging out with Kerry and Paige and their crew.'

Megan turns to Mark. 'What has she been through?'

But Debbie answers. 'Dave Waycott, Kerry's father, was a trawler skipper. Winter before last he drowned in a really bad storm.'

'That's the story,' says Mark. Debbie subdues her husband with a not-in-front-of-the-children look.

Megan goes back to Amber. 'Does Kerry have a boyfriend?'

'Not anyone at school. She wouldn't stoop to that. They hang out in town, use fake ID to get into bars.'

'And they post titty pictures online,' says Kyle with a giggle.

'Kyle!' says his mother.

'What? Everyone looks at them.'

'And I'm looking at your plate,' says Debbie. 'Eat that broccoli.'

'It's gross.'

'I like it,' says Ruby. 'It's good for you.'

'It's like eating a tree. How can that be good for you?'

'Giraffes eat trees. And koala bears,' says Ruby.

Once the meal is over and the plates cleared, Megan joins her brother-in-law on the narrow terrace. He's having a sneaky cigarette. He offers the packet to Megan. She hesitates, then takes one. He lights it for her.

She inhales and grimaces. 'My first in six months.'

'Everyone's entitled to a small vice, even cops.'

'What is the real story about the Waycotts then?'

Mark sighs. 'Depends where you want to start. It's the fishing industry. Quotas, run-ins with the French. Dave was like many independent trawler owners, family boat, he inherited it from his dad. But it's a struggle making ends meet. He got into serious debt, hard to see a way out.'

'Sounds like you knew him quite well.'

'It's a tight community. He was a bit older than me, but I worked for him on his boat now and then. He was a fair bloke. Paid you your share of the catch.'

Megan stubs out her cigarette, the sharp tang of the nicotine leaving a sour taste. 'So some skippers don't give you your share?'

He shrugs. 'Everyone's just trying to make a living.'

'And how did Dave Waycott die?'

'As Debbie said, there was a storm and he drowned at sea. But he was an experienced skipper. Friends who knew him think he went over the side. He'd had enough. Plus that way his family still got the insurance.'

'I met his wife. She seems in a bad way.'

'Heather. Yeah, well, I reckon she knew. Too much grief in that family already. Years before, his dad died in an accident. The boat was just coming into dock, his old man stepped across to the jetty, slipped and missed his footing, fell down between the boat and the dock. Got crushed between the two. Dave had to pull him out. Died in hospital.'

Megan exhales. 'That's horrible.' The image of Sheila Waycott, arms folded, face impassive, comes into her mind. The woman had buried her husband and her son, but was still standing. If Kerry Waycott was acting out to gain attention it was understandable.

Mark shakes his head. 'I've seen Kerry and her mates in and out of the pubs in town. She may only be fourteen but you'd never know it. She's well out of hand.'

'That doesn't mean to say she's not vulnerable,' says Megan. 'In fact if she's not as emotionally mature as she looks it puts her more at risk.'

He nods. 'Oh I know. There's plenty of blokes who'll get a few pints inside them and look at a girl like her and think "why not". Have you got any leads?'

'I spent the afternoon with my DC going through every bit of CCTV we could find. Unfortunately the cameras along the south side of the quay aren't functioning. The council's supposed to be replacing or repairing them. But there's no money in the budget for it until next year. There's a camera near the beach that does work but it points the wrong way.'

The frustration of it had left both Megan and Vish despondent. If they had found a shot of Kerry with someone it wouldn't have been evidence of rape on its own. Slater would've still dismissed it. But it might've persuaded Kerry to name her attacker. Megan feels instinctively that they were the couple she saw walking along beside the harbour. Right time, right direction. Which means Kerry knows him.

She looks at her brother-in-law, a trawlerman like Dave Waycott, working several jobs to pay the bills. What if he tips over the edge? She pushes the thought away. Mark has a sturdiness about him that she envies. He and Deb together are a formidable duo. It makes her wonder where things went wrong in her own life, why she's never succeeded in finding such a relationship for herself. Her own marriage ended in a messy divorce.

'Amber's pretty smart,' he says, 'but I still worry about her. I worry about all three of them. Then there's all this online stuff, I don't get it myself. But they're glued to it. It's how they communicate with their mates.'

'They seem happy, well-adjusted kids to me,' says Megan. 'So you must be doing something right.'

He laughs. 'Yeah, well, maybe.' His brow darkens and he says, 'Y'know, Meg, it's brilliant what you do. I don't know where we'd all be without people like you, who can deal with all the nasty little bits of human nature that no one else wants to look at.'

Megan smiles. So they've been talking about her. She can feel her sister's anxiety in this attempt at a confidence boost.

'I've been thinking of jacking it in,' she says. 'The panic attack. It's scary.'

'If you weren't scared, you'd be stupid, wouldn't you? But that's no reason to stop.'

'If my bosses found out they might not agree.'

'They'd have to go a long way to find someone as good at the job as you. My guess is they know that.'

Megan smiles to herself. For the second time in one day a man has flattered her. Perhaps things are looking up.

CHAPTER ELEVEN

A fitful night's sleep leaves Megan weary. The Waycotts invaded her dreams. Kerry, a kid caught between the burden of family grief and a desire to be someone in her own right and simply to be noticed. Sheila, doggedly trying to hold it all together. And the despair of a man who saw no way out but to throw himself into a stormy sea.

When she woke with a start, the clickety-clack of the boss's heels still echoing down an endless corridor in her mind, it hit her. She was overwhelmed by the Waycotts' sorrow. She couldn't tell where her own pain ended and theirs began.

It takes two mugs of black coffee to get her up and functioning. The traffic is slow and sluggish and by the time she arrives at the mortuary for the post mortem Brittney is waiting in the car park. The mortuary has the appearance of a sad sixties office block in need of renovation. She and Brittney show their ID at reception and are directed to a small waiting room.

Brittney is brimming with enthusiasm. Although she's seen plenty of bodies in her previous career as a paramedic, the idea of seeing one carefully dissected obviously excites her. She's also keen to bring Megan up to speed with her research.

Holding up her phone, she says, 'So here's a YouTube clip of Georgia and Damian all loved up on their wedding day. The venue was a French chateau.'

Megan glances at the screen. Laughing faces, tinny music, it's impossible to discern much else. 'How long ago is this?' she asks.

'About six years. Before she was killed off.'

'Killed off?'

'In the TV series she was in, *One Fine Day*. Georgia was married to the producer, Eric Russell. He was her first husband. They split up when she got it on with Damian. He worked on the show as a lighting technician. Then Eric Russell killed her character off, wrote her out of the show. A lot of people thought it was revenge.'

'Because she'd gone off with another bloke?'

'A much younger bloke too.'

Megan sighs. 'I don't know about telly, her life sounds like a bloody soap opera.'

'Yeah. And it didn't work out well for her. Damian dumped her and Georgia accused him of stealing a ton of money.'

'And you still haven't tracked him down?'

'No. They split up at the beginning of the year. For a while it was in all the tabloids. Pictures of him at clubs and restaurants with various different women. Pictures of Georgia miserable and drunk and falling out of taxis. Then it became old news. Then she accused him of stealing her money. But by then the papers had lost interest and it was just the gossip mags.'

'You think he's disappeared?'

Brittney shrugs. 'I can't say for sure. I talked to a couple of the girls he was photographed with. No one's seen him since the summer.'

'He could've gone abroad. Living the life somewhere on Georgia's money.'

'Georgia went really loopy for a couple of months, after the money thing,' says Brittney. 'Spent some time in rehab "grieving" apparently.'

'Grieving for what?'

'She said her lost love, the man who betrayed her. Then everything seemed to go back to normal.'

'Perhaps she got bored,' says Megan. There's a silliness about all this that annoys her. Compared to the rape of a kid it feels trivial.

Brittney has a twinkle in her eye. 'What if it's him in the tank?'

Megan frowns. 'Could a woman of Georgia's age have managed to kill a younger man and stuff him in a septic tank? Seems a bit unlikely.'

'She'd need some help.'

'Okay, it's not impossible. Once we've got a time frame for the death we can see if it correlates with his disappearance. Can you pin down the last time anyone saw him?'

'I'm working on it. We need permission to access his bank accounts, track his phone.'

'I'll ask Slater to authorise it.'

Megan smiles wistfully at the young cop. Somewhere in the recesses of her brain, memories lurk of a time she was in Brittney's shoes, excited by the chase, driven to solve the puzzle. Back then there was no emotional baggage, being a detective was fun.

Her thoughts flip back to the Waycotts. She looks at her watch and comes to a decision.

'Listen, Brittney, this post mortem will take hours and I need to check something out on another case.'

Brittney shrugs. 'Okay, you want me to stay here?'

The DC probably thinks she's bottling it. It is years since she's attended a post mortem and after her recent experience with the rats, who knows? Maybe she is.

'Yeah, are you all right with that? You're on top of this, you've done most of the work and you know what we're looking for. I'll be back in an hour or so.'

'Fine,' says Brittney.

Megan hesitates. 'You can cope?'

Brittney puffs out her chest. 'No problem.'

As Megan walks out of the building and towards her car she tries not to dwell on what the DCI would say. But if she ends up getting a bollocking so be it. If she's going to do this job again, it has to be her way, not Slater's.

The school is on the edge of the town, low rise, modern and surrounded by fields of sheep. It has an idyllic feel to it which seems to Megan to belong to a simpler time. She's more accustomed to the bunker mentality of London schools with metal detectors at the front gate.

After introducing herself at the office she doesn't have to wait long before the headteacher appears.

She's tall and willowy, with rimless glasses and red lipstick. 'Linda Kovacs,' she says, holding out her hand to shake. 'What can we do for you, Sergeant?'

'I'd like to talk to you about one of your pupils, Kerry Waycott.'

'Ah, yes,' says Kovacs. 'We have been wondering if anything would come of that.'

'Of what?'

'This rape thing. The kids are all talking about it because it's all over Snapchat. Simon Jones, our head of year nine, has been monitoring the situation. But half the time it's impossible to tell fact from fiction with social media. So is it true?'

'We're looking into it.'

Megan follows Kovacs into her office and accepts the offer of a cup of coffee while they wait for Simon Jones to join them.

He's all smiles, no more than thirty, chinos neatly pressed, a tie covered with dolphins. 'Poor Kerry,' he says with a sad shake of the head. 'She's been through a lot. Lost her dad. He drowned at sea. You know about that?'

'Yes.'

Megan studies him. The teachers she remembers from her schooldays were always old, weary and morose. He seems youthful and determined to be jolly.

'I gather what happened to Kerry is being talked about on Snapchat,' says Megan. 'Can you tell me about that?'

'Snapchat,' he says. 'Okay, most parents find it deeply annoying, but on planet teenager it's essential. For communication, for identity, for hierarchy. And what it offers someone like Kerry is the space to, well, be herself. Express her feelings. Because at home the rule is silence, emotional shutdown.'

'Has she been posting about this herself?'

'I gather, from what I'm hearing, that her friend Paige is her proxy.'

'But you think it's coming from Kerry?'

'I should think so. They're very tight, those two.'

'Would you say she's attention-seeking?'

'She's a fourteen-year-old girl, they're all attention-seekers,' he replies with a dismissive wave of his hand. 'Their chosen method depends on their level of distress. Performing in front of a camera gives a kid like Kerry the permission to feel.'

Megan glances at Linda Kovacs, who's listening attentively.

'Is this the sort of thing you want to know?' says Jones with a bright smile.

It sounds like claptrap to Megan but she refrains from saying so. She notes the dampness on his upper lip. There's something about him that's off but she can't put her finger on it. Perhaps he's just a gobby bloke. She remembers the sergeant who trained her back in her days in uniform. *Check your prejudices at the door*, that was his mantra. And gobby blokes given to mansplaining are high on her list of prejudices.

'What I need to know,' says Megan, 'is would being a rape victim give Kerry status on social media?'

He inhales as he considers this. 'Probably. In the value system of her network and peer group, suffering and speaking about suffering enhances her profile.'

'Meaning she would have a motive to lie?'

His face crinkles with a frown. 'Motive? It's not the sort of language I'd use, but I suppose so.'

Walking back to her car, Megan can't shake off her sense of annoyance and dissatisfaction. Perhaps Simon Jones had simply pissed her off. But what is she trying to achieve here? Slater's right, she's not a social worker. She's just going round in circles.

A text from Brittney pops up on her phone. *Murder confirmed. Waiting for time frame. See you back at office?*

CHAPTER TWELVE

Wednesday, 10.45am

Shirin stands by the kitchen window, staring out. Her nerves are jangling. She's hardly slept. Until well after midnight vehicles were ploughing back and forth, churning up the grass down the hill towards the septic tank. Big arc lights had been set up and around a dozen people came and went in a range of strange costumes. A uniformed PC had given them strict instructions to stay in the house and he remained outside to ensure they did. But now it's all quiet. The trucks and the white suits are gone. The area around the tank remains taped off and two officers are in a squad car on the track to stop anyone who approaches.

Georgia sits at the large pine table carefully coring an apple and cutting it into segments.

'Do you think they'll come back?' she says.

'Beats me,' Shirin replies. 'They made enough of a racket last night.' *Keep calm. Hold it together.*

'I just took a couple of temazepam.' Georgia offers the slices of apple to Noah, who sits on a chair beside her. 'There you go, darling.'

The boy takes the fruit, arranges it in a circle on his plate then starts to eat it piece by piece.

'What do you say?'

'Thank you, Auntie,' the child whispers.

Georgia gets up, takes the knife over to the sink and rinses it. 'Well, we can't just sit here and do nothing.'

Shirin looks at her employer. Managing Georgia and her moods can be a pain. She's not stupid but she is volatile and that could ruin everything. *When in doubt*, Shirin reminds herself, *you kick the can down the road, it always works. That's how you stay one step ahead of disaster.*

'I think that's exactly what we should do,' she says. 'It's up to them to prove a crime's been committed.'

'Oh for goodness' sake, Shirin, what do you think all that nonsense out there is about? There looking for something. Evidence. I don't know.' She shakes her head and sighs as if trying to erase an unpleasant memory.

Shirin scans her. *What's going on? Does she know more than she's letting on?*

'So there's a body. But we don't know who it is, do we?' Shirin says. 'I think I should take Noah to nursery. Keep to a normal routine.'

Georgia is pacing. 'I'm going to call my lawyer.'

'And say what?' She fixes Georgia with a steely glare. 'Is there something you're not telling me?'

'Me not telling you! That's rich.'

Georgia exhales loudly and folds her arms. She's spent so many years gurning for the cameras that, it seems to Shirin, she can't help but signal every emotion.

'Okay,' says Georgia with another huff. 'Here's what I think. If we're going to protect you-know-who—' She tilts her head in Noah's direction. *As if he doesn't know exactly what's going on.* 'We should get things started now with the adoption.'

Shirin stares at her; so this is her game. She may be as clueless as Shirin about the identity of the body but they can both guess who put it there. Why else would she be suggesting this now? Georgia thinks she can exploit the situation.

'No,' she replies firmly. 'I'm not ready.'

'Shirin, we have a deal. Now's the time. The best way out is if I adopt him.'

The idea that any competent authority would regard Georgia O'Brien as a responsible parent is farcical. But money talks, Shirin's well aware of that. Georgia's been through two husbands and now, in her early fifties, she's got it into her head that having a child of her own will bring her the love and affection she craves. But can she protect him?

Shirin smiles at Noah. Those intense, dark eyes, staring at her, reminding her every time she looks at him. At least he'd grow up rich, with a private education, all the advantages she never had. And she would get her chance. That's the trade-off. It's tempting.

'I've kept my part of the bargain,' she says. 'I've worked my guts out on your bloody books.'

'Darling, I'm not saying you haven't. And you'll get the recognition.'

'When?'

'I'll talk to them, I promise.'

Georgia's reinvention of herself as a children's author was in its infancy when Shirin first came to Winterbrook Farm. Georgia had been through two ghost writers already. Shirin had no idea if she could write a kids' book. But the opportunity was there and she'd seized it. They'd both been surprised by the results. Three years down the road and that, at least, has been a complete success. Georgia tours the country doing readings and signings, Shirin does the rest.

'We agreed,' says Shirin. 'The deal is my name on the cover too but I get to say when you can adopt him.' She's been kicking this can down the road for months. Does the stupid woman really believe she would give away her little boy?

Georgia flaps her hand in the vague direction of the window. 'Circumstances have changed. We have to protect the child.'

'You're just using all this.'

'I'm not. You know what's happening as well as I do. It's him. He's out there. He's sending us a message.'

Shirin feels her tears welling. She swallows them down. She doesn't want to admit that Georgia's right. She could run but what then? Back to square one. Three years' hard graft down the drain. Georgia owes her. And where else could she run to? It feels like she's been doing that her whole life.

CHAPTER THIRTEEN

Wednesday, 11.55am

Megan is slotting her jacket over the back of her desk chair when she sees Slater beckoning her. There's no sign of Brittney. She can feel the frostiness even before she reaches the DCI's doorway.

Slater is standing behind her desk. She doesn't invite Megan to sit.

'I've just had a call from a school in Berrycombe,' she says. 'Linda Kovacs?'

'What on earth does she want?'

'She's worried about some kind of hysteria breaking out in her school around "recent events" so she's planning a rape awareness day. She'd like our help.'

Megan sighs. 'I'm sorry, boss.'

'No you're not. I don't care that you went to the school when I specifically told you not to. You may have a good reason that you're planning to share at some point.' There's a tartness in the DCI's tone, sarcasm is her weapon of choice. *Predictable*, thinks Megan.

Slater laces her fingers. She's controlling her anger, which is not a good sign. Most of Megan's bosses have been male, some have been shouters, but usually they said their piece and it was over. In her experience women bosses can be far more venomous. Megan braces herself. She probably deserves it.

Slater picks up her pen, uncaps and recaps it. 'What I do have a problem with is you walking out on the PM.'

'I didn't walk out—'

'Don't interrupt. I'm SIO, Senior Investigating Officer, presumably you remember what one of those is?'

'Yes, ma'am.'

'Which means I issue the actions and you carry them out. I told you that if this turned into a murder investigation, which it has, I wanted to be on top of it.'

'I know, ma'am, you're right.'

'But that's hardly the point any more. I've just been told by Brittney Saric that the property owner and therefore a possible suspect for this murder is Georgia O'Brien. Don't you think you should've flagged this up sooner?'

Megan frowns. *Is this really her issue?* 'Well, she's only a suspect if the body's recent and once we had the results of the PM I was going to—'

Slater puts the pen down with an irritable snap. 'You do know who she is?'

'Yeah, some actress?'

'Some actress? What planet are you living on? Georgia O'Brien is an A-list celebrity. She's a national treasure. The daughter of Dame Heidi Soames. Now she's a famous children's author too. I read her bloody books to my kids every night. And according to Brittney we're considering questioning her over whether she murdered her husband and stuffed him in her septic tank. Once this becomes public knowledge, can you imagine the shitstorm that's going to erupt?'

Now it makes sense.

'I don't watch much television. I didn't realise.'

The DCI sighs. 'Seems to me there's a lot you don't realise, Megan.'

Megan stares at the laptop, the notepad and neat array of pens on the desk. Slater's right of course. An ordinary DS living a normal life would be tuned into such things. She feels sorrowful and aberrant.

She looks Slater in the eye and says, 'I know you've been persuaded to take a chance on me. And I suspect it wouldn't have been your choice.'

'That's irrelevant.'

'No it's not. I've completely ballsed things up. To be fair to Brittney she did try and make it clear to me who this woman was. But I wasn't paying attention, I got sidetracked by the kid who says she was raped.'

Slater shakes her head, folds her arms. Megan's surprised to see how uncomfortable she is with an open expression of remorse. She would've preferred her DS to get stroppy and argue. That would be easier for her.

'Okay,' she says. 'It's your first week back on the job. I know you were injured in the line of duty. I don't know what that was about although I can take a guess because you got the QPM and Barker's gone out on a limb for you. But this is a team. I run it. And there's no room for a star centre forward.'

Megan exhales. Now they're getting to the nub of it. 'That's the last thing I want to be, ma'am, I promise you. I just want to fit in. But if you don't think I'm up to it then I'll—'

'It's not what I think, Megan. It's what you think. I have no idea what's going on in your head. This was a stupid mistake but you're a capable detective, that's clear. I think we both need to see if you can actually do the job. Or if you even want to.'

Megan nods. Does she want to? *Slater's sharp. She's put her finger on it.*

He left her in that cellar for a reason. He could've just killed her. But he wanted to destroy her first, to make her welcome death.

If she walks away now he's won.

CHAPTER FOURTEEN

Wednesday, 2.30pm

Megan stands in the corner. It seems appropriate, she feels like a naughty child. Laura Slater paces up and down checking her phone. They're in the viewing gallery at the mortuary waiting for the pathologist to complete the post mortem. Brittney stands close to the glass and watches eagle-eyed. Megan's seen too many corpses reduced to meat and viscera, it doesn't interest her that much.

The DCI is taking ownership of the investigation and stamping her authority on it as SIO. Megan can hardly blame her. It's easy to imagine her phone conversation with the Detective Super. Rob Barker will not have been happy to learn that they were probably about to embark on a difficult high-profile murder investigation that would bring the national media circus to town.

Slater turns to face Megan. 'When you went round, what was your initial impression?'

'Weird set-up,' Megan replies. 'Shirin Khan supposedly works for Georgia. But the power balance feels complicated. There was a lot of tension. They definitely had something to hide.'

'Works as what?'

'Didn't say.'

'And you said there was a child?'

'A boy. About four. He's Asian or mixed race so I assume he belongs to Shirin.'

Slater nods. At least the DCI doesn't appear to be a sulker, which is a relief.

The door opens and in comes a large man in blue surgical scrubs. His face mask dangles round his neck and is tangled in his beard. Megan hates beards and therefore her first impression of Dr Yannis Kakos is not favourable.

Slater steps forward and shakes hands. 'Dr Kakos, I'm DCI Slater.'

'I'm so sorry to keep you ladies waiting,' he says with formality and a heavy accent.

'Post mortems take time, we're used to that,' says Slater with equal politeness. 'What can you tell us?'

'The body is decomposed in part. Has been in this tank, covered in—' He wrinkles his nose as he searches for the correct English term.

'Effluent,' says Megan from her corner.

Kakos looks at her, smiles and dips his head. 'Thank you. My English is a little... simple maybe. Last week I'm in Athens removing appendix, now I'm here.' He laughs. 'Life is full of surprises, eh? I try so long to get a job here. I think maybe A&E but my English not good enough. Okay, they say, you can be a pathologist.' He chuckles again.

Megan can feel the boss's rising impatience. She can already predict the phone call to Barker and the carefully worded complaint. A high-profile investigation like this and the Home Office sees fit to send a Greek locum.

'Well,' says Slater, 'I trust our CSI, that's the crime scene investigator, briefed you thoroughly on the conditions in which the body was found.'

Kakos nods, his eyes twinkle, and Megan gets the impression that the new pathologist might have a mischievous streak. 'Well,' he says, mirroring Slater, 'yes, lots of these tanks in Greece, in countryside, favourite place to put body. At university where I worked we do many autopsy on such cadaver for the government.'

Megan smiles. She's beginning to like him.

Slater is smart enough to realise she's had her nose tweaked but her smile is coldly polite. 'Based on your experience, therefore, how long would you say the body's been there?'

'I say weeks, not months. Some flesh still, gases from tank speed up process and animals come to feed.'

The swishing of the rats' tails leaps into Megan's mind, she bats the image away.

'Is a man, we measure one eighty-three centimetre, is tall. Tall as me. Age I think is thirty-five to fifty-five, hard to be more precise. His death, I think, is by stabbing. In chest. Fractures to rib cage and laceration to remaining flesh on torso. Someone don't like him much. They stab him many times. Maybe ten at least.'

'Thank you,' says Slater. 'That's very helpful. 'We obviously need to identify the body—'

'Some fingerprint on right hand. We get them. Jaw intact, so teeth is good. I take DNA samples. Eyes is gone, but structure of skull and face bones, so you maybe make facial… er…'

'Facial reconstruction?' says Slater.

'Yeah, is enough for that.'

'Thank you, Dr Kakos.' Slater can't wait to get out the door.

'Don't worry, Detectives,' the pathologist says with a cheeky grin. 'My report in writing much clearer. I have good translation app. Made in China.'

'Well,' says the DCI, as they walk across the car park to their respective vehicles, 'he's different.'

Megan and Brittney exchange looks; difference is clearly not a compliment in Slater's book.

Clicking the fob to open her car she adds, 'First priority, we need to move them out of the house and secure the whole property as a crime scene.'

Megan nods. 'My guess is she'll kick off at that but then get lawyered up pretty quickly.'

'I'll talk to the CSM,' says Slater. 'You can go and give Georgia the good news.' She meets Megan's eye. 'We need to keep it low key for as long as possible, certainly until we identify the body. How's that going?'

'We need some permissions for financial and phone access.'

'That's fine. Just get on with it.'

'Understood, boss,' says Megan. She's tempted to tug her forelock but Slater probably wouldn't see the funny side of that.

She and Brittney watch the DCI reverse and drive away.

Behind her owl glasses Brittney looks sheepish. 'I'm really sorry if I dropped you in it,' she says. 'He just announced it in the first five minutes, that it was definitely murder. I didn't know what to do. I thought I should tell someone.'

'Hey, it's not a problem,' says Megan. 'I'm the one with my head up my arse. You did the right thing.'

CHAPTER FIFTEEN

Wednesday, 3.15pm

Megan stands shoulders back, hands crossed neatly in front of her. It's a pose designed to make it clear she's the one in control. It reminds her of her days in uniform, the thin blue line facing the rowdies and the protestors and the drunks. Life seemed a whole lot easier back then.

'No, that's ridiculous. Absolutely not.' Georgia O'Brien faces her with a mulish expression. A few rays of pale autumn sunshine are filtering through the French windows and dancing across what looks to be an expensive Persian rug in the drawing room at Winterbrook Farm. *Who even has a drawing room?* thinks Megan. It's an old farmhouse, not a mansion.

'I appreciate that it'll be inconvenient,' she says, 'but our crime scene investigators will have to do an extensive search of the whole property and you'll probably be more comfortable in a hotel.'

'I have deadlines for my next book, I have work to do. I have no intention of abandoning my home to a bunch of strangers in plastic suits. There are some extremely valuable items of antique furniture in this house.'

'I can assure you the premises will be completely secure,' says Megan with a smile. Cat and mouse with a potential suspect is not a game she's played for a while. But after her dressing down from the DCI she has to get this right.

'What if I need something?' Georgia strolls round the room as she speaks. 'I find it impossible to work without my things around me.'

Megan has noticed that she rarely delivers a line standing still. On the other hand, Shirin hardly moves. She stands, shoulders hunched, head down, like a scolded child. Megan wonders how she's going to get under the carapace of this double act. Where are the cracks? She has to find one.

She glances at Shirin. 'I think it will be far safer for your little boy. Children are naturally fascinated by unusual activity and we wouldn't want him to come to any harm.'

Shirin meets her eye. 'I don't understand why you have to search the house. A body has turned up in our septic tank. Which is halfway down the hill. Anyone could've put it there.'

'That's absolutely correct,' says Megan. 'Which is why we have to examine the immediate vicinity in detail so we can establish how it came to be there.'

'Are you suggesting we're involved?' says Georgia.

'I'm suggesting nothing. Our inquiries are at an early stage. Once we have the results of the post mortem and can establish the identity of the deceased we will be in a position to move forward.'

'And that's police gobbledegook for what?' snaps Georgia. She fiddles with the numerous bracelets on her wrist. Megan notices Shirin trying to catch her eye. But Georgia continues. 'You think I don't want to know who's stuffed a dead body in my septic tank? I mean, when are you people going to start doing your bloody job?'

Bingo. Megan says nothing.

'Y'know,' says Georgia, 'I could call up any national newspaper and tell them how I'm being treated. They would be down here like a shot. And your chief constable would be hauling you over the coals.'

Now she's on the back foot and rattled. Megan smiles and says, 'I can only apologise for the inconvenience, Miss O'Brien.'

'And so you should. This whole thing is preposterous.'

'In these circumstances it's standard police practice to examine the whole of a potential crime scene. We treat everyone the same.'

'I shall be going to stay with my mother.' Georgia turns her back on Megan.

'That sounds sensible. If you wouldn't mind giving us her address, DC Saric can note it down.'

Brittney beams and gets out her notebook.

'It's at Maidencombe overlooking the bay. Elsinore House. I've no idea what the bloody postcode is.'

Brittney makes a note and says, 'We can look it up.'

'Before we go,' says Megan, 'it would also be helpful if we could get in touch with your husband.'

'Damian? Former husband.'

'Are you actually divorced?'

'We will be when my lawyers can track the thieving bastard down and get back the hundred grand he stole from me.'

Megan gives her a quizzical look. 'You don't have a forwarding address for him?'

'He's probably shacked up with Laetitia Woods. That's who he went off with.'

'Is that Laetitia Woods the model?' says Brittney.

'No, it's Laetitia Woods the brain-dead, anorexic clothes-horse,' says Georgia.

Megan is aware of Brittney at her side trying not to smile. She imagines the DC recounting this exchange to her nan.

'And when did you last see him?' says Megan.

'I've really no idea.' Georgia turns to Shirin. 'Do you remember when he was last here?'

'At least a year ago,' says Shirin.

Her dark eyes don't leave Georgia's face. Megan can feel the effort she's making, willing Georgia to be calm. But it's not working.

Whatever the unusual power dynamic between them is, Megan concludes, Georgia is the weak link.

CHAPTER SIXTEEN

Wednesday, 5.05pm

Megan and Brittney get back to the office to find the place is still a hive of activity. Even Ted Jennings appears to be beavering away. The briefing room has been cleared out and a large whiteboard erected. Slater is standing in front of it talking to Hilary Kumar, the senior CSI.

Megan approaches.

'Have you two met?' says Slater.

Hilary Kumar has spiky cropped hair and looks way too young and cheerful for someone who spends their life around dead bodies. 'Hey,' she says, giving Megan a friendly nod. 'Welcome to the bucolic country life. Don't you just love septic tanks?'

'I've been in some London sewers that are pretty grim,' says Megan.

'Last week we got a machete out of a fatberg in the sewer system in Newquay,' says the CSI proudly.

'Lovely,' says Megan.

'You seen an actual fatberg? They're really gross. And huge.'

Slater frowns and Megan senses her impatience. She's beginning to realise that the DCI only does small talk when she has to.

'How did Georgia react?' she says.

'Rattled, bit rude, she's going to her mother's.'

'We'll cordon the house as soon as they're out,' says the CSI. 'But the underwater team's coming back tonight and we'll start to sieve the contents of the tank. Anything in particular we're looking for?'

'Died from multiple stab wounds,' says Slater, 'so we're probably looking for a knife.'

'It may be her ex-husband,' says Megan. 'Watch, jewellery, anything we can identify as personal to him.'

'Clothes will have probably rotted but we might get lucky,' says the CSI.

Brittney joins them. 'Just got a response from Damian Conrad's credit card company,' she says. 'His cards were maxed out, no payments for three months so they've frozen them. He's not responded to their emails.'

'Plenty of people do that,' says Hilary Kumar. 'Well, I'm off.' To Megan she seems upbeat for someone about to dismantle a septic tank on a freezing hillside in the dark.

Slater turns to the DC. 'Any friends or family you've managed to contact?'

'Parents are dead, no siblings. I talked to a couple of casual girlfriends. They last saw him in the summer.'

'Georgia's just told us he went off with a model called Laetitia Woods,' says Megan. 'We'll try and contact her.'

The DCI raises her eyebrows. 'Think I've seen her in *Vogue*. She's very striking.'

Megan has to avoid Brittney's eye. *She would read Vogue.*

The DC continues, 'Vish has been trying to trace his phone. We got a number from one of the girlfriends but it's dead.'

'Maybe the phone's in the tank,' says Megan. 'We'd better tell CSI to add it to their list.'

Slater nods. She seems distracted. Megan wonders what calculations are going on in the boss's mind. For an ambitious SIO this could be a career-defining case. Megan's glad she's not the one carrying the can. Being a DS has its advantages.

Returning to her desk, she finds a yellow Post-it stuck to the computer screen. It says: *Sheila Waycott phoned*. Megan sighs. She scans the room. Over at the coffee station Brittney and Vish are giggling.

'Vish,' she says. 'Did you take this call?'

He strolls over. 'Yeah. She says she's got new information but she'll only talk to you.'

'Oh shit. That's all I need.'

Megan decides to visit the Waycotts on her way home. Through the lit bay window she sees Sheila and her granddaughter blank and zombified in front of the television.

Opening the door Sheila says sourly, 'Didn't think you were coming.'

'I'm sorry it's so late, Mrs Waycott,' Megan replies. 'It's been one of those days.' An understatement.

'Well, I've talked some sense into her, I think.'

'Okay.'

Kerry is curled up on the sofa. It looks as if she hasn't moved since Megan's last visit.

'Hello, Kerry.'

The girl stares up at her with undisguised hostility.

'Tell her his name then,' says Sheila.

The girl's lip trembles. 'He said he'd kill me, cut me with a knife.'

'Did he have a knife?' says Megan.

'Dunno.'

'This is someone you know?'

'That doesn't mean to say he didn't force her to it,' says Sheila.

'I know that, Mrs Waycott.'

Kerry rubs her face. She looks like a frightened child and that, Megan reflects, is what she is.

Megan perches on the armchair opposite. 'What do you think will happen if you tell me?'

'It'll be my word against his. You lot'll do nothing because you'll go, "there's not enough evidence" and he'll get pissed off and come after me.'

This is a surprisingly adult analysis of the situation and, Megan has to admit, close to the truth.

'I'll be honest with you,' she says. 'Rape can be hard to prove.'

Kerry shoots her grandmother a baleful look. 'See, I told you.'

'No one's gonna come for you, Kerry, because he'll have us to deal with if he tries that lark,' says Sheila with vehemence.

'What am I s'posed to do, Gran? Never go out?'

'Okay,' says Megan. 'What if we do this in stages? You tell me his name. But I won't do anything now, tonight. We'll start to make some inquiries and see if we can build a case. But keeping you safe will be our priority at all times. If we find out more about him, believe me, that will lessen the possibility of him threatening you.'

Kerry's eyes brim with tears, she's back in child mode.

Megan waits. Sheila turns away. At least she's resisting the temptation to bully the girl further.

Finally Kerry sighs and says, 'His name's Jared.'

'Jared,' says Megan. 'Do you know his second name?'

'Not sure. Clarke or something like that?'

'How d'you know him?'

'He works at Mayhem, behind the bar.'

'Where is this bar?'

'It's down on the quay,' says Sheila. 'Used to be a pub called the Prince of Wales. It's been shut up for a while. Couple of months ago some bloke from London bought it. He's doing the whole building up. But they've opened up the bar downstairs.'

'If Jared's a barman,' says Megan, 'he must be over eighteen. Do you know how old he is?'

Kerry shrugs. Having made her accusation she seems to have collapsed and retreated into a private space of her own.

Megan's not sure what she's going to do with this information. It needs to be recorded in a formal interview. But she can predict what Slater will say. She decides that's an argument for tomorrow.

CHAPTER SEVENTEEN

Wednesday, 7.30pm

Once the stupid cop has left, Kerry persuades the old girl to let her go home. They both know that Heather will be out of it on her latest cocktail of booze and pills. Her younger brother and sister may or may not be tucked up in bed. They may or may not have been fed.

'I need to check on the littl'uns,' says Kerry.

Sheila nods. She opens her purse. 'You'd better take a taxi.'

Kerry is tempted by the fiver being offered. Then she feels guilty. 'Save your money, Gran. It's only a ten-minute walk.'

'Remember what I said. You see him, you ring me. Your uncle Justin'll—'

'No, Gran. Please. I did what you said and told that cop. You said we should give them a chance. I don't want Uncle Justin involved.'

Sheila nods. 'Best to stay on the right side of the law, I suppose. It's what your dad would've wanted.'

Kerry nods. She's been feeling stir crazy for hours. She just wants to get out. Paige has been texting, asking loads of questions. When is she coming back to school? After two days banged up at her gran's even the prospect of school is attractive.

She loosens her hair and runs down the hill into town. She runs hard until she's out of breath. For the first time in days she feels free. But instead of heading for home she continues on towards the harbour.

The tide's out, boats close to the quay rest at odd angles on the mud. A family of swans is roosting on the slipway. There's a chilly wind coming off the bay and few people about.

She plonks down on an OAP bench and texts Paige:

im out.

A reply pings back in seconds.

where?

down the quay where you?

be there in 5

Paige Tucker is her best friend and when she came to the school a year ago Kerry's life certainly changed for the better. Paige wasn't stupid and boring like the kids she'd grown up with. But, more importantly, to Paige she wasn't *poor Kerry Waycott whose dad died.*

Kerry'd had a bellyful of that. And of the stupid counsellor she had to see once a week at school, her mum going mental, her gran laying down the law then expecting her to cook and clean when her mum couldn't.

She missed her dad, obviously. But he'd been weird for a while before he died. Sometimes they'd still cuddle up on the sofa and watch the football. Other times she'd say something and he'd completely ignore her. She thought he was depressed but when she said that to her gran she'd got her head bitten off.

Paige said she had potential. That was something no one had ever said about her before. And Paige showed her how to perform for the camera. They practised making little videos on their phones, just the two of them. And they laughed a lot. Paige said that there were girls who had become millionaires on social media who weren't prettier or smarter than them. Paige reckoned they could do it. Paige had ambition. Kerry liked that.

She sees her friend appear around the corner, baseball cap on, hood up. Behind her on a leash she's towing a small Yorkshire terrier. Kerry rushes forward to meet her. They hug, the dog and his leash get tangled, he yelps.

'Sssh, Oscar,' Paige says sternly.

'Babes, I have been going mental,' says Kerry.

'Why did you stay at your gran's for so long?' says Paige. 'You should've just left.'

'She wouldn't let me.'

Paige shakes her head. They return to the bench and sit. Her friend smiles at her and says, 'So, you all right?'

'Yeah, sort of.'

Squeezing her hand Paige says, 'Oh babes, must've been awful.'

'Yeah.'

'But I've been posting. Feedback's great. It's created quite a buzz.'

'People think I'm a slut.'

'No they don't. Well, the boring ones do.'

'It really wasn't my fault.'

Paige pushes back her hood and sighs. 'What happened? I didn't even see you leave the bar.' The dog settles at her feet.

'We just went for a walk.'

'Are you stupid or what? What have I told you?'

'I thought he liked me.'

'Yeah, durr-brain. I told you how to play it. If they get really frisky, you give them a hand job. Jack them off quickly, it shuts them up.'

'I don't really know how to do that,' says Kerry.

Paige sighs. 'What did you tell the Feds?'

'Nothing really.'

'You said they came round twice.'

Tears well up in Kerry's eyes. She brushes them away. 'My gran, she just wouldn't shut up and she wouldn't let me go home.'

Paige gives her a sidelong glance. 'Kerry, what did you do?'

'I had to give them a name.'

'Oh, for fuck's sake.'

'P, I had to.'

'No you didn't. You could ruin everything.'

'I had no choice, I promise.'

'What did you actually tell them?'

Kerry wipes the back of her hand across her nose and says, 'I told them it was Jared.'

Paige leaps to her feet. 'Jared! You said Jared? Why?'

'I dunno. I had to say someone.' Even though Paige is her best mate there's stuff she can't say. It's too dangerous.

Her friend stares at her in disbelief and then the anger erupts. 'Why would you do that to him? Why? Cause he prefers me and you're just a jealous little bitch?'

'No! I'm really sorry. But what else was I supposed to do? I had to say something. I thought you'd understand.'

Paige yanks the dog to its feet. 'Yeah but not Jared.'

'I'll take it back. I'll tell them I was wrong.'

Paige is seething. Kerry's never seen her like this. There's a stillness about her, a coldness that's frightening.

'You are a complete moron,' she says. 'I don't know why I've wasted my time on a minger like you.'

Kerry's tears are flowing now. 'Paige, please, don't say that. You're my best friend.'

'What? You think I wanna be friends with a stupid, lying piece of shit like you? We're done! Don't ever speak to me again.'

Paige flips her hood up and walks away, dragging the dog after her.

'Please, Paige, I'm begging you. I'm sorry.'

Without stopping or turning Paige raises her middle digit and gives Kerry the finger.

Kerry slumps forward. She feels sick. Her head is spinning. The rape was bad but this is worse. Without Paige how will she survive? She puts her face in her hands and sobs.

CHAPTER EIGHTEEN

Thursday, 6.45am

It's dawn as Megan parks and walks down to the beach. The wind has been howling since the early hours; it's changed direction. Now it's onshore, from the north east, raw and gusting. The sea is churned up, there's a heavy swell and the waves crash on to the shore.

Megan has guessed it will be too rough to swim but she's come anyway. She's not sure why. Perhaps simply for the peace. As daylight slowly leaches through the louring clouds she sits on the concrete wall and watches the gulls stirring and strutting, stretching out their necks to emit their harsh screeching calls.

This is the part of her new life she does like, living by the sea. But the job? She's well aware that the adrenaline rush of undercover work is addictive and she was hooked. It ruined her marriage. Slater is snippy, has her down as a prima donna but she doesn't know the half of it. No one really does.

Having spent her teenage years truanting from school, out on the edge, taking care of her younger siblings, Megan can easily empathise with a girl like Kerry Waycott. She too was fatherless, although hers simply walked out of the door because he'd had enough. Her mother also functioned with the aid of prescription drugs and alcohol.

But what are the chances of bringing charges and mounting a successful prosecution for rape in this case? The Crown Prosecution

Service will demand a realistic prospect of a conviction. And even if she can persuade them and the DCI, she still has questions in her own mind about Kerry. A confused kid, a liar, an attention-seeker; she could be all those things.

Megan is in the office by eight thirty but finds the DCI already at her desk, glued to her laptop and clutching a mug of coffee. It doesn't look like her first. She's pale and her eyes darkly underscored; Megan concludes she's feeling the stress.

'Morning, boss.'

'CSI found a Gyuto Japanese chef's knife like this one in Georgia O'Brien's septic tank,' says Slater.

She swivels her laptop to show Megan the picture.

'You could do a lot of damage with that,' says Megan.

'They sell for around a hundred and sixty quid. Hilary Kumar reckons it's the right size for the murder weapon. It's gone to the lab. Hardly a speck of rust on it.'

'I've been thinking, boss. If I was going to kill my ex-husband, would I dump him in my own tank at the bottom of the garden?'

'Perhaps she had no choice,' says Slater. 'Most domestic murders involve anger and therefore an element of panic.'

'Then having done it, only weeks later, I hire a contractor to come and fix the tank? I'm just saying, doesn't make a lot of sense.'

'Murder isn't sensible,' says the DCI, 'which is why we follow the evidence. But we must bear in mind that statistically, in these circumstances, it's most likely to be the property owner.'

'She does appear to have a missing husband.'

'Any more leads on his whereabouts?'

'Last sighting of him was back in the summer. We're waiting for the bank to get back to us about activity on his account. And Brittney's asked the intelligence unit to run a check on his passport to see if he's skipped abroad.'

'What we really need is something concrete that links directly to the body. Any luck with dental records?'

'Brittney's working on that. Talking of which, boss. The Waycott case.'

'Waycott?' Slater is still scrolling through images of knives. 'People pay thousands for these things.'

'Looks to me more like the sort of knife a proper chef would have. Or that you'd find in a restaurant kitchen.'

'Possibly,' says Slater. 'But for someone like Georgia it could be about snobbery and having the best money can buy.'

Megan shrugs. 'She's rich enough, I suppose. On the teenage rape. Her grandmother called me and I went round there last night. Kerry is now saying she lied because she was scared. It wasn't a stranger rape, it was a barman she knows.'

'Well, Sexual Offences can have it back then. It's no longer our remit.'

'I thought at least we should bring him in for questioning. She is fourteen. And she's frightened.'

Slater leans back in her chair, gazes up at Megan and sighs. 'If I say no, it's not our job, leave it to the specialist rape team, you're going to think I'm a cold-hearted bitch who doesn't care, aren't you?'

Megan shrugs. 'Wouldn't have put it quite like that. But I have built up some rapport with the grandmother and I just feel I should carry on.' She lapses into silence.

Slater's hair is not quite as perfect as usual and Megan wonders if she's been up all night, waiting for some news from the CSIs.

'My first job as a DC,' says Slater, 'I was twenty-five and thought I was going to change the world. It was an eighteen-year-old student, in her first week at uni, went out and got very drunk. She was gang raped by three other students who thought because she was drunk and they were drunk it was just a bit of fun. Jury agreed and acquitted. A week later she jumped off a motorway bridge in front of a lorry.' She folds her hands. 'What I learnt from this was you can't get emotionally involved and do this job effectively. It's one or the other.'

Megan isn't inclined to argue. Her list of justifications for the things she did whilst working undercover wouldn't stand up to any moral scrutiny. But when it comes to emotional detachment, she's walking round with her brain in a sling. Choosing one or the other isn't an option for her. Sometimes she feels totally detached, other times sick with sorrow at the misery around her. Dr Moretti could probably explain this with some medical jargon. But what the hell use is that?

Vish appears in the doorway. 'Excuse me, boss. Just got a call through from the control room. Response officers were called out to a vulnerable misper. Sheila Waycott has reported her grand-daughter missing. They think she disappeared last night. Her bed wasn't slept in. The family are very worried. Sexual Offences have flagged it up to us.'

Slater throws up her hands and laughs. 'Well, there you go. I think you win this round, DS Thomas.'

It seems for all her fancy qualifications and focused determination under pressure there's a brittleness to Laura Slater.

'I don't think it's a competition, ma'am,' says Megan.

CHAPTER NINETEEN

Shirin has only visited Dame Heidi Soames's coastal mansion on one previous occasion. Set on a wooded slope above a rocky cove, the modernist structure comprises glass and steel and seems to hang from the hillside above the sea. Everything is light and spacious and minimalist, it couldn't be more different to Winterbrook Farm. But Shirin already knows that whatever her mother does or likes, Georgia favours the opposite.

Dame Heidi's housekeeper escorted her and Noah to one of several guest suites when they arrived the previous evening. On the bedroom wall there's a large black and white photo of a youthful Dame Heidi playing Ophelia at the RSC. The large, doleful eyes and delicate frame are still apparent fifty years later. She walks with a stick now, but it's Shirin's theory that she doesn't really need it; it's just an effective prop for the role of eccentric old lady with a stick. She's just had a cameo doing exactly that in a new Netflix series.

Shirin wakes much later than usual to find Noah has already disappeared from the king-sized bed. If she lets Georgia have her way this place will be his one day.

She only has to press a button to open the electronic blinds and the room floods with a sombre grey light. The vista is dominated by sea and sky. The rolling waves crested in white seem to beckon and draw you. To Shirin, who grew up on a run-down, inner city estate, it's mildly intimidating. The walk-in shower is as large as most bathrooms and she stands under the pulsing jets for some time. She concludes that she may as well make the most of the luxury lifestyle while it lasts. Soon the house of cards will come crashing down. He'll make sure of that.

A long sweeping staircase winds down through the central atrium and from it Shirin can see Noah perched at the breakfast bar in the open-plan kitchen. The housekeeper is feeding him cereal and juice. He looks like he owns the place already.

When she gets to the bottom of the stairs she becomes aware of voices, not loud but confidential, coming from a smaller room off the huge hallway. The housekeeper doesn't appear to have noticed her so she creeps closer to eavesdrop.

The door to the room is open. Georgia is slumped in an Eames armchair. Her mother is standing over her, gesticulating with her stick.

'Listen to me, Georgia. You can't be stupid and melodramatic about this. This is serious. You have to get your priorities straight.'

'Oh, Mummy, I don't know what to do. It doesn't make any sense.' Georgia's voice is small and whinny and pathetic.

'That's the trouble with you, you get involved with the wrong sort of people and never realise until it's too late and then you come whimpering to me to sort it out.'

'I'm sorry.'

'Well, I've told you what to do. Stop panicking. We will handle this.'

'But what if—'

'There are no what ifs.'

Shirin glances over her shoulder in the direction of the kitchen. The housekeeper is out of sight round a corner but she can still glimpse Noah's tousled head bent over his bowl. She catches his eye and smiles. He smiles back.

From within the study: 'I spoke to Henry Crewe last night and he's coming down. He's been my lawyer for thirty years, he knows everyone who's of any importance and he will deal with the police.'

Edging closer to the open doorway, Shirin can see the back of Dame Heidi. The old lady is fully dressed but Georgia is swathed in one of her Japanese kimonos. Next to her mother she looks like a sumo wrestler.

'This really isn't my fault,' bleats Georgia.

'I warned you years ago. Told you not to get involved. Then none of this would've happened.'

'I know. I'm so sorry, Mummy. I should've listened to you.' Now she's blubbing like a baby.

'Well, Henry's people'll sort it all out. At least now you are listening. That's something. So let's talk about the girl.'

'I need Shirin. She writes the books and, I have to say, she's really quite good at it.'

'You don't need her. There are plenty of other people out there who can ghost a book for you. They're only kids' books. How hard can that be? What sells them is your name and your brand.'

'I do enjoy doing the readings,' says Georgia meekly.

'I've published three autobiographies and two theatrical memoirs. They were all written by different people and they were all number one bestsellers. I'll get my agent to find someone to replace Shirin.'

'But I did promise her that—'

'More fool you. You owe her absolutely nothing, Georgia. You took her in, her and the child. You gave her a comfortable home and a decent wage. But now circumstances have changed. You've allowed her to become too powerful. We have to draw a line under all this. Understand?'

'Yes, Mummy.'

Shirin catches a flash of movement in her peripheral vision. It's the housekeeper coming round the corner with a tray of coffee.

Two swift steps take her back to the bottom of the stairs where she pauses.

'Shall I take that?' she says, smiling at the housekeeper.

The housekeeper smiles back and hands over the tray. On it is a large cafetière, two white bone china mugs and a small jug of milk.

Shirin carries it to the door of the study, stops, raps on the frame and walks in. 'Morning, ladies,' she says brightly.

Dame Heidi gives her a baleful look but Georgia jumps up.

'Darling,' says Georgia. 'How did you sleep?'

'Like a baby. This really is a lovely house, Heidi.'

Shirin places the tray on the desk and faces the two of them – Georgia, large and blowsy beside her malevolent pixie of a mother.

'Well,' says Shirin, 'here's what I think. We do need to draw a line under all this. But what exactly is this? You know the identity of the body, don't you?'

'Darling, don't be ridiculous,' says Georgia. 'How could we?'

'That I don't know. But if you're thinking of sidelining me, think again. Because you're right, we're in this together. And you need to remember that. I've been in the system, I've been locked up. Trust me, Georgia, the lifestyle wouldn't suit you.'

CHAPTER TWENTY

Thursday, 9.35am

Megan and Vish park the Škoda on the quayside and walk across the road to the stone building that was formerly a large harbourside pub. This is where Jared Clarke works; he's the barman Kerry says raped her. The front is criss-crossed with scaffolding and a tarpaulin hangs down over the upper stories. But downstairs there's an open door and a painted sign saying *Mayhem* with an arrow.

Megan is consumed with nagging guilt. If she'd acted on the information the previous evening when Kerry told her, would the kid even be missing?

As they reach the door to the bar there's an almighty crash and the sound of smashing glass. Exchanging looks, they step inside.

A big man, six three at least, solid muscle with a weightlifter's neck, is wielding a broken chair leg in his right hand. On the floor at his feet, prostrate and bleeding, a smaller individual cowers.

Whacking the chair leg down on his victim's trembling back he screams, 'Where is she? You tell me or I'll fuckin' kill yer!'

Vish launches himself forward. He matches the man in height but he's half the size. He grabs the man by the shoulder. The man, surprised at the onslaught, hesitates then swats him aside. Vish is knocked backwards to the floor.

Megan is on her phone, calling for back-up. Then she pulls out her warrant card, holds it out in front of her and shouts, 'Police! You're under arrest!'

The man blinks at her. His face is sweating, the chair leg still clutched in his hand.

'Don't even think about it,' says Megan. 'Put it down, kneel down, hands behind your head. Now!'

Vish is scrambling to his feet, winded from the blow.

Megan glances at him. 'You all right?'

He nods and pulls out a pair of handcuffs.

The man sighs, drops the chair leg. It clunks to the floor. He sinks to his knees. Vish grabs his wrists and forces his hands behind his back as he cuffs him.

Megan turns to the victim on the floor, squatting down beside him. He's barely conscious, his nose is smashed and his face is bleeding. He groans.

'Try not to move,' she says. Then she turns to Vish. 'Tell control we need an ambulance.'

'I'm on it,' the DC replies.

Standing up, Megan faces the assailant. 'You're under arrest for assaulting a police officer,' she says. 'You do not have to say anything. But it may harm your defence if you do not mention when questioned something you later rely on in court. Anything you do say may be given in evidence.'

'Oh yeah,' he says sourly. 'Nick me. If you tossers could do your job I wouldn't even be here.'

'What's your name?' says Megan.

'Justin Waycott. And that little turd is a rapist and has got hold of my niece Kerry. And he would've told me what he's done with her if you morons hadn't intervened.'

Megan glances at the man on the floor and concludes he must be Jared Clarke. He's not moving.

'Whatever he's done or you think he's done,' she says, 'does not justify your actions.'

'Get over yourself, copper,' says Justin. 'I know who you are now. The one who came round last night to see my mum. So you could've stopped this. You knew it was him cause they told you. If you'd nicked him last night when you should've, Kerry wouldn't be missing now. Whatever's happened to her, whatever he's done to her, is on you. Your fault. So don't lecture me. You got no right.'

Vish glares at him. 'You're in a lot of trouble, mate. I'd shut it if I was you.'

'Yeah, really?' sneers Justin. 'You're not from these parts, are you?'

Megan shakes her head wearily. She's met plenty of versions of Justin Waycott. Blokes brimming with resentment, on a hair trigger most of the time and looking for someone to blame. But her fear is, he's right about Kerry.

She goes back to Jared. He's breathing but his eyes are firmly shut.

'Jared,' she says. 'Can you hear me?'

Waycott huffs. 'Course he can hear you. Give him a good kick, that'll get his attention.'

Three uniformed response officers in stab vests and armed with Tasers come rushing in.

'Over here, lads,' says Vish.

'Get him out of here,' says Megan.

They take charge of Waycott. 'You find her,' he shouts, as they escort him out. 'Cause if she's harmed it's on you, copper. Remember that.'

Megan scans Jared Clarke. She doubts he's feigning it. His face is a bloodied mess. His right hand looks as if it's been stamped on. He wears a t-shirt which says *Surfers Against Sewage*. She sighs. He won't be answering questions any time soon.

A tall figure appears in the doorway. Silhouetted against the grey morning light, his features are hard to make out. He sends a visceral shiver through Megan; for a brief moment she feels as if she knows him. But that's impossible.

He comes striding across the room. 'Bloody hell,' he says. 'What happened here? Jared? My God!' He's broad-shouldered, black hair braided into neat cornrows and a sculpted beard. Megan feels the pheromones ping which is the last thing she expects or needs.

He looks anxiously at her. 'You the cops? I'm Leon Hall. I own the place. The guy from the cafe next door phoned me, said it was all kicking off. What the hell happened? A robbery?' He shakes his head. 'I just seen uniforms putting some thug in the back of a van.'

'I'm DS Thomas,' says Megan. He's not looking at her any more and she wishes he would. 'This is DC Prasad. We're not sure yet.'

Leon kneels down beside Jared, puts a gentle hand on his shoulder. 'Hang on in there, man. It's gonna be all right.' He glances up at Megan, he seems shaken. 'You got an ambulance coming? Shit, he don't look good.'

'They're on their way. What's his name?' She needs to check. Waycott could've got the wrong person.

'Jared Clarke. He's one of my barmen. Things can get a bit lairy on a Saturday night and we're prepared for that. But half nine on a Thursday morning, that's mental.'

'Is it usual for him to be here on his own?' asks Vish.

'He comes in early to clear up a bit. He's a really good lad, a real worker. Aww, this is just awful.' He seems distressed, Megan glimpses a tear welling in his dark eyes. 'Stupid thing is, the till's empty. I don't keep money on the premises overnight.'

'We're actually looking for a fourteen-year-old girl who's disappeared. Kerry Waycott. We have information that Jared might know her.'

Leon shrugs. 'Could do. I wouldn't know. You probably can't tell at the moment but he's a good-looking boy. He's always got girls running after him. Where's this bloody ambulance? Can't you hassle them?'

'I'll go and check,' says Vish.

'We've also been told that Kerry comes here to your bar,' says Megan.

Leon rocks back on his heels and sighs. 'Listen, Sergeant,' he says. 'We card every kid. Every single one. We have to. It's more than my licence is worth. But you know as well as I do, it's not foolproof. Fake IDs you can buy online nowadays, even your lot'd need a bloody microscope to tell the difference.'

'I appreciate it can be difficult for licensees. You've never heard of this girl, Kerry?'

'No, name doesn't ring a bell.' He gives her a quizzical look. 'What is this actually about?'

'I don't think this was a botched robbery, Mr Hall,' says Megan. 'The attacker is the uncle of the missing girl. Jared's been accused of raping her.'

Leon gives her a disbelieving look. 'What? Nah, he's not like that. No way. How old you say she was?'

'Fourteen.'

He shakes his head. 'No. Not Jared. Someone's got their wires crossed.'

Vish returns with two paramedics in tow. Leon steps back to let them work.

Leon folds his arms and stands beside Megan. His presence is brooding. His concern is focused on the boy on the floor. She's close enough to feel the heat of his body. It's a hard thing to admit to herself but he's the first man she's felt in any way drawn to for quite a while. They watch the paramedics put a collar on Jared and carefully lift him on to a stretcher. The boy groans.

'Pisses me off,' Leon says, 'I'd've been down here myself an hour ago, but I had a meeting with the builder. We're doing the rooms upstairs.' He sighs. 'If only I'd been here.'

'Was Jared working last night?'

'Yeah, all evening. We opened up at six, shut the doors at eleven. I locked up about half past and gave him and a couple of the others a lift home.'

'Where does he live?'

'He shares a flat with another lad, Harry, who also works for me. They're kite surfers. Bar work gives them a chance to get out on the waves during the day. They're both really good, compete at a national level.' He sighs. 'Look, I don't know who's pointing the finger at Jared but it's bollocks. I know him. He's no rapist.'

'It's one line of inquiry,' says Megan.

But his attention is already on the stretcher as it's being lifted and carried out of the door. 'I'm going to the hospital with him if that's okay.' He starts to follow the paramedics.

'Of course,' says Megan.

He doesn't look back.

She stands in the middle of the bar room and looks around. It smells of floor cleaner and beer. What is the matter with her? She's forty-two. He must be ten years younger. At least. He's a tattooed mixed-race guy who runs a bar. What is this? Some kind of weird nostalgia for her past London life? She's not that woman any more. Nor does she want to be.

CHAPTER TWENTY-ONE

Sheila Waycott's sitting room has turned into an informal co-ordination centre for the search. Friends, family, neighbours with dogs are coming and going, collecting printed maps. A zoned-out Heather is dispensing drinks in the kitchen.

Megan stands in the hallway and watches. The official police search is being run from a mobile unit in town. But this is where the energy is and the urgency. Megan bumps into her brother-in-law, Mark, as he comes out.

'Oh,' he says, 'well, I thought I should do my bit. For Dave, as much as anything. The family's been through so much.'

Megan just smiles and nods. They both feel the awkwardness; he retreats to the kitchen. The community is turning out for one of its own and out of respect for the memory of Kerry's dead father.

Hovering in the doorway, Megan waits until she catches Sheila's eye.

'Well, well,' Sheila says bitterly. 'I didn't think you'd show your face. Too busy nicking honest men who are just trying to make a difference.'

'Sheila,' says Megan. 'You know as well as me that having your son beat a suspect half to death is not the answer.'

'Oh, so you're here to nick me too? I didn't tell him what to do. But Justin feels responsible for Kerry since her dad died.'

Megan sighs. 'I'm not here to nick you. I'm here to ask you to let us do our job.'

Sheila throws out her arms. Her face is gaunt, she's obviously running on caffeine and anxiety. 'What?' she says. 'You don't want all these people looking too?'

The surly attitude is understandable and Megan knows she must suck it up. But Sheila Waycott can't make her feel any worse. She saw Kerry that night, knew something was wrong but did nothing. That's when she should've intervened.

'We welcome the help,' she says. 'But that's not what I'm talking about.'

'Used to be the case,' says Sheila, 'that if a kiddie went missing, the local constables from the police station in town would be in charge. Someone that we know and that knows us. But all of that's been done away with.'

Yeah yeah, nostalgia's not what it used to be.

'I'm not going to waste time with a discussion of how things have changed,' Megan says briskly. 'I need Kerry's phone number. I need all and any information you have about her social media accounts and her email address. Has she got a bank card?'

'I've got her phone number. You'll have to ask Heather about the rest.'

'And I presume you've been calling her?'

'Since six o'clock this morning. I woke up and I just had this horrible feeling. I should never've let her go. I went round to Heather's and woke her up. We discovered that Kerry hadn't been home. She left here last night not long after you. So where did she go? Then I went to her friend's house.'

'Paige Tucker?'

Sheila shakes her head with disdain. 'The mother's a right snotty cow. "We've got money", you know the sort.'

Megan does.

'It was seven by then. I forced her to let me speak to Paige. She hasn't seen her or heard from her. Then I got really worried. Cause there's only one answer, isn't there? She went to him.'

'Why do you think she'd do that?'

'She's a child. She wants people to like her and she felt bad about telling you about him.'

So there was no evidence, the Waycotts were just jumping to a whole load of conclusions.

'I got the impression she was scared of him,' says Megan. 'There are lots of other possibilities of what she could've done, Sheila. Maybe she got on the last bus somewhere? We've got officers going through the CCTV round the town looking for sightings. Whether or not Jared Clarke raped her may well be a separate issue from her disappearance.'

'What's he said about it? Does he deny it?'

'He's said nothing yet. He's in hospital, unconscious. DC Prasad is at his bedside waiting for him to wake up so he can be questioned.'

Sheila looks at Megan and her chin trembles. If she's capable of remorse, this is it.

'Look, Justin didn't mean to really hurt him,' she says. 'But he's got a temper.'

'I know, I've seen it.'

'I didn't tell him what had happened to Kerry before because I know what he's like. When we lost Dave everything went to pieces.' She swallows down her grief. 'His big brother kept him in line. My eldest son was a good man.'

'I'm sure he was, Sheila.'

'And Justin worshipped him. He got so mad when he heard about Kerry because he felt he'd let Dave down. And there was no stopping him.'

'If he gets himself a good lawyer I'm sure they'll say all this in mitigation. But the priority now is to find Kerry. Wouldn't you agree?'

Sheila nods. 'Do you think she's dead?'

'I think she's missing and vulnerable. But there's no reason to assume she's come to harm. We'll find her, Sheila.'

It sounds convincing but is it true?

CHAPTER TWENTY-TWO

Thursday, 11.45am

After a futile attempt to find out about Kerry's social media accounts from Heather Waycott, Megan comes out of the house to find a group of men standing round the Škoda. One is sitting on the bonnet smoking. Megan counts seven in total. They range in ages from early twenties to forties a couple wear high-viz vests, most have work clothes and heavy fishermen's jackets.

The bonnet sitter jumps up, tosses his fag and steps forward. 'You the bitch that nicked Justin?'

'I'm DS Thomas and I arrested Justin Waycott for a serious assault. I suggest you all step back from my car or I may end up nicking you too.'

But the man moves towards her; he's young and not as big as some of the others. He needs to prove he's tough. It's the gang mentality, Megan's seen plenty of that. His beard is ginger, still downy and soft, but his eyes are full of hatred.

'You lot,' he says, 'you just think you can treat us all like shit and we'll take it. Well, me and the lads take another view.'

'Do you?' says Megan. 'I'm here to find Kerry Waycott and you are stopping me from doing that.'

Another older man pipes up. 'We'll find her but you need to let Justin go and drop the charges. He ain't done nothing wrong, he was just protecting his family.'

Megan takes a deep breath. She's alone, without back-up because they're short-handed and Vish has gone to the hospital. She knows staying calm and keeping her nerve will determine what happens next. Placing her focus on the pack leader, she stares him out.

'Listen,' she says. 'I'm sure you'd all agree with me that the priority is to find Kerry.'

A third man, small and weaselly with a woolly hat pulled low over his forehead, chips in. 'That's our priority. And Justin's. Fuck knows about you lot. You just want to tick your boxes. Make it look like you're doing the right thing.'

'We've already got officers, dog handlers and drones deployed looking for Kerry. We're also tracking her mobile phone. That's a large commitment of resources. I don't call that box-ticking.'

'She's just saying that. Bitch is clearly lying,' says the ginger beard.

The staring has worked, he's less confident.

'Yeah,' says the weasel. 'If you was really on our side, you'd let Justin go.'

'That's not an option,' Megan replies evenly. 'The man he beat up, who may or may not have any involvement in Kerry's disappearance, is in hospital in a serious condition. I don't call that self-defence or protecting your family, I call it an intentional assault resulting in grievous bodily harm. And it's against the law.'

Sheila Waycott appears on the doorstep, scowl on face, arms folded, feet planted in battle-axe mode.

Megan glances over her shoulder in Sheila's direction. Back-up comes in unexpected forms.

Turning to the men crowding round her she says, 'Are you going to let me get on with the job of finding Kerry or not?'

A tall man at the back of the group calls out, 'Is she telling the truth, Sheila?'

For a moment Sheila says nothing. She regards Megan with a gimlet eye. Then she sighs and says, 'All I know is, my son's in jail and she's protecting a rapist.' With that she disappears back into the house.

Megan feels the tension rippling round the group. Like a pack of feral dogs they're waiting for the first to strike. Megan's guess is it will be ginger beard, he's itching for it. He's also the youngest, with the most to prove. She braces herself.

Then she hears a familiar voice.

'What's going on here, lads?' It's Mark. He's just come out of the house and is walking towards them.

'Mind your own business, Markie,' says the weasel.

'What you planning to do? Think about this. She's a police officer.'

'Whadda you care?' says ginger beard. 'You shagging her?'

'She's my sister-in-law,' says Mark. 'She's just doing her job. And you lot need to back off right now. You're not helping Justin and you're certainly not helping Kerry.'

'Your fucking sister-in-law!' The comment comes from the back of the pack accompanied by a guffaw.

'You always was an arse-licking toe rag, wasn't you, Markie,' says the weasel.

Mark stands next to Megan. 'And you always was a brainless, lazy piece of shit, Billy. You still beating your wife and kids and spending her wages on booze?'

Billy wags his finger. 'One of these nights, mate. Just you and me.'

'Yeah,' says Mark. 'I don't think you got the bottle. Now piss off, the lot of you!'

There's some mumbling and a degree of sidling about before they start to walk away.

Mark turns to her. 'You all right?'

She smiles. 'I am now. Thanks.'

He shrugs. 'They're the worst elements. The low-lives. Every town's got them. Don't judge us by them.'

'I don't,' says Megan. 'And I'm glad you were here.'

He seems embarrassed but he smiles. 'Deb would never have forgiven me. And she's the boss in our house.'

Mark Hayden has been married to her sister for sixteen years but Megan doesn't feel she knows him that well. At first glance he's a rugged bloke, rough round the edges, and in appearance not so different from Justin Waycott. But there any similarity ends. Mark lets his wife do the talking for both of them but he's the solid presence behind her. Debbie and the kids are the bedrock of his existence. He's a shy man. Megan's ex-husband, Paul, had found him boring. So family get-togethers had been tricky.

A memory of Paul jumps into her head. Funny, always telling stories. Full of mercurial energy. Her ex-husband was brimming with the social confidence that Mark lacks. But he wasn't dependable, not in the way Mark is. When she returned home broken by the job, he couldn't cope. He wanted a wife who mirrored him, reflected his brilliance. In less than a month, he left her.

Megan's phone buzzes, breaking the awkwardness of the moment. She glances at the screen. Linda Kovacs?

She answers. 'DS Thomas.'

The headteacher sounds tense. 'Some of the students have come to me,' she says, 'with a video on Snapchat. It's Kerry Waycott. She's saying she's going to commit suicide.'

'Can you tell where she is?'

'Not really. Near the sea on the cliffs I think. She says she's going to jump and live-stream herself doing it.'

CHAPTER TWENTY-THREE

Thursday, 12.05pm

Megan is en route to the school when she gets the call that the drone unit has identified a lone figure on a remote part of the headland near Berry Head. The coastguard has been alerted.

DCI Slater comes on the car speakerphone. 'It's a favourite suicide spot,' she says. 'High and difficult to access. Uniformed response are a couple of minutes away but my nearest trained negotiator is in Exeter. Do you think she'll do it or is this attention-seeking?'

'I couldn't say, boss.' Megan is glancing at her satnav. 'I can be there in less than five myself, let me have a go at talking her down. At least she knows me.'

'Okay,' says Slater. 'I've got a meeting with Georgia O'Brien's bloody lawyer. He's coming down from London. But keep me posted.'

'Will do.'

Narrow lanes with towering hedgerows wind upwards towards the clifftop. Then suddenly the road turns into a track and the vista opens up to uneven pasture with a few low windswept bushes.

Megan can see a patrol car parked up ahead. She pulls up next to it.

One officer stands beside the car, feeding back information via the radio. She looks absurdly young and nervous. Megan flashes her ID.

The PC looks relieved. 'This is my first jumper,' she says. 'My mate's trying to talk to her but she's climbed down onto a bit of a ledge.'

'Right,' says Megan. 'Report back to the coastguard that we might need some help to winch her up.'

The PC nods, glad to be doing something useful.

Megan heads up a short incline towards the cliff edge. The wind buffets her. It's been blowing hard for most of the day but inland it's not so noticeable. Added to that there's now a fine drizzle. Out to sea, the horizon is shrouded in mist.

The other PC is lying on his belly in the wet grass. Megan squats on all fours next to him.

'I'm DS Thomas,' she says. 'I've dealt with this girl already. Is she saying anything?'

'Just told me to eff off,' he replies sheepishly. 'Be careful,' he adds. 'The edge here is very crumbly. Whole bloody thing could just go. There's been landslips all along these cliffs.'

Megan lies down flat and peers over. The ground falls away steeply but is covered in thick vegetation which seems quite brambly and sharp. A few feet below her she can see the back of Kerry Waycott's head. She's sitting hunched forward with only a small scrubby bush between her and the sheer drop. Waves are crashing on the rocks far below. Her denim jacket is soaked and her hair is plastered to her scalp.

'Go back to your mate,' Megan whispers to the young PC, 'and tell her we definitely need the coastguard and winching gear. ASAP.'

'Will do.' He crawls back from the edge.

Megan takes his place. She can feel the wet seeping through her shirt from the sodden grass beneath her and rain trickling down her face and neck.

'Hello, Kerry,' she says. 'It's Megan, Megan Thomas. I came to talk to you at your gran's last night.'

At first there's no response, then the girl cranes her neck to look up.

'Hey,' says Megan. 'You've got yourself in a bit of a pickle. But I'm here to help you.'

'No one can help me.' Her voice is barely audible.

'It may feel like that at the moment. But you and me, we're going to sort this out.'

'Everyone hates me, thinks I'm a skanky bitch.'

'I don't. Your mum and your gran don't. Your friends don't. Everyone's really concerned about you and wants you to come home.'

'Thing is, I am a bitch.'

'Whatever you're worried about, Kerry, we can sort it out, I promise you.'

'No, you can't. You're lying. I'd rather just jump and get it over with.'

'Haven't you got a little brother and sister? They'll be so upset.'

'They'll get over it. They'll have to. Like with Dad, you just have to get over it.'

'Things have been really hard for you, I know that. My dad went off when I was a teenager so I do know what it's like. He didn't die though, he just walked out.'

'Where did he go?'

'I've no idea. I didn't care. Then my younger sister went looking for him years later. He'd moved to Manchester, had a new partner and two more kids. A whole new family.'

She's hooked the teenager's attention. Kerry is looking up at her.

'What happened?'

'He was really angry that Debbie – that's my sister – had found him. He didn't want his new partner to find out what a complete shithead he was.'

'Did you go and see him?'

'No, I already knew he was a lying shit.'

'You could've gone to his partner and told her. Dobbed him in.'

'Believe me, I thought about it. But I decided I just wanted to get on with my own life. Find a way forward. And however dark and depressing things look there is always a way forward, Kerry.' Her way forward was to marry Paul, which didn't turn out so well. But she doesn't mention that.

'Not for me,' says Kerry.

'There is. I promise you. You just have to find it.'

Megan glances over her shoulder. A coastguard vehicle has pulled up beside the squad car and two men are getting out and starting to unload their gear.

'Paige hates me,' says Kerry. 'I really thought she was my friend.'

'Friends fall out. But she's worried about you too.'

'That's a lie. I've seen what she's been posting. I know what she wants. She wants me to jump because then she can be in the spotlight. She can be the grieving best friend of the girl who jumped off the cliff. She'll get loads more followers.'

'Well if that's the case then she's not worthy to be your friend. Do you know my niece, Amber Hayden? She goes to your school. I've met some of her mates, they're really nice.'

'I was at primary with Amber. She thinks I'm a slut too. All that lot do.'

'Have you thought that perhaps it's because you're friends with Paige?'

'Paige is really cool. Everyone likes her.'

'You sure? I don't think Amber likes her.'

Kerry sighs. 'I dunno. I'm confused.'

'And wet and tired. I know. So here's my plan. You just sit tight and we're going to get you up and out of there. Get you nice and warm and dry. You fancy a mug of hot chocolate?'

Megan beckons to the coastguards. They come trotting towards her.

'Yeah.' Megan can see the hint of a smile on the side of Kerry's upturned face.

'Do you like it with all the marshmallows and stuff?'

'Yeah.'

'Me too. Real sugar hit,' says Megan.

'I think I can climb back up,' says Kerry.

'No, stay still! Wait—'

Kerry stands up and the bush in front of her gives way. Losing her footing, she screams and grabs onto the tussocks of grass above her. Megan seizes her wrist.

The first coastguard officer leans over Megan, pinning her down, and stretches over her to catch hold of Kerry's arm. The second officer lies down next to her and grasps the other arm. They hoist Kerry up in one fluid movement and roll her over onto the grass. The first officer pulls Megan away from the edge. They all end up in a heap.

'Well,' says the first officer. 'Health and safety won't be too impressed by this.'

'I won't tell if you don't,' says Megan.

Kerry looks as shocked as she feels.

'You all right?' Megan asks.

The girl nods. She's shivering, her face pale and lost and desolate. Megan puts an arm round her. 'It's going to be okay.'

'No it isn't,' says Kerry. 'Paige is right, I'm a complete moron.'

'Believe me, we all make mistakes. It's not just you. But it doesn't make you a bad person. You have to remember that.' They both have to remember that.

The young PC arrives with a space blanket. Megan wraps it carefully around Kerry.

They walk back towards the squad car. Megan is cold and wet but it doesn't matter. She's dodged another bullet. Relief floods through her.

CHAPTER TWENTY-FOUR

Thursday, 12.30pm

Laura Slater places a mug of coffee in front of her guest. Is she making a point? she wonders. Keeping it informal, not succumbing to the game that Sir Henry Crewe is hoping to play with her?

'I'm so sorry for keeping you waiting,' she says. 'I've just been co-ordinating a cliff rescue.'

He inclines his glossy white patrician head and says, 'I would've thought that was a job for uniform and the coastguard, not you, Detective Chief Inspector.'

'Ordinarily, yes. But the girl in question is part of an ongoing inquiry. We have a lot on our plate at present.'

'In which case I'm extremely grateful that you're sparing the time to talk to me.'

Laura sits down across the conference table from the lawyer. She doesn't mention that she's seen him before, when he gave a talk to her class at university. Afterwards all the high-flyers had queued up to pay court to the great man. His firm – called simply Crewe and Partners – took only three law graduates a year. And they took the best. A First was mandatory to even get an interview. Back then Laura was toying with the idea of a legal career but she didn't have the nerve to approach him.

Nowadays he's a PR man as much as a lawyer. His clients are the great and good; he sorts out the fallout from their sexual peccadilloes, their messy divorces, their financial indiscretions. The knighthood came from a grateful former prime minister. Crewe had helped smooth over a scandal involving party funding.

'So what can I do for you?' says Laura. She tries to imagine that she's talking to an annoying neighbour who's knocked on the door at an inconvenient moment, not to a legal grandee who's consulted on cabinet appointments.

'I'm here on behalf of Georgia O'Brien,' says the great man. 'As I'm sure you're aware, her mother is Dame Heidi Soames and Heidi is a great friend of mine.'

'Heidi Soames the actress? No, I wasn't aware Ms O'Brien was her daughter.' If Sir Henry is going to try and lean on her then at least she can make him work for it.

He scans her face. Can he tell she's lying?

Steepling his fingers, he says, 'My information is that there was an unfortunate discovery in Georgia's septic tank.'

Laura stares at him with a blank expression. She says nothing. He returns her gaze; he must be close to seventy but his eyes are still cornflower blue.

Then she smiles. 'I have two small children,' she says. 'They love all the Disney movies. Wasn't Heidi an old witch who helps some kids escape from a dragon in... oh, I can't remember the title of the film. But we loved it.'

'In all probability,' he replies. Those hooded blue eyes are now regarding Laura sharply.

Game on, thinks Laura.

'One of my younger associates, Jonathan Cooper, says he knows you from university.'

'Really,' says Laura. Upper-class tosser known to all the girls on her course as a groper. 'I don't think I recall him. But perhaps we weren't in the same year.'

'He remembers you. Says you were remarkably able. There was some surprise that you didn't opt for the Bar.'

'I was always interested in criminal law,' says Laura. 'I did an MSc in Criminology and that persuaded me that a career in the police might be more interesting and challenging.'

'Excellent,' says Sir Henry, sipping his coffee. 'I'm sure your chief constable is extremely glad of that.'

Now they're getting down to it. *Here comes the veiled threat,* thinks Laura. She decides to take the bull by the horns.

'You want to talk to me about the body found in Georgia O'Brien's septic tank,' she says.

'Indeed.' He sighs dramatically. 'To be perfectly candid, Georgia is something of a worry to her poor mother. Over the years she's made some poor decisions.'

He's worried but how much does he know?

'I suppose that sometimes,' he continues, 'having a famous parent who's been very successful is not an advantage.'

Dumping your kid with a series of nannies while you live a rackety life between lovers probably doesn't help either. Laura has read the background brief that DC Brittney Saric prepared.

But she makes no comment. If it does turn out to be the husband in the tank, this is going to be a tough one to explain away, even for a skilled operator like Sir Henry. She's curious as to how he'll do it.

'It's not generally known,' he says, 'but over the years Georgia has had issues with her mental health. Two difficult marriages. Ups and downs in her career. Depression. An over-reliance on prescription drugs. Some unwise liaisons.'

Diminished responsibility. Is that going to be his fallback position?

'She seems to have found considerable success in her own right as a children's author,' says Laura.

'Yes indeed,' he replies. 'Which is why this is all rather unfortunate. I understand Georgia has been evicted from her home and it's being treated as a crime scene, so I presume you're taking this quite seriously.'

'When a body's found and the death is unexplained we always take it seriously. But we're following routine procedure and our inquiry is in the very early stages. There's little else to say at present.'

'You do realise that given Georgia's profile, this may attract some attention from the media. I think it would benefit us both to get ahead of that particular game. I was wondering if a joint statement would be useful?'

'Saying what?'

'A body was discovered on Georgia's property, she has no idea how it got there and that she's co-operating fully with your inquiries.'

'She's been rather awkward actually. And rude to my officers.'

'I'm sure. But, as I've explained, she has her issues.'

'Sir Henry, do you mind if I speak frankly?'

'I wish you would.'

'I'm going to do my job; I will investigate, collect evidence and follow procedures to the letter. It's not part of my job to help you do your job. You don't want any of this to impact negatively on your client, which is understandable. But I can't help you in that regard. You can take the matter up with Detective Superintendent Barker or with the chief constable. But we will issue a statement to the press when we're ready and have something to say.'

Sir Henry Crewe smiles and shakes his head wearily. Laura feels a surge of excitement. The look on his face says she's got him on the back foot.

He seems to be pondering, considering a change of tactics possibly?

'You're looking for Damian,' he says. 'What if you don't find him?'

They know the identity of the body. And it is Damian.

'Do you have any information as to his whereabouts?'

'I've honestly no idea.' He hesitates, then he adds, 'Look, all I want is a heads-up. Let me bring Georgia in voluntarily to answer questions.'

'She'd be interviewed under caution.'

'Of course. I understand you don't want to be rushed. But you must have the results of the PM by now. So you probably know how this person died and how recently, even if you haven't identified them yet. Your CSIs are all over my client's property because they're looking for a murder weapon. I'm just trying to make a difficult situation as easy as possible for my client. And that's me doing my job.'

He smiles, the blue eyes twinkle. *He thinks Georgia murdered her old man.* But now Laura needs to prove it. She feels a surge of adrenaline.

'Do you want to bring her in tomorrow morning?' she says. Damage limitation appears to be his new strategy.

'Thank you,' he replies. 'Would eleven o'clock be suitable?' It sounds as if he's arranging a dental appointment.

'Yes, that's fine,' says Laura.

He rises, offers his hand to shake and sails out of the office.

Laura stands behind her desk savouring the moment. Is it too much to hope that Georgia O'Brien might actually confess to murder? They still don't have the evidence to prove the body is Damian Conrad. But if she talks that might not matter.

CHAPTER TWENTY-FIVE

Thursday, 1.15pm

A bedraggled Kerry Waycott sits in the back of an ambulance and Megan keeps her promise of a hot chocolate, sending the young PC to get one from the cafe next to the lighthouse on the headland.

Megan leaves it to the paramedics to check Kerry over. She phones Sheila Waycott to tell her that her granddaughter has been found.

'Found where?' says Sheila. 'You said that bastard was in hospital.'

'She was planning to jump off the cliffs near Berry Head. She thinks everyone hates her.'

The other end of the line remains silent.

'Sheila? You still there?'

The phone goes dead.

Megan sighs. She understands where Sheila's attitude is coming from but that doesn't make it any easier to stomach. Her shirt and the front of her trousers are soaked through. Her brand new suit jacket, bought for the job, is plastered in mud. She feels shivery. The euphoric rush of saving the girl is fading. She needs a change of clothes.

Returning to the ambulance, she finds Kerry settled in the back, scooping the pink and white marshmallows from the top of her hot chocolate with her finger.

'How you doing?' says Megan.

'My gran is going to go mental, isn't she?'

Quite likely in Megan's view but she says, 'Listen to me, Kerry. These guys are going to take you to the hospital and get you checked over. You need to talk to the doctors about how you've been feeling and the things that led to this. Because then they can arrange to get you some proper support and help. Okay?'

Kerry nods. She seems absurdly young, bundled up in the space blanket like a cherubic toddler.

'You're right about Paige,' she says. 'She's not a proper friend. If she was, she'd've never walked off and left me.'

'Left you when?'

'Last night. I went down the harbour. She came and met me, said some pretty nasty things.'

Sheila told Megan she'd been to the Tucker house that morning looking for Kerry and Paige had said she hadn't seen her.

'You're right, mate,' says Megan. 'Paige is bad news and I'd steer clear if I was you.'

After a quick visit home for a change of clothes, Megan drives to the school. Vish is in the car park waiting for her.

'You all right?' he says.

Megan didn't think she looked that bad.

'Only you've got mud on your face.'

She licks her fingers, squats down and peers in the door mirror to clean herself up.

'Better?'

He nods.

'So has Jared Clarke regained consciousness?' says Megan.

'I only had the chance of a quick word. They were taking him to theatre. His nose is so badly smashed he can't breathe.'

Megan shakes her head wearily. 'What did he say?'

'Complete denial. Says he was working that night but I don't think he's that sure who Kerry is. But he knows Paige.'

'Has he given a DNA sample?' says Megan.

'Yeah. No problem. He asked specifically if we could use it to clear his name.'

'Okay, we need to wrap this up.' Slater's words are ringing in Megan's head: *we're not social workers.*

As they approach the main doors the bell goes for the end of the school day and the place erupts. Pupils come hurtling down the corridors, from tiny year sevens in baggy blazers they've yet to grow into, to cool year thirteen girls with silky manes and super-short skirts.

It takes several minutes for Megan and Vish to navigate their way through the flood to the headteacher's office.

Linda Kovacs is waiting for them. She looks stressed. Her red lipstick is smudged.

'She's all right then?'

'Yes,' says Megan. 'She's been taken to hospital to be checked over. But physically she's fine.'

'Thank God. I had a suicide at my last school. Sixteen-year-old boy. It was awful.'

There's a tap on the door and Simon Jones appears. No dolphin tie today, just sober stripes. He looks straight at Kovacs, who nods and says, 'She's okay.'

'This is a bit of a knot to untangle,' says Megan. 'We have an allegation of rape and an attempted suicide. It also seems to me that there could be some bullying involved.'

'Bullying?' says Kovacs defensively.

'There seems to be something of a power imbalance between Kerry Waycott and her friend, Paige Tucker.'

'I don't think this can be laid at Paige's door,' says Jones briskly. 'Kerry is the attention-seeker. She's latched on to Paige, who is far more mature and frankly a smarter girl.'

This is not how Amber described her, thinks Megan. More middle class, maybe.

But she says, 'The barman who Kerry alleges raped her doesn't seem to know her name but he knows Paige.'

Simon Jones shifts from foot to foot. He's irritated. Megan watches as Kovacs tries to catch his eye to subdue him.

'Look,' he says, 'all I'm saying is, Paige shouldn't be dragged into this.'

Kovacs steps forward. 'I think you can leave it to us to deal with the dynamic between these girls. Obviously rape is a matter for the police. But I think that, with a girl like Kerry, there's a good chance this whole thing is a story she's made up to gain attention. To gain sympathy from friends like Paige and to use on social media to gain even more sympathy and attention.'

'Our forensic team does have semen that we can check for DNA,' says Megan.

'I'm not saying she hasn't had sex,' says Kovacs.

Megan notices Simon Jones's reaction. Suddenly he's still. It's as if he's holding his breath.

The headteacher glances at him then focuses back on Megan. 'I'm aware how busy you must be, Sergeant. The Waycotts are not easy people to deal with and the tragedy of the parents has fallen heavily on Kerry. But I will tackle the matter and get some proper counselling for this poor girl.'

'The grandmother appears to be in control, do you think she'll agree?' says Megan.

'I've dealt with Sheila Waycott before,' says Kovacs. 'You just have to talk to her in the right way.'

Megan tries to imagine that conversation: the supercilious headteacher versus the angry trawlerman's widow. But Kovacs is right; there doesn't appear to be enough evidence to prosecute so realistically there's nothing more the police can do. Kerry Waycott is someone else's problem.

As she and Vish walk out of the school and across the car park she says, 'Is it me or was that weird?'

'There was a weird vibe,' Vish replies.

'What's the deal with Mr Jones?'

Vish shrugs. 'I had a teacher like that at school. He was creepy too.'

Megan sighs. 'Perhaps we're just being too suspicious. Suggesting there was bullying going on in their school is bound to make them defensive.'

'Maybe,' says Vish. 'My dad says since I became a cop I've become cynical and suspicious of everyone.'

Megan unlocks the car and they get in.

'The team's got a full-time analyst, hasn't it?' says Megan.

'Kitty. She's a laugh.'

'I think we should ask her to run a check on Mr Jones. Just to be thorough.'

CHAPTER TWENTY-SIX

Thursday, 5pm

It's getting dark, that encroaching teatime darkness of autumn. The orange glow of a street lamp filters through the blinds. Megan sits in the low-slung armchair facing Dr Moretti.

She sighs and says, 'Thanks for fitting me in at such short notice.'

Moretti gives her the annoying, lip-curl smile. 'Busy week?'

'And it's only Thursday,' says Megan.

They both laugh.

The shrink sits with her hands neatly folded. Megan knows she's waiting. At the time she called, wet through from leaning over the edge of a cliff, it seemed like a good idea. Now she's not so sure.

Stop being such a bloody child!

'Okay,' she says. 'I think maybe I had a panic attack. One of the officers I was with used to be a paramedic. She said it was.'

Moretti nods. 'When was this?'

'Monday. First job I went on.'

'How long did it go on for?'

'I don't really know. A few minutes, maybe less. This officer I mentioned, she got hold of me, told me to just breathe. I thought I was having a heart attack.'

'Panic attacks can be very frightening. Do you know what the trigger was?'

Megan nods. She's about to reply. Then from nowhere at all the tears come. She never cries. Hasn't for years. But now she's choking with sobs and can't seem to stop. Moretti passes her the box of tissues.

Her mind seems oddly blank, she's not even thinking about the rats. What's consuming her is a sense of utter despair. Her brain is fogbound by the feeling. But then comes another sensation. It's rising up inside from her guts, up her gullet, into her throat. She gags on it. Anger. Pure rage. And now she sees the rats, with their sharp incisors and their scurrying claws.

Moments pass. Could even be five minutes. Moretti says nothing, does nothing. She's watching Megan with a steady, gentle gaze.

Megan plucks a tissue from the box and blows her nose.

Eventually she says, 'There was this dead body in a septic tank. The contractors fixing the tank found it and called us. My first job. It felt like a test. I didn't want to do the wrong thing. Calling out a whole forensic team is expensive. And I know that Slater doesn't really want me on the team, feels she's been lumbered. I didn't want to give her any ammo. So I stuck my head down into the tank to take a look. And there were rats eating the corpse.'

She swallows hard. Now she sees them again, sliding silently between the bones. Slick muzzles, shiny swishing tails.

'Deep breaths,' says Moretti. 'Slowly in, then out.'

Megan inhales and exhales.

'That's good. Concentrate on your breathing.'

It seems odd to Megan that such a simple thing, that we take for granted, can be so soothing.

She looks at Moretti. 'Sorry,' she says.

'For what?'

'I don't know. I feel embarrassed.'

'This is what I'm here for.'

'It's made me think, can I even do this job?' says Megan. 'What if it happens again? Am I just fooling myself?'

'Do you think you are?'

'I really don't know. I was determined to come back because I couldn't imagine what else I would do.'

'Is that the only reason?'

'I used to think I was good at it. But half the time it feels like I can't trust my own judgement any more.'

'Maybe you are good at it,' says Moretti. 'Other people seem to think so, but perhaps you need to rediscover that for yourself.'

'What if I keep having panic attacks?'

'There is medication.'

'No,' says Megan firmly. 'I don't want that.' Ever since she could remember her mum was on tablets of one sort or another. For her nerves, for her blood pressure. When she died at sixty-two the GP had tried to explain it away with jargon. Megan believes, in the end, it was the combination of all those bloody pills that killed her.

Moretti tilts her head. 'You saw rats eating a dead body. Pretty horrible. It also means your fear is rooted in logic and experience. To my mind, that could make it easier to manage.'

'How d'you mean?'

'Avoid rats.'

'It's that simple.'

Moretti smiles. 'No, it's not simple. But with practice it's doable. Where you live, do you worry about them?'

'Not really. My sister has a dog. He chases anything that moves.'

'We all need strategies to navigate the world and keep ourselves safe. But the neuroplasticity of the human brain is amazing.'

'What does that mean?'

'It means you can teach an old dog new tricks,' says Moretti. 'I'm not saying you'll never have another attack. But it seems to me the trigger is quite specific, so it can be managed.'

'If I avoid rats?'

'Of the rodent variety. The ones you arrest are a different matter.'

Megan stares at her. Dr Diane Moretti, her inscrutable shrink, is making a joke.

CHAPTER TWENTY-SEVEN

Friday, 7.30am

For the first time in a long while Megan sleeps through the night. As pallid shafts of dawn light percolate through the blinds on her attic window she is instantly awake and alert. The harbour below looks calm enough but she checks the coastal forecast app on her phone, which informs her the tide is high with a moderate swell. Too rough to swim? Her mood is buoyant. What's life without a little risk?

She usually drives to a nearby beach which sweeps round to encompass a large sheltered bay. But she received a text from Slater the previous evening asking her to come in early. So she opts for a beach in the town only a short walk down the hill. It's on the far side of the breakwater and as she wades into the crashing surf it occurs to her that this is the place Kerry Waycott said she was raped.

Getting through the breaking waves is a struggle. She dives in and under a couple until she can begin to swim. But the swell is heavier than she expected. It crosses her mind that this was a stupid move. She's a reasonably strong swimmer but this is rough water. A surfer with a board to keep them afloat would manage it. A lone swimmer is taking a serious risk of being thrown on to the nearby rocks.

She changes her mind and turns back towards the shore. But suddenly it's much further away than she thought. She pulls with all her might but is making little headway. Could she be caught in a riptide? Is an unseen current dragging her out? She feels a sense of panic rising. Water in her mouth. Too much. Salty, it chokes her. She spits.

When she was in the cellar, paralysed by terror, she'd remembered something she once heard on a TV show – bravery is not about being fearless, it's about knowing how to manage your fear. She'd focused on creating an imaginary barrier around herself to keep the rats at bay. As they approached, she monitored them, waited, then she'd kick out. And mostly it worked. They scattered. Isn't this, in effect, what Moretti was talking about? How bloody ironic to think of this just before she drowns!

Focus. She relaxes into a float. Then she realises if she can ride one of the approaching breakers, it'll carry her to shore. Keeping relaxed but horizontal, she watches an approaching white crest and swims with it like a surfer as it rushes towards the beach. It breaks and crashes and dumps her on the shingle. On her hands and knees she crawls forward out of the sea and staggers up the beach. Relief turns to elation, a buzz which she knows can easily become addictive.

Arriving at work an hour later Megan is still reflecting on her own idiocy. Her ex-husband once told her she had a death wish and she told him he talked bollocks. But somewhere in there was a sliver of truth.

The parking area reserved for MCT is already full, not with cars but with vans topped with satellite dishes. The press pack has arrived and are setting up camp. Megan decides to steal a parking slot belonging to the timber merchants across the road.

As she enters the office she bumps into an excited Brittney.

'What's going on? Slater told me to come in early.'

'We think Georgia O'Brien's coming in to confess,' says the DC.

'You're kidding me,' says Megan. 'Have we ID'd the body?'

'Nope. But it has to be Damian. He's completely disappeared.'

'Are we sure about this? Feels to me like we're jumping the gun.'

Brittney shrugs. 'We've ticked quite a few boxes. Still waiting for full access to his bank account but no activity on his credit cards. His phone's dead. Plus he left a car parked on the street which the finance company repossessed.'

'What about Laetitia whatsit, the model?'

'Says she hasn't seen him.'

Megan shakes her head. 'It's still a bit thin. He could've just done a runner.'

'I have hassled the intelligence unit about checking his passport. Someone's off sick and it got missed.'

'And Slater's okay with that?'

Brittney sighs. 'Yeah. I s'pose.'

Slater is in her office in one of her sharper suits, hair neatly pinned.

Megan taps on the door. 'Morning, boss.'

The DCI smiles. 'Morning,' she replies. Her make-up is immaculate. She's pumped and ready for action. 'Are you up to speed with all the material Brittney's put together on Georgia O'Brien's background?'

'No. Sorry.'

'Not to worry. You've got time. Brittney's done an excellent job. But she's never done an interview of this kind. So I want you to lead it.'

'Okay,' says Megan. 'Why do we think she's going to confess?'

'Her lawyer's bringing her in. It looks like he's decided to go for a diminished responsibility plea. He might even succeed in keeping her out of jail.'

'Why would he do this now? Doesn't make a lot of sense to me. What evidence have we got? We can't even prove it's the husband yet. He must know that. If I was her brief I'd be advising her to just hang on in there and wait and see.'

'Her brief is Sir Henry Crewe.'

'Never heard of him.'

'I think he's acting to protect her. We don't know what state she's in. If she's falling apart at the seams it may be the smart move.'

'She's a bit flaky and likes to put on a show. But she struck me as quite a robust character. Have you seen the TV crews outside? Someone's tipped them off.'

'What are you telling me, Megan? You don't think you're up to conducting this interview?' Slater's look is fierce.

Megan holds up her palms and says, 'No. I can do it. If that's what you want.'

'Fine,' says Slater. 'They'll be here at eleven.'

Megan goes off in search of coffee. She pours herself a large mug. Brittney is at her desk, her owl glasses shining.

'Right,' says Megan. 'Tell me everything I need to know about Georgia O'Brien.'

CHAPTER TWENTY-EIGHT

Friday, 10.50am

A black, chauffeured Mercedes pulls up and a cacophony of cries and commotion rises up from the car park at the front of the building.

'Georgia! Over here! Hey, Georgia!'

Megan and Brittney get up from their desks and walk over to the window, as does everyone else in the office. They're looking down from the first floor.

Below, Georgia O'Brien and Sir Henry Crewe are pausing on the steps. Camera flashes are going off and a forest of microphones is being thrust towards them.

Brittney grabs her phone and starts to video the back of the suspect's head. The fizz of grey curls has been pulled back from her expertly made-up face and tied with a black silk scarf. Her coat is scarlet with a fake fur collar, also red. *Some kind of statement?* Megan wonders.

Sir Henry Crewe raises his hand and the pack falls silent. Brittney opens a window so they can hear.

'I'm going to read a short statement,' the lawyer says, placing his half-moon spectacles on his nose.

'My client is a law-abiding citizen who has led a blameless life. To many people she is a much-loved actress, to others a talented children's author. When a dead body was discovered on her property she immediately informed the authorities. She has come here today voluntarily to speak to the police about it. I hope you'll understand that's all I can tell you at present. Thank you, ladies and gentlemen.'

'Is she being interviewed under caution?' shouts a reporter.

'Is she a suspect?' hollers another.

Sir Henry gives a regal wave of the hand and shepherds his client into the building.

Megan frowns and turns to Brittney. 'Look at all these television crews. All the major broadcasters.'

'I know, it's exciting, isn't it?' says the DC.

'Yeah, but who told them to come?'

'Good bloody question,' says Ted Jennings, who's on his second doughnut of the morning. 'They must've had a tip-off last night. Far as I know, we haven't even put out a statement about the discovery of a body.'

Megan meets his eye. For all his laziness he's a canny old bugger and Megan can quite see why he's steering well clear. She wishes she could do the same. It feels to her like they're being set up in some way. Surely Slater can see that.

Georgia and her legal adviser have been settled in the interview room, coffee provided in ceramic cups. The amazing coat has been draped, by Georgia, over the back of her chair. The cameras are set up to digitally record the interview. Slater will watch a live-steam in her office, where she's been joined by Detective Superintendent Rob Barker.

Entering the room, Megan and Brittney take their seats.

'Good morning,' says Megan. 'Thank you for coming in.' She taps the touch pad to start recording. 'Could we go round the table and all say our names for the record?'

They do so. Henry Crewe omits his title.

Megan turns to Georgia. 'This is an interview under caution in order that we may ask you specific questions about the body found in your septic tank. You do not have to say anything. But it may harm your defence if you do not mention when questioned something you later rely on in court. Anything you do say may be given in evidence. Is this all clear to you?'

'Back in the day,' says Georgia, 'I did two seasons of *The Bill*. I played a feisty young DC. It was great fun.'

Megan meets her gaze. She doesn't look like a woman broken by remorse who's about to confess to the murder of her husband. She has a jaunty twinkle in her eye. Under the red coat her outfit is all black – a delicate silk blouse revealing several inches of cleavage, a calf-length skirt and leather boots. It's a costume but who's the audience? Megan can only wonder at the discussion going on in the office between Slater and Barker. It must be clear, even to Slater, that they're being played.

'Can I begin by asking you how the body was discovered?' says Megan.

'Well, we had a leak. I'm really not technically minded. I think there was a smell. Shirin dealt with it.'

'Shirin?'

'Shirin Khan, my personal assistant.'

'She lives with you?'

'Yes.'

'Does anyone else live on the premises?'

'No other adults, just her little boy, Noah. Come to think of it, he does wander about. He's a very bright little fellow. He might've seen something and told her.'

'Then what happened?'

'She called someone. I don't know, some firm or other.'

'She didn't discuss the matter with you?'

'No. Why would she? That's what I pay her for. To sort these things out. I knew nothing about it.'

'You didn't see these workmen and wonder what they were doing?'

'No. I was busy at the time. I meditate in the mornings, I don't like to be disturbed.'

'When did you learn about the discovery then?'

'Not sure. Shirin must've come and told me. And of course I was completely shocked. I said at once that we must call the police.'

'And did you?'

'I told her to.'

'We were contacted by Tony Wilson, the contractor,' says Megan.

Georgia shrugs. 'She must've told him to do it.'

'You didn't speak to Mr Wilson directly?'

'As I said before, why would I? That's what I have a personal assistant for.'

'Okay,' says Megan. 'Let's turn to the body. Do you have any idea how it got there?'

Georgia sighs and leans back in her chair. 'Well, it seems to me quite obvious. Someone put it there. Planted it, I suppose you'd say. I live in the middle of Dartmoor, the septic tank is a good distance from the house—'

Brittney leans towards Megan and whispers, 'It's three hundred and twenty meters.'

'Exactly,' says Georgia. 'And right down the hill. Anyone could've driven up at night, dumped the body and not be seen from the house. There's no razor wire or anything to stop them, it's just an open field.'

'You had no knowledge of it then before you were informed by Shirin Khan?'

'No.'

'Let's turn to more personal matters,' says Megan. 'Are you married?'

'Separated.'

'Your husband's name?'

'Damian Conrad.'

'And do you know Mr Conrad's current whereabouts?'

'Well, I didn't. Because the thieving bastard ran off with a hundred grand of my money which he filched from a joint bank account. However, I've discovered he's been hiding in Toronto.'

Megan meets her eye, notes the smug expression. As she suspected, they've been suckered. Sir Henry Crewe is staring straight ahead of him with a small twitching smile.

'Toronto?' says Megan. 'How do you know that?'

'A reporter at one of the tabloid newspapers phoned me.' She sighs dramatically. 'You know what they're like. Morals of an alley cat. Anyway, they set a private investigator to track Damian down. Offered him money to come back and face the music.'

'Face which music?' says Megan.

'The theft of the hundred grand, obviously. You see, he thinks he's entitled to it. Because we were married and it was in a joint account.' She glances at her elegant TAG Heuer watch. 'In fact, his plane should be landing at Heathrow right about now.'

CHAPTER TWENTY-NINE

Friday, 11.30am

Megan stands in the entrance to the MCT office block. Across the road Sir Henry Crewe is holding an impromptu press conference. Georgia is beside him, swishing her coat and posing for photographs. Camera crews and reporters are crowding round and blocking the road. The lads from the timber yard are leaning over the fence and taking pictures on their phones.

Vish joins Megan and holds up his phone. 'Here it is, on the paper's YouTube channel. Damian Conrad arriving at Heathrow.'

She shakes her head and says, 'Where's Brittney?'

'In the toilets,' says Vish. 'She was crying when I saw her. Thinks it's all her fault.'

'Well it isn't,' says Megan. She knows exactly whose fault it is but reins in her impulse to criticise the boss to a junior colleague.

'We could nick them for blocking the road,' says Vish.

'I don't think that would help. Can you hear what he's saying?'

'They've got it on upstairs. One of the news channels is carrying it live.'

They turn and go back into the building. 'What's the DCI doing?' says Megan.

'She was in a huddle in her office with Barker.'

Megan wishes she could be a fly on the wall for that conversation.

Upstairs in the office, a TV monitor has been tuned to Sky's live bulletin. Everyone, including Slater and Barker, is standing round watching.

On screen Sir Henry Crewe is in full flow: 'To say that the police acted precipitously is an understatement. My client tried to co-operate but she was driven from her home and treated like a criminal. This has been a botched investigation from start to finish. At no time have the police addressed the question of the kind of danger Georgia could be in. Clearly she is being targeted, possibly for the purposes of blackmail. But the police saw only a celebrity that they wanted to bring down. And the absolutely absurd notion that the body in the tank was her husband is melodramatic nonsense and yet further proof of the total incompetence at work here. I shall be writing to the chief constable and asking for a personal guarantee that there will be no further harassment of my client and that she can return to her home.'

A question comes from a reporter in the crowd. 'What does Dame Heidi think?'

'Heidi is as shocked and devastated as any mother would be that her daughter has been treated in such an appalling fashion. The police have clearly exceeded their authority and need reining in. I hope senior officers are taking note.'

Megan glances at Laura Slater: she looks pale, her lips are tightly pursed.

Barker has his hands in his trouser pockets and a resigned expression. He's a large bear of a man, balding and paunchy round the middle.

'Okay everyone,' he says. 'Show's over.'

The television is turned off. People drift back to their desks.

Barker beckons. 'Megan, you got a minute?'

'Sir.' She follows him into Slater's office.

'What's your take on this?' he says.

Megan glances at the DCI, who's standing in the corner, arms tightly folded. Slater gives her a baleful look.

'Well, boss,' she says. 'I still think Georgia and her sidekick are lying. Obviously we asked about Conrad's whereabouts and I'd say Georgia was deliberately evasive. We just got set up by a smart lawyer.'

'Henry Crewe is known for this sort of thing,' says Barker. 'But is this just a random corpse that's been dumped there?'

'I think Georgia and Shirin definitely know more than they're letting on. But until we get an ID on it I couldn't say. It's only been there a few weeks. Not sure I buy their assertion that someone could've planted it without being seen.'

'What about the contractors? Have you looked into them?'

'They were questioned. They do this sort of work all the time. There was nothing to arouse suspicion.'

'This is the thing,' says Slater, the tension rising in her voice, 'I'm trying to run a murder investigation without the resources. I've got no DI because Jim Collins is on long-term sick leave. Megan was off on some wild goose chase with a supposed rape victim who decided to throw herself off a cliff. I'm not blaming you for this, Megan, I'm just stating the facts.'

Megan meets Slater's eye. It's pretty clear that she is blaming her and flagging it up to Barker.

Slater ploughs on. 'I've got an enthusiastic but inexperienced DC, who was unsupervised and went off at a complete tangent, suggesting that the body was the husband and Georgia O'Brien had motive.'

'I'm sorry, ma'am,' says Megan firmly, 'but I don't think you can put this on Brittney. She didn't go off at a tangent, she just did the research. You want someone to blame, blame me. I should've been more on it.'

Slater's surprised look suggests she wasn't expecting to be challenged and for an instant Megan glimpses the raw fear behind her polished façade. It seems that when crossed the DCI can be a dirty opponent.

'Okay,' says Barker, raising his hand. 'This gets us nowhere. The media are now going to be a big factor in this case, which is what Crewe was up to here today. But I will deal with that. He thinks he can use a public outcry to force us to back off. The other way to look at this is to ask, why did he go to all this trouble? It could confirm our suspicions. But if Georgia is in the frame we need to be sure of our facts. Very sure.' He shoots a look at Slater. 'There may be no quick result here so we have to be patient. And I hear what you say, Laura. A DI will be seconded to you on a temporary basis. Probably from Exeter. I'll have to see who's available.'

'Thank you, sir.' She glares at Megan.

'Right,' says Barker. 'I need to go and brief the deputy chief on all this. Let's keep in close touch.' And with a curt nod to the two women, he heads out.

Megan looks at Laura Slater. She's clearly struggling with a toxic brew of anger and embarrassment. Being made a fool of publicly would upset most people but Megan can see how corrosive it is for an ambitious woman like the DCI.

'I think perhaps, boss,' says Megan carefully, 'you should speak to Brittney and tell her this is not her fault.'

Slater gives her a mulish look and shakes her head. 'You're supposed to be the DS. You can tell her.'

CHAPTER THIRTY

Megan walks out of the building at the end of her shift on the dot; she's on autopilot, blank with exhaustion.

Damian Conrad's bank finally replied to their request for access to his financial records. But it was all too late. A report came in on the Japanese chef's knife found in the septic tank. It told them little. The dimensions of the blade made it a potential murder weapon. But it was also a cheaper version and far more common than Laura Slater had assumed.

She had remained closeted in her office all day, licking her wounds. Megan had to prise Brittney out of the women's toilet and take her down the road to a nearby cafe to calm her down. They sat amongst the fry-ups and sipped steamy black coffees.

'Do you think I should resign?' asked the sorrowful DC.

'Absolutely not,' said Megan.

'Do you think I'll be investigated?'

'I doubt it, and once Slater gets over herself, she'll probably have a word.'

'I did tell her how sorry I was.'

'Brit, listen to me,' said Megan. 'This is not about you. You did your job and provided the information. Slater decided to take a punt on the assumption that Damian Conrad was dead. She knew we couldn't prove it.'

'I did try for his dental records but they were supposedly lost.'

'That should've told her something.'

'What do I do now?' said Brittney.

'Learn from this and move on. The boss thought she had the drop on Georgia's high-priced lawyer, turned out to be the other way round.'

'Is that what you think happened?'

'Probably,' said Megan. 'Why else do you think Slater's walking round with a face like a slapped arse?'

Brittney cracked a smile, a hint of her normal breezy disposition returning. She had the makings of a good detective and Megan hoped that in time she'd learn to ride out the office politics. She also knew the vanity of bosses and the blame game that tended to accompany it took most people years to master. Megan herself still hadn't. But she knew she had a problem with authority. Her school reports always harped on about that. Working undercover, outside the constraints of the system, had suited her much better.

Megan arrives home to find her sister in the kitchen stirring a pot of lamb stew and looking equally worn out.

'Hey,' says Debbie. 'You went out at the crack of dawn. Hope you didn't try and swim.'

If it was anyone else Megan would lie but she just gives her sister a sheepish look.

'Meg! Really? These are dangerous waters. Every year people drown.'

'I know. I do take care.'

Debbie shakes her head, tastes the stew and adds more salt. 'You eating with us tonight?'

'I hope so,' Megan replies and pulls a bottle of red wine from her bag. 'My first week back on the job. I thought we should probably raise a glass.'

'You bet,' says her sister brightly.

Megan gives her a quizzical frown. Their lives have been too entwined for her not to sense when something's off-kilter with her sister.

'What's going on?' she says.

'Nothing,' Debbie replies. 'Hassle-y day.'

'Okay.'

Megan waits.

Debbie sighs. Unlike Megan, she's never been able to hold in her feelings for long. 'Friday afternoons,' she says, 'I try and help out for a couple of hours at the food bank. I hear you nicked Justin Waycott, and I'm not saying there's anything wrong in that, because he is a complete headbanger, but it's caused quite a stir.'

'Your friends and neighbours are waking up to the fact that the sister who's living with you is a cop?'

Debbie turns the heat down and puts a lid on the heavy cast-iron pot.

'I don't give a monkey's what any of them think,' she says. 'And Mark can stand up for himself. I just worry that the kids might get picked on. The Waycotts are a bit like the mafia round here, they're connected to all kinds of people. And because Dave died… well, you know what people are like.'

Megan sighs. 'Yes, I do. And we always said, once I got settled in the job, I'd move out and get my own place.'

'No! That's not what I want.'

'Isn't it?'

'No, it bloody isn't. I'm not like you, Meg. When people get upset with me I feel guilty. I know it's stupid and makes no sense—'

'I'll find a little flat.'

'Oh for fuck's sake! I knew if I told you, you'd be like this. I don't want you to do anything. I just need to be able to talk about it. This isn't London. You can't just shut your front door and assume people will ignore you. Various people are asking me questions, y'know.'

'About Kerry Waycott?'

'Yeah, and I don't know what to say. And Amber says you were down at the school.'

Megan sighs. 'The last thing I want is to put any of you in an awkward position.'

Debbie grabs her arm. 'Meg, don't be like this, all snooty and detached like a cop.'

Are cops snooty?

'I just need to learn how to do this better. What to say to people.' Debbie gives her *the look*, she's been doing it since she was five years old. The puzzled and trusting look of her baby sister. When there was nothing in the fridge and their mum was crashed out on the sofa with a bottle of vodka, this was her expression as she waited for her big sister to tell her what to do. To find them food. It's a long time now since either of them have been truly hungry but poverty leaves its mark. In Debbie, it's turned into a determination to cook. No matter how tired she is, she'll always make a proper meal for her family. And usually way too much. They have a freezer full of leftovers.

'I understand how you feel,' says Megan. The truth is she doesn't. This is her world and she's been an insider since she was nineteen. She married an insider, although that didn't turn out well. Before she went undercover most of her friends had been cops. In many ways she's more at home with the sick jokes that fly round the office and the competitive resentments of Laura Slater than her own sister's civilian awkwardness.

'Listen,' she continues, 'all you need to say is, you've no idea. Once people realise you've got no gossip to pass on they'll leave you alone.'

Debbie shrugs. 'Okay.' She doesn't seem satisfied.

But the appearance of Amber and Ruby, who've been out walking the dog, ends the conversation. The removal of coats and boots, the towelling of a muddy dog, the squabbling over who should do what, consumes Debbie's attention.

Megan lays the table and opens the wine.

As they all settle at the table and Debbie starts to dish up the food, Amber slides into the chair next to her aunt and whispers, 'Can I show you something?'

Megan nods.

Amber clicks her phone on. It opens to Snapchat. She hands it to Megan.

On screen, Paige Tucker is lounging on a divan in what looks like her bedroom. Hair long and loose, she's heavily made-up, but her mascara is dramatically streaked and she clutches a tissue. The pose looks staged.

Her tone is mournful. 'The predators are out there. They're stalking us. Girls like us, we're their prey. Kerry won't go out. She was brutally raped but no one believes her. I just want to reach out to my friend, to my sister. I want us all to reach out and give her comfort.'

Megan hands the phone back. 'How long has this been going on?'

'All evening.'

'Is Kerry posting anything herself?'

Amber shakes her head. 'It's all Paige. Talking about how upset she is for Kerry. How we're all in danger but she's probably next on his list. She's really just getting off on the whole thing.'

'You should take no notice,' says Megan. 'Mrs Kovacs said she's going to deal with this.'

'That's a laugh,' says Amber with a huff.

'What d'you mean?'

Amber crosses her fingers. 'Paige and Jones are like that. She's teacher's pet and then some. He drools over her – it's disgusting to watch them.' She adopts a mocking tone. 'Paige is such a *genius*, supposed to be going to *Oxford*, so he has to give her books of poetry to read.'

'Really,' says Megan.

Looking round, she realises that Debbie, Mark, Kyle and little Ruby are all sitting and staring at them. Her sister seems tense and close to tears. Mark squeezes his wife's hand.

'Sorry,' says Megan. 'Not a suitable subject for the dinner table.'

Ruby frowns. 'Is giving someone a book of poetry disgusting, then?'

CHAPTER THIRTY-ONE

Friday, 7.30pm

Shirin stares out of the vast plate glass window; she can see one or two specks of light from container vessels passing way out at sea. The night is starless and black, spectral trees running down to an invisible shoreline. It sends an involuntary shiver up her spine.

Georgia is stretched out on one of the sofas snoring. She's drunk as a skunk. Two empty bottles of Cristal are upended in an ice bucket on the floor. She's spent the afternoon celebrating. Heidi had promised that her posh lawyer would deal with the police and he did. In Georgia's mind it's all over. Shirin thinks that's naive.

By the time Georgia and the lawyer returned from the interview, the Internet was buzzing with pictures and videos of Georgia. The red coat was her mother's idea. Dame Heidi had done enough red carpets and premieres to know how to hook the media's full attention. The coat had been brought down from London in the early hours of the morning by special courier. A make-up artist had arrived at breakfast time.

The headlines screaming from the websites and the front pages of tomorrow's newspapers are versions of *Police accuse Georgia – is she the scarlet woman?* Sir Henry Crewe's PR team had done the reporters' jobs for them.

He was a cool customer. He'd sat at Heidi's black ash dining table with his two assistants beside him and lectured Georgia like a stern headmaster. Shirin enjoyed that bit. She wondered how much he knew. But did that even matter? His job was to stop the police in their tracks and he was undoubtedly being well paid to do it.

Turning away from the window, Shirin realises she's being watched. A beady-eyed Dame Heidi is standing beside the sofa, leaning on her stick.

'Well,' she says, glancing down in some disgust at her daughter, 'that's sorted the police out. Now what about you?'

'Me?' says Shirin. 'What do you mean?'

'I really can't have you holding us to ransom.'

'It's hardly that. We made a deal. Georgia wants to adopt Noah. I don't know if she's told you that?'

'My dear girl, in the end she tells me everything.'

Shirin meets the old lady's gaze. It's like having a conversation with a witch. Or perhaps that's just Dame Heidi's talent, she can morph into whatever she pleases and her aim, at this moment, is to intimidate Shirin.

'Okay,' says Shirin. 'Today you pulled a clever stunt but you know and I know the fundamental problem hasn't gone away. Eventually the police will identify the body.'

'My guess is the two of you are in it together,' says Heidi.

'The two of us?' *What's she talking about?*

Raising her stick, Heidi points it at Shirin. 'I know all about the visits from your friend.'

'He's not my friend.'

'You sure about that?'

'Very sure.' *If only she knew.*

Dame Heidi wags her finger. 'If you two think you can blackmail us—'

'Blackmail?' says Shirin. 'How do you figure that?'

'You must think I'm completely naive, my dear.'

'I don't know what you're thinking, but whoever has ended up in that tank, it's got nothing to do with me.'

'Really?'

'I'm not a criminal.'

'Nor am I. Tell your friend that when you next see him.'

Shirin stares at her. The amazing bone structure of that beautiful face is hollowed out by age but still intact. The eyes are still arresting. *Nor am I.* It makes no sense. Until it dawns on Shirin what the old lady is actually saying.

'You don't just know about him, do you? You've met him.'

Heidi chuckles. 'Now you're being ridiculous.'

CHAPTER THIRTY-TWO

Saturday, 2.10pm

Megan walks down the high street, stopping to glance in estate agents' windows. A one-bedroom flat would meet her needs. She's thinking modern and functional, perhaps with a view, plus a car parking space. A practical and sensible approach is what's required. As she browses, she wonders about going in and registering. But the hollow feeling in the pit of her stomach won't go away. If she's honest the prospect of living alone is daunting.

She sat at the dinner table the previous evening and scanned the faces of her family. Her sister's family to be more precise. She is the divorced aunt, the damaged, middle-aged sister who has to see a shrink, the cop with a job they don't fully understand. They love her, want to help her and had made a place at their table. But it wasn't an easy situation either way.

The wine helped mitigate the awkwardness of the meal. Debbie drank a couple of glasses, they laughed and reeled out a few anecdotes about their shared childhood, the ones with a PG rating suitable for her kids' consumption. But Megan knew it was time: she had to let them off the hook.

The ambling Saturday afternoon shoppers all seem to be in company: elderly couples happily wandering, parents wrangling pushchairs and kids and dogs. She wonders about getting a dog, isn't that what lonely divorcees do? But it would hardly be fair on the animal to be shut up in a flat all day waiting for her to come home from work.

If she had never taken the undercover job, would her marriage have survived? She and Paul colluded in the idea that the stress of the job was to blame. They had always planned to have a family but it never happened. In their mid-thirties, they tried several rounds of IVF. But by then their relationship was frayed and Megan knew her husband's eye was already straying. Had she let him off the hook too? Maybe she had. At the time it had felt like the easiest thing to do. It meant their divorce was civilised. He tried his best to support her when she was rescued from the cellar; she told herself that but in her heart she knew it wasn't true. His mind was on promotion, climbing the greasy pole, and he was already screwing a young DC who worked for him.

Paul was a bloke always at the centre of things. Great at telling jokes and bouncing with energy, but the attention and the drama had to be focused on him. His upbringing had been as tough as hers, like her he bunked off school. Still he managed to persuade everyone that he was smart. He'd turned Megan into the wife, the sidekick, the background to his glory. Her job was always to support him. She wonders now if going undercover was her act of rebellion, a way of escaping a marriage in which the power imbalance was never talked about. Paul wore the trousers, called the shots; surely that was the natural order. In the world and in the job, such narcissism became leadership potential. Paul was a detective chief inspector by the time he was thirty-five.

It may have been Megan's old boss in the Met who'd recommended her to Barker. But she suspected that, behind the scenes, Paul had had a word with him and encouraged him to do it. This was her ex-husband's guilt coming out, his sop to the damaged and broken wife he'd traded in for a better model. She knows she's bruised and bitter and she works at not letting it show. But she never imagined that at forty-two she'd be alone, looking for a little one-bedroom flat.

Walking along the quay, she's surprised to see the folding doors of Mayhem standing open. Metal tables and chairs are arranged outside, a woman seated at one is pouring her companion a cup of tea.

Megan hesitates and peers inside. Then she sees him. Leon Hall steps out of the dark interior and gives her a wave.

'Hey,' he says. 'How you doing?'

'I'm surprised you're open,' Megan replies.

He holds up his hands. 'Wanna see my liquor licence, Officer?'

She laughs.

'Actually,' he says, 'I probably make as much money selling tea and cakes on a Saturday as I do selling booze. Can I tempt you?'

'Depends on the cake.'

He smiles. He does have a disarming smile. 'Come and take a look.'

She follows him inside.

On her previous visit she didn't have much opportunity to observe the place. The room is a cavernous oblong and goes straight back from the bi-fold glass doors which cover the whole of the front. The bar is on the right-hand side with a kitchen behind it. The decor is quirky and retro. The theme seems to be eighties bling.

Glancing up at the wall, Megan finds herself being overlooked by a bright blue stag's head with enormous antlers. Leon presses a switch on the wall and the eyeballs glow red.

'Interesting,' she says.

'Shot him myself.' He laughs. 'Nah, just kidding. Got him from a geezer on the Old Kent Road who bought up old props from the Royal Opera. I think he brings a bit of class to the place.'

'Is that where you're from?'

He gives her a side-eyed glance. 'South London, round and about, yeah. You never stop being a cop, do you?'

'I worked for a bit in Lewisham.'

'Think our paths crossed?'

'I don't know. Do you?'

He grins. 'Perhaps I wasn't always quite the upstanding businessman and solid citizen you see before you today.' The tone is flirty but feather-light. His look is direct, the eyes teasing but she doesn't mind. Is it because she fancies him? she wonders. All that longing and anxiety and pain, does she even want that again?

'So,' he says, leading her over to a glass-fronted display cabinet, 'we have chocolate brownies to die for. We have New York-style cheesecake, carrot cake, three-tier Victoria sponge. And, I should mention, none of this is out of a packet. I've got a lady who bakes for me who makes Paul Hollywood look like an amateur.'

'Okay, I'll try the chocolate brownie.' She knows they're playing a little game but that's okay. It's not as if she has anything else to do on her day off.

'Good move. And some tea?'

'Earl Grey just with lemon?'

Megan gets out her purse but Leon waves it away.

'Nah, this is on the house. Say thank you for rescuing my boy.'

'How is he?'

'He'll pull through. Might take a while before he's back out on the water again. Once he gets out of hospital his mate, Harry, is going to drive him up to his parents' place in Bristol. He's staying there until he's properly recovered. I hope that toe rag goes down for a serious stretch.'

'Have you had any trouble from Waycott and his mates?'

'They know better than to come round here when I'm around. I grew up in North Peckham, so I reckon you know what that's like.'

'Yep, I know.'

She watches him put the brownie on a plate using tongs. Her youth was full of lads like him, roaming the estate. The run-down sixties blocks would've been demolished when he was still a teen.

But poverty simply moved down the road. Some ended up in gangs, others chose the army. And a few lads, like her ex-husband, went into the police.

Is that why she's attracted to him? He reminds her of Paul, mixed race, big and tough, but with a roguish smile.

Why do we repeat the same behaviour over and over? she wonders. *It's stupid. You can't turn back the clock. Go back and do it again but get it right this time?*

She gives him a polite smile, picks up the cake and goes to sit at one of the metal tables outside. She needs to stop fooling herself. But he's right about one thing: the brownie is excellent.

CHAPTER THIRTY-THREE

At the start of her second week Megan makes a point of getting into the office early. She's settling into a routine with her morning swim, weather permitting.

Over the weekend she had a quiet chat with her niece about Simon Jones, the head of year nine. Out of earshot of her parents, Amber was explicit.

'Jones is weird,' she said.

'Creepy weird?'

'Yeah. When he talks to you he always stands really close, know what I mean?'

'Yes,' said Megan. *But a fourteen-year-old shouldn't.* 'Has he ever tried anything on with you? Touched you inappropriately?'

'Don't think I'm his type.' Amber is energetic and sporty, she plays football for the school team and belongs to the junior gig rowing club down at the harbour.

'What is his type, then?' said Megan.

Amber swooped the back of her hand dramatically across her brow. 'Oh, y'know. Actressy types and stick-thin ballerinas with big sad eyes who float around quoting stuff from stupid books they've read. He says stuff to them like, "you can always talk to me about your problems". He likes girls who have problems.'

'I thought you did ballet for a while?'

'Nah, dropped it for football.'

'Well, steer clear of him.'

Amber gave her a sardonic look. She is reassuringly canny for her age. 'All I ever get from him is grief for not giving in my homework on time.'

Megan smiled. 'You're a girl after my own heart.'

Mug of coffee in hand, Megan switches on her computer and starts to search various databases. She knows she should be focusing on the O'Brien case but Kerry Waycott's desolate, half-knowing half-innocent face dominates her thoughts.

There are several Simon Joneses on the Police National Computer. She follows through to the individual forces but none of the mugshots match. Although she knows the basics, Megan's data analysis skills are definitely rusty. So when the unit's civilian analyst, Kitty, arrives in Lycra shorts and a cycling helmet, Megan jumps up and offers to get her a coffee.

Apinya Hughes is half Thai and half Welsh, her parents run a Chinese chippy in Merthyr Tydfil. But her gamer tag is *kittyka-trap666* and so Kitty is the name she goes by. Her work station is festooned with cat pictures and evil-looking cartoon felines. A pink plastic moggy with blue eyes and long lashes dangles from the corner of her computer screen.

Kitty gives Megan a deadpan look; they've been introduced but haven't spoken. 'You want bumping up my to-do list this morning,' she says, 'the usual bribe is doughnuts. I run on sugar.'

'Okay,' says Megan. 'I owe you a box of doughnuts.'

'A box?' says Kitty, removing her helmet. 'Rush job then.' She's small and elfin and doesn't look as if she ever eats more than a raw carrot. 'Is this the teacher dude that Vish was talking about last week?'

'Simon Jones, yeah.'

Kitty flicks on her screens. Her fingers skate across the keyboard at lightning speed. 'I did take a quick look.' She pulls up a file and perches on the edge of her chair. 'Here you go. A bit of an odd thing. I was going to go back and dig but I haven't had time.'

'What?'

'He got his enhanced DBS check when he came to the school two years ago. But before that it looks like he doesn't exist.'

'How d'you mean?'

'He's appeared out of thin air. I cross-checked DOB, no credit cards and I can't find a national insurance number.'

'You think this could be a fake identity?'

'I wouldn't mind betting. He buys a fake driver's licence online, plus a council tax bill or bank statement, and uses that to get his DBS check. Mocks up some references for the school.'

'So how can we find his real name?'

'If he's fronting this just to the school, he's probably running two IDs, real and fake, using the same initials. It's more difficult to fake credit cards and bank stuff, so he'd use S. Jones with his real first name for some things, and a different first name with the same initial for the fake driving licence and the DBS check.'

'That's risky. Wouldn't the school realise if they're paying him? Or HMRC?'

'It's all automated,' says Kitty. 'I use my real first name for some things, Kitty for others. Who actually checks these things? If you think he's definitely been a bad boy I can go through all the S. Joneses on the PNC but that would take time and then we'd have to match it with a picture.'

Megan nods. 'Sounds complicated.'

'Not really.'

The open-plan office is filling up with the day shift. Megan notices Laura Slater going into her office with a smartly suited and booted bloke in his thirties. It seems Barker has kept his promise and she's got her reinforcements.

Kitty is still tapping away at her keyboard, eyes glued to the screen.

'Here we go,' she says. 'School's website, head of year nine, Simon J. Jones. That him?'

Simon Jones grins at them from the screen.

'Yep,' says Megan, although her attention is hooked on the meet-and-greet dance going on in Slater's office.

'Nice tie,' says Kitty. Jones is sporting the dolphin print.

'It'd be great,' says Megan, turning to give the analyst a warm smile, 'if we can come up with something I can use at this morning's briefing. Also I know a place that does the perfect chocolate brownie.'

Kitty smiles. This seals the deal. 'Okay,' she says. 'If not Simon, then… what's your favourite name?'

'I dunno. Sam, Steven, Stanley.'

'Bit young for a Stanley.'

'Sean, Scott, Seth.'

'Too old for Seth.'

'I don't know. Try a few.'

The DCI comes out of her office and stands at the front of the room, which falls quiet.

'Morning, everyone.' She looks as bright and brisk as usual.

On the surface she seems to have recovered from her mugging at the hands of Sir Henry Crewe. But the weekend papers have been full of carefully engineered headlines on the theme *Police dub Georgia the Scarlet Woman,* and a smattering of articles accusing the police of incompetence.

'Just a quick introduction,' Slater says. 'This is DI Richard Montieth. He's been seconded to us and will be focusing on the O'Brien investigation. I've brought him up to speed but, Megan' – she shoots a chilly smile across the room to locate the DS – 'perhaps you'll fill in some of the detail.'

Megan nods, although it's hard to fathom exactly what details the boss means. He can read the briefing for himself.

Tucked away from the DCI's sightline behind her computer screen, Kitty is still tapping away.

'Score!' she mutters.

Megan glances at Kitty's screen. In the mugshot he's younger, leaner and sullen but it's definitely him.

'Steven John Jones,' Kitty whispers. 'Three years for sexual activity with a child and breach of trust. Offence took place in Manchester. Served eighteen months and was put on the Sex Offender Register.'

Megan stares at the picture. Perhaps Kerry Waycott didn't make it up? Could this be the sexual predator who raped her?

CHAPTER THIRTY-FOUR

Monday, 10.35am

When Megan presents the information about Jones at the briefing, Slater is brisk. 'Yeah, follow it up, obviously.'

'Can I take Vish?'

'Fine. Well done.'

'Actually, boss, it was Kitty who dug this up.'

'Good work all of you.' There's a bright blankness about Slater. *Is she on something?*

In the presence of the new DI, she seems determined to present a capable and co-operative team.

As soon as the briefing is over Megan discovers why. Montieth makes a beeline for her. He's all smiles and holds out his hand to shake. The sharp suit, worn with a green tartan waistcoat, the sandy buzz cut and the firm grip all smack of an ambitious man on the rise and in a hurry. Snapping at Slater's heels, perhaps?

'I've heard a lot about you,' he says in a soft Glaswegian burr.

Megan smiles. 'Not all bad, I hope.'

He laughs as he follows her gaze towards the DCI's office. 'I think the boss has huge respect for your abilities.'

Megan's not about to be flattered into submission. She waits.

'And,' says Montieth, 'I think I might know your husband.'

'Ex-husband. How?'

'I've played a few rugby matches against the Met.'

Megan's heart sinks. That's all she needs. To hear she was the subject of locker room banter.

'Sorry. Didn't know you'd split,' he says. 'But Paul was really proud of you. I gather you got the QPM for an undercover job.'

Trust Paul to blab about it, use her to make himself look good and compromise her security.

'I was just part of the team. Obviously I can't talk about it.'

'Obviously.' Montieth shrugs and grins. 'But, hey, you've got stuff to do. I'll let you get on. Just wanted to say that I think we'll work well together. We can talk later about the septic tank and the actress.' He raises his eyebrows and laughs. He's trying to keep it light and Megan finds herself appreciating the effort. In the face of Slater's resentments he might become a useful ally.

It's late morning when Megan and Vish arrive at the school. Once they're closeted in Linda Kovacs's office with Jones, Megan lets Vish take the lead.

Asked if his real name is Steven John Jones, the teacher slumps down on a chair.

'This is not how it looks,' he says, shooting a beseeching look at Kovacs.

She stands rooted to the spot, colour draining from her cheeks.

'And you were convicted of sexual activity with a child and breach of trust and placed on the Sex Offender Register?'

He buries his face in his palms.

'Could you answer the question, Mr Jones?' says Vish.

He nods and hangs his head. Linda Kovacs folds her arms tightly as if holding herself together. But she can't take her eyes off him.

'And subsequently, using the name Simon, you falsified documents to obtain a DBS check?'

Ignoring the police, Jones focuses on the headteacher. His tone is whiny and pleading. 'I was young,' he says, 'and I made a stupid mistake. I had an affair with a fourteen-year-old which was wholly consensual. But I've served my time. Eighteen months in prison. And, believe me, I've learnt my lesson. Is it fair that I should be banned from teaching, from a job I love and I'm good at, for an error of judgement made when I was an inexperienced young fool?'

Kovacs glares at him. For a moment Megan wonders if she's about to throw a punch. The fury pulsing off her is palpable.

She starts to speak but the words stick in her throat. 'I want you—' She has to cough. 'I want you out of my school now.'

'Linda, please—'

'Now!' She turns to Megan. 'Could you please just get him out?'

Megan nods. She glances at Vish.

The DC takes Jones by the arm.

He pulls away. 'What? Am I under arrest?'

'We'd like you to come with us voluntarily to answer further questions,' Vish replies. 'And, in the circumstances, I think that's a good idea, don't you?'

Jones shakes his head. 'You've got to believe me, Linda, it was a one-off. It's in the past.'

'Come on,' says Vish.

'And I'm so sorry. I can't tell you.' His voice cracks.

The headteacher turns her back on him. Shoulders hunched, Jones allows Vish to shepherd him out of the room.

Megan looks at Linda Kovacs. 'Are you all right?'

For a moment she doesn't reply.

Finally she says, 'I can't believe I let this happen. I thought Simon was so—' She exhales with a shudder. 'But then he's not Simon, is he?'

'No.'

'Where did this happen?'

'The offences took place in Manchester. He was convicted three and half years ago.'

Kovacs sighs. 'That doesn't even make him that young. Maybe twenty-six. Certainly old enough to know he shouldn't be taking advantage of a fourteen-year-old.'

'Now I have to ask,' says Megan, 'whether he could be having sexual relations with any of your pupils?'

Kovacs swallows hard. Her eyes brim with tears. 'I would've said no way. But now—' She shakes her head. 'The truth is, I've no idea.'

'Do you think he's taken a particular interest in Paige Tucker? Or Kerry Waycott?'

'Oh my God! No! Really?' Linda Kovacs claps her hand over her mouth and sobs.

CHAPTER THIRTY-FIVE

Monday, 12.36pm

Kerry Waycott is in pyjamas on the sofa, curled in a foetal ball round a fluffy pink elephant, when her mother escorts Megan into the room. The corner television is showing a jaunty property make-over show.

Heather's face is grey, her hair unwashed and sticking out at odd angles. 'Says she won't go to school. Says I can't make her.'

'Hello, Kerry,' says Megan. 'How you doing?'

Kerry glares at her. 'You should've let me jump.'

'Would've been a bit final. What if you'd changed your mind?'

Kerry sits up, still clutching the elephant. It's threadbare in parts and one of its ears is hanging off. 'I can't go to school,' she says, 'cause everyone hates me, thinks I'm a liar. My gran's really angry because of what happened to Uncle Justin.'

Megan moves two pizza boxes off the armchair and settles on the edge of it. 'I don't think you can be held responsible for your uncle's actions, Kerry.'

'Yeah? Try telling that to the old girl. Once you lot had gone she screamed at me for about ten minutes.'

Heather squeezes on the end of the sofa and says, 'I've offered her some of my pills to make her feel a bit better.'

'That's probably not a good idea,' says Megan. 'They're prescribed for you. If you think she needs something you should take her to the doctor.'

'I'm not going to the bloody doctor's and I don't want none of your stupid zombie pills, Mum.'

Megan smiles at the teenager. Her feistiness is a good sign.

'And I don't wanna have to see someone,' she adds with contempt.

'Believe it or not,' says Megan, 'I know how you feel.'

'No you don't. I'm not an idiot. You're like all the rest of them. You say stuff, like, *it's all gonna be all right*. Then once I'm doing what I'm told, off you pop.'

'Fair enough,' says Megan. 'But you can't sit on the sofa for the rest of your life, can you?'

'Why not?'

'You'll get bored.' Megan points at the television. 'You may learn how to fit a new kitchen. But is that really what you're interested in?'

The hint of a smile plays around the teenager's mouth. She's enjoying the banter. Heather's eyelids are drooping, she's dozing off.

Megan waits for a moment then she says, 'So why did you tell me that it was Jared who raped you? Because that is a lie, isn't it?'

Kerry gives her a sulky look. 'It's complicated.'

'I can do complicated. Try me.'

'Gran was on at me. I had to say something but I was frightened.'

'Frightened of who, Kerry?'

Kerry buries her face in the elephant's fake-fur back. Megan scans her. Her narrow, hunched shoulders underscore her vulnerability. It is hard to tell what's true and what's a pose with her. She's still a kid, imitating the behaviour she sees around her, particularly online and on the television. Is the fear genuine? Or is it an act, a teenage game to stick two fingers up to the grown-ups? Her mother lies beside her on the sofa, head lolling, absent in every sense that matters.

'Okay,' says Megan. 'Let's talk about school.'

'Let's not,' says Kerry, raising her head.

'You hate it that much?'

'I dunno. That's complicated too. I like hanging out with my mates. When I had any mates.'

'What about the teachers?'

'Some are cool. I like Miss Kennedy. She does art. I like designing stuff.'

'What about your head of year, Mr Jones?'

Kerry smiles. 'Old Fishface, that's what Paige calls him, cause he's got these stupid ties.'

'Paige doesn't like him?'

'She plays him.' Kerry adopts a mocking tone. 'Oh, sir, I'm really in an emotional state today cause my hamster died and I've got my period. I need to be let off my homework.'

Kerry's a good mimic. It's easy to imagine her and Paige practising their riffs for the camera.

'I've met him,' says Megan. 'He's not bad-looking. Do you think perhaps Paige secretly fancies him?'

'Yuk! Fishface? She'd rather die.'

'Is he really that much of a joke?' says Megan.

'Paige's mum likes him cause she wants Paige to go to Oxford and do English.'

'What does Paige want?'

'I dunno. Become a star on the net. But her parents are rich so she probably will go to uni and just hang out.'

'So let's be clear,' says Megan. 'Have you ever been persuaded to have sex with Mr Jones?'

Kerry laughs out loud. 'You think I was raped by Fishface, don't you? That's so amusing.' The superior toss of the head is perfect. In the melodrama stakes, Kerry Waycott could give Georgia O'Brien a run for her money.

Is this just a game?

Megan tilts her head. Or could it be some elaborate deflection to protect Simon Jones because Kerry is terrified of him? It doesn't feel like that. But Megan thinks of her niece, Amber. Knowing, smart, vulnerable. Half child, half woman. It would be naive to assume that a fourteen-year-old is not capable of such an elaborate ploy.

She sighs. 'I don't know what to say to you, Kerry. If you won't trust me how can I protect you? You came to the police with an allegation of rape.'

'Only cause of my gran.' Her face is sombre now.

'We're not without resources. We can protect you.'

Kerry purses her lips. She seems to be fighting an interior battle. Or has she just flipped into another role?

Finally she says, 'I rat him out, he'll know.'

'How?'

'Because he makes the rules. Cops are a joke to him. He'll kill me then my whole family.' Now she's in a gangster movie.

Megan's thoughts skip back to her time undercover. A kid like Kerry has no idea about real gangsters. They look like accountants not thugs and lethal force is simply part of the business plan.

'Trust me, Kerry. We make the rules. Not criminals.'

Kerry stares at her, the unlined face of a child, but the haunted eyes of a damaged woman. Her chin quivers but she says nothing.

Megan stares back. It's impossible to get to the truth with Kerry. *He'll kill my whole family?* This has to be nonsense.

CHAPTER THIRTY-SIX

Monday, 2.30pm

On her return to the office, Megan finds the place in some turmoil. The incident room is being expanded to include the empty office next to it. The additional space is not large but desks are being rearranged and a workman with a tool box is fixing digital locks to both doors. After the media drubbing in the tabloid press over the weekend, Slater is not risking any leaks. Montieth is overseeing the operation, while chatting to the CSI, Hilary Kumar. He gives Megan a friendly nod as she passes.

Megan finds Vish at his desk. He's holed up in a corner looking disconsolate as things are shifted around him.

She leans on the adjacent window sill. 'I talked to Kerry. She says it's not him. And I'm inclined to believe her. Where is he?'

'In the custody suite,' says Vish. 'Haven't done a formal interview. I was waiting for you. But all the way here in the squad car he didn't shut up. And guess what he's saying?'

Megan ponders. 'If I had to guess,' she says, 'I'd say there's something going on between him and Kovacs.'

'How the hell do you know that?' says Vish, flopping back in his chair.

'Come on. Think about her reaction. She took it all very personally. It was a personal betrayal. His pleading was to her, not to us. Ordinarily I wouldn't expect a headteacher to end up crying in that situation, would you? Pissed off, yeah. But floods of tears?'

Vish sighs. 'No, I suppose not. Makes sense when you explain it.' He looks downcast. 'But why didn't I get it?'

'Did he mention Kerry at all?'

'Yeah, he said if we're trying to hang that on him, the night she was attacked he was sleeping with Kovacs.'

Megan looks around her. 'Bit chaotic round here. If that's his alibi, we'd better go and check it out.' She sighs. 'But the boss is right. We've done what we can. Probably time we parked this up. He may be guilty of fraud but that's not going to be Slater's priority.'

Vish drags himself from his chair and follows her out.

'What's put a bug up your arse?' says Megan.

'It's nothing.'

Two removal men have a desk wedged half in and half out of the lift so they take the stairs. Vish clatters down them ahead of her, he's always got energy to burn. But his moods are boyishly transparent. Happy or sad, he can't disguise it.

'Haven't seen Brittney this morning,' says Megan as they head out of the main doors.

Vish shrugs and says, 'Think Montieth's got her and Kitty doing a deep dive into Georgia O'Brien's past.'

'Well, Damian or no Damian, they've still got to be our prime suspects.'

She gives the young DC a side-long glance. The rivalry between him and Brittney is friendly most of the time. But if she's been picked by the new DI he will be jealous even though her research skills on the computer are superior.

They arrive at the Škoda. Megan offers him the keys. 'Want to drive?'

'If you like.'

She wonders why she's placating him. It's a bad habit of hers, smoothing things over, but it does make life easier.

They get in the car. He starts it up and says petulantly, 'Maybe if I go and cry my eyes out in the bog I'll get put on the murder team too.'

School is over for the day and the place is deserted. They find Linda Kovacs tidying her office. And she seems to be expecting them.

'I thought you'd be back,' she says. 'I've been writing my letter of resignation to the governors.'

'What's prompted that?' says Megan.

'Isn't it a week ago today that Kerry Waycott was attacked? On the Monday night.'

'Yes,' says Megan. 'Sometime around eleven.'

Kovacs sighs. 'He— I don't even know what to call him. Simon?'

'Steven Jones is his real name.'

'When you ask him, he's going to say he was with me. That he stayed the night at my house.'

'Is that true?' says Megan.

Kovacs shovels her hair out of her eyes. 'Y'know, when I realised how this was going to play out, I thought to myself, I'll deny it. Act shocked. My word against his. I'm a respectable headteacher, he's a convicted sex offender. I get to keep my job. He gets what he deserves.'

Megan scans her. She's been crying. Her eyes are red, mascara-smudged. But now the tears are gone. Megan glances at Vish. He's watching intently too. It's compelling seeing a woman like Kovacs unravel.

'It was very tempting,' she says. 'Can you imagine what people are going to say when they find out? Poor stupid old Linda, middle-aged divorcee, having a secret affair with a colleague ten years younger. People might accept that. But not when they find out the rest. What he actually is. It's the lies that get to me. All those lies. Do you think wanting revenge is wrong?'

'We all want it,' says Megan. 'That's only human. Depends what you do to get it. There's no harm as long as it remains a fantasy.'

'I'm not going to lie. I've decided. The truth is the truth. He's not going to rob me of my self-esteem as well.'

'That's probably a good decision.'

'Is it? I wonder. I've worked for years to build my career and my reputation. Now, in one day, it's all gone. Oh, I'll get a job somewhere, back in the classroom, but I'll never get back to where I was. Who's going to trust my judgement? I'll have to sell my house. Move away.' She laughs bitterly. 'But in the end, he's not even the one you're looking for, is he? And anyway, the girl's probably lying.'

Megan says nothing.

'Or there's another selfish lying bastard out there who thinks if a fourteen-year-old child bats her eyes at him she's fair game.'

'We really don't know.'

'I don't think I'd want your job, Sergeant,' says Kovacs.

CHAPTER THIRTY-SEVEN

Monday, 9.23pm

Megan is frustrated; after the conversation with Kovacs, Steven Jones was released under investigation. The evening is cold and dry and a raw north-easterly breeze has driven most people off the streets. Megan has her snug new jacket; it's probably time to break out a hat and some gloves. She's bone weary but restless. Given the options of slumping in front of the television with the family or retreating to her room and watching a Netflix film on her laptop, she's offered to walk the dog.

Scout is such an amiable creature, he makes the perfect companion. He stops politely by a lamp post and takes his dump, then waits while she bags it and deposits it in the nearby dog bin. Who trained this animal to poo only yards from the bin? Megan smiles at him in amazement. In acknowledgement of his prowess he raises his head so she can stroke his silky muzzle.

They walk down into the town and along the quayside. It could be unnerving, walking alone between the pools of lamplight but she feels more comfortable because of the dog. There's a tang of seaweed in the air. The tide is out, the mud of the inner harbour is exposed and halyards clank relentlessly in the dark. Red and white lights glitter on the moored boats in the outer harbour.

The frustrations and blind alleys of the job are aspects she forgot about during her adrenaline-pumped undercover years.

The daily slog of an investigation which simply won't yield the proof. She suspects the O'Brien case will turn into that, as Barker has already predicted: a game of patience, a careful sifting of each scrap of forensic evidence and the painstaking task of matching the corpse with an ID. Except now every move they make will be scrutinised and chewed over by the media pack. This is prime fodder for the tabloids and soon enough the police will be under attack for failing to make progress.

She walks past Mayhem. The dimly lit interior shows that the bar is open but on a Monday night it looks pretty empty. There's music playing, the muted thumping of the bass. Should she stop off for a drink? In recent months, as part of her recovery, she's been keeping a tight rein on her alcohol intake. Some wine with dinner is fine. But vodka shots to take the edge off her nerves? Weaning herself off that particular habit has taken some determination.

She could have a beer. *Will he even be there?*

Scout looks up at her, she looks down at him, smiles and says, 'You're right, mate, it's a seriously bad idea.'

She and the dog complete their walk. Returning home, she finds her sister making hot chocolate. She accepts a mug, retreats to her room, lies on the bed and sips it as she stares out of the window at the patchwork of lighted windows on the hillside opposite. Perhaps being a detective gives her too much exposure to the pain and crookedness of other lives, she misses out on the kindness and joy. The end result for her has certainly been loneliness and cynicism. Maybe she should jack it in and find some other way to earn a living? But what the hell would she do? Become a security guard or private investigator? It wouldn't be any different.

Falling asleep fully clothed, she wakes in the early hours shivering. She undresses, slips under the duvet and falls into a fitful doze. She's been a poor sleeper for as long as she can remember. The need to be wary, to keep watch, was etched on her psyche long before she became a police officer. Moretti has offered her pills. Isn't that all doctors ever do? But she hates the brain fog that goes with them.

Sleeping, then waking, then sleeping again, her mind is full of shadows – her failed marriage, the cases never solved – and ghosts – her dead mother plus a helter-skelter of accusing faces. Her consciousness zigzags in and out of darkness.

She wakes with a start when her phones rings. It's seven am and she realises she forgot to put an alarm on. A grey dawn light floods the room.

The phone is registering an unknown caller. She answers with a curt hello.

'Megan,' says a male voice. 'It's Richard Montieth. Sorry if I've woken you.'

'No, it's fine.'

'I'm duty DI. Got the shout from comms. Some mackerel fishermen have discovered a body on the rocks near Ellwood Cove. It's a teenage girl. Could possibly be your rape victim, Kerry Waycott? Wondered if you'd come down and take a look.'

Megan's guts lurch. Kerry? No, no, not that. Was she that depressed? Bored, maybe. But why would control contact CID for a suicide?

Jumping out of bed she feels dizzy, then sick. 'Yeah, sure,' she says. 'I don't get it. Is it suspicious?'

'Yep,' says Montieth. 'Her throat's been cut.'

CHAPTER THIRTY-EIGHT

Tuesday, 7.35am

The track down to the cove is steep and muddy. A uniformed officer is guarding it. Megan shows her ID and he directs her via the designated route. The crime scene investigators have already set up on the foreshore. Their four-wheel drive vehicle and the coastguard's Land Rover are the only ones allowed down the rutted track.

The beach itself falls away sharply. A large section of it has already been cordoned off. The access route is a narrow strip round the edge. Scrambling down a bank of pebbles, Megan stumbles and slides. She lands in a heap. Montieth turns from his conversation with Hilary Kumar, the Crime Scene Manager, and steps forward to help her up.

'Easy does it,' he says with a friendly smile.

His grip is firm as he hauls her to her feet.

'Sorry about this,' he adds. 'One of the response officers was on your cliff rescue, thought he recognised the girl. But he wasn't sure.'

Megan nods. 'Okay.' She's feeling sick.

At a casual glance it looks as if someone is having a party on the beach. Two small white marquee tents have been erected. Except it's dawn on a cold autumn morning, everyone is wearing plastic jumpsuits and most of the cove from the rocks to the tideline is criss-crossed with yellow tape.

Megan has thrown on jeans, a sweatshirt and jacket. In the larger tent she takes off her jacket and struggles into the obligatory white suit.

The smaller of the two tents is leaning at a precipitous angle a short distance away over the rocks. This is to protect the body, which is still in situ. But a glance at the rising tide makes it clear that they need to work fast. Half a dozen CSIs are already on their hands and knees doing a fingertip search of the beach.

'I'm going to go and phone the pathologist again,' says Hilary. 'But I doubt he can get here in time. So we're going to have to move her anyway.'

'Right,' says Montieth. 'Your call.'

'I presume the body was washed up?' says Megan. Joining in the matter-of-fact professional conversation helps her cope.

'No, I don't think so,' says Hilary. 'The pattern of lividity on her back and the backs of her thighs would appear to carry the imprint of the rocks and bunches of seaweed that were underneath her.'

'You think this is where she died then, on the rocks?'

'Yeah. Maybe she was running away? The PM will soon tell us if she did drown or not, but I'd say not.'

'The body's snagged on the rocks,' says Montieth. 'The tide's been in and out once probably since it's been there. But we're assuming she was killed here. Luckily, the pebbles on this beach are quite large and round. We think we've got what might be blood spatter on some that have escaped the tide.'

They pause outside the tent.

'Okay?' says Montieth.

Megan nods and takes a deep breath. She's seen plenty of corpses. She's been reminding herself of this on the short drive here. This will be no different.

Montieth lifts the tent flap.

The first thought that comes into Megan's head is of mermaids. It's the long fair hair, matted with seaweed, lying across a large jagged rock. The face is turned away but the throat is severed and, even in such a short time, various sea creatures – crabs, eels and fish – have been making the most of the open gash.

Megan has to climb round and step across the body to get a proper view. The eyes are gone but she was expecting that. What's left is like a chalk-white mask in the rough shape of a face. The innocence is still there and a hint of the cheekiness. But perhaps Megan is imagining that.

'Yep,' she says briskly. 'It's her. Kerry Waycott.'

'Thanks,' says the DI. He puts a hand on her arm to steady her. They step out of the small tent.

Megan feels better than she expected. No hint of a panic attack. Dead bodies are never pleasant. But she's dealt with it.

'Next of kin?' says Montieth. 'I'll do the knock if you like.'

'The family situation is complicated. I'll do it, if you don't mind.'

'Okay,' he says. 'If you're sure.'

She's far from sure. But it's the least she can do for the Waycotts.

As she makes her way back up the beach, her legs begin to shake. Once out of sight of her colleagues, she crouches down and allows the tears to come. This should never have happened. She should never have let it happen. Kerry needed her and she walked away. Desolation engulfs her.

CHAPTER THIRTY-NINE

Tuesday, 7.55am

It's early and Megan wonders how difficult it's going to be to rouse Heather Waycott. In the event, as she approaches the small terraced house painted sunshine yellow, she sees the kitchen light on and Kerry's mother framed in the window. She's filling the kettle at the sink. This will probably be the last thing she does before her already chaotic life is thrown into even more turmoil.

Ringing the doorbell, Megan tries not to plan out what she's going to say. It's better to play it by ear. The door is opened by a boy. He's eight or nine, blond with sandy brows and lashes like Kerry. Megan has only glimpsed her younger brother and sister before, playing in the garden.

She smiles at him. 'Hello,' she says. 'I'm Megan. Is Mummy there?'

'Mum, it's that cop,' he calls over his shoulder.

Megan follows him into the house. Heather appears in the kitchen doorway. She wears an old Coldplay concert t-shirt and some frayed men's pyjama bottoms. Her skinny arms hang limply at her sides. For a frozen moment she stares at Megan, then her mouth gapes open and she drops to her knees with a feral howl of pain.

Her puzzled son puts his arms round her and tries to hug her. 'Mum?' he whimpers.

Megan has done this too many times, as a young PC and as a detective. She waits a moment then helps Heather to her feet and shepherds her to the sofa in the living room. The boy and his younger sister, who looks to be about five, stand and stare forlornly until their crying mother gathers them into her arms and clutches them tight.

Returning to the hall Megan makes a quick phone call to Sheila Waycott; she manages to hold back the information and ask her to come round.

Then she sits down on the same armchair as the evening before. The pizza boxes are on the floor beside the chair where she put them. She waits for the questions that will come. But Heather says nothing. She doesn't even ask if her daughter is really dead. If they're sure it's her.

Megan would prefer shouting and accusations to the heavy silence. Now the initial shock is wearing off, her own abject failure to save Kerry is flooding through her like a toxin.

It takes about ten minutes for Sheila to turn up in a black Mitsubishi Trojan pick-up driven by her son, Justin. He's been released on bail. She lets herself in with a key.

Megan stands up to face her.

'She's dead, in't she?' says Sheila. 'That's why you're here.'

'Yes, I'm afraid so,' says Megan.

'How? She kill herself?'

Witnessing the intense pain on the old lady's face, Megan guesses that's her preferred option.

'There'll be a post mortem later today probably,' says Megan carefully. 'And the result will tell us more. But, at the moment, we're not treating this as a suicide.'

It takes a moment for the implications to sink in.

Heather raises her head. 'What? I thought… she was just so upset. She told me she'd had enough. But you're saying… what? I don't understand.'

'All we can say at the moment is that she was probably unlawfully killed.'

Justin stands behind his mother, towering over her. 'What the fuck?' he says. 'Who was it? That piece of shit rapist that I gave a good hiding to?'

Megan fixes him with a steely glare. 'If you're talking about Jared Clarke,' she says, 'he's still in hospital. So, no, it couldn't have been him.'

Justin clenches his fist 'If you bloody lot of morons had the least fucking clue what you're doing—'

'All right, Justin!' says his mother sharply. 'We've had quite enough of that. It don't help no one.'

Justin folds his arms. He's too big for the room. He can't stand still and bangs into the dining table. Like a caged bear tugging on its chain, he's furious with everyone. 'I'm going outside for a smoke,' he says and disappears out of the door.

Sheila looks at Megan. Megan looks at Sheila. She wonders which way the old lady's anger will fly but she can take a guess.

Sheila shakes her head. 'I should've made her come and live with me. Insisted.' She shoots a baleful glance at Heather. 'Then I could've kept a proper eye on her. And as for you lot… Justin's right. I dunno what we pay our bloody taxes for.'

'Mrs Waycott, I was here last night and I did my level best to persuade your granddaughter to tell me who she was so scared of. She wouldn't say. I tried. But not hard enough. You think that doesn't haunt me now?'

The old lady turns a bitter eye on Megan. 'How should I know how you people think?'

'For crying out loud, shut up, Ma!' screams Heather. She stands up abruptly and faces her astounded mother-in-law. The two children cling to her. 'Kerry didn't wanna live with you cause you fucking bullied her. Dave would never have stood for the way you treat us. And if you'd done what he asked and lent him the money he needed for the boat, he'd still be here and none of this—'

She collapses back onto the sofa with her face in her hands.

Sheila stares at her. Her pouchy face is red, sweat beading on the forehead and she's shaking. She brushes the back of her hand briskly across her nose, erasing the only hint of a tear. 'Well,' she says. 'I think I'll go and put the kettle on.'

She turns and walks, somewhat unsteadily, Megan thinks, through to the kitchen. Megan sighs. Watching the Waycott family implode is not easy.

Heather looks up at Megan and says, 'What happens now?'

'You'll be assigned a family liaison officer. It'll probably be a woman and she'll be here to help you through this. But it would help, if you can manage, if you tell me some more about what happened after I left last night. You mentioned Kerry said she'd had enough.'

Heather struggles to compose herself. She clasps her younger daughter. The child looks both puzzled and petrified. Finally Heather says, 'She got a bit stir crazy. Said she had to get out. I told her no. But she wouldn't listen. She went and got dressed.'

'Do you know where she went or was intending to go?'

'I know she was texting Paige. But Paige has been funny with her. Kerry wouldn't really talk about it but I think they'd fallen out.'

'Was she intending to meet Paige?'

Heather puts her hand over her mouth. 'This is all my fault. I'm her mother. I should've stopped her.'

CHAPTER FORTY

The Tuckers' house is a blue rectangular box cantilevered onto the steep hillside overlooking the harbour. Megan leans on the doorbell, she's not in the mood to be polite.

Emma Tucker opens the door. A tall, willowy woman in expensive Lululemon gym kit, she looks at the dishevelled figure on her doorstep with faint distaste.

Megan holds up her ID and says, 'Detective Sergeant Thomas, Mrs Tucker. I need to talk to your daughter. Now.'

'I'm sorry, what's this about?'

'I'm from the Major Crimes team. This is an extremely serious matter.' She fixes the woman with a hard stare. 'Mind if I come in?'

Emma Tucker leads her unwanted guest into the vast open-plan living area. It has a panoramic view of the fishing port waking up to a grey, overcast morning. The kitchen is to one side and an older man, around sixty, perches on a stool at the breakfast bar, eating a croissant and scrolling through messages on his phone.

'This is my husband. Darling, the police want to speak to Paige.'

He looks at Megan over his tortoiseshell specs and says, 'Oh really. And what's this about?'

'I'd like to ask her some questions about her friend, Kerry Waycott.'

'Oh, not that wretched girl,' says Mrs Tucker with a huff.

'Yes, that wretched girl,' says Megan. 'I have reason to believe your daughter may have been the last person that she spoke to, or who saw her alive.'

The Tuckers stare at one another. He removes his glasses and gets off his stool. He looks to be a man in the habit of taking charge of difficult situations. Holding out his hand to shake he says, 'Roger Tucker.'

'DS Thomas.'

'Can we offer you a cup of coffee, Sergeant?' he says.

Megan would love a cup of coffee. She can smell the aroma coming from the cafetière on the counter.

'No thank you,' she says. She's about to repeat her demand to speak to Paige, but then she notices that the girl is peeping round the corner at them.

Mrs Tucker scurries over and puts an arm round Paige's shoulders. 'Darling,' she says. 'This is a police officer and she's brought some bad news. Poor Kerry is... well, erm, dead, I'm assuming?'

Megan doesn't speak. She's scanning Paige for her immediate reaction.

For a teenager, she seems unusually composed. Her hair is long and straight and golden. It obscures half her face until she carefully tucks it behind her ear. Her glance goes from Megan to her father then her mother. Then – on cue, Megan feels – she starts to cry quietly.

Emma Tucker pulls her daughter into a hug. 'Sssh, baby! It's all right, Mama's here.'

Megan waits for the performance to be over. Roger Tucker appears to be doing the same.

He folds his arms. 'Well,' he says, 'this is all rather unfortunate. Is this the girl that was suicidal? Tried to jump off a cliff. What actually happened?'

'I can't go into details at present. But I would like to see your daughter's phone.'

This gets Paige's attention. She pulls away from her mother. 'My phone? Why? I mean, is that even legal? If Kerry's killed herself, that's not my fault.'

'If you have nothing to hide I don't see why you'd object,' says Megan with a smile. 'But we can obtain a warrant if necessary.'

'Of course she has nothing to hide,' exclaims Mrs Tucker. 'Paige, get your phone.'

Paige glares at her mother, who seems to have stepped neatly into Megan's trap.

'I'll have to go and find it,' the teenager replies.

'Try the pockets of your hoodie,' says Megan.

Paige fumbles in her pocket and pulls out a brand new iPhone. 'Oh, yeah,' she says flatly. 'I forgot. But there's loads of private stuff on it.' She looks pleadingly at her father. 'Daddy, do I have to?'

'Yes, sweetheart,' he says. 'I think if this poor girl has killed herself, you want to be as helpful as possible, don't you?'

Paige nods. The colour has drained from her face. The upset has become genuine.

'Right,' says Megan, 'I'd like you to open your phone and read to me the texts you exchanged with Kerry last night.'

Paige glances at her father for support. He's frowning but nods.

She opens the phone and says, 'She texted me on and off all day. But I was at school so I didn't reply.'

Emma Tucker gives her an approving smile.

Sighing, Paige ploughs on. 'So, I dunno, about eight o'clock she says – you want me to actually read it out loud?'

'Yes,' says Megan.

Paige takes a deep breath and reads from the screen. '*Feds been round again. I am so screwed. Meet me. Begging you babes*. I replied: *can't*. She said: *please. You my only friend*. I said: *I ain't your friend*.

No way. Jared's in hospital. All your fault you skanky bitch. Just cause he wants me not you.'

'Who on earth is Jared?' says her mother.

'Let's leave that for now,' says Roger Tucker. 'Carry on, Paige.'

'She said…' Paige swallows hard. 'She said: *I'm desperate*. I said: *Fuck off, bitch. Blocking you now*. And that's what I did.'

'You blocked her number and had no further contact with her?' says Megan.

The girl nods.

Roger Tucker has his hands in his pockets. His wife stands stiffly, holding her head upright.

Paige gazes imploringly at her parents and whispers, 'I'm really sorry.'

'That's that, I suppose,' says her father briskly. 'I'm sure no one could've foreseen that the poor girl would end up doing harm to herself. We will of course be sending our condolences to her family.'

'This wasn't a suicide,' says Megan. 'Our assumption is Kerry Waycott was unlawfully killed. We'll know more when we have the results of the post mortem. I will arrange for you to bring Paige in for further questioning and to make a formal statement. I'm assuming, Mr Tucker, that you're happy for your daughter to help us with our inquiries.'

He stares at Megan. Part of her is glad to have finally wiped the smug look off his face.

'My God,' he says, 'you think this is murder? Could Paige be in danger?'

'No reason to think so. Unless you know something you're not telling us, Paige.'

Paige is staring down at her pink fluffy mules. She shakes her head.

'We'll be in touch,' says Megan.

Roger Tucker sees her out. He says nothing.

Megan walks towards her car. Her nerve endings are zinging. She knows she's rattled Paige Tucker's cage as hard as she dares. But it feels justified. She's one of the few people who knew enough about Kerry's life to also know who she was so scared of.

The white bloodless mask of Kerry's dead face is imprinted on Megan's brain. It leaves her with little sympathy for a manipulative vixen like Paige.

CHAPTER FORTY-ONE

Tuesday, 10.45am

Shirin holds the phone to her ear. 'Listen,' she says. 'I don't know what's going on here. I want you to stop calling me.'

She's standing outside the back door and it's icy cold. A biting wind is sweeping across the moor. Winterbrook Farm is freezing inside and out; since the police booted them out, the heating's been off. Down the hill, the yellow tape round the septic tank is flapping in the wind.

He's angry, she can feel it. But he doesn't shout. He's never been a shouter. He's far more dangerous than that.

'Sugar,' he says, the tone silky and seductive. 'You know the way out of this. We was always good together, you and me, childhood sweethearts, the dream team.'

'No,' she says emphatically. 'I'm not going back to that life. Never.'

'It'll be a different life. I've changed.' More lies.

She says nothing.

'Hey,' he says, 'I'm a patient man. You'll come round in the end. You and me. It's what Aisha would've wanted. The three of us together. You know that.'

Aisha. She's not going to go there. She can't, not today.

'Listen to me,' she says. 'I didn't put the stupid body there, and if you've done it to piss me off and make my life harder—'

'Why would I wanna piss you off?'

'To threaten me.'

'I would never threaten you, sugar. Ain't my style, you know that.'

Not much, thinks Shirin. But she says, 'Then what the hell are you playing at? Some game of yours, except I get to deal with the fallout.'

'You know me, Shirin. I'm a helpful dude. There was a problem. I helped them out.'

'What do you mean? Helped them out?'

'This is all gonna work out fine. I know what I'm doing. You'll see. Don't worry. Give the boy a kiss from me.'

He hangs up. Shirin realises she's shaking. It's tempting to think the conversation went well. But she's known him for too long. When he sounds at his most reasonable, that's the time to worry. The lull before the storm.

In spite of the cold she walks up and down. She needs time to think, to decide on her next move. Georgia must know more than she's letting on. That's become clear.

Going back into the house, she finds Georgia in the sitting room – or 'drawing room', as she insists on calling it.

Georgia flings out her arms. 'The whole place smells,' she says. 'Absolutely stinks to high heaven.'

'Stinks of what?'

'I don't know. A hundred farting policemen.'

Shirin smiles. It's hard not to envy Georgia and the blithe stupidity with which she sails through life. It's all about where you're born, blind luck really. Those that have shall receive all the goodies.

'We need to get some contract cleaners in,' says Georgia. 'Deep clean the whole place. Do you think the police will pay for it?'

'No.'

'They've violated my home. I could ask Henry. I'm not moving back in with it like this. I think we've scared them into realising they can't treat me like a common criminal and get away with it.'

'Georgia, don't be naive. All your mother and her fancy lawyer have succeeded in doing is pissing them off. Now they're going to dig in.'

'What do you mean?'

'They're not going to give up and go away.'

'Henry says crimes go unsolved all the time. Particularly now, when they're short of skilled manpower and resources. Something else'll come up and take their attention. You said it yourself: it's up to them to prove a crime's been committed. Now they know they've got a battle on their hands with us, they'll go for something that gives them an easier result. They'll go through the motions for a bit, then it'll become a cold case. Everyone'll forget about it.'

'Do you really believe that? And what about him, his reaction?'

Georgia ignores the second question.

'Nowadays, with most burglaries, they don't even bother. You just claim on your insurance. A friend of Mummy's lost thousands of pounds worth of jewellery and antiques, the police did nothing. The insurance company hired some private security firm to sort it out.'

'This is a dead body, which is different.'

'Is it? Darling, now who's being naive? Anyway, no one gives two hoots about him.'

'What's that supposed to mean?'

Georgia flaps her hands dismissively. 'Nothing.'

'You know who it is, don't you?'

'Now you're being ridiculous.' *Exactly what Heidi said.*

Shirin sighs. 'Am I?'

Georgia tosses her head and says, 'It would be more useful, Shirin, if you'd do something about this ghastly smell.'

CHAPTER FORTY-TWO

Megan goes home for a shower and a change of clothes. By the time she gets to the office the morning briefing is nearly over. She slides in at the back of the room. Detective Superintendent Barker has turned up to take charge of proceedings, which is no surprise. The room is fuller than usual. Additional officers, both uniforms and detectives, have been drafted in and there's the sense of seriousness and anticipation you only get on a big op.

Laura Slater is standing beside the boss and she registers Megan's arrival. Their eyes meet for a second but it's impossible to read Slater's look. Is she feeling sick and guilty and responsible like Megan? Probably not.

'…and obviously,' says Barker, 'this will mean pressure and overtime. Richard will be SIO on the Waycott murder, Laura will remain SIO on O'Brien and, as head of the team, she'll pick up anything else that comes in. Any questions?'

Megan raises her hand. 'Sir, will the higher vaginal swab that Sexual Offences took from Kerry Waycott after she was raped now be fast-tracked for DNA analysis?'

Barker glances at Montieth. 'Richard?'

'Top of my list, obviously. Thanks for flagging that up, Megan.' He smiles. Slater doesn't.

'Right, thanks everyone,' says Barker. 'And I know I don't need to say this, but we now have two high-profile, media-sensitive investigations going on. I don't want any leaks. If they hassle you when you're out and about you refer them to the press office. Those of you who are new to this type of inquiry may be surprised how persistent they can be. From offers to buy you a drink to cash bribes. Don't talk about the details of the case at home. Don't be fooled by concerned neighbours who appear from nowhere and just want to be reassured their kids are in no danger. Bear in mind witnesses may well be selling their stories to the tabloids. Let's keep this watertight. Okay?'

As the meeting breaks up, Megan makes a beeline for Montieth. He's pouring himself a coffee.

'Good point you raised. I didn't know that hadn't been done,' he says.

'We were hanging fire. We thought she was lying about the rape.'

He shrugs and shakes his head. 'There's nothing you could've done, Megan. Don't blame yourself.'

She nods curtly. The last thing she wants is sympathy. That could crack her open and so far she's holding it together. *Focus. Do the job.* It's the mantra to get her through this.

'I went to see the Waycotts,' she says. 'The mother hasn't much of a clue what her daughter was up to.'

'Vish says the father's dead.'

'Yeah. He was a trawler skipper. Accident at sea. But there's a bit of a question mark as to whether it was suicide. Family's a mess, basically.'

'What about this teacher you nicked?'

'He's got an alibi for the rape. After the Waycotts I called in on Kerry's supposed best friend, Paige Tucker.'

Montieth gets out his notebook and scribbles down the name.

'She's a piece of work but I'm fairly convinced she can tell us loads more about what she and Kerry got up to. She may even know the rapist. So where do you want to start?'

'Megan, you need to have a word with the DCI.'

'Why?'

'I want to work with you on this, of course I do, but it's not my call.'

It feels to Megan as if she's been sucker-punched. Then she sees red. Turning on her heel, she storms across the room to Slater's office. The DCI and Barker are in the middle of a conversation when she bursts in.

'Sorry,' she says. 'Why are you taking me off the Waycott case?'

The two senior officers exchange looks.

'It's a question of resources,' says Slater. 'I need you to stick with O'Brien. They're tricky people to deal with, and you've already got the measure of them. We simply don't have another DI to put in at the moment. So I need you to step up.'

'Until we ID the body, we can't really move forward. And Brittney's on that. Just give me a couple of days on Waycott—'

Does it sound too much like she's begging? She is begging.

'Megan, I can't. I know it's tedious trying to get an ID on the body. We need to find some dental records that match and we need to keep on it. Failing that, we'll have to do a facial reconstruction.'

'That's a phone call to the lab. One of the DCs can do that. I'm just asking for a couple of days out. What difference is that going to make?'

Slater sighs. 'Also I've just had social services on the phone, we've got a possible cuckooing. It's a vulnerable addict who's been targeted by a drugs gang before. I need you to check that out too.'

Megan feels her panic rising. 'Oh for Chrissake, Ted can do that, surely. In between snacks.'

It comes out all wrong. Surly and unprofessional.

'Ted will be working with Richard,' says Slater.

'Him instead of me, that's ridiculous.'

'Calm down, Megan,' says Barker. 'Laura takes the view, and I agree, that you're far too emotionally enmeshed in the Waycott case.'

'Of course I'm bloody enmeshed! I read the kid all wrong and now she's dead.'

'Richard's a very experienced homicide officer,' says Slater evenly. 'He's in the best position to take a step back and evaluate the evidence.'

'So why can't I help him? I know more about Kerry than anyone else here. Who's bringing him up to speed?'

'Vish Prasad can do that.' She sighs. 'Believe it or not, Megan, I'm trying to protect you.'

Protect yourself, more like. Megan manages to bite back the riposte. She glares at Laura Slater. The DCI's stillness and composure are the most annoying things about her.

'Also,' she says, 'in terms of you and Ted, you're the better DS, so you should step up.'

Megan turns to Barker. 'Sir, please. I know you think this is too personal but sometimes personal works. I'm the one who let Kerry down, you have to let me help find her killer.'

Barker sighs. 'You're right, it is too personal and that clouds judgement. This is Laura's decision and one I'm not going to override.' He glances at Slater then back to Megan. 'We all make mistakes and sometimes they have dire consequences. But, if you want to stay in this job and make a success of it, you deal with it and move on. Talk to Moretti. That's what she's for. You're not the first police officer to suffer guilt. But we can't run an inquiry around assuaging your conscience. Understand?'

'Sir.'

He checks his watch. 'I should've left twenty minutes ago. I've got a meeting in Exeter.'

He picks up his coat and strides out.

Slater and Megan are left facing each other.

The DCI shrugs. 'As he says, we all make mistakes. But we suck it up and move on. That's the job. Think you can do that?'

CHAPTER FORTY-THREE

Tuesday, 12.20pm

The furrowed track winds alongside a tributary of the River Dart through a patch of ancient woodland. The river is full to bursting, the recent rain bouncing over the boulders and rushing under a tiny stone bridge built for the age of the horse and cart.

The squad car navigates the bridge but the police van following has barely inches to spare. Megan rides in the back of the lead vehicle with two of the young response officers. She wonders why half the uniforms on response look like teenagers even though she knows the answer. Many older officers got axed or retired in successive rounds of government-imposed cuts.

Fortunately, the girl driving is focused on keeping the car on the bumpy track but her partner, Kieran, a chubby and enthusiastic young man, has kept up a monologue since they left the office.

'Yeah, I'd love to get a transfer to the Met, I mean, don't you miss it?'

'No,' says Megan. She could've added, *but I'm burnt-out and cynical*. 'Is it much farther, cause I feel like I might puke.'

He laughs nervously and says, 'Sorry, I know it's a bit of a rough ride but we're nearly there.'

'Okay,' says Megan, 'tell me about this woman again.' *Suck it up and move on.* She's going through the motions. 'Cuckooing' makes it sound so quaint, one little bird takes over another's nest.

The reality is a vicious drug gang invading the home of a vulnerable person, often an addict, and using it as a base to distribute drugs. It's a serious problem but not as urgent as taking a rapist and murderer off the street.

'Well,' says Kieran. 'Lizzie Quinn. We try and keep an eye on her. She's really old, maybe sixty, and she's been an addict for years. It's surprising she's still alive. Her social worker says she's come off her methadone programme and that usually means one thing: she's found some new friends and a new source of supply.'

'I gather she's been targeted by County Lines drug gangs before?'

'Yeah, several times. She's sort of an old hippie, just thinks everyone's her friend. Well, you'll see.'

The track opens into a small clearing and at its centre is a low ramshackle cottage overhung with a cathedral canopy of trees. Apart from a couple of towering conifers, most have shed their foliage and the ground is a carpet of red and yellow and brown leaves. The setting is idyllic, the river nearby; at first glance it's like stepping into a woodland fairy tale. Until you look more closely.

Megan gets out of the car. The van with two more response officers pulls up behind them.

The roof of the cottage has a gaping hole, half of the slates are missing, exposing bare rafters, and on closer inspection, it appears to be derelict. But to the side of it there are two old caravans, one set on bricks. Parked next to the caravans there's a rusty Vauxhall Astra with a flat tyre and a bright blue Nissan Juke.

'That's a new addition,' says Kieran. 'Brand new.'

'Check the reg,' says Megan.

The larger of the two caravans has a rickety metal chimney pot sticking out of the side and a thin wisp of woodsmoke curls from the top of it.

Megan raps on the door. Several moments pass then it opens and a woman peers out at them through round John Lennon glasses.

'Hello, Lizzie,' says Megan, holding up her warrant card. 'I'm Megan, I've come to have a chat if that's all right.'

Lizzie tilts her head to one side. Her grey hair, white in places, is braided and beaded into a heavy curtain of dreadlocks that hang halfway down her back. She smells strongly of patchouli oil.

'Right, okay,' she says. 'Megan,' she repeats, as if saying it helps her process and remember. Then she smiles, displaying gappy front teeth. 'I'm Lizzie.'

'I know. All right if I come in?'

'Sure,' says Lizzie.

Megan steps into the surprisingly cosy interior of the caravan. She hits her head on a wind chime which hangs in the doorway.

'Wind chime,' says Lizzie with a dreamy smile. 'To ward off evil spirits.'

'That's useful,' says Megan. 'Do you find it works?'

The small kitchenette comprises a short run of cabinets with a sink and a gas hob. It's cluttered without being dirty. Various items of drug paraphernalia are laid out carefully on the draining board. For a smackhead, Lizzie seems quite organised.

The remainder of the caravan is filled with three heavily cushioned divans forming three sides of a square. Lounging on the divans are a boy and a girl, scowling at Megan.

'Hello,' says Megan, 'and who are you?'

'These are my mates,' says Lizzie. She pauses and then points to the boy. 'This is Connor.' She smiles at him, nods, then turns to the girl. 'And this is Lexi.' The kids don't smile back.

Connor has one eye on the door. He seems to be calculating whether to make a run for it. But Megan is in the way.

'How old are you, Connor?' says Megan. He's small and skinny, jet black hair, olive skin and angry eyes. His face is smooth and beardless. He can't be more than twelve or thirteen.

'No comment,' he says with a Scouse accent.

'Liverpool, eh?' says Megan. 'You're a long way from home.'

'Fook off, copper. I'm saying nuttin.'

'They're my friends,' says Lizzie with a nod and a smile.

'I can see that. Cause they bought you a nice new car, didn't they?' says Megan. 'So you can drive them around.'

'Yeah,' says Lizzie. 'They did. How did you know?'

'Shut up, yer stupid bint!' says Connor. 'You don't have to tell 'em nuttin.'

'That's a bit rude,' says Megan. 'Not exactly how you talk to a friend, is it?'

'No comment,' says the boy.

Megan turns to the girl. Although bigger than Connor, she's probably a similar age, with long mousy hair and freckles. She wears shorts which emphasise her gangly legs and big feet. Megan smiles at her and says, 'I'm guessing, Lexi, that you're from Liverpool too.'

The girl wrinkles her nose. Then, without any warning, she leaps up and launches herself at Megan. Like a feral cat she flies straight for the face and before Megan can step back, her claws draw blood.

Megan screeches and shoves the kid back on the divan. Kieran comes busting through the door.

'Bloody hell!' says Megan, clutching her cheek.

'You all right, Sarge?' says Kieran.

'I dunno,' says Megan, lifting her hand.

He peers at her. 'Oh, that's a nasty scratch. It's drawn blood.'

'Cow just assaulted me,' says Lexi. 'I'm pressing charges.'

Megan sighs. Her face is throbbing. 'Get these two out of here and into the van.'

A search of the property by the uniformed officers produces a sizeable seizure of cocaine and cannabis, bundles of cash and several phones. There's also a quantity of heroin. But Lizzie Quinn insists this is for her personal use. The new car, unsurprisingly, is registered in her name, although Lizzie says she's borrowing it until her Astra is fixed.

Megan has a frustrating phone call with a social worker called Charlie.

'Can't you get her a place in rehab?' says Megan.

'What would be the point of that?' he replies. 'Lizzie likes her drugs, she doesn't want to get clean. Who are we to force her? She's not an ordinary smackhead. How do you think she's lived so long? She knows more about drugs than a chemist.'

'This is the fourth time she's been a target of cuckooing. She's a vulnerable adult. What are we supposed to do? Leave her here in the middle of the bloody woods until the next bunch of scumbags come along? Can't you find her some better accommodation where she gets proper support?'

'She loves the woods. She won't leave.'

'At least come down here and talk to her and get her back on the methadone programme.'

He sighs. 'I'll try. Later in the week. I'm a bit busy.'

Megan hangs up on him.

Lizzie is sitting on the steps to her caravan smoking a rollup cigarette. Megan notices she has tears in her eyes.

'You all right, Lizzie?' she says.

'I'm always sad when you take my little elves away.'

'Come on. They're kids, not bloody elves. They're here to sell drugs. And who's driving them around to facilitate that? I can nick you, you know that.'

Lizzie smiles and gives Megan a dreamy faraway look. 'Best gear I ever had was in jail.'

'Who brought them here and gave you that nice new car?'

Lizzie huffs and frowns. 'Look,' she says. 'I don't ask them their names. I don't want no trouble. Not from you lot, not from them. People ask me for favours. What am I supposed to do? I try to be friends with everyone.'

'People who use you aren't your friends.'

'Don't you think we all just use each other? You can call it fancy names, like capitalism or business or trade. It's how the world works. It's not my fault. It's why I prefer the woods. Trees are kinder. They love you back.'

CHAPTER FORTY-FOUR

Tuesday, 6.20pm

Megan sits at the kitchen table and lets her sister bathe her cheek with TCP.

'Ouch! That stings.'

'It's a nasty scratch, you don't want it to get infected. Are your tetanus shots up to date?'

'Yeah, I think so.'

'So are the rumours true?'

'What rumours?' says Megan.

'About Kerry Waycott.'

Megan notices her niece, Amber, hovering in the doorway, listening.

'C'mon,' says Debbie. 'Police have been all over Ellwood Cove for most of the day. They're saying a body's been found.'

'You know I can't talk about this stuff.'

'She tried to jump off the cliffs and you talked her down. But Ellwood Cove is wooded right down to the beach. There are no cliffs there to jump off. So what happened?'

Amber steps into the room and says, 'Mr Foxton made an announcement in our year group assembly. Said Kerry was dead and the police want to talk to her friends.'

'Who's Mr Foxton?' says Megan.

'Deputy head. He also said Mrs Kovacs has left and so has Mr Jones. What's going on?'

Megan sighs and fingers her cheek. 'The truth is, I don't know because I'm not working on the case.'

Debbie scans her sister. 'Really?' she says. Then she wags a finger at her daughter. 'So you're not to go out after dark. Got that?'

'I've got football practice after school tomorrow.'

'You need a lift, call your dad.'

Megan shoots her niece a speculative look. 'Is Paige posting about it on Snapchat?'

Amber shakes her head. 'Nope. Nothing. She's off school too. Probably having a nervous breakdown so she can make a vid about it.'

Debbie turns to her sister and says, 'Should we be worried, Meg? You would tell us, wouldn't you? None of this police bullshit.'

Megan meets her gaze directly. 'I don't think Amber is in any particular danger because I don't think this a random thing. Okay? But, nowadays, it's always a good idea to be sensible.'

'I am sensible,' says Amber.

The doorbell rings. Debbie huffs and shouts, 'Mark, can you get that! Right, dinner.'

'How about fish and chips?' says Megan. 'My treat.'

'Yeah!' says Amber. 'But can I have a battered sausage?'

Mark walks into the room with a sombre face and says, 'Megan, you've got a visitor.'

Sheila Waycott follows him in. The woman looks hollowed out. Her eyes are red and darkly underscored, her face ashen. 'Sorry to come round like this,' she says. 'Could we have a word?'

There's a moment of awkwardness. The old lady stands there desolate and waiting, like a homeless bag lady no one can bear to look at.

Megan sighs. There's no polite way to refuse.

Debbie picks up her purse and says, 'Okay. We'll go to the chip shop.' She ushers her daughter out.

'Come and sit down,' Megan says. She leads Sheila through into the sitting room.

In a day Sheila Waycott seems to have aged years.

'Mark knew my old man,' she says, as she settles in a chair. 'And he can tell you, we're not bad people.'

'I've never thought you were,' Megan replies.

'There's no excuse for Justin. His temper gets the better of him. But since we lost Dave…' She reins herself in. 'Anyway, I'm not here for that.'

'Okay,' says Megan. 'But I should tell you, Sheila, I'm not working on the case.'

'Why not?'

'It's a question of resources. But DI Montieth is a very experienced officer.'

'The Scotsman. Yeah, I've met him.' Her jaw tenses. Megan can feel the fury. 'And you know what he asked me? Him and his fat sidekick. How many different blokes was my fourteen-year-old granddaughter having sex with? We're scum so she's scum, that's his assumption.'

Megan sighs and puffs out her cheeks. Could Montieth really have been so tactless? She wouldn't have thought so.

The old lady shakes her head bitterly. 'They may as well have gone the whole hog and asked if she was on the game.'

'Sheila, I can see you're upset. And I know that some of the questions we ask can seem insensitive. But to get to the truth we have to look at every possible option.'

'Kerry was a child! This wasn't her fault.'

'I know that.'

'Can't you do something? Tell them! He walks into my house, that bloody DI of yours, in his fancy tartan waistcoat, and he's judging us! I can feel it. And judging Kerry. Making out she's a slapper and somehow caused this. Well, she didn't!'

It's the first time Megan has seen Sheila Waycott cry. But the tears are finally flowing. It occurs to Megan that this is what Sheila herself secretly thinks but can't accept. She blames Kerry.

Megan glances round, finds a box of tissues and hands them to her. Then she waits.

Sheila blows her nose and says, 'Mark knows we're decent people. You ask him. He'll tell you. They shouldn't be treating my little girl like this.'

Reaching out, Megan pats her hand. 'Okay, listen to me. No one's judging your family. This is about finding out what happened. Isn't that what we all want?'

Sheila sniffs and nods.

'Here's what I think. I think Kerry was scared of someone. This was the person who attacked her. And she probably knew him. How, we don't know. But that doesn't make it her fault in any way.'

Sheila shakes her head as if to erase the thought. 'If she was frightened of some bloke why didn't she just tell us?'

Because she was more frightened of you?

'You've already answered your own question,' says Megan. 'Fourteen. That's grown up in lots of ways but also hugely naive. So you're right, she still thought like a child and she was out of her depth. That's what paedophiles rely on.'

'You should be in charge of this, not him. Can you tell your boss that?'

'Thanks for the vote of confidence, but that's not going to happen.'

Megan manages a few more reassuring platitudes and finally Sheila Waycott leaves. Closing the front door behind her, Megan is consumed by a sense of defeat. Slater's decision to take her off the case reflects her failure, not just as a police officer but her failure to win the trust of a confused teenager who desperately needed her help.

This murder could have been avoided, should have been avoided. Someone should carry the can for that. You can't just blame the system and do the usual inquiry followed by *the lessons must be learned* bollocks. Megan got too many things wrong. She was bull-headed, insisting she could walk back in and do the job, no problem. She wasn't being honest with herself or anyone else. And Kerry had paid the price. Facing the truth is hard. Sticking instead of quitting is harder. But that's what she must do. She owes it to Kerry.

CHAPTER FORTY-FIVE

Wednesday, 9.05am

Ted Jennings, giant coffee mug in hand, has his back towards Megan as she walks across the office to her desk. He's at the coffee station talking to Vish.

'…and I'll tell you, mate, I wouldn't say this in front of this lot, but working for a bloke again, fuck me, it makes life easier.'

Vish catches Megan's eye. He looks embarrassed. She smiles to herself.

'Morning, Ted,' she says. 'How's the diet going?'

Frowning, he turns to look at her. 'I'm not on a diet,' he says.

'Oh, I thought that's why Slater wanted to get you out from behind your desk. Running round after the DI. So you get more exercise.'

Megan has the pleasure of seeing him try to puzzle this out. But she also knows it could be the high point of her day.

Steeling herself, she heads for Slater's office. The door is ajar. She taps on it.

'Morning, boss.'

Laura Slater looks up and gives her a tepid smile.

'First up, the cuckooing,' says Megan. 'Handed over two kids to the child protection team yesterday afternoon. The girl's already in the system, a vulnerable misper from Liverpool. They're shipping her back today. We're still trying to get an ID for the boy. He's an old hand at this, seems to be using a false name. Nothing useful from Lizzie Quinn on the gang behind it that targeted her. But if the kids are from Liverpool, that's probably where they're based too. I'll find out who to liaise with up there.'

'Okay. I gather you seized a large quantity of contraband. Well done.' Slater's smile looks genuine enough. But Megan still feels as if she's walking on broken glass with the DCI.

'Second thing, boss,' she says, 'is a bit more delicate. Last night Sheila Waycott came knocking on my door.'

'Not her bloody son again.'

'No, she's upset about the way she says that she and her family were questioned by the DI and the assumptions that she feels are being made about Kerry.'

Slater frowns. 'What?'

'I'm not saying it's Richard's fault, she's a bloody difficult woman to deal with. Unpredictable and sometimes vindictive.'

'What did she want from you?'

'I don't know. A chance to sound off? She's an angry woman and that was before what happened to her granddaughter.'

Slater waves her hand dismissively. 'Leave it with me, I'll speak to Richard.'

Megan hesitates then she says, 'I'm not saying this, boss, because I want back on the case. Although obviously I still feel… well, anyway, I thought you should know. If the press get hold of her—'

'Yeah, okay,' says Slater. 'Any ID on the body in the tank yet?'

'Brittney's run the DNA against all our databases and there were no hits. So he's not got a criminal record.'

The DCI sighs. 'Too much to hope for, I suppose.'

'Well, it does suggest that we're on the right track and it's not a random corpse. I think Shirin Khan is the one to get to. She's next on my list.'

Megan wanders back to her desk where she finds a fresh mug of coffee. She looks round and sees Vish smiling at her. He walks over.

'Got you a coffee,' he says, ''cause, well, y'know—'

'You don't want me to think that you're entering into some sexist male conspiracy with Ted?'

'I think you should be on the Waycott case,' says Vish. 'Everyone does, including the DI.'

Megan doesn't want to ask but she can't help herself. 'How's it going?'

'We're pulling Steven Jones in again later today.'

'But he's got an alibi for the rape.'

'Maybe not. Monty did a formal interview yesterday with Linda Kovacs and she ended up admitting that although she went to bed with Jones that night and they started to have sex, he couldn't actually get it up. Afterwards she fell asleep. Woke up in the morning and he was gone. She's no idea what time he left.'

Megan wants to kick herself. How could she have missed all that? *Always interrogate the evidence.* She was too distracted by Linda Kovacs's self-pity to question her properly.

'So what's the theory?' says Megan. 'He couldn't have sex with Kovacs so he went looking for a kid who would arouse him?'

'That's what the DI thinks,' says Vish.

It makes sense. And she missed it.

'And where was Jones on Monday night?' she says. 'Did he have an alibi for the time of the murder?'

'Holed up alone in his flat, feeling sorry for himself and brooding about the total collapse of his career? That's what we're thinking,' says Vish.

'And blaming Kerry? Motive and opportunity. He ticks the boxes.' Megan smiles. 'Looks like the DI's cracked it.'

'We're doing a trawl of all the ANPR cameras in the area. There aren't that many but with CCTV we might be able to find Jones's car, possibly the pick-up point and plot the route he took to the cove.'

'How did he get in touch with Kerry? Have you got her phone?'

'No sign of it. Anyway, I should get back.'

Megan watches him disappear into the incident room. Is that where she should be? She'd still like to be part of it. But if Montieth really has tied it up this quickly then it's the best result for everyone. When Megan talked to her, Kerry hadn't seemed scared of Jones. But it looks like she read that wrong too. More evidence of how scatty her judgement has become? But, as the boss reminded her, she needs to suck it up.

She spends the next hour talking to Liverpool CID, phoning children's homes in the North West and sending them mugshots of the boy who calls himself Connor in the hope that someone might recognise him. It feels to her that there are too many kids who have been cast adrift. Whether it's through bad luck or bad parenting, left to their own devices they find trouble or trouble finds them. She's well aware that, in another time, her own life could have taken a different course. She and her sister were often truants who hung around on street corners. They nicked food and sweets from shops but managed not to get caught. Is that all that makes a difference in the end, chance?

Richard Montieth comes out of the DCI's office and Megan clocks him looking across the room at her. He hesitates for a moment, then strides towards her.

'Morning,' she says. 'I hear congratulations might be in order.'

The tartan waistcoat is unbuttoned, he looks harassed.

Putting his hands on his hips he says, 'Are you taking the piss?'

'No. Vish said—'

'Ah yes,' he says sourly, 'office gossip. You girls like all that, don't you? Well, let me make one thing perfectly clear to you, Sergeant, I deal with people straight. If I've something to say, I say it to their face.'

Megan leans back in her chair. 'Richard, hang on. What is this about?'

'Your cosy little chat with Sheila Waycott last night.'

'It wasn't a cosy chat. She came round to my house. She knows my brother-in-law.'

'Then why didn't you come to me this morning? Tell me, instead of running straight to Slater with some tale about how much I'd upset the Waycotts?'

'It wasn't like that.'

'Wasn't it? C'mon, Megan, you've been caught out. At least have the decency to admit it. You're convinced you're the only one who can crack this case. Only you know how to talk to the poor old Waycotts.'

'No, that's not true.'

He looms over her. 'Isn't it? Because you're a London cop you think that makes you special. And you can't stand the fact that you're out of the loop. So you go sneaking to the boss behind my back.'

'I wasn't sneaking. You weren't around—'

'Oh really?' He gives a curt nod. 'I've got your number, lady.'

As Montieth walks off, Megan's gaze travels round the room. Brittney and Kitty are glued to their computer screens, trying to look busy. A couple of the uniforms are shooting her surreptitious looks. Other people's rows are always delicious and cringey in equal parts. Megan glances in the direction of Slater's office where an unseen hand snaps the door shut.

CHAPTER FORTY-SIX

Although Megan has been in this room a few times before, this is the first time she's noticed the flowers. The grey stoneware vase is simple. It sits on the low glass table between the two chairs. The flowers themselves are an eclectic arrangement of blooms and grasses in autumn colours. The sort of thing a posh florist might put together and charge twenty quid for.

'Nice flowers,' she says.

'They're from my garden,' says Dr Moretti. 'I think it's good to be reminded how much beauty there is in the world.'

Megan considers this. Does she ever think about beauty? How do you even do that when the only image that sticks in your mind is of a dead girl's dead white, eyeless face?

'How was your day?' says Moretti.

'Okay.' She could say long and boring. Going through endless missing persons reports to see if any of them could possibly fit the description of a male, aged thirty-five to fifty-five, height one hundred and eighty-three centimetres. The problem was, too many did.

'Any more panic attacks?' says Moretti.

Megan shakes her head.

'You seem different. What's going on with you?'

How does she even begin to explain? Montieth's bitter accusation still smarts. She could bleat about the unfairness of it, but what would be the point in that?

'I made a mistake,' she says.

'What sort of mistake?'

'The sort of mistake where someone dies.'

Moretti raises her eyebrows. 'Okay. Tell me some more.'

'A fourteen-year-old girl said she was raped. A messed-up kid, bit of an attention-seeker. She told me about someone she was really scared of, but wouldn't name him. The boss thought she was making it up. I went along with that. But turns out she wasn't and now she's dead.'

'Murdered, you think, by this person?'

'The DCI took me off the case. Said I was too "emotionally enmeshed". My colleagues made an arrest this afternoon.'

'Sounds like the DCI might've been right.'

'Trust you to bloody well agree with her!' says Megan.

Moretti smiles. 'You wanted a chance to vindicate yourself, that's perfectly natural.'

Scowling, Megan folds her arms. 'It's not about me, not what I wanted for me—'

'There's nothing wrong in that. Come on, be honest. What did you feel?'

'Angry.'

'And?'

'I don't bloody know! Guilty? Worried because I can't trust my own judgement.'

'What about shame? When our mistakes are exposed that's usually what we feel. Ashamed.'

Megan shakes her head and exhales. What she feels is that she's being accused. Again. First Montieth takes a pop at her, now the doctor, who is, after all, supposed to be on her side.

'I don't know,' she says. 'What does shame feel like? I'm just bloody furious with myself for fucking up and I'm wondering if I can even do this job. Maybe this whole thing, coming down here from the Met, is a huge mistake. I haven't been a proper detective for years. I've been undercover, pretending—' She hesitates: old habits die hard, some secrets still can't be told. 'Well, pretending to be someone I'm not. Now, all of a sudden, I'm a cop again. Asking the right questions, gathering all the evidence, that's the nitty-gritty that makes a case. And I'm totally out of practice. I've been running around like a headless chicken. Missing stuff I shouldn't. My boss thinks I'm a liability and basically she's right.'

'Walking away from it all would be a relief, I imagine.'

'Yes!'

'Do it then,' says Moretti. 'It's your life, your choice.'

Megan stares at her, this is not the answer she was expecting.

'Really? Just jack it all in?'

'Why not?'

'Well,' says Megan. 'That's not what I thought you'd say.'

'You need my permission? Or for me to say this is the right thing?'

'No.'

'What, then?' It feels as if Moretti is deliberately winding her up.

The scent from the flowers fills the room. Megan realises that the more she notices them the more apparent they become. The colours, the smell. It's oppressive. Is this some clever little trick to stop you wallowing in self-pity? A version of 'wake up and smell the coffee'? Beauty? What bollocks! If you get to spend your days sitting round and listening to idiots moan, and get well paid for it, then maybe you've got time to think about beauty.

Moretti continues to look at her. She's waiting, letting the silence open up until Megan feels compelled to fill it. Well, fuck that! She's not playing that game today. Lacing her fingers, she rests her gaze on the top corner of Moretti's chair above her right shoulder and stares. She doesn't have to wait long.

The shrink tilts her head and says, 'You're not a stupid woman, Megan. You knew this wouldn't be easy. We're fragile creatures; put under too much stress our bodies break, our minds break and there are no easy fixes. Healing is a slow process. I can prescribe you an analgesic for physical pain but I have no pill for suffering and doubt, although plenty of people go to their doctors asking for exactly that. And when they're refused, they self-medicate and end up addicted to opiates as a result. This is the life you have now, so this is where you start.'

'Meaning what?'

'Meaning this is where you start. With the anger and the doubt.'

CHAPTER FORTY-SEVEN

Shirin comes tearing down the sweeping staircase. She's agile enough that her bare feet skip over the glass treads. Georgia is below, perched at the breakfast bar in one of her more elaborate kimonos. This one has a dragon on the back. She has a spoonful of granola halfway to her mouth.

Gazing up at Shirin, she says, 'What the hell's the matter with you?'

'I can't find Noah.' There's a tearful tremor in her voice.

'He's probably playing somewhere.'

'I've searched the whole of the upstairs.'

Georgia puts down her spoon and sighs. 'He's probably with Agnese.' Agnese is Dame Heidi's Latvian housekeeper. 'I expect they've gone to the shops. Or he's helping Paco clean the car. All those soap suds, he loves splashing around.'

Shirin has reached the bottom of the stairs. She glares at Georgia and says, 'I warned you about this but you wouldn't listen.'

'What do you mean?'

'I said he'd come and take the boy.'

Georgia shakes her head and sighs.

'That's rubbish. I think you're panicking unnecessarily. How would he even get in here? There's an alarm system and cameras.'

'I knew he was gone as soon as I woke up. I could feel it.'
Clasping her hand to her mouth, she gulps back a tear.

Georgia frowns. 'He's a little boy. He loves to hide. I'm sure
we'll—'

Agnese walks round the corner carrying Dame Heidi's breakfast
tray. She places it by the dishwasher.

'Agnese,' says Georgia. 'Have you seen Noah? Did you give
him breakfast this morning?'

'No, madam,' says the housekeeper. 'Not see him at all today.'

'When did you last see him?' says Shirin.

The woman gives them a wary look, the tone of accusation in
Shirin's voice is obvious. 'I don't know,' she replies. 'Yesterday.'

'How much did he pay you,' says Shirin, 'to hand the boy over?'

Agnese gasps. 'What? No! I don't do nothing.'

'Hang on, Shirin,' says Georgia. 'You're jumping to a lot of
conclusions here. We're not even sure he's gone.'

'Who's gone?' says Dame Heidi. The old lady wanders into the
kitchen area from her own private wing of the house.

Agnese rushes over to her, head bowed. 'Please, madam,' she
says, 'the little boy. I don't do nothing, I swear! I would never
harm him.'

'Of course you wouldn't,' says Heidi. 'What tommyrot!'

'Then who let him into the house?' says Shirin. ''Cause someone
did. It's got to be either her or the chauffeur. And the shit wages
you pay her, Heidi, who could blame her for being tempted?'

'Oh for heaven's sake,' exclaims Georgia. 'I can't believe this
is happening.'

Heidi raises an imperious hand and says, 'Be quiet, all of you!
Agnese, stop snivelling. Not one's accusing you. Have you done
a thorough search?'

'I've looked upstairs,' says Shirin. 'But he must be gone. If he
was here he'd be wanting his breakfast. He's always hungry.'

Georgia exhales. 'She's right. Oh my God, he's gone.'

'Agnese, go and have a proper look round downstairs,' says Heidi. 'And tell Paco to search outside.'

The housekeeper looks grateful for the opportunity to escape.

Shirin glares at Heidi. 'I told you not to underestimate him. He's sending us a message. A warning.'

'Don't you think you're being rather melodramatic?' says the old lady, but her voice lacks conviction.

'Oh Mummy!' wails Georgia. 'I can't bear it if I've lost my little boy.'

'Darling, we'll find him,' says Dame Heidi, pulling her daughter into a hug.

Shirin watches them. The diminutive mother swamped by the oversized, blubbering child. What ridiculous buffoons they are.

CHAPTER FORTY-EIGHT

Lying awake into the early hours gave Megan time to think. Anger eats you if you let it. The doubt certainly does. Is that what Moretti was on about? Hard to know. But the shrink was right about one thing, Megan always knew this wouldn't be easy. As dawn broke, she drove down to the beach but she didn't swim. The wind was offshore so it wasn't rough, just cold and miserable. An Atlantic low had brought in the latest burst of squally showers.

She concluded that to be a winter swimmer she'd need a wetsuit and to continue being a cop she'd need to buckle down and relearn the skills she'd forgotten. Or just walk away? *Admit he's won.*

Living life on an emotional rollercoaster is tough. Blankness and detachment followed by bouts of emotion laced with panic and anxiety and guilt. PTSD can make you reactive and egotistical. But she doesn't want to make excuses and she doesn't want her colleagues to know how weak and damaged she is. In that cellar she lost all dignity, everything. Now, at least, she can try and claw some of that back.

Montieth thinks she is a prima donna. It's easy enough to see why he assumed she'd deliberately gone behind his back. And he'd probably had a little malicious pointer from the DCI. But the truth is, he's succeeded where she'd failed and he deserves credit for that.

Walking into a half empty office she settles at her desk, switches on her computer and starts to review all the notes and forensic reports on the O'Brien case. As the place begins to fill up she greets each of her colleagues in turn with a friendly smile. It's not that hard. No one blanks her.

Vish arrives and gives her a nod. He has a small box of hand-made chocolates tied with a bow and he places it carefully on Brittney's desk.

'Is it her birthday?' says Megan.

'No. But she's been really down in the mouth. Just wanted to cheer her up.'

Megan frowns. 'Is she still blaming herself for the dead husband thing?'

'Not just that,' says Vish. 'She thinks now everyone assumes she's a crap detective.'

He disappears into the incident room. Megan looks at the chocolates, a kind gesture from a mate. All of a sudden she feels tears welling up, which is ridiculous. From composure to sorrow in a heartbeat, all her emotions jangle round inside her. She hates it.

She forces herself back to the report she's reading: Brittney's background research on Georgia O'Brien. It's detailed and thorough, referenced with links to press reports and video clips.

When Brittney eventually appears, she does look depressed.

'Sorry I'm late,' she says.

'Not a problem,' says Megan.

Brittney picks up the chocolates, purses her lips and dumps them in the waste bin.

'They're a present from Vish to cheer you up,' says Megan.

'If I eat them I'll put on more weight. That's not going to cheer me up, is it?' she replies.

Megan glances at her and ponders. One of those young women who've hit thirty and are everyone's friend but no one's lover. Liked for her personality. But Vish is seriously good-looking. Megan can imagine the sort of girls he'd chase and it wouldn't be Brittney. To her, his well-meaning gesture could be painful. The hidden desires and undercurrents of office life, glimpsed in a look on the DC's face. More things she's out of touch with.

Brittney takes her coat off, rummages in her bag and plonks down into her desk chair.

'I'm going through all the stuff you dug up on Georgia,' Megan says.

'Oh,' says Brittney. 'Why?'

'Because that's where we're going to find the answer to this. Can the body be linked to Georgia or Shirin? That's the basic question.'

'Given the time frame, it's a fair assumption.'

'We need a list. What are your thoughts about the first husband, Eric Russell?'

Brittney swivels round in her chair. 'I dunno, really.'

'For years he produced the TV show Georgia was in, then she has an affair with Damian. She divorces Eric. He kills her off in the show and effectively ends her career.'

'Yeah,' says Brittney with a sigh. But behind the owl glasses the eyes have come to life.

'What's he up to now?' says Megan.

'A year after Georgia left, the show got axed anyway. He struggled to get another gig in telly. He's directed a couple of plays in London. I've left messages on his phone.'

'So you haven't been able to contact him?'

Brittney shoots her a defensive look. 'I have been trying. But no, not yet.'

'Calm down. I'm not having a go at you, mate. I'll get Kitty to check if he's come up as a misper.'

'Sorry. I should've done that.' To Megan's eye she's young and sad, like a confused puppy.

'Do you think the DCI hates me?' Brittney whispers.

Megan chuckles. 'I can assure you I rank far higher up her shitlist than you.'

This produces the hint of a smile.

Megan leans back in her chair and laces her fingers. 'Have you considered,' she says, 'that we picked the wrong husband?'

'Yeah, it's crossed my mind. Then I thought if I go and suggest that to Slater now…'

'And you're probably right. Even so.'

'You really think it could be him?'

'Let's try it out as a hypothesis. He ruined her acting career out of spite. Gives Georgia motive. The question is, why now?'

Brittney smiles. 'She's probably been brooding on it for years. After being dropped from the show, she didn't really work again as an actress. She'd been quite a big deal, then all she could get were bit parts and cameos. She even did a couple of pantos. But then things picked up for her when she started writing kids' books.'

'So her motive is revenge. What about opportunity? CSI found this fancy Japanese chef's knife in the tank. She's into Japanesey stuff. Post mortem found he was stabbed multiple times with an implement of a similar size.'

Brittney shrugs but she's warming up. 'He comes to visit, they have a row, she loses it, stabs him. Perhaps it's like her samurai sword.'

Megan shakes her head. 'Maybe. But then how easy would it be to get the body into the tank? Whoever he was, PM says he was one hundred and eighty-three centimetres, about six foot. That's a big bloke.'

'Shirin helped her?'

'Then, only weeks later, they call the contractors in to fix the tank? That's the bit that's never made sense. If they'd killed him and dumped the body there, why would they do that? It's the last thing they'd do, surely?'

'Okay,' says Brittney. 'They're telling the truth and it's a random body someone else dumped there.'

'It's always a temptation,' says Megan, 'to want suspects you don't particularly like to be guilty. That's what my old boss in the Met said. We once spent months building this murder case against a drug dealer we thought killed a gang rival. Turned out the victim's very sweet and innocent girlfriend did it because he'd cheated on her.'

'So we're back to square one.'

'Not necessarily. It's a theory that half works.'

'Stick with the body then.'

'Yeah,' says Megan. 'But we may have been unfair to Georgia. So I think we should go and apologise.'

'Are you kidding? We upset her again, Slater'll go mental.'

'Who said anything about upsetting her? If it is a random body, then we do owe her an apology. Grovelling puts her off her guard. But this is still a murder investigation. And it gives us another chance to ask questions, apply more pressure. Remind her we haven't gone away.'

CHAPTER FORTY-NINE

Thursday, 10.05am

Megan and Brittney walk down the sloping drive to the stark brutalist concrete façade of Elsinore House, dubbed locally 'the car park' because of its resemblance to a multi-storey. And a car is parked on the slope: a sleek black Mercedes with tinted windows. A man has his shirtsleeves rolled up and he's soaping it down with a sponge and bucket of suds. It doesn't even look dirty.

'Wonder what it's like living in a place like this?' says Brittney.

'On your own, like Dame Heidi, possibly a bit lonely.'

Brittney smiles at the chauffeur. He gives them a nervous glance and turns away. 'She's got staff. Being famous must be weird though, people know who you are, feel they know you, but you don't know them.'

Megan rings the doorbell. 'Maybe it's a way of hiding in plain sight,' she says.

The door opens abruptly and the tiny figure of Dame Heidi stares up at them. Megan holds up her warrant card. 'I'm DS Thomas and—'

She doesn't get a chance to finish. Dame Heidi beams and says, 'Well, you can never find a policeman when you want one. But now here you are. Do come in, Officers!'

Brittney and Megan exchange looks and follow the actress into the house.

Georgia is collapsed on one of the large sofas, Shirin standing over her. She shoots a look of surprise at Megan and Brittney.

'The police are here,' says Dame Heidi brightly.

'Oh, thank God!' exclaims Georgia. 'You'll find him, won't you? You'll get him back.'

'Find who?' says Megan.

'Shirin's little boy is missing,' says Dame Heidi.

'He's probably just wandered off,' says Shirin. She's frowning and is definitely put out by the arrival of the police.

'Don't be ridiculous,' says Georgia. 'This is not a house a four-year-old can wander off from. He's been kidnapped.'

'Georgia, you're overreacting,' says Shirin. 'He must be here somewhere.'

Megan watches the interchange with interest. What on earth is going on? The power struggle between Georgia and her supposed assistant is being played out yet again.

'Have you done a complete search of the house and grounds?' Megan says.

'Yes,' says Dame Heidi. 'And my housekeeper is still looking. So's the gardener and the two men that work for him. And the chauffeur.'

But he's washing the car. There's definite ambiguity in Dame Heidi's concern. Shirin may be in denial. The only person who seems genuinely upset is Georgia.

'When was the boy last seen?' says Megan.

All eyes turn to Shirin. 'I put him to bed last night about eight o'clock.'

'Where does he sleep?'

Shirin folds her arms tightly and begins to rock.

'Sometimes with me,' she says. 'But he was tired, so I put him in the other guest room.'

'Can we take a look?' asks Megan.

'There's nothing to see but an empty bed.' As she rocks, Shirin begins to cry. 'Oh my God, Georgia's right, he must've been taken. Aren't you going to do something?'

'Okay,' says Megan. 'If a child is missing we obviously take that very seriously. DC Saric will put out an alert. We'll get some officers down here and start a search.'

Brittney takes her phone out and walks into the hallway to make the calls.

Shirin's lip is trembling. Now she seems as upset as Georgia, who's avoiding her eye. Dame Heidi is watching from the sidelines with a smug grin. Megan can't help feeling that this whole situation is a hair's breadth from cracking wide open. Do they know what's happened to him? Or just suspect? There's a strange vibe and three quite different reactions to the disappearance of the little boy.

'When we came to Winterbrook Farm,' she says, 'I met Noah. He's a lovely little lad. I need to ask, is there a custody issue here, Shirin? Could Noah have been taken by his father?'

'No. He has no father,' replies Shirin emphatically.

'Oh. Only he told us that sometimes his daddy comes and brings him Haribos.'

Shirin hardly blinks. Now she's icy calm. 'It's his fantasy,' she says. 'His biological father has never been in the picture. He's never known him so he makes things up. Pretends he's a soldier or a superhero, as kids do.'

'You've always been on your own with your son then?' says Megan.

The young woman stares straight through Megan. She seems to have made a decision.

'He's not actually my son,' she says.

'Oh. But you're his guardian?'

'For the time being,' says Georgia. 'I'm in the process of adopting him.'

'I'm a little confused,' says Megan. 'Whose child is he, then?'

'He's my nephew,' says Shirin. 'My sister became pregnant when she was only fifteen. My parents threw her out. I didn't get on with them, I'd already left home. I took care of Aisha and the baby when he was born.'

'Where's your sister now?'

Shirin takes a deep breath. Her eyes are hard and blank.

'She committed suicide. When Noah was still a small baby. After that I came down here and brought him with me. Georgia kindly gave me a job.'

Georgia beams. 'When I heard what had happened, obviously I wanted to help.'

CHAPTER FIFTY

Thursday, 11.40am

Megan slips into the back of the incident room. Montieth, Slater and Ted Jennings are variously leaning and lounging in front of a bank of three monitors. A live interrogation is being streamed from the interview suite; each monitor displays a different camera angle and audio comes from a single speaker in the middle. Montieth is making notes. Slater stands next to him, arms folded, watching.

In the interview suite, Paige Tucker and her father sit at the table opposite Vish Prasad and a female DC Megan doesn't recognise.

Paige sits demurely, hair in neat plaits like a little girl, folded hands resting in front of her on the table. 'I always felt uncomfortable around him,' she says. One camera is focused on her in a head and shoulders close-up.

'Did you and Kerry talk about it?' says Vish.

'Kerry liked to wind him up.'

'How did she do that?'

'She'd talk in class, act up, then when he told her off, say cheeky things to him.'

'How did he react?'

'Told her to wait behind after class.'

'Did she talk to you about that?'

Roger Tucker is watching his daughter like a vigilant Rottweiler. But he's got little to worry about.

Paige casts her gaze downwards shyly. It's quite a performance.

'I preferred to stay out of it,' she says. 'I just wanted to concentrate on my work and focus on the grades I need for university.'

Megan tuts. She can't help it. Slater turns and glares at her.

'Sorry, boss,' she says. 'Just need a quick word about O'Brien. Some interesting developments.'

The DCI seems edgy. Running two high-profile cases must be getting to her. 'Okay,' she says. 'Hang on a minute.'

Montieth turns to look at Megan. 'Why don't you believe her?' he asks. Megan meets his gaze. He seems neither friendly nor unfriendly, simply detached and professional. *Blokes can be a lot easier*, thinks Megan. *They have a row then it's over.*

'Kerry's account suggests it was the other way round,' she says. 'Paige liked to wind Jones up.'

'She could've been lying,' says the DI.

Megan sighs. Does she want to get into this? If they've nailed Jones does it even matter?

But she shrugs and says, 'My impression, and obviously it's a subjective judgement, is that Paige dominated Kerry, possibly even bullied her. Paige is smarter, much more canny and probably a consummate liar. You only have to look at the Snapchat footage.'

Montieth strokes his beard. 'You saw that?'

Megan nods.

'I think you're right about her being canny,' he says. 'What would you ask her?'

'I'd ask about Jared Clarke.'

'The barman that Justin Waycott beat up?'

'Yeah, when Kerry was forced to give us a name, she falsely accused him. Question is, why him? I wouldn't mind betting that led to a bust-up between Paige and Kerry.'

The DI nods. 'Okay. We'll give that a try. Thanks.'

The look is still completely neutral. Megan returns it.

'No problem,' she says.

He gets up and goes out. The DCI has watched the exchange; she seems uncomfortable.

'What are these interesting developments?' she says.

'New theory, boss. The little boy that we found at Winterbrook Farm has gone missing. Georgia and Shirin are clearly at odds over it. I think it indicates we have another player here. Possibly the child's father. I'd also like to explore the possibility that our body is Georgia's first husband, Eric Russell.'

Slater frowns. 'If we're going down that route again I want it watertight.'

'Understood. Can I have authorisation to track his phone, financial transactions, social media, do a complete profile?'

'Are we looking for this missing child too?'

'Yep, uniforms are on it.'

The DCI nods. She hesitates then says, 'You seem to be getting on top of this. I'm glad to see that.'

Megan meets her gaze. *Patronising cow.* Now she's feeling bad. Does she think that Megan hasn't guessed it was her spitefulness behind Montieth's outburst? She let him believe that Megan was a sneak and she's feeling awkward and guilty.

In her years undercover Megan may have forgotten about the routine elements of police work but instead she acquired a special skill: how to sniff out an opponent's emotional weakness and exploit it. Slater has thrown down the gauntlet. It's tempting to pick it up.

'Thanks, boss,' Megan says with a smile. 'I'm think I'm getting a handle on things round here.'

CHAPTER FIFTY-ONE

Thursday, 5.30pm

An afternoon spent digging into the financial trails of Eric Russell, theatre director and former TV producer, revealed that his debit card was last used six weeks previously at a cash dispenser in Exeter. On three consecutive days money had been drawn out up to the card's daily cash limit of £1000. This had thrown up an alert on the bank's fraud system. They found his Facebook page but there were no recent posts. No one had reported him missing, so he probably lived alone.

Kitty offered to lend Brittney and Megan a hand, as she was used to liaising with fraud teams. She discovered that Russell's bank had attempted to contact him by email, text and phone. They'd drawn a blank on all fronts. They froze the debit card but they'd had no contact with him and there were no further transactions on any other accounts or credit cards. They also revealed that he was running a large overdraft.

Megan is still mulling all this over. Six weeks is about the right time frame and no one can live on fresh air. Eric Russell has either run off with three grand of his own money, or, more likely, someone else has.

Brittney was excited. The possibility that they were closer to proving their theory turned her day around and Megan was glad for her. It also raised the possibility there might be CCTV footage of someone using the card. And if Russell is dead, that person will, at the very least, be implicated in his death.

An extensive police search involving dogs, a helicopter and the coastguard failed to turn up any sign of Noah. Megan didn't really expect it would. It was an expensive operation but they had no choice. No doubt it will hit the early evening news and Georgia will probably be front and centre stage again. Megan has to step back and let it play out.

She feels better, having spent the day calmly and systematically pursuing the evidence. Proper police work. She's weary but it's an untainted exhaustion, the sort that dirt-under-the-fingernails manual labour can produce. Effort, followed by result, followed by a sense of achievement.

This is what's possible, she tells herself as she collects a trolley at the Co-op in Berrycombe. *This is normal life.*

She lets her brain idle as she pushes the trolley round the supermarket. Debbie's working overtime so Megan's offered to throw together a pasta bake.

'Hello,' he says, causing her to jump out of her skin.

Leon Hall has a trolley piled with bottles of spirits. He grins. 'Manic day. Couldn't get to the cash and carry and we're running out of stock.'

Megan smiles. His sudden appearance creates a deliciously fluttery sensation in her belly. 'Can't have a bar without booze,' she says.

'It's mainly gin and vodka for the cocktails.'

'Oh well,' she says. 'Essential, then.'

They stare at each other. His dark eyes are compelling. The beard is not as neat as before, she notices he has several days' stubble on his cheeks. If anything, it makes him more attractive. She knows she should say something polite and walk away. But she hesitates. A small siren voice in her head whispers: *why the hell not?*

'Listen,' he says. 'This is a bit awkward but I want to ask a favour.'

'Okay,' she says. He's going to chat her up. A tingle of excitement runs up her spine.

'Jared got out of hospital today.'

'How is he?'

'Still pretty banged up. And, y'know, we've been hearing things. About the girl. The one that accused him.'

'Kerry Waycott.'

'That's the one. News said she's dead. Murdered.' He shakes his head. 'Terrible.'

'I'm not involved in that investigation.'

'Jared's upset. Worries he might be in the frame again.'

'He needn't.' She smiles. 'Being incapacitated in hospital is a fairly convincing alibi.'

Leon nods, the grin widens. 'Yeah, I know but, well, just to reassure him. You got any idea who you're looking for?'

The sensation that passes through Megan is akin to being hit by a freight train. For about five seconds she stops breathing. He's staring right at her. The smile is benign and friendly. But those eyes. Why didn't she see it before? The cold, pitiless void behind them. Or maybe she did. She recalls the visceral shiver she felt when she first met him. The whispering recognition. How could she be so stupid? She's been here before. She knows that look only too well. And she knows what it means.

He seems to be waiting for an answer. His gaze is going straight through her like a laser. Part of her wants to run. Part of her doesn't. What she mustn't do is show panic. Instead she coughs, pretends to choke and puts her hand up to her mouth.

'Sorry,' she says hoarsely, 'got a bit of a sore throat, think maybe I'm getting a cold.' As diversionary tactics go, it's pathetic. He must see straight through it.

Tilting his head, his eyes narrow, and he says, 'Hot whiskey, that's what you need. Take care.'

With that, he turns on his heel and walks away.

She's left swaying. She grasps the trolley. She feels as if her legs have been kicked from under her.

CHAPTER FIFTY-TWO

Megan has about three dishes she can cook from scratch. Pasta bake is one of them. Left to her own devices she's a convenience shopper – ready-meals straight into the oven, salad in a bag. She's made a tomato-based sauce with peppers and aubergine, but as she stirs the pot she realises that in her anxiety to get out of the supermarket and away from Leon Hall, she forgot the mozzarella.

Debbie comes through the door to find her at the table with her head in her hands, crying.

Debbie scans her anxiously. 'You all right? What's up?'

Megan raises her tear-stained face. 'I forgot the bloody mozzarella!'

'Okay,' says Debbie. 'There's probably some cheddar in the fridge. That'll do.'

'It won't do! It won't. Nothing will do!'

Putting a hand on her sister's shoulder, Debbie says, 'Hey, Meg, it's all right. Calm down. We can sort this out.'

'No,' says Megan. 'Not this time. It's a mess.'

'I'm guessing we're not talking about food. What the hell happened?'

'I should've known. I should've seen it straight away. But I fancied him. Jesus Christ, Deb! Even fantasised about having sex with him. What the hell is wrong with me? Why am I attracted to men like that?' She knows why. This is ground zero for her.

Debbie sits down next to her. 'Who are we talking about here?'

Megan doesn't answer, she's mired in her own misery. The encounter with Leon has been spinning round inside her, throwing everything off balance. And the vortex created is sucking her downwards, back to a place she thought she'd escaped. *Rinse and repeat.*

'I don't understand why I'm like this. Why do I always pick bad men?'

'You don't.'

'Don't I? When I met Paul at Hendon, it seemed simple. We just fell for each other. I felt I could trust him. He was fun, always joking around. When we got married I was so happy.'

'I know,' says Debbie. 'I was there.'

'Why did it all go wrong? Because we couldn't have children? I wanted kids as much as him. I don't know why we gave up on the IVF.'

'You were pretty young when you got together. Sometimes that works. But sometimes people change, grow apart.'

'He didn't change. He was always a selfish shit, I just didn't see it. And then when I did, I didn't want to admit it. He wanted a woman who could give him kids. I no longer fitted the bill.'

'Oh, Meg!'

'So I threw in the towel.'

'Maybe that was for the best,' says Debbie.

Megan looks at her sister, a genuinely good person. A mother, a wife. Her life has been tough, but she's stuck at it. Made things work. Why isn't Megan like that? It makes her despair.

'Was it?' she says. 'What's wrong with me, Deb?'

'Nothing, sweetheart.' They both know that's not true.

'When they asked me to go undercover I agreed because I thought it'd be exciting. And I ended up playing the girlfriend of a gangster. But as time went on, it wasn't playing. That's the sick part. In the end I really fell for him. The man was a psychopathic killer and I slept with him. And I liked it.'

Saying it doesn't make her feel any better. She'd hoped it might.

If her sister's shocked, and who wouldn't be, she doesn't show it. Debbie grasps her hand. She has tears in her own eyes. 'Oh Meg, they should never have put you in that position.'

'No one had a plan. The job was to get close to him. It just happened. The more involved I got with him, the more he trusted me. I thought I was winning. Breaking the law, but for all the right reasons. It's sick.'

Debbie wipes her eyes on her sleeve. 'Why have you never told me any of this before?'

'Sometimes I wish he had killed me. I betrayed him. I certainly betrayed Paul.'

'No! Don't say that. Your bosses, they're the ones at fault here. They betrayed you. How could they put one of their own in such a situation?'

'Necessity and a need for results. They were never going to convict a man like that by conventional means. It was easy for them to turn a blind eye. And I did volunteer. Once I got in too deep, I lied to my handler. It became a very secret, very toxic game.' *Be honest, you enjoyed it.*

Debbie envelops her sister in a hug. 'Oh my poor baby, it's just horrible, all of it.' She strokes Megan's head.

'I hate what it's made me.' *That, at least, is true.*

'Yeah, but that's not who you really are underneath. And that's what this shrink is for, surely. To help you get over all that stuff and get back to the real you. You were just playing a part.'

Megan pulls away, rakes her fingers through her hair. 'I'm not sure I could even tell Moretti what I've just told you.'

'Well, maybe telling me is a start.'

'What makes it worse is that today I realised I'm still like that.'

'How do you know?'

Megan gets up and walks across to the window. Outside it's already dark and the lights twinkle across the harbour. It gives the impression of being such a safe place.

The tears have drained her; what's left is a hollow desolation. 'There's this man,' she says, 'he runs a bar down on the quay. Mayhem, it's called.' *Mayhem!*

'Used to be the Prince of Wales pub?'

Megan nods. 'We were investigating, went in there, I met him. And straight away I was hooked. He's good-looking enough. But it was more than that. One of those zingy feelings you can't explain. I should've known then, but I didn't.'

'We all fancy people. It's normal.'

'Not like this.'

Debbie takes her jacket off and folds her scarf. Megan gets a whiff of her sister's weariness.

'Earlier I bumped into him in the Co-op. Well, he may have deliberately followed me in. And he asked me something about a case. And as soon as he did, I saw the look he had.'

'What sort of look?'

'It's hard to explain. But once you've seen it, you know. Psychopaths have a way of staring.'

Debbie is frowning. A stressful day, now this. Megan can see she's reached her saturation point.

'C'mon,' she says. 'Staring people out is a trick. You look at someone and focus right into the backs of their eyes, you can make yourself seem scary. I've seen the blokes do it to each other at parties. They have a competition.'

'It's not like that,' says Megan. 'It's something you feel as well as see. It's eerie.'

'What are you saying? You think this guy's a psychopath?' There's a tinge of impatience in her sister's voice.

'I don't know what I'm saying. He reminds me of Zac. Same feeling.'

'The gangster? Does he look like him?'

'No, not really.'

'Meg, I think you've just freaked yourself out.'

Megan observes her sister. She's fidgety, glancing at the clock. She's wondering where the kids are. When Mark will be home. Debbie has two jobs, in summer three. Today she's been driving a delivery van for a local courier firm. It's hard work on a tight schedule. Now she's come home to this. Megan feels a rush of guilt.

'You're right,' she says. 'I'm sorry.'

'For what?'

'For dumping on you yet again. You don't need my crap.'

Debbie goes to the pot of sauce on the hob and gives it a stir. 'What you've told me, I think you should talk to Dr Moretti about it,' she says. 'I know it's not going to be comfortable. But she's properly trained. She'll know how to help you deal with it.'

Megan paints on a smile. 'Yeah. You're right.'

Debbie pauses to look at her. How can she understand? She can't. Megan wonders if anyone can. This was a mistake.

'Hey,' she says, 'give me that spoon. Don't mess with my pasta bake.'

'You're upset. I can finish it for you.'

Megan steps forward and takes the spoon from her sister. 'No. I'm fine. I can do it. Just find me some cheese from the fridge.'

CHAPTER FIFTY-THREE

Friday, 9.35am

Drinking most of a bottle of red wine was not the best strategy for Megan to adopt, but it wiped the spectre of Leon from her thoughts for a while. The resulting hangover provided her with a pain specific enough to distract, plus a reason to feel sorry for herself. But she can't stop brooding. She's an excellent liar. She's had loads of practice. Last night she fumbled it. Why? She gave herself away. The question is, did he notice? She suspects he did.

She arrives at work late, zoned out on painkillers and with no idea what to do next. The feeling she was on top of things and doing the job well had lasted for about a day. The office is already busy, most of the shift are at their desks.

Brittney greets her with exuberance. 'Guess what?' she says.

'You've cheered up,' says Megan.

'Me and Kitty were here until seven and we got Eric Russell's dental records.'

'How?'

'Long story. Kitty is officially a genius.'

Kitty swivels round in her chair, she and Brittney slap hands like teenagers. Little and large. The dynamic duo. Megan watches them with envy. Brittney is resilient, she bounces back.

'I sent them to the pathologist first thing,' says Brittney. 'They've arranged for a forensic odontologist to come in later this morning and we should have his report by lunchtime.'

The DC is beaming expectantly.

'That's brilliant,' says Megan. 'So we'll know if our corpse is Eric Russell. Well done, both of you.' On the outside she sounds upbeat and normal, inside she feels like shit. But she's doing what she knows. Having a convincing façade was the basic survival skill of her undercover life.

Kitty wags an accusing finger. 'You owe me, dude. On Monday you promised me chocolate brownies. "The perfect chocolate brownie," I think you said.'

This sideswipe isn't intentional. But being reminded of her visit the previous weekend to Leon's bar turns a knife in Megan's gut. He was reeling her in and she fell for it. The self-reproach kicks in again; it feels as if it may never stop.

'Sorry,' says Megan. 'They sold out. I'll get you some doughnuts.'

'Are you going to tell Slater about Russell?' says Brittney.

Megan glances across the room at the DCI's office. Inside, Laura Slater is facing DI Montieth. Slater shakes her head in annoyance and turns away. Even at a distance the tension between the two is discernible. It hooks the attention of Megan's ragged brain.

Turning back to Brittney, she says, 'What's going on? Do you know?'

The DC shrugs.

Kitty chips in. 'Results of the DNA on the Waycott case came in.'

'And?' says Megan. Her synapses are snapping. Something has happened and it's not good. It's there in Slater's body language.

'They were fast-tracked. DNA results arrived from the lab last night. But there's some problem,' says Kitty. 'I don't know what.' Like most offices, rumours are always slithering around.

Slotting her jacket over the back of her chair, Megan walks across the room. The DCI's office is in the corner next to the double doors that lead out into the corridor.

Pretending she's heading for the corridor gives Megan a moment to eavesdrop.

'…it doesn't make any bloody sense,' says Slater. She sounds peeved.

The corridor doors fly open and Detective Superintendent Barker comes sailing through.

'Morning, sir,' says Megan.

'All right, Megan,' says Barker with a nod. His face is set, it's clear he's not going to stop. He disappears into Slater's office and the door slams behind him.

Megan's panic is rising. It's all going wrong. She wants to follow, burst in behind him. This is about Kerry and she needs to know. What the hell is happening?

She strides down the corridor to the toilets, does a U-turn and comes back. Her head spins. The washed-up body caught on the rocks; cold dead flesh, holes instead of eyes. She owes a debt and it must be paid.

Returning to the main office, she sees Vish at the coffee station. She makes straight for him.

Without preamble she says, 'So the DNA results on Waycott are in?'

He gives her a conspiratorial grin. 'It's a complete shitshow.'

'Yeah? How?'

'Monty sent the vaginal samples from the original rape kit plus the post mortem swabs for analysis. Results were checked against the database this morning.'

'Don't say you got two different hits?'

'Oh no,' says Vish. 'One hit. Same perpetrator. But it's not Steven Jones. He's in the clear. Well, theoretically.'

'Why theoretically? If it's not his DNA—'

'There's a problem with the hit we did get. According to the National DNA Database, Kerry Waycott was raped and then murdered by a person who's deceased. PNC says he died four years ago.'

'That's bizarre.'

'It could be a glitch in the system. The samples were mishandled in some way? The Detective Super's taking it up with the Home Office. Meanwhile they don't want to release Jones. CPS says we have to.'

'If his lawyer gets wind of it they'll have no choice,' says Megan.

'Monty thinks the match is legitimate but it's the records that are wrong. You ever hear of that?'

'Yeah,' says Megan. 'I've heard of cases in the Met. A busy shift, a fairly minor offence. The person gives a false name when their DNA is taken. No one checks.'

'If Jones is off the hook,' says Vish, 'we're going to be looking for a needle in a haystack. Because we've got no other leads. You want a coffee?'

Megan's thoughts are in overdrive. 'No,' she says. 'I'll catch you later.'

CHAPTER FIFTY-FOUR

Friday, 10.20am

It's morning break when Megan parks outside the school. The hubbub from kids in the playground rises over the hedge and is strangely soothing. Her racing thoughts have settled. She can't ignore what she knows. The choice is made. In fact there is no choice, not one she can live with. It'll probably cost her the job but she accepts that. She's calm and composed. The anger and doubt Moretti talked about hasn't gone away. But she's channelling it and she's doing it for Kerry.

Sitting in her car, she texts her niece Amber:

Is paige in school?

The reply pings back:

Yeah

Tell her you just saw me coming in to talk to her

Ok

Megan only has to wait five minutes. Paige Tucker comes striding out of the main gate, head down, school bag over her shoulder. She doesn't notice the car until Megan gets out.

'Get in the car, Paige,' says Megan.

'Get lost!' says Paige. 'You can't make me.'

Megan smiles. 'I've arrested loads of people for obstruction. Want to see how it's done?'

Paige glares but the bluff works. 'What do you want?'

'Just a chat without you lying for Mummy and Daddy's benefit.' Megan opens the passenger door. 'Now get in.'

The teenager obeys, clutching her bag on her lap. Megan gets in the driver's seat.

'This is kidnapping,' says Paige.

'Except we're not actually going anywhere.' Taking out her phone, Megan clicks it to record and places it on the dashboard. 'I'm just going to ask you some questions. This is DS Megan Thomas with Paige Tucker.'

'You can't interview me without an appropriate adult present.'

'Very true. So let's call this an informal chat.'

'My dad's gonna go ballistic.'

'We'll cross that bridge when we come to it.'

'I thought this was all over. You've arrested Mr Jones. I always knew he was a slimeball. Doesn't surprise me he attacked Kerry.'

'Why doesn't it surprise you?'

Paige gives her a sullen stare. She's weighing her options. For a fourteen-year-old she has huge confidence. Up against her Kerry was a waif, she never stood a chance.

'Look,' says Paige with her trademark pout, the one she uses on Snapchat, 'I've done nothing wrong. None of this is my fault.'

'Is that what Daddy's been telling you? Your treatment of Kerry has in no way contributed to this whole situation? You were supposed to be her friend, but when she was at her most desperate you dumped her flat. Directly afterwards, she threatened suicide. You're old enough to know what moral responsibility is.'

'I didn't know she'd do that! You can't lay that on me.' The eyes are fierce but her chin quivers.

'Someone has power over you and they make you feel bad, it hurts, doesn't it?'

The girl nods. Megan wonders if she's finally getting under the carapace. She presses the point. 'Maybe that's how Kerry felt. Picked on.'

'I never meant…' Paige wipes the back of her hand across her nose. 'You don't know what a total pain she could be. Always whining.'

'Okay,' says Megan. 'Do you want to do something now that will help make sure her killer faces justice?'

'Yes. Course I do.'

'Then answer my questions truthfully.'

Paige swallows and nods. Her hair is in plaits today, she's definitely playing the innocent schoolgirl.

'You and Kerry went underage drinking in town, didn't you?

'Yeah.'

'Did you talk about this when you were formally interviewed?'

'How could I? I didn't want my mum and dad to know. They're strict about all that.'

'Where did the two of you go?'

'Mayhem. Down on the quay. If you're a girl it's easy to get in without being carded.'

'How did that work?'

'Once they knew you, if you dressed up, looked good, like you could be eighteen, you could get on the guest list.'

'And both you and Kerry were on the list?'

'Yes.'

'The list meant you were admitted without question?'

'Yeah.'

'How often did you go?'

'Most Fridays and Saturdays. Sometimes in the week if we could get out.'

'And you drank alcohol?'

Paige gives a knowing chuckle. 'C'mon, how old were you when you started drinking? Eighteen? I don't think so.'

'Actually, I've never been a beer drinker and I hated wine until I was about twenty-five.'

'Wine tastes like shit. Vinegar. That's why cocktails were invented.'

'Who told you that?'

'Leon. He liked us so we often got drinks on the house. He'd try out his new cocktails on us. See if they were girl-friendly. That's what he said.'

'Tell me about Leon.'

'He owns the place. Really cool.'

'Did he ever come on to you in any way?'

Paige laughs. She's flipped from surly teen to confiding woman of the world.

'God, no. He must be practically thirty. He's just a cool, friendly guy. He wanted more pretty girls like us in the bar so blokes would come. Good business. That's what Jared said.'

'Jared's the barman?'

'That's why I got so pissed with Kerry. She told you lot that Jared had raped her, which was ridiculous. So unfair. And I thought she was being a bitch because Jared fancied me not her.'

'Are you going out with Jared?'

'We're mates. I think he would've asked me out eventually. We were getting there. Guys sometimes need a bit of handling, if you know what I mean. I'm sure you do.'

Megan watches her. The transformation is remarkable. And frightening.

'Maybe he was worried because of your age?'

'Maybe.'

'What happened the night Kerry was raped?'

Paige turns towards Megan and makes direct eye contact.

'I honestly don't know,' she says. 'We were sitting up at the bar, chatting to Jared and Harry, the other barman. Place was a bit empty. Leon was experimenting with a new sort of cocktail. Had tequila in it, which I think is gross. But he was mixing it with juices and asking us to try it. In the end it was so sweet you couldn't really taste the tequila.'

Is this really what happened that night? Kerry had refused to say. Megan feels she's finally putting together the pieces of the puzzle.

'How many drinks do you think you had?'

'I don't know because it was a sip of this one, then that one. I did end up feeling quite pissed.'

'Cocktails can be lethal. What happened then?'

Paige tilts her head to one side as if casting her mind back. But Megan has an uncanny feeling that she's being played. Suddenly it's all too easy. Paige is talking to her as if recounting an escapade to a mate. Is she imagining talking to a camera, staring into the back of the lens, addressing all her fans out there in the electronic ether?

'I felt sick,' says Paige, 'so I went to the loo. I wasn't sick. Just giddy. So I sat in there for a while. Came back into the bar and Kerry had gone home.'

'How do you know she'd gone home?'

'Jared said. He said I should go home too. He called me a taxi.'

'You had money for a taxi.'

'Used my card.'

'This was a Monday night, a school night. What did you say to your parents?'

'They thought I was at Kerry's making videos. I let myself in. They were watching telly. I just called hi and went straight up to my room.'

'When you came out of the loo and Jared said that Kerry had gone home, who else was there?'

'Just the guys.'

'The guys? Harry, was he still around?'

'Yeah, I think so.'

'What about Leon? Was he still making cocktails?'

'I think he was doing the till. Cashing up, whatever you call it.'

'They were closing up?'

'Yeah. The taxi came and I left.'

'When Kerry told you she'd been raped that night, what did you think?'

'I wasn't sure.'

'So you didn't think that she'd gone off with someone instead of going home?'

Paige sighs. 'I tried to be her friend. I really did. But Kerry was mental. She was always doing stuff. She lied about stuff. She lied about Jared – that was typical. She could stay out all night and her mum wouldn't even notice. She was a mess. She could've met someone on the way home. It could've been Jones, I honestly don't know.'

'And that's all you know?'

Paige smiles and shrugs. 'Yeah, I've told you everything. I promise. Now can I go back to school? It's double maths, my favourite.'

CHAPTER FIFTY-FIVE

Friday, 12.14pm

Megan is hammering up the M5 to Bristol when her phone rings. She answers it on hands-free. Brittney is excited.

'It's him! Eric Russell,' she says. 'Dental records confirm. He still had most of his teeth. So it's a definite.'

'Okay, that's great. Well done.' Megan doesn't mean to sound distracted but she does. Checking Paige's story is her priority. Russell's not going anywhere, nor is his killer.

'So where are you?' says Brittney.

'In the car. I've got an appointment. A medical thing.' Lying on the hoof is a talent. 'Tests. Nothing to worry about. Although obviously I'm feeling a bit stressed.' Megan knows only too well how to be casually convincing.

'Oh, I'm sorry to hear that. Can I do anything to help?' Brittney's warm concern needles Megan's conscience.

'It's fine, I didn't want people to know. I'll be back this afternoon,' she says. *Lies, lies, lies.* It can't be helped.

Brittney sighs. 'Look, it's a bit chaotic round here. Senior officers in and out. I can sit on this until you get back. No one will notice.'

Megan hesitates, going off-piste herself is one thing, but making Brittney complicit?

'Well, I don't know. Maybe—'

'Megan, it's fine. I don't expect I could get to speak to Slater straight away even if I tried.'

'I don't want to put you—'

'No. Not a problem. Don't worry. Focus on yourself. And good luck with the tests.'

'Thanks.'

Megan hangs up. She glances in the rear-view mirror. She'd like to feel bad but she doesn't. Being a consummate liar is a useful skill but not one she can write on her CV when looking for a new job, which she soon will be. But, she tells herself, this is about the bigger picture, the greater good. In her heart she knows that's hogwash. It's about ego and her pathetic need to slay her demons by being the one to crack the Waycott case. Her hunch about Leon Hall is just that, a gut feeling, which could be completely wrong. What she needs is evidence.

Jared Clarke's home address is simple enough to find from the details Vish took at the hospital and put in the case notes. The Clarkes live in an elegant, three-storey Georgian terrace in the Clifton area of Bristol. The street is soggy with drifts of autumn leaves from the magnificent lime trees. They fill the gutters between parked cars, which are mostly high-end hybrids and large four-by-fours.

Megan has to run the gauntlet of Jared's polite but protective mother. He's lying on a sunlounger in the conservatory at the back of the house with a snoozing ginger tomcat curled up beside him. One arm is in plaster with a sling and his face is swollen with bruises in shades of mauve and yellow. 'Banged up' is a fairly accurate description.

Mrs Clarke hovers, offering tea. Megan gets rid of her by accepting and identifying herself as the concerned officer who rescued her son from Justin Waycott.

'It's appalling the kind of casual violence that's out there nowadays,' says Mrs Clarke. 'I don't know what's the matter with people. I think the police have a horrible job.'

Once she's gone, Megan sits in a basket chair opposite Jared. 'You haven't told your parents about Justin Waycott's supposed motive for the attack then?'

Jared sighs. 'They worry. They're shocked enough as it is. I didn't want to make it worse.' With his uninjured hand he rubs the cat's head. 'It's horrendous what happened to Kerry.'

Clicking her phone to record, Megan says, 'Yes, it is. So are you happy to answer some questions?'

He looks at the phone and nods but it's clear he isn't.

'How well did you know Kerry Waycott?'

'She was a girl who came into the bar. I didn't know her second name.'

'A fourteen-year-old girl. Did you know that?'

He dips his head. 'Well, yeah. It was obvious. But I don't make the rules.'

'Who makes the rules?'

'Guy I worked for, Leon. He owns the place.'

'Leon Hall? What's he like? A good boss?'

'He's okay.'

'Even though he has a policy of allowing underage girls to drink.'

'To be fair to Leon, it's pretty standard practice. I've worked in other seaside bars. It's usually a young crowd, that's what you're looking for, and some of the girls are likely to be underage.'

'You know Paige as well?'

'Yeah. She and Kerry were mates. Always came in together.'

'Paige thinks you had plans to ask her out. Is that true?'

Jared huffs. 'No. I'm not that daft. Okay, you flirt a bit with all the customers. That's the job. But I'm really not into kids. And to be brutally honest, there are plenty of older girls that come in.'

Megan scans him. In spite of his bruises he's a fit, blond surfer who could have his pick of women.

'How old are you, Jared?'

'Nineteen. This was supposed to be my gap year. Work a bit, surf a bit, have fun.' He gives her a sour look.

'Why do you think Kerry accused you?'

'I've no idea.' He sounds tetchy. 'Am I still a suspect?' There's an edge to his annoyance that strikes Megan. And suddenly a thought jumps into her head.

'Do you think you were being used as a scapegoat?'

Jared is still, he stops petting the cat. She's struck a nerve.

'How d'you mean?'

'You know what a scapegoat is?'

'Well, yeah, but why would I be?' He fidgets with the sling, readjusts it. Unlike her, he's not a good liar.

'Tell me exactly what happened on that Monday night in the bar.'

'There's not much to tell. Me and Harry were clearing up. I was emptying food out of the chill cabinet, taking it to the fridge in the kitchen. Came back in, both girls were gone.'

'Were they drunk?'

'Tiny bit, maybe. Kerry more than Paige. Paige doesn't really drink. She's quite an ambitious kid, focused on what she wants. Likes to stay in control.'

'So you didn't call her a taxi because she was drunk?'

'No.' He seems surprised.

Megan hesitates, who should she believe? Paige or Jared? Why would Paige bother with an elaborate lie? To add to her plausibility, perhaps?

'Where was Leon?'

'Upstairs in the office, I think. Took us a while to finish clearing up. He came and locked up, gave me and Harry a ride home.'

'Anyone in particular chatting the girls up that night?'

'No. It was Monday. Pretty quiet.'

'They sat at the bar and talked to you?'

'No.' The tension in him is rising. Megan can feel it. He seems an ordinary, straightforward young man. But he's struggling. Fear versus the truth, that's usually the dilemma.

'So, what were they doing?' she says.

He shifts his arm, winces. He doesn't want to answer.

Finally he says, 'They were sitting at a table with Leon working on their playlist.'

'Their playlist?'

'Leon was going to let them do a DJ set. Try them out in a guest slot on Friday night. The idea was to video it and stream it on YouTube. They were really excited. Thought they were going to be social media stars.'

Megan frowns. 'Was Leon in the habit of doing this? Promoting local talent?'

'I'm a sports guy. I like music but it's not my thing. I wasn't involved.'

'Is it Leon's thing?'

Jared shrugs. 'You run a bar, you gotta have music. I don't know. Maybe he knows what he's doing. He could turn a couple of schoolgirls into DJs.'

'That's what he was planning to do?'

Jared hesitates. 'It's what he told the girls. Got them all excited about it.' *Is this what Paige wanted to conceal?*

'As in, hooked them?'

'I just worked there.'

'You said you're really not into kids. But what about Leon?'

Jared stares down at his plastered arm. 'Look, I don't know about any of that.'

'Any of what?'

'You work for a dude like that, you don't ask questions.'

'Because you're scared of him?'

Jared says nothing. He sighs.

'While you and Harry were clearing up,' says Megan, 'could he have left the bar with Kerry then come back later to lock up?'

'I don't know. Maybe.'

'How long did you spend clearing up before he came to lock up?'

'Half an hour, bit more, I'm not sure.'

'Do you think Leon could've raped Kerry that night?'

Jared fingers his bruised cheek. 'I don't know. I can't tell you anything else. I'm sorry.'

The young man is cradling his broken arm; he looks burdened and desolate.

'What are you going to do now?' says Megan. 'Once you've recovered, are you coming back to Berrycombe?'

'No.'

'That sounds pretty definite.'

Jared looks down at the cat, who looks back at him. Then he turns to Megan. She senses a shift.

'You asked if I thought I'd been made a scapegoat,' he says. 'I think it was probably more a diversion.'

'How do you mean?'

'I didn't know Kerry and Justin were related. But I knew Justin Waycott. He worked on the door sometimes on a Saturday night when we were busy.'

'Leon employed him as a bouncer?' Megan tries to keep the surprise out of her voice.

'Yeah. He did all sorts of stuff for Leon. They were tight. Good mates. Okay, Justin's a hothead but he'd never've come steaming in there and beat me up unless he'd been given the nod by Leon.'

'Leon set you up by letting Justin think you'd raped his niece?'

'No way I can prove it but, yeah, that's the only way it makes sense.'

It makes sense to Megan too. When she and Vish arrested Justin, Leon had pretended not to know him. Maybe Kerry was told to point the finger at Jared? Leon was worried Justin would find out he'd raped Kerry. And after the savage beating Justin gave Jared, Megan can see why.

CHAPTER FIFTY-SIX

It feels to Laura Slater as if her morning has been one long damage limitation exercise. The same could be said of the last week. Since Sir Henry Crewe suckered her into believing Georgia O'Brien would confess to murder, she's been like a bear with a sore head – at least that was her husband Alex's opinion.

In the office she's worked hard to maintain her composure and a professional attitude. Underneath, she's been seething. But the real source of her upset is that she fell for it. He outsmarted her and that hurts. He read her as an over-ambitious but silly female, hungry for a high-profile result. He dangled a dainty morsel and relied on the fact that she'd be so tempted she wouldn't stop and think for long enough to see the trap.

Rob Barker's comforting words did little to appease her.

'Laura, he's a grade A arsehole. He's known for it. And he's been doing it for years. His rich clients pay him a lot of money to get them off the hook and he uses every trick in the book. Don't take it personally.'

Laura does take it personally. What is it that Crewe exudes that she hates so much? He possesses the supreme confidence of male-ness, the privilege of being the definer, not the defined. He's the gentleman who grasps your elbow and guides you safely through the door. And she's been fighting the spectre of men like that her whole life, coercion under cover of concern. Her grandfather prided himself on being a gentleman. He was a GP but persuaded her mother to become a nurse not a doctor, because it was a more suitable career for a girl.

Now there are policies and procedures everywhere to stamp out sexism but do they even scratch the surface? Laura hates always feeling at a disadvantage. But it's the worm inside her own head. No one else is doing it to her and that makes it worse. She goes on senior management courses, where the men stand around, hands in pockets, glasses in hands, throwing back their heads and laughing at shared anecdotes. Watching, she feels diminished. An outsider. Colleagues regard her as capable but starchy. Laura Slater can't take a joke, she's not one of the boys.

In the safety of her own home and the privacy of her own bedroom she sobbed and Alex comforted her. Then she put on her suit, pinned up her hair, kissed her children and stepped back out into the fray.

Checking her watch, she sees that it's time for her meeting with the Waycotts. Technically she's still the SIO, although Montieth has been acting up, and she feels she should explain to them personally why Steven Jones is being released.

Family liaison have arranged the meeting. But when Laura walks into the room, only the grandmother and uncle have turned up. Richard Montieth accompanies her. Justin Waycott gives the DI a hostile look, assuming he's the power in the room.

Settling at the table and folding her hands, Laura calmly explains the intricacies of DNA testing. She addresses Sheila Waycott, who, she's been warned, can be difficult.

But Sheila's gaze is vacant. Whatever fight was in the old lady is gone.

'So you're letting the bastard go?' says Justin.

'The DNA tests exonerate him, Mr Waycott. He didn't do it,' says Laura.

'First it's the boy in the bar, then, nah, not him. Then it's the bloody teacher. Do you lot even know what you're doing?'

'We will find the culprit, I assure you.'

'Assure my arse! It's a bloody joke,' says Justin.

'Justin,' says his mother. 'There's no call to be offensive.'

'I'm sorry that you feel we've let you down,' says Laura.

'Heather thinks your sergeant did her best for Kerry after she was raped,' says Sheila. 'She wasn't an easy kid to deal with. I don't think we knew the half of what she got up to.'

'Megan's a good officer.'

'Yeah,' says Justin, glaring at Montieth, 'she knows how to talk to people without looking down her nose at them.'

After the meeting Laura and Montieth walk back to the office side by side.

'I looked up his record,' says the DI. 'A bit too handy with his fists is our Mr Waycott. Mostly bar-room brawls.'

'Are you thinking he might have done this to his own niece?'

'He's a thug but he doesn't strike me that way. But he's on the PNC so we can certainly run his DNA. Have we got any more feedback on the other hit?'

'Barker's been talking to the mortuary, the lab and the Home Office. It'll take time but every stage in the procedure is being double-checked.'

'Meanwhile we're looking for a dead man.'

'So it would seem.' She hesitates then says, 'How you finding Ted as a DS?'

They both know what she's really asking.

Megan Thomas has been a problem for Slater since she arrived. A few years older than Laura, she's tough and street-smart with an obvious disdain for the rules. Although it doesn't appear intentional, she creates ripples in her wake and the younger officers naturally defer to her.

The Superintendent put it to Laura in terms of a favour, a favour he wanted to do for an old mate in the Met. But was there really any choice? Barker had decided she was joining the team. All Laura was told was that Megan was a former undercover officer who'd received the QPM. Maintaining her anonymity meant there was no discussion of the work she'd done. Laura suspects it was an important case.

Megan looks you in the eye but there is always cynicism in her gaze. To Laura she seems like an old fighter, always wary and on her guard for the next punch. Knowing even how to talk to such a woman, let alone manage her, is proving an uphill struggle.

Montieth glances at the DCI and smiles. 'Ted's an experienced officer. Don't worry, boss, we'll get there.'

Passing through the double doors into the office, Laura can't help noticing Megan and Brittney having a discussion. And the DS turns and heads straight for her.

'Got some news to cheer you up, boss,' Megan says. An impatient energy seems to pulse off her. It feels like facing a whirling dervish.

Laura steps back and says, 'Come into my office.'

Once she's got the desk between them, she feels more at ease. 'Right,' she says.

'We've got dental records and confirmed the ID on the body. Eric Russell. Georgia's first husband. So we were on the right track all along.'

'Well done.'

'Brittney and Kitty deserve the credit. We've got an address for him, a village outside Exmouth.'

'Possibly a good idea to search that first before confronting Georgia.'

'I agree. We've also been doing an ANPR search on his car to see if we can place him anywhere near Winterbrook Farm.'

'That's good work.'

Megan is skewering her with that penetrating stare. She seems about to say something more. There's a hesitation but she says, 'Thanks, I'll keep you posted,' turns on her heel and disappears.

Laura relaxes in her chair. So the body in the septic tank is Georgia's ex-husband. She's going to enjoy sticking that to Sir Henry Crewe.

CHAPTER FIFTY-SEVEN

Friday, 3.25pm

Guided by the temperamental satnav, Megan and Brittney drive down a single-track lane towards the estuary of the River Exe. They turn a corner and a sudden break in the high hedgerow shows them a panorama of mudflats and the mercurial thread of the river dazzling and flashing with shafts of late afternoon sun.

'Wow!' says Brittney.

'Do you think we're going the right way?' says Megan with a frown. She still has the city mindset which gets nervous when there's grass in the middle of the road.

Brittney is driving. 'Quite a few places round here. You just don't see them, they're tucked away behind the hedges.'

Megan sighs. This is not what she wants to be doing but there's little choice. She needs to be strategic, do one job properly in order to access the information she needs for the other. It crossed her mind to tell the DCI what she'd found out but Slater looked irritable so she decided to bide her time until she has something solid. Still she's ticking with impatience. Trust Georgia's ex-husband to live in the back of beyond.

The track finally dwindles to almost nothing and there's a gateway.

'This is it,' says Brittney confidently.

They turn in to find a large cottage-style modern house, painted white with a slate roof and gable windows. It faces a grassy slope with a cinematic view of the estuary.

Megan gets out of the Škoda and strolls around. At the other side of the house she finds a carport and, sitting under it, a white Audi TT. There's a smattering of twigs and garden flotsam strewn over the bonnet and dead leaves have bunched round the wheels. Megan runs her index finger through the film of grime covering the windscreen.

Brittney joins her.

'This hasn't moved for quite a while,' Megan says.

The DC consults her phone. 'It's his reg. Last ANPR hit we could find was nearly two months ago in Exeter.'

'Excuse me! Can I help you?' The imperious voice is coming from behind a large laurel hedge. Through a gap a stooped figure appears. He's leaning heavily on a wheeled walking frame.

Megan pulls out her ID and steps forward. 'Good afternoon, sir. Detective Sergeant Thomas. I presume you're Mr Russell's neighbour?'

The old man gives a curt nod. 'Fisher, Ronnie Fisher. Eric's away at the moment.'

'Did he tell you where he was going, Mr Fisher?'

'No. But he tends to go away this time of the year.'

'Do you have a key to the house?'

Fisher chuckles. 'No, no. Eric's quite a private type, if you know what I mean. Used to be married to that actress. I forget her name.'

'I'm sorry to be the bearer of bad news, Mr Fisher,' says Megan, 'but Eric Russell has passed away.'

The old man sighs and shakes his head wearily. 'Oh that is a shame. Poor old Eric. A young man too, can't have been more than fifty.'

'Can you recall the last time you saw him?'

Fisher is still slowly shaking his head. He raises a gnarled knuckle and rubs his cheek. Megan and Brittney exchange glances. He looks ancient and not entirely steady on his feet.

'I'm afraid I don't recall,' he says. 'I do try and be neighbourly, keep an eye on things since he's away so much. Goes to London quite often to direct plays. I hadn't seen him for a day or two so I presumed he was doing something like that. I didn't see him leave but he had some chaps come in to do some work.'

Megan raises her eyebrows. She thought she'd be spending a few hours treading water here. Could this be a lucky break? Surely she's overdue one.

'When was this?' she says.

'Weeks ago now.' He ponders. 'But I can probably tell you exactly, because it was the day my youngest granddaughter came and that'll be on my calendar.'

'Can you tell us more about these men, Mr Fisher?' says Megan.

'Please do call me Ronnie,' he says, 'everyone does.' His eyes are pale and rheumy but they glint with intelligence. 'If you're detectives, I gather something serious is afoot.'

Megan smiles. 'How old are you, Ronnie? If it's not rude to ask.'

'Ninety-six. I flew Liberators in the Far East during the war. Taught me to stay sharp and keep my eyes open. My late wife said it was just an excuse to be a nosey old bugger.'

'We like nosey old buggers,' says Megan. 'So what can you tell me about these workmen?'

'Two big chaps, well over six feet. The one I talked to was very friendly. Had a tight woolly hat on and he was, well, not sure how you're supposed to say it nowadays: he wasn't completely black but he wasn't completely white.'

'He was mixed race?'

'That's the ticket. He said Eric wanted them to shift some furniture.'

'You remember what sort of vehicle they had?'

'Big sort of American-style thing. Cab at the front with a flat bed at the back covered over.'

'A pick-up truck?' says Brittney. She's scrolling rapidly on her phone.

'Yes, that is what they're called. My age, you forget so much.'

'You're doing brilliantly,' says Megan. 'Most people a quarter your age walk round and see nothing.'

Brittney shows him a picture of a silver Mitsubishi pick-up on her phone. 'Similar to that?' she says.

He nods and rubs his chin. 'Come to think of it, it was dark. Maybe black.'

'How long were they here?'

'Not sure I can answer that. I came round because I heard raised voices. They were having a bit of a barney about something. Soon as I appeared the other one got back in the truck. He was upset. The one I talked to was all smiles though, quite charming. Explained what they were doing. I noticed them leaving a bit later. They'd put some rolls of carpet in the back. Persian rug from what I could see.'

'Okay,' says Megan. 'Don't suppose you have such a thing as a crowbar, Ronnie?'

The old man beams. 'You want to break in? Course I have!' He turns his frame on one wheel and heads for his house.

'I think we've made his day,' says Brittney.

While Brittney goes with Ronnie to fetch the crowbar, Megan gets some vinyl gloves from the car and dusters for her feet then she peers through the windows. She shouldn't be doing this. She should call the Crime Scene Manager and wait for them to get a locksmith. But that would take hours and she's feeling impatient.

The interior is in deep shadow and it's difficult to see. She walks round to the back of the house where French doors open straight onto a small patio and the garden. There's more light filtering through and it's possible to see that a coffee table has been moved to one side. To do what? Roll up a Persian rug?

Returning with the crowbar Brittney says, 'According to Ronnie's calendar these guys were here seven weeks ago to the day. Could fit our time frame.'

'Right,' says Megan. 'There's a door at the side that looks like it goes into a laundry room. We'll break in there. But just me. If this is a crime scene we want as little contamination as possible. We'll use our phones to communicate. Ring me.'

The DC nods.

The lock on the laundry room door yields to the crowbar with a sharp crack. Megan steps inside the house. The room is tiny but leads to the kitchen. A heavy, stale odour assails Megan as she moves cautiously forward. Just the stuffy smell of an empty house? Megan flicks the light switch on. The floor is made of modern composite tiles, flecked to seem like granite. But the white grouting between them is streaked with dark lines. Megan squats down; there's a faintly ferrous smell. She pokes a section with the end of a pen. The dark lines extend halfway across the kitchen floor.

She holds her phone in one hand. 'Brittney,' she says, 'call the office. Looks like someone's tried to clean up blood on the kitchen floor. We need CSI down here pronto. I'd say there's a fairly good chance that Eric Russell was murdered in this house.'

CHAPTER FIFTY-EIGHT

It's after dark by the time Megan and Brittney hand the scene over to CSI and Hilary Kumar. They've shared two cups of tea and a packet of Hobnobs with Ronnie Fisher and heard the story of his long life.

'I had tickets for Phoebe Bridgers in Bristol tonight,' says Kumar. 'She rarely comes over from the States. And I know she'll be awesome.'

'I'm really sorry for spoiling your weekend, Hilary,' says Megan.

'You'd better prepare yourself for a bollocking. Slater's hacked off with you.'

'Because I broke in instead of calling you lot? I wanted to be sure and I don't think I compromised the scene.'

'That's cause you're a bloody impatient, headbanging detective,' says Hilary with a smile. 'Slater's also pissed because if Russell was killed here, it rather lets Georgia O'Brien off the hook, doesn't it?'

'Not necessarily.'

The CSI shrugs. 'If someone trucks his body thirty odd miles down the road to dump it in her septic tank, it tends to support the argument that they were out to set her up, doesn't it?'

Megan knows she could be right. But what about Noah? He's still missing. A large number of officers are out searching for him. It seems clear to Megan that someone has taken him. But who and why? Could he have been taken as a warning to Georgia?

*

The main office is quiet and the DCI's office empty by the time Megan gets back. She left Brittney in the car park and told her to go home.

Settling at her desk, she feels too wired to do that herself. Although she's glad to have moved the O'Brien case on, it's not Eric Russell's ghost that's haunting her.

She's considering whether to take the bull by the horns and go on a recce to the bar since Friday night is club night, when Richard Montieth wanders into the room. Sleeves rolled up, waistcoat unbuttoned, he still manages to look spruce. The shine on his shoes remains immaculate.

'Well,' he says, strolling over. 'You've had a result this afternoon. Good breakthrough.'

'Thank you, sir,' she replies. She's deliberately formal. It seems the best way to deal with the bad blood between them.

He smiles and shakes his head. He's doing his 'I'm not a bloke for bullshit' act.

'Listen,' he says. 'Think I went over the top a bit the other day. And I'd like to apologise.'

Megan shrugs. 'Okay,' she says. What he revealed was a short fuse and a nasty temper, which she won't forget in a hurry. But now he's on the back foot she sees her opportunity.

She waits, increasing his discomfort. It works.

'I've been watching events unfold,' he says. 'You're not really that hot on the chain of command, are you? Or procedure.'

'Probably not. But I really wasn't trying to undermine you or piss you off.'

He nods thoughtfully. 'I get that now. But you seem to have a knack of rubbing people up the wrong way.' He means Slater but Megan doubts he's going to say that.

She sighs. 'I am trying to fit in.'

He folds his arms and perches on the corner of the desk. 'How long did you work undercover? Am I allowed to ask that?'

'Four years.'

'Same target?'

'Yeah.'

'That's tough. And tough trying to slot back in.'

'A bit.'

He holds out his hand to shake. 'I think you and I should start over. Clean sheet.'

'Fair enough.'

She grasps his hand and matches the grip. Blokes are such simple creatures, she reflects. They have a punch up, they shake hands and it's over. But that's all to the good.

'In which case,' she says, 'can I ask about the Waycott case?'

'Ask away. I never saw the sense in excluding you.'

'Slater thinks I'm over-emotional and have too much to prove and she's right. It's my failure.'

'I think the Waycotts were a seriously dysfunctional family before you ever came along. The girl lost her dad and her mother became a prescription drug addict, that's when her life started to go pear-shaped.'

'I still fell short.'

'Megan, we all fall short. Okay, so what do you want to know?'

'What's happening about this hit on the database?'

He huffs, rubs his close-cropped head. 'We're still trying to sort it out. Someone's cocked up but doesn't want to admit it. The individual whose DNA came up was a London thug and drug dealer called Trevor Pearse. He had a recall to jail outstanding and fled to Bulgaria three years ago where he upset the locals and died in a gang-related shooting. An inquest took place. The Foreign and Commonwealth Office accepted the findings of the Bulgarian police that he was shot dead by an unknown assailant. His body was cremated over there by his Bulgarian girlfriend.'

'Mind if I check out the mugshot?'

'Of course. Type him in.'

Megan turns to her computer screen and taps in the details. Her nerve endings are zinging as her fingers bounce off the keys. Some sixth sense is telling her what she'll see even before it pops up. The horror is in the anticipation. But when she looks into those familiar eyes they still send a convulsion of shock straight through her.

Montieth glances at her with concern. 'You recognise him, don't you?'

Remember to breathe.

She inhales sharply and says, 'Yes. He's using the name Leon Hall and running a bar in Berrycombe. Kerry Waycott was a regular and knew him. And he's very much alive.'

CHAPTER FIFTY-NINE

APOLOGIES TO OUR PATRONS. CLOSED UNTIL FURTHER NOTICE. The text is neatly printed on a sheet of A4 paper and pinned to the door of Mayhem. The corner flaps up and down in the stiff onshore breeze.

It's cold and dark. The quay is deserted. A refrigerated lorry trundles by en route to the port. The windows of the pub on the corner are lit but even the smokers have abandoned the outside wooden tables. A curious springer spaniel sniffs at the armed police officer crouching in a cafe doorway; his owner is waved briskly on. Half a dozen armed officers are deployed in the deep shadows either side of the door to the bar.

The sergeant in charge of the armed response team pulls the notice off the door, trots across the road and hands it to Montieth. He's sitting in an unmarked car, at a discreet distance, with Megan beside him.

Montieth reads it. 'What d'you make of this? Has he got wind we're coming?'

Megan's heart sinks. Her first thought is Jared. Or did she give herself away in the supermarket? Trying to cover it with a stupid coughing fit. The horror of realisation must've shown on her face. Little more than twenty-four hours after that encounter and he's gone.

The notice could read as a challenge, a middle finger stuck up at the police. If he left in a hurry why bother to stick up a note at all? Is he taunting her?

This is ridiculous, she's indulging her paranoia.

'Does he live on the premises?' says the DI.

'I think he has a flat upstairs,' says Megan.

'Right,' Montieth says to the sergeant. 'We've got a section eight warrant. Go in, search the place.'

A nod and he's running back across the road.

The DI turns to Megan. 'Could someone have tipped him off?'

The possibilities, her own culpability, it's all churning in her head.

'Jared Clarke, the barman,' she says. 'Could be him. Although I'd be surprised.'

They watch the armed response team wield an enforcer and smash open the door to the bar with one blow. The officers pour inside.

A Range Rover Discovery pulls up directly behind them. A man Megan doesn't recognise is driving, but DCI Slater gets out of the passenger seat. She's wearing jeans and a hoodie, hair loose on her shoulders; in civvies she looks a different person.

Getting into the back of their vehicle she says, 'Have we got him?'

'Maybe not,' says Montieth. 'Megan thinks the barman could've alerted him to our interest.'

Megan braces herself for an avalanche of difficult questions. She's already come clean to Montieth and admitted she went to Bristol to see Jared. She's not sure what's been passed on to the DCI. But the boss says, 'Put out a general alert, get his mugshot to Border Force and out nationwide. Plus the name he's using. If he's got a convincing fake passport he could've skipped the country already. But we may get lucky.'

The response team sergeant emerges from the building and signals to Montieth with a negative sweep of his gloved hand.

'Unfortunately not yet,' says the DI.

'Go and lean on this barman, see what you can find out. And well done, Megan. Good call.' There's a looseness and ease about the boss which Megan hasn't encountered before. Megan wonders what the DI has actually said to her. It can't have been anything near the truth.

But Slater gets out of the car before Megan can respond. She returns to the Discovery and is driven off. The idea that Laura Slater has another life with a husband who drives her and where she slobs around in jeans and a hoodie seems perverse.

Montieth chuckles. 'Amazing what a couple of glasses'll do, isn't it?' he says.

'What did you actually tell her?' says Megan.

'Just that you recognised his mugshot.' He shrugs. 'He's a London gangster. She didn't question it. Let's go and have a poke round in his lair, shall we? See what we can find.'

The upper floors of the building are being renovated but there's a makeshift office, and a small kitchen and bedroom which have obviously been in use. The whole place has the anonymous feel of a hotel room, as if its occupant had always assumed he'd have to pick up at a moment's notice and vanish into thin air. The property will need to be forensically examined but Montieth decides that can wait. He leaves it to be secured by local uniforms.

Megan feels a curious lassitude. Having steeled herself for a confrontation she's now drifting and mentally exhausted. Guilt and doubt prickle the fringes of her psyche. It probably doesn't help that all she's eaten since breakfast are two Hobnobs.

Montieth drives them to Bristol and she falls asleep in the car. The image of Leon gnaws at her as she drifts in and out of consciousness. If he is Trevor Pearse and faked his own death once to escape the law, he'll already be gone. On a ferry from Plymouth, a flight from Exeter, he'd've had plenty of choice. But a drug dealer wanted on a recall to prison… why open a bar in Berrycombe? Surely a bolt hole in North Cyprus or Turkey would be a safer bet?

Jared Clarke has also been easing his nerves with alcohol. The effect on him is to make him obstreperous.

'Fuck it,' he says. 'You think I'm gonna get up in a court and testify against him! Few years' time he gets out and comes looking for me.'

'No one has suggested the need for that yet,' says the DI.

'He called me. What was I s'posed to say? I've been beaten up once already.'

'When did he call you?' says Megan.

'I dunno. This morning. Maybe lunchtime. After you'd been I was freaked out. I spoke to Harry. Ten minutes later, Leon phoned up. All I said was you'd been here asking questions. I swear.'

Hours. They missed him by hours.

'You always knew it was him, didn't you, Jared?' says Megan. 'Then Justin attacked you and that confirmed it.'

'I don't know. Don't remember.'

'We will need to take your phone,' says the DI.

Megan gets home at eleven, dog-tired. Standing in the corner near the front door is an enormous bouquet of lilies. The pungent smell of them hits her empty stomach. Pollen from the heavy orange stamens has stained the floor.

Debbie puts her head round the kitchen door. 'You must be knackered,' she says with a sympathetic smile. 'There's some cold pizza in the fridge.'

'These things stink,' says Megan. 'I hate lilies. Funeral flowers.'

'That's a pity,' says her sister, 'because they're for you. Came about six o'clock, special delivery.'

Megan stares down at the flowers. There's a small, white envelope tucked in the top. It has a black border. She picks it up and opens it. The card is tastefully printed with the message *RIP*. Underneath, a personal message has been typed in: *Hey, Megan. Wish I could have got to know you. Stay safe.*

She was right about one thing: the notice nailed to the door of the bar was personal.

Her head starts to spin, whether from panic or lack of food is impossible to tell. She slumps down on her knees. This isn't her paranoia. Leon Hall or Trevor Pearse, or whoever he is, he's out there and he's laughing at her.

CHAPTER SIXTY

Saturday, 10.08am

A uniformed officer stands outside the broken wooden door of Mayhem, which is criss-crossed with police tape. His gloved hands are folded behind his back, he shifts from foot to foot. It's a cold and boring job, Megan knows, she's done it. She watches him from the other side of the harbour as she walks along with the dog.

Scout is perky and glad of a proper morning walk instead of the usual round-the-block sprint that he gets from Mark. Megan is grateful for a companion who won't interrogate her mood or her disturbing thoughts. She's cancelled her appointment with Dr Moretti, scheduled for this morning; she knew, even as she made the phone call and delivered the lie, that wimping out was a mistake. Moretti merely replied politely that she hoped her stomach bug cleared up quickly.

The route around the harbour and along the breakwater is a regular trail for local dog-walkers. Scout encounters several canine friends and they stop to sniff and greet.

The fear and paralysing anxiety filling Megan's head through an endless, sleepless night begins to dissipate. Realising that Leon could be Kerry's killer, followed by the failure to arrest him has left her squirrelly. But exercise helps. At closer inspection, the grey sea is striated with colours from purple to green. The daytime world in all its banal but noisy detail is reassuring. She can tell herself the flowers were a sly gesture designed to unnerve her. But he's a criminal on the run; he knows the score, he's gone.

Vish Prasad was in the office overnight co-ordinating the search for Trevor Pearse. Megan finds it hard to think of him as that; in her mind he remains Leon.

Around four am, unable to settle, she called Vish for an update.

'A sighting at Dover,' said Vish. 'And a drunk driver pulled over on the M4, both possibles that came up negative.'

'Oh well,' she said. 'I'm sure he's long gone.'

'I'm really, really sorry, Megan,' said Vish.

'For what?'

'I saw the mugshot when we got it through from the Met after the DNA hit. I should've recognised him.'

Their visit to the bar was nine days ago but it feels like another age.

'Vish, you'd just been whacked by Justin Waycott.'

'I've still got the bruise.'

'It knocked the wind out of you. I'm surprised you could stand up, let alone remember anything. And you went out to look for the ambulance while I talked to him.'

'Yeah, but if I'd made the connection when I should, as soon as we got the picture, we'd've had him. It's my fault he had time to do a runner. I feel really bad.'

Megan feels the burden of guilt is hers alone; she's not willing to share it.

'What came up on the PNC were the details of a dead man,' she says. 'I've seen them. And in the mugshot the hair was different, he was a lot younger and he didn't have a beard.'

'You still recognised him.'

Megan hesitated. How could she explain that she already knew, that some dark intuition had alerted her? It begged too many questions she couldn't answer, even to herself.

'These things happen,' she said. 'We all miss stuff we shouldn't. It's part of the job. Don't beat yourself up.'

As she walks down the long breakwater wall that protects the sanctuary of the harbour from the choppy sea, she wonders why she can't take her own advice.

We all fall short. Even the DI said it.

But self-blame leads to self-pity and that's a comforting place to wallow. Perhaps that's why it's attractive. A place to rest up, evade action and retire from responsibility. Is that what she's doing now?

The job holds her life together, that's the simple truth. She's a lonely divorcee, no partner, no children, no one to accompany her on the weekly supermarket shop. A temporary lodger in her sister's house. Even the dog beside her is borrowed.

Reaching the end of the breakwater, she and Scout do a brisk turn and head back. In the channel through the outer harbour a sizeable motor yacht cruises past them towards the open sea. A sleek forty-footer, mostly white with a metal trim, it's a millionaire's toy. But standing in the cockpit grasping the helm is Justin Waycott.

Megan does a double-take. She pulls out her phone and videos the passing boat. His eyes are on the harbour exit and he doesn't seem to notice her.

When she gets home, Megan shows the video to her brother-in-law and asks what he makes of it.

Peering at the screen on her phone, Mark says, 'Can't quite read the name. Looks like the *Sea Serpent*. One of Terry Benson's boats.'

'One? He has several?'

'Owns a fish processing business. He has several of everything.'

'Does Justin Waycott work for Benson?'

Mark laughs drily. 'I doubt it. Want me to find out?'

Megan nods. 'Do you mind?'

'I went to school with Terry and we're still mates.' Mark takes out his own phone and goes into the sitting room to make the call.

Debbie is standing by the kitchen sink, munching a piece of toast. 'If you can be mates with someone who's loaded,' she says sardonically.

Megan watches her sister. Most Saturdays she works at least part of the day. Picking up extra shifts keeps the family finances afloat.

'I'll clear up,' says Megan. The sink is piled with breakfast dishes.

Her sister smiles, kisses her forehead. 'Thank you.'

Amber appears in the doorway. 'Mum, Kyle's shoving Ruby around. I've told him to stop. He says they're just playing. But I think he's being too rough.'

'Oh for Pete's sake!' says Debbie.

'I can thump him if you like,' says Amber, 'but then I'm the bully.'

Her mother goes out into the hall and hollers up the stairs. 'Kyle!'

Megan starts to stack the dishwasher. *The joys of family life*, she thinks; still she envies her sister with every fibre of her being.

'Did you hate being the big sister?' Amber asks.

'It had its advantages,' says Megan with a wry smile.

Returning, Mark says, 'Mystery solved. It's Kerry Waycott's funeral this afternoon. Terry's lent Justin the boat so the family can scatter her ashes at sea. So she'll be with her dad.'

CHAPTER SIXTY-ONE

Saturday, 3pm

The village is several miles up the coast from Berrycombe. The ancient church commands an imposing hilltop location, although now it's surrounded by static caravan parks. The churchyard is overgrown and contains no recent interments. But it's also full of Waycotts going back more than a hundred and fifty years and Kerry was christened there, so they've agreed to hold the service prior to the private cremation elsewhere.

Justin and Sheila lead the cortege up the hill on foot. Between them they are supporting Heather Waycott. Other friends and relatives, that Megan doesn't know, follow with Kerry's confused younger siblings.

The turnout of local well-wishers, the curious and the press, is into the hundreds. Uniformed officers are discreetly deployed and Megan stands shoulder to shoulder next to Laura Slater and Richard Montieth at the side of the road outside the church.

Justin Waycott scowls at them as he passes, following his niece's white casket. He's a big man, uncomfortable in a suit; the collar and tie chafe his neck and he runs his index finger round it obsessively.

Slater has a number of specialist officers mingling with the crowd, making an unobtrusive record of the event. She stands stiffly next to Megan, an inch or two shorter, shoulders back and chin up.

When Megan phoned to ask if she could attend, the boss seemed surprised.

'Don't see why not,' she said. 'If you actually want to. I hate having to do these things.'

Megan hastily borrowed a black leather jacket from her sister. Next to Slater's full-length black cashmere coat and Montieth's dark three-piece suit, she looks like she's strayed in from a bikers' convention.

During the service they squeeze into a pew at the back of the church. It's standing room only, with a crowd jammed in the doorway. Megan notices Linda Kovacs and catches her eye. Mr Foxton, now acting head at the school, reads badly from the Bible in a slow and monotonous voice. Paige Tucker sits sandwiched between her parents having a sneaky peek around.

A large photograph of Kerry is displayed on an easel to one side of the altar. It's the standard school portrait of a hopeful teenager with a sunny smile and must've been taken more than a year before her death.

A nervous cousin steps up to the lectern, reads the poem 'Do Not Stand at My Grave and Weep' and has a coughing fit in the middle.

Megan wonders what other option there is apart from weeping. Justice won't be coming any time soon.

'Must've been the first bloody thing that came up when she googled funerals,' mumbles Montieth under his breath. 'Could've found a decent poem.'

Glancing at him, Megan is nonplussed; is he a man of literary tastes? He seems more the type for rude rugby songs in the pub. After working alone for so long, making buddies of colleagues is an alien process to her now. Everyone feels distant and transient. Now more than ever.

The vicar invites them all to kneel and pray. Next to her, Slater appears to be doing just that. She knows the responses, unlike Megan, who's rarely been inside a church.

Megan's eye wanders across the backs of bowed heads and down the nave. How many of those present actually knew Kerry? But the community has turned out in force to make a statement about one of its own, a lost child they want to reclaim.

Drifting down the aisle her gaze comes to a shuddering halt. The shoulders are broad, a tight-knitted black skull cap pulled low on the bowed head. Recognition hits like a fist in the gut. She cranes to see the face, which is in his hands. He wears black leather gloves.

'Shit!' she hisses. 'I think it's him!'

'What? Where?' whispers Montieth.

Slater's eyes snap open.

Leaning to one side in her seat she tries to point. Montieth stands up but, at the same moment, so does the rest of the congregation. The pallbearers hoist the coffin onto their shoulders and begin to process back down the aisle.

Montieth squeezes out and tries to edge through the crowd at the back and make his way round to the other side of the church. But it's hard to get through, the place is rammed. Megan tries to keep her eye on Leon. She jumps up to stand on the pew but in the sea of people and faces before her it's impossible to pick him out. He's melted away.

Slater pulls out her phone and issues instructions. The whole area needs to be sealed.

'You sure?' she asks. 'Did you see his face?'

'I thought I was sure,' says Megan calmly. Inside she feels like a crazy woman.

CHAPTER SIXTY-TWO

The cordon thrown round the church had the effect of corralling the disgruntled mourners for nearly half an hour. The funeral party and family were allowed through quickly for their appointment at the crematorium. Everyone else was required to file past an improvised checkpoint. There was no sign of Trevor Pearse.

Megan watched the laborious process with a heavy heart. Had her imagination got the better of her? It looked that way. She received no words of recrimination from her colleagues but she felt deeply embarrassed.

'Better to call it than not. Even if you weren't certain,' said the DI. 'I'm sure the boss agrees.'

Whatever Slater's opinion, she didn't share it.

Later, the covert footage shot at the funeral was examined frame by frame. Kitty, Brittney and Vish were among those who racked up a weekend of overtime reviewing all the material. It yielded nothing of interest.

By Monday morning they're all back at their desks, the work stations still strewn with takeaway cups and chocolate wrappers, the atmosphere a little stir-crazy.

As Megan walks into the office she finds them having a giggle.

'Look at this one, Brit,' says Kitty. 'Left or right?'

They appear to have moved from reviewing the funeral footage to Bumble, a dating app.

Brittney peers and wrinkles her nose. 'Left, no, oh, I dunno. Actually he looks a bit like my mum's hairdresser, which is weird.'

'I swipe right on everyone,' says Vish. 'Then weed out the losers later.'

'Yeah, but you're gross,' says Kitty.

'It's a technique which gives you the choice,' he replies.

'Yeah, I've heard about your techniques, mate.' Kitty has a deep, dirty laugh.

'I get few complaints,' he says with a toss of the head.

Seeing their shared camaraderie, Megan feels an outsider. And old. She's not of their generation, she doesn't share their concerns or get their jokes.

'Morning, Megan,' says Brittney with a warm smile.

And they feel sorry for her. Which is worse.

Slater walks in to begin the morning briefing, flanked by Montieth. The dating app goes off and they all click back to work mode.

'Right, listen up,' says the boss. 'We've got a lot to get through today.'

There's a general shuffling and settling. Kitty whispers to Vish, he sniggers. Slater flings them a schoolmarmish look. She doesn't notice Ted Jennings yawning.

'First on the agenda,' she says, 'Trevor Pearse remains our prime suspect for the rape and murder of Kerry Waycott. It's seems fairly certain he's fled the jurisdiction. Monty is going to liaise with colleagues in Organised Crime in the Met, see if we can track any of his criminal connections.'

'We'll be applying for a European Arrest Warrant too,' Montieth adds.

Slater's gaze skates around the room and comes to rest on Megan. As usual, it gives her an uncomfortable feeling.

'In the O'Brien case,' Slater continues, 'we have confirmed that the body in the septic tank is that of Georgia O'Brien's first husband, Eric Russell. CSI have examined his house near Exmouth and we now know he was murdered there and the body moved. They also found some other knives that match the one recovered from the tank and a knife block with an empty slot. Thanks to good work by Megan and Brittney, we have a description of a vehicle and two men. These are likely to have been Russell's attackers. The question is, do they connect with Georgia and, if so, how?'

'We talked to Eric Russell's neighbour,' says Megan. 'According to him, Russell had boasted that he was putting on a play in London and Dame Heidi Soames, Georgia's mother, would be starring in it.'

'Any confirmation of this?' says Slater.

'Probably just a boast,' says Brittney. 'His career had been going down the pan for a few years. He recently applied to increase his mortgage, got turned down. Seems very unlikely that his ex-mother-in-law would've agreed to work with him. They weren't even on speaking terms.'

'Is this just tabloid gossip?' says Montieth.

'No,' says Megan. 'It's a fair assumption. When Georgia left Russell for husband number two, who was twenty years younger than her, Russell retaliated by dumping her from their successful TV show. He was the producer. In effect, it ruined her acting career. After that, it's hard to imagine Heidi would've wanted to work with him.'

'The TV show was later cancelled,' Brittney adds.

'Let's get Georgia in then,' says Montieth.

Megan scans Slater; the mauling they received from Georgia's lawyer must still smart.

The boss exhales. 'Unfortunately the situation is compounded by the disappearance of the child, Noah Khan. An extensive search of the area has been carried out. No sign of him. Four-year-old children either wander off or they're taken. So we must assume the latter. Does anyone have a theory to offer on that?'

'Shirin Khan is the boy's aunt not his mother,' says Megan. 'When we first met the child he spoke of being visited by his father. Shirin dismissed this as a product of his imagination. However, is it a stretch to wonder if one of these two men is also Noah's father and that's how he comes into the picture?'

'Okay,' says the DCI. 'What are you saying? Georgia is involved in a conspiracy to murder and used this man?'

'Makes sense,' says Megan. 'You've got to consider Georgia's character. This is not a woman who does things for herself. She's rich, a successful children's author, used to having her own way. She gets other people to do things for her.'

'Why would they put the body in her tank?' says Montieth.

Megan shrugs. 'A falling out between conspirators? Georgia has said she wants to adopt Noah. But then if one of these men is the boy's father, perhaps he wants his son back? He wants to pressurise her? I don't know.'

'We need to be crystal clear this time that Georgia has motive,' says Slater, shooting a critical look across the room at Brittney. It seems spiteful. The young DC dips her head in embarrassment. Megan's annoyed. Why does Slater do this? But the boss continues. 'So I'd like some better evidence. Also her lawyer has kindly informed me that Georgia is giving interviews to press and television this morning, appealing for help to find Noah, who's now being described as her adopted son.'

'Oh for Chrissake!' says Montieth. 'They're having a bloody laugh.'

Megan agrees with him, although she can see why the DCI is being cautious. They don't want to face the accusation that not enough is being done to find Noah. And that's undoubtedly the lawyer's next play. Slater doesn't intend to get sandbagged again.

'We can focus on nailing down the vehicle that the two men drove,' says Megan. 'Our witness described a dark pick-up, possibly a Mitsubishi. We know the day it was there. We can drill down through all the ANPR for the vicinity.'

'Good idea. Kitty, can you organise that?'

'Already on it, boss,' says the analyst.

Brittney pipes up. 'We also suspect someone used Russell's bank card to withdraw cash. We can check for CCTV on that.'

Megan smiles to herself. The girl is fighting back. She feels oddly proud.

'Fine,' says Slater in a chilly voice. 'Oh and one last thing. The director of social services is having a fit. Has a social worker called Charlie Adams been trying to contact you, Megan?'

He's left five messages on her phone.

'Possibly,' she says with a sigh. 'He wants us to check on Lizzie Quinn. But I don't see why I should do his job too. When I spoke to him before, he refused to do anything. I suggested he find a rehab place for her.'

'Now they're making it a safeguarding issue. Saying she could be targeted again. So you'll have to follow up.'

Megan huffs. 'He's just scared to go into the woods on his own. Probably thinks it's full of hobgoblins.'

'He could be right,' says Slater drily.

Laughter ripples round the room, breaking the tension of the meeting.

'A volunteer to back up Megan?' says Montieth jovially. 'Save her from the kelpies.'

'I will,' says Vish. 'I'm not scared. Although I don't know what a kelpie is.'

Megan forces a smile. The meeting is over. And her opportunity to mention the flowers she's received from Leon is gone. Hobgoblins? Where did that come from? She wonders about her own mental processes. Moretti could explain the connection. It leaves Megan feeling twitchy and paranoid.

CHAPTER SIXTY-THREE

Monday, 10.23am

Shirin stands on the terrace and stares out to sea. There's a biting wind. Below her, the steep cliffside tumbles away, the winter wood covering it stripped of leaves. Only the stark conifers remain. But she's glad to escape the fug of the overheated house.

Rival local and national news teams, with all their paraphernalia and personnel, have been trooping in and out all morning. Sir Henry Crewe and his two assistants, plus laptops and phones, have taken over the dining room. Furniture in the open-plan living room has been rearranged to create the best light for filming.

Georgia is waiting in the wings, eager for her next performance. Sir Henry's PR minions have written the script: the touching tale of a middle-aged woman, lacking children of her own, deciding to open her heart and home to a small orphaned boy.

Shirin wonders what Aisha would make of all this. Her dead sister was angry throughout the pregnancy, refusing to nurse the child once he was born. An adoption might have suited her. Georgia's cash certainly would. But when Shirin asked what she wanted, Aisha just screamed, 'I want my fucking life back!' The irony was, in the end she chose death. But Shirin knows why. It was to escape him.

The sliding doors open and Dame Heidi steps out. She's wearing an elegantly embroidered pashmina. Shirin wonders what it's like to always have what you want, but more than that, to feel you deserve it. Her own mother told her – it was the last time they ever spoke – that she deserved to suffer for the humiliation and disgrace she'd brought upon her family. She was a bad daughter, fit only to be cast out. Bad and broken.

'My goodness,' says Dame Heidi, 'aren't you freezing out here?'

'Only in my soul,' says Shirin.

'You're a strange girl,' says Heidi, fixing her with a quizzical eye. 'But I don't dislike you. You have grit. Georgia can be distressingly spineless.'

Shirin has no intention of being fooled by her.

'You really think this will work?' she says.

'Don't you want the boy found?'

'Do you?' says Shirin.

The two women face each other. Shirin has the advantage in youth and height. But the old lady has an iron will, disguised by the easy charm celebrity can confer. In many ways Shirin admires her and wonders: was she born with that chip of ice in her heart or is it something she's cultivated? Shirin would love to know how, even to take lessons.

'What do you plan to do when they identify the body?' she says.

'Whatever the police think happened, it's up to them to prove it. Beyond reasonable doubt. That's what Henry says.'

'Having your first husband's body in your septic tank does raise questions.'

Heidi smiles. 'Oh, so he told you.'

Not exactly. Shirin has thought hard about what Georgia let slip. 'No one gives two hoots about him,' she'd said. Knowing Georgia that points to one person and Heidi just confirmed it.

'Did he explain our deal too?' says Heidi. She seems unconcerned.

'You agreed to give him Noah,' says Shirin. It's a guess but a shrewd one. 'Georgia must be upset about that,' she adds.

'She doesn't know that part,' says Dame Heidi. 'And I'm sure we both want to keep her happy, don't we? And more important, on an even keel. With you writing her books for her.'

'And getting proper credit and half the money.'

Heidi grins. 'Obviously. And in return we keep this little part of the puzzle to ourselves, don't we?'

Shirin stares at Dame Heidi, into those enormous Bambi eyes the camera loves. 'I know Eric shafted Georgia,' she says, 'but why did you want him dead? That's extreme.'

'I didn't want him dead. That was never the arrangement. He was a nasty, vicious, disgusting little nonentity. Georgia met him at drama school. She should never have married him.'

'I'm sure you told her that.'

'I did. But now, after all these years, the fool thought he could blackmail me. Get me to do some awful play of his.' The expression on the old lady's face is one of sour contempt. A glimpse, perhaps, of the real Heidi? 'But, I told you, I will not be blackmailed. Your friend—'

'And I told you he's not my friend.'

'He offered to explain that to Eric in terms that would be unambiguous.'

Shirin nods. He's certainly done that.

'You've made a deal with the devil, Heidi. Do you realise that?'

'My dear girl, I've been in this business fifty years. It's hardly the first time. Do you know how many cocks I've sucked?'

'This is different.'

'How? He's got what he wants: his son. The police have got zilch. Henry doubts the CPS will let them even bring charges. Now we can all get on with our lives.'

'Except Georgia. She hasn't got what she wants.'

'She'll get over it.'

'This charade is for her, isn't it? To keep her sweet.'

'What's the harm in that? You can see how much she's enjoying herself.'

Shirin scans the old lady, a fierce but diminutive figure wrapped in a shawl. She seems harmless, even kindly. 'Having someone beaten up is one thing,' she says. 'But this is murder.'

'Which was never my intention. What do you think I am, a monster? The situation simply got out of hand. Eric was never that smart.'

'You think you can get away with it?'

Dame Heidi seems to weigh this in her mind.

Finally she says, 'Yes. I can. Happens more than you think, according to Henry.'

'I admire your confidence.'

'Do you know the reason my daughter never succeeded in becoming a real star like me? I have tried to explain this to her. It's why most people never make it. It's not about knowing who you truly are inside and all that self-indulgent claptrap. It's about deciding what to be, now, in this precise second. Total control of yourself, of your instrument, moment by moment. Once you can do that you can convince anyone of anything.'

Shirin scans her. She's met some scary people, mostly petty hustlers and drug dealers. But only one she'd call evil. Until now, that is.

'You believe that?' she says.

'My dear, I know it. In my blood and in my bones.'

CHAPTER SIXTY-FOUR

Monday, 11.34am

The lane to Lizzie Quinn's cottage has become a stream and close to impassable in places. Vish drives; he manoeuvres slowly round the submerged potholes that pepper the flooded track. The overhanging trees form a dense, dripping corridor of foliage either side. The whoosh of water echoes everywhere.

Megan feels as if they're travelling down a tunnel to a secret portal. The dankness and gloom of the woods creates an eerie sense of foreboding. It would be easy to imagine eyes among the trees, watching. *His eyes.* But she needs to rein in such dangerous flights of fancy and stay grounded. Conjuring up Leon at the funeral caused enough problems. *Keep it real*, she tells herself.

'When is this rain going to stop?' she says.

'I can see why the social worker didn't fancy this,' says Vish.

'Last time I came down here was too fast, in the back of a squad car and I practically chucked up. You're a much better driver.'

'Thank you,' he says. 'And also for what you said to me on the phone.'

'Hope it helped,' says Megan.

'It's my first big murder case,' says Vish. 'Didn't want it to end like this.'

'You think it's ended?'

'We're never going to nick him, are we?'

'Sometimes it's a long game,' says Megan. *Lifelong.* But she doesn't want to depress the young DC by adding that.

When they finally reach the clearing round the cottage, it seems deserted. The rusty old Astra hasn't moved but the Nissan Juke is gone. It's been impounded.

Megan wonders if Lizzie Quinn is even at home. The walk to the main road must be over a mile. The nearest shop is farther. The isolation of the place disturbs Megan, she couldn't stand it. How does Lizzie get food? Is there even mains water and a proper toilet? Megan doubts it.

Getting out of the car, she sees a fine wisp of woodsmoke drifting from the metal chimney of the larger caravan. She can smell the sharp tang of it, like a bonfire.

She raps on the door and waits. As before, she expects Lizzie to take her time. She hears a giggle inside the caravan. Is the damned social worker right? Has Lizzie got herself some new elves already? That's just annoying.

Megan raps again sharply. The door to the caravan swings out towards her and she finds herself face to face with a much smaller child than she expected. It's Noah, beaming at her.

She stares at him in disbelief. 'Hello, Noah,' she says. 'What are you doing here?'

He retreats into the cosy interior and Megan follows him in. Lizzie is sitting cross-legged on one of the divans, a roll-up in one hand, playing cards in the other, chuckling. Noah jumps back on to the divan beside her and picks up his stack of cards.

'Hello,' says Lizzie with a benign smile. 'We're playing animal snap. I only just taught him. But he's much faster than me already.'

Beating a smackhead at animal snap is probably not that hard, thinks Megan. But she just smiles.

Vish appears behind her in the doorway.

'Look who we've found,' says Megan.

The DC does a double-take. 'Hello, mate,' he says. 'What you up to?'

'Playing snap,' says Noah. He giggles gleefully. 'I'm winning.'

Megan and Vish exchange looks. She casts her eye swiftly around the caravan. The needles and drugs that were in evidence before have disappeared. There's a half-eaten packet of biscuits on the side with a carton of orange juice. Noah doesn't appear to have come to any harm. He seems positively happy.

'So, Lizzie,' says Megan. 'How come Noah's here?'

'I'm babysitting.'

'Right. How long's he been here?'

'I dunno. Few days.'

'We had baked beans and sausages for breakfast,' says Noah. 'I never had a sausage before. Auntie says they're bad, made of donkeys. But I don't believe her.'

Vish perches next to Noah on the divan. 'You've got lots to say, haven't you, little fella. You been having a nice time?'

The child nods vigorously. 'Yesterday I climbed a tree.'

'A tree. Awesome. How high up did you get?'

'He was like a little monkey,' says Lizzie. 'No fear.' She gives Noah a hug. The child hugs her back.

'Thing is, Lizzie,' says Megan, 'loads of people have been looking for Noah. He's missing.'

'He's not missing. He's here. I'm babysitting,' says Lizzie. She sounds affronted.

'Who asked you to babysit?'

She frowns. 'I'm not supposed to say.'

'Why not?'

'It's a secret. Obviously.'

*

It takes half an hour to cajole and gently coerce Lizzie and Noah into the car and head back to MCT's base. After several futile attempts to get a signal, Megan manages to phone Slater.

The boss's initial surprise is replaced by rapid calculation.

'We need to think about this carefully,' she says. 'Is he anxious, wanting his mum?'

'No, he's fine. It's the happiest I've seen him. He referred to Auntie, which is maybe what he calls Shirin. Or could be Georgia?'

'I think we'll get Shirin here on her own. See if we can unravel this.'

'Okay.'

Megan hangs up and checks her charges in the back seat. Noah is snuggled up next to Lizzie, who's staring out of the window and humming softly to herself.

By the time they make it to the office Shirin is in an interview room, brought in by uniform. She hasn't been given any explanation and is understandably tetchy.

As Megan ushers Lizzie and Noah in, Slater is waiting.

'Take them straight in,' Slater says, indicating the interview room.

'Am I being nicked?' says Lizzie. ''Cause I haven't done anything.'

'You're helping us with our inquiries,' says Megan. 'Remember, you agreed to do that?'

Megan opens the door. Shirin is sitting tensely at the table. She looks up, sees Lizzie and Noah, is surprised but not that surprised. She stands up and smiles; Noah rushes into her arms. Scooping him up, she hugs him tight.

'I climbed a tree, Mummy! A big tree,' he squeals.

'Did you, babe? That's brilliant.' She buries her face in his dark curls.

'Can I stay at Lizzie's? I like it much better than Auntie's.'

Shirin puts him down, looks at Megan and sighs. Megan meets her gaze. The dark eyes remain hard and inscrutable but there could be a hint of relief in her face. Is it simply for the return of her child or something more?

Lizzie shakes her head wearily. 'God, I need a fag.' She smiles at Shirin and shrugs. 'Sorry, kiddo. They just turned up out of the blue.'

'I presume you two know each other?' says Megan. 'How?'

'I try to keep in touch with my little elves if I can, even when they grow up,' says Lizzie. 'Can I smoke in here?'

'No,' says Megan.

Shirin sits down on the chair, lifts Noah on to her lap and rocks him. He curls into her arms and sucks his thumb.

Megan stands in front of her. They make a touching picture.

'So you took Noah to Lizzie's and asked her to look after him?'

'Yep,' Shirin says.

'Why?' says Megan. 'And why did you lie to us?'

Shirin gazes up at her. Megan sees she has tears in her eyes.

'Because it was all getting crazy,' she says, 'and it was the only thing I could think of to keep him safe.'

CHAPTER SIXTY-FIVE

Monday, 1.35pm

The interview is conducted under caution by Megan and Vish, streamed and watched by Slater and Detective Superintendent Barker on the monitors in the incident room. At the least Shirin is guilty of wasting police time, and she could be an accessory to murder. She waives her right to a solicitor, a small relief. No one wants Sir Henry Crewe in the mix, including Shirin.

Noah and Lizzie are being looked after in an adjacent room and have embarked on another round of animal snap.

Megan watches Shirin as they go through the caution and the formalities. Her hands are neatly folded on the table in front of her and she seems composed. There's resignation and relief in her tone of voice. But Megan senses an element of calculation too.

'I was fifteen when I first came down to Devon,' she says. 'Nobody had heard much about County Lines then. London gangs were just getting into it. Getting out of the city, developing new supply lines, new territory. Staying with Lizzie in the woods was brilliant. Like going on holiday.'

'But you were here to sell drugs?' says Megan.

'Yeah. I was maybe fourteen when I left home. Rows with my parents. They were religious, bigoted. I wanted to be a normal kid, like my friends at school. They saw that as bad. I got a boyfriend. They said I had to choose. I chose to work for a gang selling drugs.

To me, back then, it was freedom.' She gives her interrogators a defiant look.

Megan wonders if this is Shirin coming clean or simply another game. Now she's the savvy city kid, the opposite of the self-effacing skivvy and personal assistant who opened the door to the police at Winterbrook Farm. She was a drug dealer, now she ghostwrites children's books. She's the real player, not Georgia.

'How much time did you spend down here?' Megan says.

'Came down for a few months, got nicked, taken back, banged up, let out. Rinse and repeat. So maybe I came down three times in all. Then I was put into foster care.' She smiles wistfully. 'They were great people, helped me get my head straight. Went to college while I lived with them, passed some exams.'

'Nice to know the system can work,' says Megan. She doesn't want to rush things. They're feeling each other out. If Megan's going to crack this, she needs to build a rapport with the girl.

Shirin sneers. 'Only cause individuals go the extra mile,' she says. 'The system's still shit. I turned eighteen, I got a job. Things were okay. Then my sister, Aisha, got in some bother.'

'Younger sister?'

'She was nearly fifteen, she couldn't hack it at home either. But I kept telling her, hang on in there, don't follow my example. Stick with school, do your exams.'

Megan notices a change in her whole demeanour. The chippy attitude subsides. Her shoulders droop, weighed down, perhaps, by difficult memories?

'There was this guy,' she says. 'I knew him before. Went out with him for a couple of months when I was fourteen. He got sent down for drug dealing and GBH. I split up with him, I knew he was bad news. Hadn't seen him for years. But then he got released on licence. He wanted us to get back together. I said no way. I'm not a masochist. I was working, I'd got myself straight. But he was persistent. Wouldn't take no for an answer. Followed me.

We had a fight and he got really mad. I ran out on him, hid at a mate's.' There are tears in her eyes. She exhales and says, 'So he went looking for my sister and raped her. He liked younger girls. To teach me a lesson, he said.'

'Did you go to the police?' says Megan.

'Aisha wouldn't. She was scared of him. With good reason. He got sent back to jail anyway because he beat up a dealer and stole his gear.'

Shirin's head dips. She's silent for several moments.

Megan waits. She's aware of her colleagues watching, assessing. The mood in the room feels finely balanced.

Looking up, Shirin smiles at Vish and says, 'My parents called her a whore. You'd probably agree with that, wouldn't you?'

'No,' he says softly. 'She was a victim of abuse.'

'Well, anyway, they threw her out. She came to live with me and Noah was born. That's when I thought we needed to get away from London. I started to make plans, look for another job. I was doing office work, learning bookkeeping at a firm of accountants. Georgia O'Brien was a client of theirs. She wanted a live-in personal assistant. Go back to Devon, I thought, why not? The money was shit but I blagged my way into it. Then, as I told you when you came round, Aisha never made it, she committed suicide. I didn't expect Georgia to still take me, a girl with a baby, but she did.'

'And you and Noah have been here for what, three and half years?'

Her head sinks low. 'I still really miss her.' If it's an act, she's good. Megan wonders at her own cynicism. Perhaps it's defensive. She glances at Vish, he's riveted.

'Noah seems to regard you as his mother,' Megan says. 'Does he know?'

'Sort of. But he's too young really. I show him pictures of Aisha. As he grows up, I'll make sure he understands.'

'You really love him, don't you?'

She nods, turns away, wipes her nose with the back of her hand.

Now she's emotionally vulnerable, ask the question. Megan knows the technique. 'So why would you agree to Georgia adopting him?' she says.

Shirin laughs, not what Megan's expecting.

'Oh, I was just playing her,' she says. 'Y'know, jerking her along. It's what you have to do to get what you want in this world, isn't it?' She gives Megan a knowing look.

'That's a harsh philosophy.'

'Is it? I dunno. It's what's worked for me.' There's no apology but she's not a whiner, she doesn't indulge in self-pity. Megan finds herself liking that.

'And what do you want, Shirin?' she says.

'She's making a bloody fortune out of these kids' book. But I'm the one writing them. Okay, she's the brand, the famous face everyone knows. But I've worked bloody hard and I should be getting half the money.'

'And you're not?'

'What do you think?' Her eyes are blazing. Megan can see the intelligence and determination behind them. The effort it's taken for her to survive. They have a lot in common.

Megan smiles. 'Do you want a break? Cup of coffee?'

Shirin nods and sniffs.

Vish stands up. 'I'll get you a coffee. How do you take it?'

'Black's fine. Thanks.'

As he leaves the room she smiles at Megan. 'He's cute. A cute Asian cop, that's novel round here.'

'Is it? I used to be in the Met. It's full of cute cops of every colour and creed. Including me. Though you may not agree with that.'

Shirin chuckles. The tension between them relaxes a tad.

'I know Georgia's a difficult cow and childish,' Shirin says. 'But she's got a good heart and you're barking up the wrong tree.'

Megan scans her. Another abrupt change of tone. What's this about?

'How do you mean exactly?' she says.

The girl sighs. 'This is all so knackering.'

'What is?'

'It's easy for the likes of Georgia. But for me? Always kicking the can down the road, improvising until something better comes along. Living from one crisis to the next. No security. But that's life on the streets. You wouldn't understand.'

'Maybe I would. Worrying about where the next meal's coming from, I know about that.'

'You've slept on the streets?'

'Not that. But I've been hungry. My mother struggled, she was a single parent and we lived on benefits. Most of my childhood was a scrabble to get from one week's payment to the next. I know what that feels like.'

Tilting her head, the girl fixes Megan with a steely stare.

'Okay,' she says, 'I'll tell you what you want to know, but there's a condition. You put Noah somewhere totally safe.'

'You don't want to take him home with you?'

'Cut the bullshit, am I even going home?'

'I don't know yet. But whatever happens he will be properly taken care of, I promise.'

'No, not the usual social services placement. Children's home, foster care, that's not safe. You know that as well as I do. A police safe house, secure and secret.'

'You're going to have to explain to me why.'

Shirin leans forward, elbows on the table. She nods in the direction of the wall-mounted camera.

'Hope your mates are listening carefully back there, cause here's the juice. You were right about there being a custody issue. Noah's father got out of prison and he came looking for us again. Wants me to marry him and make us into a proper family. That's what he says.'

'You don't want that?'

'God, no! He's a scumbag. A psycho. He raped my sister.'

'What's his plan? Take you and Noah back to London?'

'No, he likes it here. Wants us to stay. He's opened a bar.'

With a whoosh the air is sucked out of the room. It feels to Megan like the tectonic plates have abruptly shifted and resettled with a thunderous crash. She's talking about Leon. Of course she is.

Aware of holding her breath, Megan exhales and says calmly, 'When did he do that?'

'About six months ago. He even persuaded Georgia to invest in it.'

'How?' *You know how.*

'He can be charming if he wants. Women fall for his schtick.'

Megan wonders if Shirin is sharp enough to pick up on the shock her revelation has caused. But she seems lost in her own thoughts.

'When did you last see him?'

'Not sure when I actually saw him. He phoned me last week, on Tuesday.'

'Why did you hide Noah at Lizzie's?'

'I told you, to protect him. I suspected they'd made a deal.' Her level of tension and agitation is rising again. The shoulders sag, she stares at her fingernails. 'Then I had a conversation this morning with Heidi and she admitted it.'

'Georgia's mother, Dame Heidi Soames?'

Shirin nods.

Vish returns with a cup of coffee and an A4 print of Trevor Pearse's mugshot. He hands it to Megan.

She lays it on the table in front of Shirin and says, 'Is this him?'

'So you lot know who he is. I did wonder,' she says, fingering the side of the picture. 'He's got a beard now.'

'Drink your coffee, Shirin.'

Vish sits down and says, 'Can you tell us the name he's been using?'

'Leon Hall.'

'But that's not his real name.'

'Trevor Pearse. Trevor after his old man, he's always hated it.' She meets Megan's eye but the look is pleading. 'And now you know why Noah has to be protected from him.'

'Yes, we do,' says Megan. 'Tell us about this deal.'

Shirin takes a sip of coffee. 'I didn't know there was a body in the septic tank. There was a leak and so I called the contractors. It was the first I knew.'

'That someone had been murdered?'

'Yes, but I know Trev.' Her chin trembles, she swallows hard. 'It was just too much of a coincidence.'

'You suspected he was involved?'

'At first I thought it was someone he'd had a beef with and whacked. Put the body there to piss me off. Just to make my life more difficult because I wouldn't do what he wanted.'

'That's not something that would surprise you?'

'No.' She picks up the coffee and takes another sip. 'But Georgia was being weird, even for Georgia. You lot thought it was Damian. But she knew he was in Toronto. I couldn't figure what they were playing at, her, Heidi, the lawyer. Why didn't she just say, he's in Toronto? Then I realised it was a diversion, because she and Heidi knew it was her first husband, Eric.'

'But you still thought Trevor was involved?'

A thin smile spreads across Shirin's face. 'What's it you lot call it? When you don't know but you try and fit the evidence together?'

'Circumstantial evidence?' says Vish.

'Yeah, that's the one. A stone-cold killer turns up on the doorstep. Then the husband that shafted you is murdered. Has to be connected, right?'

'And is it?' says Megan.

'I met Trev when I was a kid. At first it was exciting being with him. I felt like a princess. But then I learnt what it meant to be his princess. I thought my parents tried to control my every move, but that was nothing compared to Trevor. Then he got nicked and put away and that was my chance to escape him. I join this other rival gang. They'd started to move out of London. That's how I first came to Devon.'

'Did that work in terms of escaping Trevor?'

'For a while. Even inside, he tried to keep tabs on me. But being part of this rival gang, it protected me. He didn't know where they'd sent me. They weren't gonna tell him.'

'He never tracked you down to Lizzie Quinn's?'

'He didn't know about her. That's why I knew Noah would be safe there.'

'What happened when you went back to London?'

'Once he got out, I was working, trying make a different life. But he tracked me down again, wouldn't leave me alone.'

'He stalked you?'

'Yes. Sent me flowers all the time. Kept asking me out. He's, I dunno, obsessive. Everything has to be on his terms. Always. It's a sickness. So I knew that if he was involved in this it was because he was getting what he wanted.'

Those damn lilies! Megan wonders what he wants from her.

'And what he wanted was Noah?'

'Yes. It's a guess but I'd say Trev figured he'd put the body in the tank in case they reneged on the deal. Like insurance. It's how his mind works. Always looking for another angle to play.'

Megan leans back in her chair and says, 'Why would Georgia agree to that if she wants to adopt your nephew?'

'Exactly. That's what I meant before. You're barking up the wrong tree. It has to be the old lady.'

'Let's be clear. You think Dame Heidi Soames conspired to have Eric Russell murdered? Why?'

'When I talked to her this morning she said that Russell was blackmailing her. Her deal with Trev was just to threaten him and make him stop.'

'Did you believe her?'

'Who knows? She says she'll get away with it. You lot'll never prove it. The case won't even go to court.' Shirin smiles. 'In some ways she's like him, expects absolutely everything to go her way. The woman's a witch.'

Vish and Megan exchange looks.

'Okay,' says Megan. 'I think we'll take that break now.'

CHAPTER SIXTY-SIX

Monday, 4.30pm

'Do we believe her or is this an elaborate con to conceal her complicity with her former boyfriend, Pearse?' says Superintendent Barker. He's standing at the front of the room, arms folded.

The office lights are on against the encroaching darkness. Montieth is in London but the rest of the team is assembled.

Megan's gaze drifts out of the window. She's finding it hard to focus. In the twilight a forklift truck is unloading pallets from a lorry for the timber merchants across the road. She's still trying to absorb and process the enormity of Shirin Khan's revelation. They all are.

Standing beside Barker, Slater seems pensive and twitchy. 'Brittney,' she says, 'what have you got on Khan's background?'

Brittney stands up. 'Her record is as a juvenile. Back and forth, County Lines stuff consistent with what she told us. No adult convictions. Kitty had a quick look at her phone and we've downloaded the records.'

'And?' says Slater.

'The call she said she received last Tuesday from Trevor was made from the landline at the bar called Mayhem,' says Kitty. 'We're running checks on all the other numbers, particularly mobiles, but I'd say he was being deliberately cautious. Making sure no one could use a mobile number to track him.'

Concrete evidence. *Leon is Trevor.* There's still a part of Megan, maybe not a good part, that doesn't want to believe it. Accepting her attraction, her desire for a man like that, means facing her shame. It takes effort to push that aside, get back to the facts of the case. But she must.

'We did ask Shirin for a mobile number for him,' says Vish. 'Predictably, the one she gave us was dead.'

'Anyone else got theories or ideas to offer?' says Slater.

Ted Jennings raises his hand and says, 'Think I'm with the guv'nor, boss. Is a girl like that likely to tell us the truth? A leopard don't change its spots. Not in my experience.'

'Thanks for that useful piece of philosophy, Ted,' says the DCI drily. 'Any other contributions based on the evidence?'

'Well,' says Megan, 'the idea of Pearse – or Leon – as Eric Russell's killer would fit the description of the man our witness spoke to at the house.'

'Thought he was about a hundred,' says Ted.

'He's ninety-six and very observant,' says Brittney helpfully.

'We can certainly get him to look at the mugshot,' says Megan. 'But I'm wondering about his accomplice. What if it's Justin Waycott?'

'Waycott?' says the Superintendent. 'How the hell do you get to that? If Pearse raped and killed his niece?'

'No reason Waycott would know that though,' says Slater. 'Go on, Megan.'

'We know from Jared Clarke that Waycott worked at the bar as a bouncer. Pearse went to some lengths to deflect blame for the attack on Kerry onto Jared. Obviously he didn't want Justin to find out. But also, when I went to break the news of Kerry's death to the Waycotts, Justin drove his mother round to Heather's house. He had a black Mitsubishi pick-up. I think it was a Trojan.'

'Kitty,' says Slater. 'Pull up DVLA records on Justin Waycott's vehicle and cross-check it with ANPR. Let's see if we can place it anywhere near Eric Russell's house on the relevant date.'

'On it,' says Kitty.

'Vish,' Slater adds. 'Take some back-up and go and find Justin Waycott.'

'In the meantime, what do you want to do with Shirin Khan?' says Barker.

The DCI paces at the front of the room. Megan is acutely aware that this is possibly the most challenging situation Slater has ever faced as an SIO. Careers are made or broken on such cases. Megan's guess is that her instinct will be to remain cautious.

'It may be true that she's trying to lead us up the garden path in some way,' Slater says. 'A conspiracy to murder instigated by Dame Heidi Soames is a pretty outrageous accusation.'

'I don't want to have to deal with the press on that one,' says Barker.

A ripple of tension-relieving laughter runs round the room.

Sighing, he adds, 'But nor should we dismiss it or be frightened off.'

'Perhaps Heidi told Shirin the truth,' says Megan. 'She wanted to get a blackmailer off her back. Sounds plausible.'

'Brittney,' says Slater. 'I want to know what kind of dirt Russell could have on Dame Heidi. Start phoning up showbiz gossip columnists on the tabloids, see if anyone'll speak to you. They always know about scandals too libellous to print.'

Brittney beams from ear to ear. Her dream job. Megan smiles at her.

'Got to be sex, hasn't it?' says Ted. 'So if you need any advice, Brit, I'm your man.'

This raises another laugh. Kitty and Brittney exchange grimaces.

'Been checking out the porn sites, have you, Ted?' says Kitty.

'Settle down,' says Barker. 'I know it's been a long weekend.' He turns to the DCI. 'What about Shirin Khan?'

Slater raises her eyebrows. 'She's no use to us in a cell, so we cut her loose, put her under surveillance?'

He nods. 'Okay.'

'But,' she continues, 'we take her at her word and keep the boy.'

'Where's he going to go?' says Megan.

'I'm not risking handing him over to social services. I'll take him home with me,' says Slater.

CHAPTER SIXTY-SEVEN

Monday, 5.47pm

Megan is given the task of transporting Noah safely to the DCI's house.

'Where are you taking him?' says Shirin.

'You asked me to keep him safe, that's what I'm going to do,' Megan replies. 'You want to change your mind? There's no coercion here. It's still your choice.'

Shirin picks up her jacket; she seems torn. Megan scans her face. The fear is barely suppressed. Shirin is either playing a very devious game or she really believes he's still around. That he wouldn't leave without Noah. Megan wonders if even an arrogant psychopath like Pearse would take such a risk. It seems foolhardy. He knows the police are after him. He'd be risking a life sentence with a hefty tariff if he went down for Kerry's murder. He must've guessed they have DNA evidence pointing to him. But, as Megan knows, a man like that doesn't have the usual attitude to risk. The error would be to judge him by normal standards.

Squatting down beside the boy, Shirin pulls him into a hug. 'You be good,' she says.

Megan watches Noah. He looks as wary as when they first saw him; an unnaturally subdued child who's become a pawn in a game.

'You going to be a little soldier?' says Shirin, ruffling his hair.

He nods. It seems likely that he's been asked this before. He knows the answer to give.

Shirin and Lizzie leave together in a taxi. The surveillance team of four in two vehicles is led by Ted Jennings. Megan watches from an upper window as the whole cavalcade sets off at discreet intervals. Shirin will surely know she's being followed. If this is Slater's strategy it seems woefully threadbare.

Since learning that Leon Hall and Trevor Pearse are the same person, Megan's anxiety has soared off the scale and so has her imagination. She has to stay real, rein in her emotions and follow the evidence. But, on the other hand, this is territory she knows. Slater may have read the books but Megan's experienced the reality of dealing with a psychopath. She escaped from one, she knows they're unpredictable. Most of the stereotypes are wrong, which will make catching him harder.

She looks at Noah. Is it in the genes? The child certainly has a guarded directness in his gaze. But perhaps he's simply frightened; children are not her speciality. She wishes Vish was coming with her; he, at least, managed some rapport with the boy.

Megan has been given Slater's address and she enters it into her car's satnav. Noah sits in the passenger seat, his dark eyes watching and waiting.

'Know how this works?' says Megan cheerfully. 'It tells us which way to go.'

'Like on a boat?' says Noah.

'I don't know much about boats.'

Megan starts the engine and backs out.

'We're going on a boat,' he says.

'Yeah? When?'

He doesn't answer. He's staring out of the window. Megan can see his sad little face reflected in the glass. He must wonder what the hell is going on.

She turns onto the main road and tries again. 'What sort of boat? Big boat, like a ferry?'

Noah gives her a puzzled look. 'What's a ferry?'

'A special boat that you can drive onto in your car.'

The boy considers this. 'A boat for cars?'

'Yeah.'

This appeals to him, he smiles and nods.

It's dark as they head north out of Plymouth. In a stream of headlights and rush hour traffic they skirt the flank of Dartmoor.

'Does Mummy like boats?' says Megan. 'Or just Daddy?'

'I'm not supposed to talk about him, or I'll be in trouble again.'

'Oh dear,' says Megan. 'Were you in trouble before?'

He nods.

'Was Mummy really upset?' says Megan.

He shakes his head. 'Not Mummy, Auntie. She shouts.'

'I imagine that's scary,' says Megan. Georgia O'Brien having a rant would probably frighten any child. And some adults.

They lapse into silence.

The Slaters live in a converted barn nestled in the South Hams hills outside Totnes. It's an area Megan doesn't know and can't see much of in the dark. But as they pull up outside the house a security light comes on. The door opens and Alex Slater appears with two little girls.

He's average height but lean and muscular, like a runner or cyclist. Stepping forward, he holds out his hand to Megan. The smile is warm and spontaneous, the opposite of his wife. 'Hey, I'm Alex,' he says. 'You found it all right, most people get lost the first time.'

'Megan.'

He gives her hand a friendly squeeze. 'Laura's talked about you loads. I feel I know you.' Moaning about her to the old man, that doesn't sound good.

Bending down in front of Noah, he offers him a handshake too. 'You must be Noah. Put it there, my man. It's going to be great to have another bloke around. I'm surrounded by girls. And this is Issie and Ava. They're really excited you're coming to stay.'

Issie is the oldest, about six; she looks unnervingly like her mother, with the same imperious tilt to the chin. Ava is blonde and bubbly and giggly, a similar age to Noah. She steps forward immediately and gives him a hug. He grins and hugs her back.

For some reason the whole thing brings a lump to Megan's throat. She has to swallow hard to stop herself bursting into tears. It's been a rollercoaster of a day. She knows she needs to get out of there and fast.

CHAPTER SIXTY-EIGHT

Monday, 7.48pm

The office is still busy when Megan returns. Most of the team have volunteered to work overtime and Barker has boosted morale by ordering in pizza for everyone.

Vish is perched on the corner of Brittney's desk tucking into a large slice.

'Vishwajeet! Watch where you're dripping that!' she squeals.

'It's just tomato sauce.'

'Drip on your own desk.'

'Did you get Justin Waycott?' says Megan, joining them.

'Nope. He's done a runner,' says Vish. 'Checked his flat, went to his mum's. She reckons he's away working on a trawler.'

'She would definitely lie to protect him,' says Megan.

'Also if he was at sea,' says Vish, 'his pick-up wouldn't have been pinging off APNR cameras outside a Sainsbury's petrol station on the edge of Plymouth late this afternoon.'

'Maybe it wasn't him driving,' says Megan.

'We thought of that,' says Brittney. 'I went down there and got hold of the CCTV from the petrol station. Want to see?'

Megan nods. Brittney brings up the footage on her computer screen. The black Mitsubishi Trojan pulls up to one of the pumps.

Brittney adds a commentary. 'Here's Justin.' Waycott has his collar up and a baseball cap pulled low across his face. He fills the tank and goes into the shop to pay. 'Pays cash,' says Brittney. 'I got the manager to match the till receipt with the number plate. But, watch now, this is where it gets interesting.'

Megan peers closely at the screen. The footage is poor quality, dark and grainy. Justin climbs back into the driver's seat and buckles up. His hands are on the steering wheel. Then there seems to be a third hand. 'He's got someone with him,' says Megan. 'Sitting in the passenger seat.'

'Exactly,' says Brittney. 'We've enhanced the footage and this is the best we can get.'

She clicks to another clip. The enlargement creates an almost abstract image. But there is a person in the passenger seat indicated by the hand movement and the outline of a torso which moves. No head or face are visible.

'Is it a man?' says Megan.

'Seems a similar size to Justin,' says Brittney.

'Shit,' says Megan. A shiver runs up her spine. *He's still around.* 'I wonder. Have you told Slater?'

'Yep,' says Brittney, 'and we've put out an alert for the vehicle. But it seems to have disappeared off the grid.'

The idea of Justin Waycott driving round with Trevor Pearse, that he may still be within their reach, is both tantalising and disturbing. But she knows such assumptions need to be resisted. They can lead to blind alleys. 'It could be anyone,' she says. 'We can't jump to conclusions. The connection between them is mostly speculation.'

'Yeah,' says Vish, 'except here's the icing on the cake. We got some footage from the bank in Exeter. Shows the person using the cash dispenser to withdraw money on Eric Russell's cash card.'

'And?'

'Not a great shot, he's wearing a baseball cap. But we think it's Justin Waycott. So you were probably right. It could've been him with Pearse.'

These are the pieces of the puzzle they need to fit together. Everyone's knackered but Megan can feel the electricity in the room. There's an atmosphere of expectation and determination, a sense they're within a hair's breadth of breaking the case.

'What about ANPR, can we place Waycott's pick-up near Russell's house?' she says.

'Still loads of stuff to go through,' Brittney replies with a sigh. 'Oh and the boss wants to talk to you.'

'Okay.'

Megan heads for the DCI's office. Laura Slater is tapping at her keyboard – she's a fast and efficient typist, obviously – and peering at the screen. Megan can't help but think of the two little girls, picture-perfect children, and the handsome, supportive husband. It's hard not to be full of envy. She wonders, and not for the first time, why some lives seem to be much luckier than others. Luckier than hers, certainly. Is it chance? Or do some people make better choices? It probably helps if you're not born with an internal self-destruct button.

Slater looks up. She's pale but that's the only indication of the pressure she's under.

'Brittney said you wanted a word.' Megan keeps the tone neutral.

'Yes,' says the DCI. 'Eric Russell's neighbour, he's pretty elderly.'

'Ronnie Fisher, he's ninety-six.'

'If he can identify Trevor Pearse and Justin Waycott as the two men who visited Russell's house, is that going to be credible?'

'He's very sharp. I don't see why not.'

'CPS are going to worry about that, because it could end up a crucial plank of the case. The defence will attack him, his eyesight, his memory. Make out he's a doddery old man led by us.'

'I don't know what we can do about that. But we've got Justin using Russell's cash card.'

'Yeah but the footage isn't good. Too much room for doubt. Let's just be sure we do the whole thing by the book.'

'I'll go and see Ronnie tomorrow.'

'Yeah,' says Slater. 'But in the morning I'm going to interview Heidi Soames. I'd like you with me.'

'Fine.' Slater's decided to bite the bullet.

'You may wonder why I'm doing it personally.'

'I get it, boss. You want to flatter her, make her think she's getting special treatment.'

Slater smiles. 'Exactly. I hope to be on top of all the detail by then. But if I miss anything, I know you won't. That's why I want you there.'

Megan meets Slater's eye. It takes a moment to sink in that the boss is paying her a compliment.

CHAPTER SIXTY-NINE

Tuesday, 10.30am

A restless night of febrile fantasies leaves Megan's nerves jangling. She can't remember her dreams in any detail, but the residual sense of dread that she wakes with is hard to shake off. Leaving the house early, before anyone's up, she walks by the sea to try and clear her head. It's too rough to swim as she hoped. It takes a double espresso to get her focused on the task in hand.

Dame Heidi arrives at MCT with her lawyer. Megan watches from a window. They turn up without fanfare in her chauffeured black Mercedes with tinted windows. The uniformed chauffeur jumps out to open the door. The lack of any media presence suggests a change of tactics. Vish is tasked with escorting the actress and Sir Henry Crewe to the interview room. Heidi wears a plain grey suit, expensive and well cut, and a sombre silk scarf.

Brittney peers over Megan's shoulder. 'Who's she playing, do you think? The Queen?'

'Where's the hat?' says Megan. 'I think this is her attempt at being normal and ordinary.'

Vish reports that the visitors are settled and have refused an offer of tea or coffee.

Megan puts her head round Slater's door. 'You want them to stew for a bit, boss?'

The DCI gets up and picks up her file. 'No, no, he thinks we're all plods, he'll expect that.'

Megan follows Laura Slater into the interview room. Handshakes and introductions are exchanged. Everyone is seated. Megan taps the touch screen to start recording.

Slater folds her hands and looks directly at Heidi Soames.

'As I hope Sir Henry has explained to you,' she says, 'this is an interview under caution because we think you may have information or knowledge relevant to the murder of Eric Russell, whose body was discovered in the septic tank at Winterbrook Farm, a property owned by your daughter.'

'Actually it's technically owned by me,' says Heidi, 'but that's detail. I am more than happy to assist with your inquiries, Chief Inspector.'

'Excellent. DS Thomas will read the caution.'

'The "you do not have to say anything" bit? I know it, you needn't bother.'

'Unfortunately, Dame Heidi, we do have to bother.' Slater turns to Megan. 'Megan.'

The caution is delivered. Dame Heidi examines her manicured nails and Sir Henry Crewe focuses his unremitting gaze on Slater. Megan can feel the negative energy his presence generates. The only other men she's come across capable of creating such an atmosphere in an interview room have been villains.

As she comes to the end of the spiel, Dame Heidi smiles at Megan and says, 'You have a lovely speaking voice, my dear. Good enunciation.'

'Thank you,' says Megan.

'Before you proceed with your questions,' says Sir Henry, 'my client would like to speak.'

'By all means,' says Slater.

Dame Heidi frowns, follows this with a skittish smile and says, 'Thank you so much.'

Megan has a vision of an invisible clapper board thwacking down accompanied by a shout of 'action'.

Inhaling sharply, then sighing, the old lady says, 'As a mother, this is the single hardest thing I have ever had to do. So I hope you'll bear with me.'

My God, thinks Megan, *she's going to throw her own daughter under the bus! Poor old Georgia. The actress and her sharky lawyer are about to blame it all on her.*

'My daughter was in need of a personal assistant. Sadly, she's never been a very good judge of character and she hired a young woman, perfectly acceptable in herself, but who turned out to have criminal connections. Somehow, I don't really know how, poor Georgia became entangled in their web. I believe they took advantage of her and her lack of emotional stability. They learnt about her first husband, Eric Russell, and Georgia's huge unresolved anger around his response to their break-up. I can only guess at what happened. I have no direct knowledge. I saw my daughter rarely during this period. However, if the body in the septic tank is Eric Russell, then I think these criminals are probably responsible. But I should emphasise, Georgia has had mental health problems for many years, including an addiction to prescription drugs. I believe they exploited her.'

Dame Heidi ends with a faraway gaze and a moistness in her eyes. Then, as if recollecting herself, she looks directly at Slater, smiles and says, 'I'm sorry I can't be more helpful. But this is everything I know.'

Slater smiles back. 'Thank you, Dame Heidi,' she says. 'These criminals you refer to, did you ever meet them?'

'No. Well, apart from Shirin.'

'Could I just ask you to take a look at this picture?' The DCI pushes the A4 print of Trevor Pearse across the table. 'Do you recognise this man?'

Opening her handbag, Dame Heidi brings out a pair of red-rimmed glasses, places them on her nose and peers. 'No,' she says. 'I have an excellent memory for faces but I've never seen this one.'

'You're sure you've never met him?'

'Quite sure.'

Megan watches the lawyer. He's relaxed, monitoring his client's performance but, from his point of view, it's all obviously going to plan.

Turning to the DCI, Megan says, 'Could we take a short break, ma'am?'

Slater raises her eyebrows but says, 'Certainly.'

Once they're outside the interview room, Megan says, 'I've got an idea. It'll only take ten minutes.'

The DCI gives her sceptical look. 'What sort of idea?'

'She's going to stonewall us. But I think I can prove she's lying. Which should at least rattle her cage.'

'Okay,' says Slater. 'Go for it.'

CHAPTER SEVENTY

Tuesday, 11.06am

It's drizzling as Vish runs across the crowded car park. Megan watches from the doorway of MCT. The black Mercedes is tucked in next to a lorry. The chauffeur has earbuds in and is watching something on his phone, so it takes several taps on the window to attract his attention.

Vish gets him out of the car and back to the downstairs foyer of the office building where Megan is waiting.

Megan smiles at him. 'Paco, isn't it? You're Dame Heidi's chauffeur?'

He's a small, sturdy man; it's hard to tell his age. His face is heavily lined by years of work and stress and sending money home to a family he never sees. He dips his head; probably where he comes from the police are to be feared.

'Yes, madam,' he says, in careful English.

'Don't look so worried,' says Megan with a smile. 'I just want to ask you a couple of questions.'

'Yes, madam, of course.' His eyes remain downcast.

They find an empty office to use. The chauffeur shifts from foot to foot. Megan can sense his tension. But she doesn't have time to do this gently. Vish gets out his notebook and pen.

'Where are you from?' she says.

'Manila, Philippines.'

'Okay,' she says. 'I want you to understand, Paco, that it's really important you tell me the truth. If we later discover you've been lying, it could impact on your immigration status. You understand that.'

He nods and swallows. He still doesn't make eye contact.

'How long have you worked for Dame Heidi?'

'Two years and one month.'

Vish writes down his answers.

'And you drive her everywhere?'

'Yes, madam, I do.'

'You know Winterbrook Farm, her daughter's house?'

'Yes, I do.'

'How often do you go there?'

Panic floods into the poor man's eyes.

Megan says, 'It's not a trick question, just tell me roughly. Once a week? Less? More?'

'Sometimes not for several weeks, then maybe two or three times in one week.'

'Okay, that's good. You're doing well. Give me some examples of other places you go.'

'To London. Dame Heidi stays at Dorchester in Park Lane. To Stratford to theatre. Umm…'

'Does Dame Heidi visit many places locally in Devon?'

'Some friends in Dartmouth.'

'Anywhere in Berrycombe?'

He shakes his head.

'Do people travel in the car with her?'

'Yes. Her daughter. Sometimes others.'

'I'm going to show you a picture of a man,' says Megan. 'I want to know if he's ever travelled in the back of the car with Dame Heidi.'

Vish hands him the printout of Pearse. Paco stares at it. He hesitates. Megan holds her breath. She's guessing here, banking on the fact Dame Heidi is unlikely to go anywhere on her own.

He tilts his head and sighs. He already knows that whichever way he jumps this will probably turn out badly for him.

'I think he has a beard,' says the chauffeur. 'I see him once.'

'Tell us about that.'

'We collect him at Winterbrook Farm. We go for a drive round Dartmoor. We stop at a parking place. They get out, walk about, talk.'

'How long for?'

'Perhaps fifteen minutes. Then we drive back to the farm and he gets out.'

'When was this?'

'In the summer. I remember the car park was busy. I always need to find safe spot so car don't get scratched. It was August I think.'

'Do you know his name?'

'She call him Leo. Or Leon.'

Megan smiles. 'Thank you, Paco. You've been really helpful. My colleague is going write up what you've said in the form of a statement and ask you to sign it. Okay?'

He nods. 'Am I in trouble?'

'Not if you've told us the truth.'

Finally he looks directly at Megan. The look is vacant and resigned. He nods. 'But now she sack me, I think.'

Megan follows Slater back into the interview room. Heidi and her lawyer have accepted the offer of coffee this time and are drinking from china teacups, which Megan has never seen around the office before.

The recording is restarted. Slater carefully adjusts the papers in front of her on the table and says, 'Dame Heidi, my officers have been speaking to a well-known columnist from a national tabloid newspaper. She was approached by Eric Russell back in April of this year with a story concerning you. Do you know about this?'

Crewe and Heidi exchange looks. She merely shrugs and says, 'No. But it wouldn't be the first time he's tried to peddle tittle-tattle about me. One shouldn't speak ill of the dead, but he was a nasty individual. When Georgia left him – and my view was that she should never have married him – he axed her from the television show she starred in and he produced.'

'He and your daughter first met each other at drama school and became friends back then? They were a similar age?'

'Yes. I wanted her to go to RADA like me. But she didn't get in, unfortunately.'

'According to this columnist, Russell alleges that you had a sexual relationship with him when he was an eighteen-year-old drama student and your daughter's boyfriend. And also that you had sexual relationships with several of his friends, one of whom was underage. Is this true?'

'Oh, poppycock!'

'The columnist also says that the newspaper's lawyers did inform your lawyers of these accusations.' Slater switches her gaze to Crewe. 'Is this true, Sir Henry?'

'I am not the one being interviewed here, Detective Chief Inspector. But what I would say is that my office often receives notice from the media about scurrilous accusations against high-profile clients such as Heidi. I do not relay them to her, because I wouldn't wish to distress her. The paper's lawyers would've wanted to know whether we'd sue and the answer would've been yes.'

'So there you have it,' says Heidi, throwing open her palms. 'Now can we wind this up, because I'm an old lady, these chairs are hard, your coffee tastes disgusting and I need to go home and rest.'

Megan catches Slater's eye. Finally they're getting under her skin.

'Of course,' says Slater. 'My sergeant just has one more quick question for you.'

Dame Heidi huffs and sinks back in her chair.

'Yes,' says Megan. She pushes Pearse's mugshot across the table again. 'You said earlier that you've never met this man. But we have a witness who says you met him last August at your daughter's house, drove with him in the back of your car, got out and had a private conversation with him on Dartmoor. What was that about, Dame Heidi? Was it, as another witness tells us, that you asked this man to stop Russell blackmailing you?'

A small smile plays around Dame Heidi's mouth. The weariness of a moment ago has evaporated, her icy control has returned. She flings an amused look at Crewe. 'Is this the bit, Henry, where I say "no comment"?'

'I think it probably is,' he replies. 'Are you charging my client?'

'We're releasing her under investigation,' says Slater.

'Very wise,' says Crewe. 'For, as I'm sure the CPS will point out to you, asking an English jury to believe such a fantastical tale against a much-loved public figure like Dame Heidi is going to require more than the testimony of a couple of… what shall we say?… n'er-do-wells.'

Slater looks directly at the lawyer. 'We'll be in touch.'

CHAPTER SEVENTY-ONE

Tuesday, 3.35pm

The DCI's corner office is compact and largely taken up by the desk, which is always neat. Laura Slater sits behind it, drumming the end of her pen rhythmically, a habitual gesture when she's feeling impatient. Montieth stands in one corner, arms folded. Megan leans on a filing cabinet in the other.

'I can't believe it, boss,' says Ted. He stands in front of the desk. 'We spent the whole night sitting in those skanky woods watching that bloody caravan. My arthritis is really playing up now.'

'Shirin Khan went to Lizzie Quinn's caravan and stayed all night?' Slater doesn't sound sympathetic. Megan watches the exchange with amusement.

'They stopped for a Chinese, taxi waited while they got it, took it back with them, never budged. Stayed all morning too.'

'No phone calls observed?'

'Not that we saw,' says Ted. 'But to be frank we didn't see much. Those bloody woods are a nightmare. Can't see anything but trees.'

'Okay, Ted, thanks,' says Slater. 'Oh and good work.' She adds this as an afterthought; he's halfway out of the door.

'Boss,' he says sullenly and leaves. He looks cold and wet. Megan almost feels sorry for him.

'Are we tracking their phones?' says Montieth.

'Yes,' says Megan. 'But they're not daft, if she does try and contact him she'll use a burner. But I believe her. I think she wants to escape him.'

It's been a long morning. Megan feels both enervated and hyped on coffee. The interview with Dame Heidi was an object lesson in the hard slog of a normal investigation. Rushing out to get the chauffeur's testimony gave her the shot of adrenaline she needed. But now that feels irrelevant. All Megan has done is ruin the man's life.

'How helpful were the Met, Monty?' says Slater.

'The Chief Super I spoke to was pretty convinced Pearse is dead. But then I talked to a DI who was SIO on a gang murder some years ago. Pearse was his prime suspect, although they never made the case. Witnesses were all scared off. He described him as an evil individual, clever and manipulative. They're going to chase up some of his old contacts for us.'

'Good,' says the DCI. 'Well, it's clear we have to amalgamate these two investigations. It'll make things complicated, so I want you both to keep pursuing your separate threads but liaising.'

'I hear you had quite a session with the grande dame herself,' says Montieth. 'Got her on the ropes.'

'Short of Trevor Pearse turning up, confessing to murder and saying "she asked me to do it", I don't think we're that far ahead,' says Megan. 'And the thing that's been lost in this is Kerry.'

Even to herself she sounds wired and irritable. She has to calm down. If she's discovered anything useful in the last week, it's that she needs to learn how to deal with frustration. And swim more. She has to play the long game like Slater. Go home at five to the family and forget about it until tomorrow. It's a great idea, if you've got someone to go home to. Megan's problem is she's always been addicted to the buzz.

'What about Georgia?' says Montieth.

'She's checked into a private clinic in Hampshire, where she's supposedly being treated for depression and addiction to prescription drugs,' says Megan.

'That's convenient.'

'Crewe's fallback position appears to be to blame Georgia,' says Slater.

Megan sighs. 'Well, I need to go and show Pearse's mugshot to Ronnie Fisher, Eric's neighbour.'

Laura Slater flashes her an unexpected smile. 'For what it's worth, Megan, I think we did well with Dame Heidi today. And your guess about the chauffeur was inspired. It showed Crewe we mean business.'

'He's right though, isn't he? What jury's going to believe Paco over Dame Heidi? I bullied him, now he'll lose his job. And for what?'

Slater smiles again. 'He'll be on a plane back to Manila with a fat wad of cash in his pocket before this ever comes to court. You've probably done him a favour. May even be home for Christmas.' She glances at Montieth. 'Am I right?'

'Almost certainly, boss.'

Are they trying to be nice to her? She's not sure. *The long game.* This is what she said to Vish. What she didn't mention is that she's crap at it.

As she returns to her desk, Brittney swivels in her chair. 'Guess what?' she says. 'Phone records from Mayhem include Kerry Waycott's mobile number. She called him. He called her back.'

'What day was that?' says Megan. 'I'm guessing the day we first went round there.'

'Tuesday. Two weeks ago.'

Megan gives her head a weary shake. 'I bet that's when he told her to name Jared.'

Brittney frowns. 'He raped her but she was calling him. It's like she was still attracted to him. I don't understand that.'

Megan says nothing. She understands. It's eerie, the thought that she and Kerry were drawn to the same man.

The DCI emerges from her office, pours herself a coffee. Montieth says something to her. They chat. Megan watches. The rhythms of a busy investigation. To all of these people this is a job. They work hard, they go home. They have another life. Kids, partners, sex, meals out, drinks with friends. That's how you play the long game. Megan wonders if she'll ever find that part of her life again. She lost it when she went undercover. The old Megan died in a cellar. Now she's a different creature, emerging from the chrysalis. And it's painful. Bound to be.

Suddenly there's a commotion in the corner of the office.

'We've got an ANPR hit,' Kitty calls out. 'He's on the move. Waycott's pick-up is on the Berrycombe/Paignton Road.'

'Let's get some response vehicles down there,' says Montieth.

Vish seizes a phone to call the main control room.

Megan grabs her jacket. Sitting in the office and waiting doesn't feel like an option. Moving is a relief.

'Hang on, Megan,' shouts Brittney. 'I've got your sister on the phone.' She holds out the handset.

'What?' says Megan. 'Tell her I'll call her back.'

'She sounds in a bit of a panic.'

Megan checks her own phone. Three missed calls from her sister. 'I'll call her back on my mobile.'

Heading out of the office, Megan clatters down the stairs. She clicks on Debbie's number. It's answered after a single ring.

'Oh, thank God,' says Debbie. 'I've been trying to get you for ages.'

'What's up? I'm in a bit of rush.'

'It's Amber. She hasn't come home from school.'

'I'm sure there's a perfectly simple—'

'No, listen, Meg! You don't understand. Kyle saw her. He says she was with her friends, then this girl came up to her. And she went off with this girl and got into a black pick-up truck.'

Megan stops dead in her tracks. She's halfway down the stairs. She feels giddy and has to grasp the bannister. 'Okay,' she says. 'I'll—' Her brain scrambles to adjust, she can't think.

'Wait!' screams Debbie. 'That's not all. The pick-up drove off with Amber in it, but the girl stayed. So Kyle went after the girl and asked what was going on. Said Amber was his sister. The girl said she had no idea what he was talking about. What the fuck's happened, Megan? Who's taken my daughter?'

CHAPTER SEVENTY-TWO

Megan hammers with her fist on the Tuckers' front door. Roger Tucker opens it and stares at her over his large tortoiseshell spectacles. He has a glass of red wine in his hand. It doesn't look like his first.

'Where's Paige?' says Megan, without preamble. She's running on adrenaline and is fit to burst.

'Is there some kind of problem, Sergeant?' he says.

'Yes,' says Megan. 'And if you don't know where she is, it just got worse. For both of us.'

He shrugs and says, 'She's here. Doing her homework, I think. You'd better come in.'

Megan follows him into the house. Paige is standing by the kitchen counter. She's tense. She's obviously been expecting this.

'Daddy,' she says, in a slightly high-pitched voice. 'You have to listen to me. Whatever nonsense she's about to tell you, she's lying. The police have been persecuting Leon. And I just tried to help him. All he wants is his little boy.'

'What on earth are you talking about?' says her father.

'They can't find out who killed Kerry so they're trying to pin it on him.'

'Is that what he told you?' says Megan.

'He's desperate. He just wants his son. He's applied for custody, done everything he should. And now because of these ridiculous allegations he's been turned down. It simply isn't fair.'

Megan takes a deep breath. Her impulse is to throttle Paige Tucker but, she reminds herself, this is a child too, who's probably as much of a victim as her niece.

'Did he ask you to bring Amber to him?'

'He thinks it's the only way he can get you to see sense.'

'For crying out loud, Paige!' says her father. 'What have you got involved in?'

Emma Tucker appears, in sports gear, earbuds dangling round her neck. 'What's happening? Why are you shouting, Roger? You know Paige gets upset if you shout at her. I hate all this male aggression.'

'Do you,' he says, draining his glass in one gulp. 'What a shame.'

Paige flees to her mother's arms. 'Mummy, I was only trying to help a friend, a persecuted friend! You always say loyalty to friends is important.'

'I know, darling, try and calm down and we'll sort this out. I'm sure there's been another misunderstanding.'

Megan's temper is simmering close to boiling point.

'Here's the misunderstanding,' she says. 'Your daughter's so-called friend, Leon Hall, is known to the police as Trevor Pearse. He has convictions for serious violence and drug smuggling. There are outstanding warrants for his arrest and we currently want to interview him in connection with two murders, including Kerry Waycott's.'

Paige clutches her mother in floods of tears. 'No, it's just not true,' she sobs. 'It can't be!'

'Oh my good God!' says Roger Tucker. Then he turns on his wife. 'I bloody told you, you stupid cow! You indulge her every whim, let her rule the roost. Look what you've turned her into. Now she's consorting with criminals.'

Emma's chin trembles and she slowly shakes her head.

'Right,' says Megan. 'I haven't got time for this. Where's he taken Amber?'

Paige is still crying. 'It's not just him, it's Kerry's uncle too. That's what I had to say to her, that Kerry's uncle wanted to talk to her. So how could Leon have hurt Kerry? Why do you even think it's him? This is all so unfair.'

Megan approaches the teenager. 'Paige, listen to me carefully. Leon is devious, he manipulates people. I think Justin doesn't know. Trusts him like you do. But forensic evidence, specifically DNA, identifies him as Kerry's attacker.'

'You could've made a mistake,' she whimpers.

'No. We haven't. So how did he get in touch with you? Did he phone you?'

She shakes her head.

'What then?'

'Not on my phone. Because that can be traced. We use a burner.'

'A burner!' exclaims her father. 'That's what criminals and drug dealers use.'

'That's what he is,' says Megan. 'Go and get it, Paige. Move!'

CHAPTER SEVENTY-THREE

Tuesday, 4.30pm

With the burner in her hand, Megan leaves the Tucker family to implode. The phone is small and basic, none of the fancy bells and whistles that come with the modern smartphone. It will have only one number in contacts.

Megan settles in the driver's seat of her car and stares at it. She faces a dilemma: if she waits there's a chance that they can get a trace on the phone the next time it's turned on. But how long could that take? She doesn't have time.

She decides to take a risk and presses the call button. Will he even answer?

After two rings the line connects. The voice is unmistakable. 'Told you to junk this, Paige.'

'Did you?' says Megan.

He chuckles. 'I knew I could rely on you to be smart. You're wasted as a cop. Hope you liked the flowers.'

'Let's both be smart,' says Megan. 'Where's Amber?'

'She's a lovely girl, your niece. Feisty as her old auntie, I like that.'

'You hurt her, Pearse, and I'll forget I'm a cop and come after you. You won't have to worry about serving time.'

'I don't worry. No way I'm going back to jail. But I want my son. You're going to get him for me.'

'He's with Shirin.'

'Don't play me. Bitches like you always have to try, don't you? You lifted her and the boy, she told me.'

'How?'

'I keep tabs on her. We had a little chat last night at a Chinese takeaway. I persuaded her to talk to me. You took Noah, where did you put him?'

He's backed her into a corner, but Megan doesn't miss a beat.

'Okay, here's the deal,' she says. 'Noah for Amber, straight swap. But you'll never get out of the country with him.'

'You let me worry about that. It's not going to be a problem.'

We're going on a boat. That's what Noah said. But now it makes sense. Justin Waycott borrowed a boat. A luxury motor yacht more than capable of crossing the English Channel. It's moored up somewhere, waiting. That's his way out. Once it gets dark it won't be that hard to slip away unnoticed.

'First I want to see Amber, check she's okay.'

'How long will it take you to collect Noah?'

'Not that long.'

'Don't bullshit me, Megan. I wrote the book. Here's how we're going to play this. You go and get my son and you call me back. I see a blue light or hear a siren, I'll slit Amber's lovely soft throat. I hear a chopper, I'll chop off her fingers one by one. You get the picture. You do not want to piss me off. I think you know I'm a man of my word.'

The line goes dead.

Megan's heart is thumping in her chest. She wants to scream but what she has to do is think. And fast.

CHAPTER SEVENTY-FOUR

The road out of Berrycombe snakes along the side of a narrow valley before cutting back towards the coast. Megan knows it well, she drives it most days. It takes her to the beaches where she swims. The afternoon light is fast fading, it'll be dark not long after five o'clock.

She grips the wheel. Amber's life will depend on her keeping cool and keeping her nerve. But she's been here before. Staying one jump ahead of a psychopathic killer is a deadly game. Probing for the weakness, watching for the opportunity. She got too close to Zac, he could read her. But this time is different. Leon doesn't know her, and will probably underestimate her. That's the advantage she must exploit.

She's got Brittney on speakerphone.

'Service provider can't get a trace on your burner. But the good news is we've received confirmation on the boat,' says the DC. 'Benson lent the *Sea Serpent* to Justin Waycott and it hasn't been returned.'

'Any more hits on Waycott's truck?' says Megan.

'Last one was an hour and a half ago. Since then, nothing. Response went up and down the road, found no trace.'

Megan scans the dark hedgerows, the snatches of buildings; a petrol station flashes past. She slows down.

'They took Amber and they turned off this road,' she says. 'It has to be Ellwood Cove. Where else could you moor up a boat like the *Sea Serpent* unseen?'

Ellwood Cove is where Kerry's body was found. Megan has avoided it ever since. A compulsion to revisit the scene of the crime, to glory in it? Some killers do that. Or is it a question of practicality?

'Another thing,' says Brittney. 'We went back over the ANPR the night Kerry was murdered. Waycott's truck was cruising round the town then out towards the cove. Maybe Sheila sent him to look for Kerry.'

'Sheila didn't know she was missing until the next morning.'

'I don't know what he was doing then,' says Brittney. 'The DCI's here. She wants a word.'

Slater comes on the line. 'Megan, you have to wait for back-up.'

'He'll see us coming a mile off, he'll freak.'

'Monty and Vish are in a car and on their way to you. And they're armed. Wait for them to get to you.'

'It'll take them half an hour at least. By then it'll be dark.'

Slater's tone remains calm and reasoned. Megan's head is howling inside. If he kills Amber – but she can't even think that. She can't allow that possibility any space in her mind.

'The Armed Response Team's been deployed from Exeter,' Slater says. 'We're holding off the helicopter, but there'll be a coastguard cutter offshore. They make a run for it, we'll get them.'

'Which will probably be too late for Amber. I'm turning off on to the track to Ellwood Cove now, so I might lose the signal.'

'Listen to me, Megan, don't be a hero.'

'I'm not being a fucking hero!' Megan shouts. 'They've got my niece!'

She clicks the phone off. She has to focus.

Hardly a hundred meters down the track it becomes deeply rutted and impossible for an ordinary car. Megan grinds to a halt.

She picks up the burner from the passenger seat, takes a deep breath and rings the number.

'Have you got him?' says that silky voice. 'Because you're running out of time.'

'I've got him.'

'Let me say hello.'

'Okay, speak.'

'Noah? You there, little buddy? Ready for that trip?'

'He's crying,' says Megan. 'He's upset and confused. I think we should just get on with this.'

There's a silence. A moment of hesitation. Megan holds her breath. Has he bought it?

'You know Ellwood Cove?' As if she'd forget. 'Bring him there to the beach. But trust me, I see anyone but you and Noah, anyone at all, your precious niece'll be dead before you get to her. I got nothing to lose. You clear about that?'

Megan hesitates but she has no choice.

'Absolutely,' she says.

CHAPTER SEVENTY-FIVE

Tuesday 4.55pm

Ellwood Cove is wooded down to the rocky margins of the shore. The low trees and salt-loving shrubs that fringe the small, crescent-shaped beach provide good cover and, in the waning afternoon light, Megan is able to creep through the lengthening shadows unseen.

There's little wind and its direction is south-westerly so there's hardly any swell. The *Sea Serpent* is riding gently at anchor no more than thirty meters out in the small sheltered bay. Two jet-skis are tethered to the stern. Only one person is visible in the cockpit, wearing a bright yellow fisherman's vest. Megan has to wait for him to turn towards her to be sure it's Justin Waycott.

A small flock of gulls is roosting on the rocks close to the shoreline – the rocks where Kerry Waycott's body washed up. The remaining light reflects like mercury off the water. The entire seaboard is bathed in tranquillity.

Megan crouches down behind the twisted trunk of a blackthorn bush. She takes a deep breath and hollers, 'Amber!'

The gulls rise up in a single body, wings flapping.

The sound carries easily in the still, dank air. Justin jerks his head round towards her and a second figure – black jacket, tight beanie hat – emerges from below to join him.

'I want to see her,' shouts Megan.

He steps down from the cockpit onto the platform at the stern. 'Where's Noah?' he shouts back.

'He's here. Look, he's waving.' Squatting down behind the dark, spectral bushes, Megan waves her hand.

'I can't see him. Come on, buddy, come out.'

'No! Not until I see Amber.'

Pearse turns and says something to Justin. He disappears below and a minute later Amber, still in school uniform, steps out onto the deck.

Until this moment a small part of Megan has been hoping against hope that it was a bluff, that this psychopathic killer didn't have her niece.

'Hey, babe,' she shouts, but her voice cracks with emotion. 'You okay?'

The reply is reedy and full of fear. 'Yeah.'

Megan looks at her watch. Her nearest back-up – Monty and Vish – could be ten to fifteen minutes away. She gets out her phone. The cove can be problematic for a signal. What she needs now is some luck, an unreliable commodity in her life at the best of times.

'You bring her to the beach, we make the swap,' she shouts.

'You kidding me!' shouts Pearse. 'And risk getting jumped?'

'Okay. I understand, you don't trust me. Send Justin.'

Megan watches, nerves taut enough to snap. How will he react? She tries to concentrate on her breathing. A discussion is taking place between the two men. She picks out the odd word, the tone suggests a disagreement. It's probably only a couple of minutes but it feels to Megan like an eternity.

Then Justin climbs down a short ladder onto the stern. He helps Amber down after him. He mounts one of the jet-skis, starts it up and she gets on the back.

As the jet-ski approaches the shingle, Megan checks the strength of her phone signal and prays.

Justin beaches the jet-ski and helps Amber off.

'She stays here,' he calls. 'You bring Noah down.'

'No, he's frightened. You need to come and get him.'

The stand-off lasts a few seconds. Justin huffs and plods up the beach towards Megan.

She stands up and steps out from behind the trees. 'Just listen to me, Justin.' She holds up her phone. 'This is an email showing an entry on the Met's database. That's the police in London.'

'What the fuck? This is a trick.'

'What's happening? What you doing?' shouts Pearse from the boat.

She puts the phone in front of his face. 'No. No trick. Look at the picture. This is the man that killed Kerry. His DNA matches that of Kerry's attacker. His name's Trevor Pearse. He raped and murdered your niece. Look closely at the picture. It's him, it's Leon.'

'What?' Justin blinks at the phone, struggling to focus. He shakes his head, glances back towards the boat.

It's going to take more to convince him. Then she realises. *The ANPR hit on Justin's truck! That's it.*

'Think back, Justin,' she says. 'The night she was killed. Leon borrowed your pick-up truck, didn't he? I don't know what excuse he gave you. But that's how he got Kerry. She was upset, wandering the streets, she saw the pick-up and thought it was you come to look for her.' Megan's guessing but she's struck a chord.

Now Justin's staring at the screen. He stands rooted to the spot. His eyes are tearing up.

'Where's Noah?' shouts Pearse. 'You think you can play me, bitch!'

He jumps onto the second jet-ski and starts it up. The engine roars as he guns it, loops round and heads for the beach.

Megan stays focused on Justin. 'I'm right, aren't I?' she says. 'He brought it back the next morning, didn't he? He killed Kerry. I'm telling you the truth.'

Justin Waycott stares at her, his face blank and bemused. Then he turns on his heel and walks away down the beach.

Megan rushes past him. 'Amber! Run!' The girl doesn't need telling twice. But as she sprints along the hard sand, splashing in and out of the breaking waves, Pearse swerves the jet-ski round and heads straight for her.

Sliding down a bank of pebbles, Megan picks herself up and runs as hard as she can. She has to get to Amber before Pearse does. Her lungs are screaming. The beach is boulder-strewn; she trips, falls, scrambles to her feet again.

Pearse beaches the jet-ski, leaps off and storms after Amber. She's fit and fast but he quickly gains on her. As she scrabbles up the steep bank of stones, he grabs her legs and drags her back.

Catching up to them, Megan seizes the largest boulder she can lift and flings it at him. It glances off his shoulder. With a furious roar he turns and throws a punch at her. A vicious right hook, it catches her under the chin and sends her flying. She lands in a dazed heap and instinctively rolls sideways to avoid the next blow. But it doesn't come.

Justin Waycott barrels into Pearse from behind like a charging bull. The two men grapple and tumble down the shingle bank towards the water's edge. Pearse is on his feet first, he grasps Justin by the throat. Justin knees him in the balls then, as his grip slackens, headbutts him, knocking Pearse backwards into the waves.

The water is less than a foot deep and the two big men are evenly matched but Justin is heavier. He throws himself down, knees on Pearse's chest, and uses his weight to hold the other man under.

Pearse kicks out, his arms flail; Justin pushes with all his might, his hand pressing down hard on the spluttering face beneath, and he doesn't let go.

Megan and Amber stand frozen, witnessing this brutal fight to the death. Megan clutches her niece and tries to shield her from the sight. Her heart is thumping and she can feel Amber trembling in her arms. She counts to ten, willing Justin to hold on, as the drowning man continues desperately thrashing. And then it stops. Justin stands up, lurches to the shore panting and collapses.

The body of Trevor Pearse bobs to the surface and floats face up, rolling gently in the waves.

CHAPTER SEVENTY-SIX

Megan can move her jaw so she concludes it isn't broken. She ignores Brittney's advice and Slater's instructions to go to A&E. Once she's delivered Amber safely home to her parents, she returns to the office.

She finds Slater and Barker in the incident room watching the feed on the monitors. In the interview suite, Montieth and Vish are trying to question Justin Waycott. Slumped in his chair, the duty solicitor beside him, the big man seems oblivious to the proceedings. He stares vacantly at the wall. He's in shock. He's just killed the murderer of his niece with his bare hands. A doctor will have seen him and pronounced him fit to be interviewed, but that seems meaningless to Megan.

'Justin,' says Montieth, 'Are you listening to me?'

It's clear he isn't. He folds his arms on the table in front of him, lays his head down on them and closes his eyes.

Montieth glances toward the camera and shrugs.

Megan turns to Slater and says, 'Mind if I try?'

The boss nods. 'Go for it.'

Entering the interview room, Megan takes Montieth's seat at the table. The DI leaves, Vish remains. She says her name and rank for the recording and then she waits.

It takes two or three minutes for Justin to register her presence. He lifts his head wearily and sighs. His eyes are heavy and bloodshot.

'I've come to say thank you,' says Megan.

'Didn't do it for you,' he says.

'Thank you anyway.'

They lapse into silence. Megan waits.

Finally Justin says, 'You asking me questions or what? Otherwise put me back in a cell so I can sleep.'

'You saved our lives. I wanted to acknowledge that. And to say that I will be giving evidence that you used lethal force in the defence of another.'

He grunts. 'What's that mean?'

'The Crown Prosecution Service will probably accept that as a defence in the murder of Trevor Pearse.'

'Okay.'

His gaze skitters away to the corner of the room. He seems lost in his own thoughts.

After several moments he turns to her and says, 'Y'know, I was thinking about my brother, Dave. When Kerry was first born, him and Heather came round to my mum's with her. I never really held a baby before that. Such a tiny little thing. Dave was so proud. I never seen him so happy. He was full of plans. Stuff he was gonna do. Fix up Dad's old boat, him and me. Make our fortunes. There was nothing he wouldn't have done for his little girl.' Tears well, he wipes his nose with the back of his fist. 'I dunno. Where did all of that go? What happened? Fucked if I know.'

Megan watches him for a moment then she says, 'Did you fix up the boat?'

'Oh yeah. She was a dream. But too small, we couldn't compete with the big boys. What with the quotas, we couldn't make the fishing pay. Both had to get second jobs. I should've realised about that bastard Leon, cause I knew what a fucking liar he was.'

'Did you? How?'

'I didn't know he was gonna kill that bloke in Exmouth, I swear. He told me we were just going there to put the frighteners on him, rough him up a bit.'

'Did he say why?'

'He said the bloke was blackmailing this actress and he was doing it to help her. They'd made a deal so he could get his son back.'

'He tell you her name?'

'Yeah. I never heard of her, Heidi something. But then I asked Ma. She said she was really famous and rich. Which made sense, cause Leon was playing her too.'

Megan can see Vish move out of the corner of her eye. She glances at him; nothing must break the flow now.

She speaks softly, the gentlest of prompts. 'How d'you mean, playing her too?'

'He told me to wait in the truck while he went in the house to talk to this guy. Then he came out and just said, "change of plan. The bloke's dead." We had to shift the body. Well, we had words. I told him, I didn't sign up for that. His excuse was, he was following instructions. The old lady wanted him dead. I didn't believe him. I thought he just lost it. I should've driven off then and left him to it. Wish I had.'

'Why didn't you?'

Justin folds his arms and huffs. 'Money. He gave me the bloke's cash card. PIN was with it in his wallet. Told me to help myself.'

'So you agreed to help him dispose of the body?'

Justin nods and sighs. 'We rolled it up in a carpet and put it in the pick-up. We're driving and the smug bastard sits there smiling to himself. Like the cat that got the cream. I was pissed off and I still didn't believe him about her saying to do it. I told him again I thought he was lying. So he says he's got this thing on his phone that proves it. When he talked to her and they made the deal, he secretly recorded it.'

Megan feels a stab of excitement. Pearse made a voice recording of his meeting with Dame Heidi Soames?

'On his phone?' she says.

'Yeah. He says to me, "I'm a genius. Stupid old hag thought I was just gonna get rid of this blackmailer for her. But once I get my son, I'm gonna blackmail her." He reckoned he'd be putting the squeeze on her for years to come, bleed her dry. A money pit, he called it.'

Megan can feel Vish's excitement, he's itching to leave. Under the table she lays a restraining hand on his arm.

'Did you ever hear this recording?' she says.

'Yeah, later he played me a bit of it. And it was true. She said, "he's scum, he should be put down". Leon said, "so you want him dead?" and she replied, "yes". He wasn't lying about that.'

Conspiracy to murder! If they can prove it.

'He had this recording on his phone?' Megan's brain is way ahead. If the phone was in Pearse's pocket when he went in the water, that could be a problem.

'He made it on a phone. But he had a copy on his laptop for safety. That's what he played to me.'

'You know where this laptop is?' says Megan.

'With his stuff on the boat. In a holdall. He was travelling light.'

Megan glances at Vish, gives him a nod to release him. He gets up and leaves.

Justin Waycott sneers, 'Now your boy's on a mission. Hope you get the bitch.'

Megan doesn't comment.

'You want a cup of tea or something?' she says.

'Nah, just sleep.'

'I'll get them to take you back to your cell.'

He gives her his trademark surly look. 'You believe me then? A copper actually thinks I'm telling the truth. That's a first.'

'We have a witness who saw you and Leon arguing at the Exmouth house. So, yeah, I believe you, Justin.'

Once she's handed him over to the custody sergeant, she goes in search of Slater.

The DCI is on her phone. 'Right, thanks,' she says and hangs up.

'Do we have it?' says Megan anxiously.

'CSI took the holdall off the boat. And, yeah, the laptop's in it. Plus several phones. It's all going for forensic examination. Vish has gone down to the lab to get a copy of the recording.' She beams. Another one of her unexpected smiles. 'Well done, Megan. The way you handled him in that interview was brilliant.'

Megan shrugs. She doesn't know what to say. Scanning the office she realises all eyes are on her, and they're smiling with admiration. She feels uncomfortable.

'I know you think I didn't want you on the team,' says the DCI, 'but now I understand why your old boss in the Met went the extra mile for you.'

'Pity, probably,' says Megan.

'No,' says Slater. 'It wasn't that.'

EPILOGUE

'Did you know,' says Ruby, 'that ducks have special feet to help them swim?'

'Webbed feet, dummy,' says Kyle. 'That's what they're called.'

'Don't call her a dummy,' says Amber. 'You didn't know that when you were seven.'

'Did too,' says her brother.

Megan is standing behind them on the pontoon at the edge of the lake. The country park is also a wildlife sanctuary. In the pale winter sunshine the flocks of waterfowl are swimming and preening. They come in various shapes and sizes and colours but, having grown up an inner-city kid, Megan finds it difficult to name any of the different varieties.

She puts a hand on Amber's shoulder, points and says, 'The typical duck-looking ones with the green heads, are they mallards?'

'Yeah, but they're the drakes or males. The more speckly ones with the brown heads are female mallards. They're ducks.'

'Confusing,' Megan says.

Amber smiles. On the outside she doesn't seem to have suffered that much from her experience. But as Megan knows only too well, appearances can be deceptive. The first few nights afterwards she had nightmares. Megan heard her crying, heard her sister getting up and comforting the child. Dr Moretti recommended a colleague and Megan insisted on paying. Amber treated it as a game: now they both had shrinks, how cool? But it has helped.

Megan has been put on sick leave. Slater insisted. Time to process, if nothing else. That's what the boss said. The CPS have brought charges against Dame Heidi and her daughter. The media are having a field day.

Noah is continuing to stay with the Slaters until Shirin can sort out their future. But Georgia is going to need her to keep writing the books and has agreed to meet her demands.

Megan went to see Sheila Waycott. It was an awkward encounter. Sheila didn't mince her words, she was glad her son had killed Kerry's murderer.

Ruby and Kyle scamper off along the path. Amber follows. Megan watches, feeling anxious and guilty about her niece. She can't seem to shake that off even though Debbie and Mark have assured her that she isn't to blame.

'The world is full of evil bastards,' said her sister. 'Encountering one, it's just bad luck. Amber knows that.'

Is it bad luck or a darker compulsion? Zac, Leon, it's no coincidence. At least this time she didn't sleep with him.

'It was because of me that he targeted her,' Megan said.

'We all have to accept what we can't control,' her sister replied.

It's what she can't control that Megan fears. But the job and the team have brought stability and purpose back into her life. And for that she's grateful.

She looks up. Behind her there's a stand of huge conifers, packed close together, their rough, lichen-covered trunks reaching up to the sky. She cranes her neck. How tall are they? A hundred feet? More? She can only guess.

'What are you looking at?' says Debbie. She and Mark have joined her; Scout, on his leash, trots beside them.

'All these trees,' says Megan. 'I'm getting used to them. But I need to do some research, learn the names of them all, like these pine trees.'

'I think these are Sitka spruce,' says Mark.

'There you go,' she says. 'I'm on a steep learning curve here.'

'I love this place,' says Debbie. 'It's great coming here on a Sunday. Living by the sea is always interesting, but I like the peace here.'

'Talking of which,' says Megan. 'I've been to the letting agent. Found a couple of quite nice flats. So I should be out of your hair soon.'

Debbie stops in her tracks and huffs. 'Oh, Meg, why? I told you it's not necessary.'

Mark tugs on Scout's lead. 'Come on mate, let's catch up with the kids, make sure no one's fallen in.'

The two sisters face each other.

'You don't have to say that, Deb. It was only ever temporary,' Megan says.

'You really want to live on your own?'

'It'll be fine. You need your space.'

Debbie is irritated. 'No,' she says. 'What I need is my free, last-minute babysitter, so me and my old man can escape once in a while. Plus I need my free dog-walker, cause you're the only one that gives Scout a decent walk and without that we'll end up with a dog blob.'

Megan laughs. 'A dog blob?'

'Yeah. Scout needs you. And the kids love having you as part of the family.'

'You don't have to say all this.'

'I'm not just saying it. It's true. And, I don't want to guilt trip you, but hey, I will. It's what Amber needs. Especially now.'

'How do you work that out?'

'She'll be fine. But I know her, she gets spooked. And she told me, she feels much safer when you're around.'

'She said that?'

'Yes. Frankly so do I. So, you're staying. Right?'

Megan smiles. 'Okay. Looks like I'm staying.'

A LETTER FROM SUSAN

I want to say a huge thank you for choosing to read *Buried Deep*. If you did enjoy it, and want to keep up to date with all my latest releases, just sign up at the following link. Your email address will never be shared and you can unsubscribe at any time.

www.bookouture.com/susan-wilkins

This is my fifth book and people often ask me, why crime fiction? Why don't you write something nice that doesn't involve horrible people doing horrible things? My answer has always been the same: look at the world. We live in challenging times and we need stories to help us make sense of it all. For me the crime genre is the most realistic form of contemporary fiction. It deals with how we live now as individuals and as a society. There have always been people who don't want to play by the rules, who think they should get what they want even if it impacts badly on others. But where do you draw the line? Morality informs our laws yet moral values can be ambiguous and contentious. Killing is wrong, most people would agree. But are there times when it's justified? Theft is wrong, unless you believe property is theft. And then we get into the murky realm of politics.

In the years I've been writing crime fiction I've met many police officers and others who work in law enforcement. The more I've discovered about what they actually do, the more my respect for them has grown. I think of my friend, GC, working in counter-terrorism in London, trying to keep one step ahead of dangerous individuals driven by violence and hate. I think of AK, working as a response officer in Brighton, turning up when the public calls, not knowing what he's walking into: a domestic brawl or a drug addict with a knife. You come to realise why it's called the thin blue line.

I've tried to create a character in Megan Thomas to fit the mood of the times. She's far from perfect but she isn't bad; like me, like you, like most of us. I hope you enjoy her adventures in the beautiful county of Devon, where I now live.

Do get in touch and let me know what you thought of *Buried Deep*. I love hearing from readers and you can find me on Facebook, my website, Twitter when I'm bored, and Instagram, where I post pictures of cute seals in Brixham Harbour.

Also if you feel like writing a review I'd be most grateful. The choice of books out there is vast and reviews do make a big difference in helping readers discover one of my books for the first time.

Happy reading!

Thanks,
Susan Wilkins

     @susanwilkinsauthor

     @susanwilkins32

     www.susanwilkins.co.uk

     susan_wilkins32

ACKNOWLEDGEMENTS

Huge thanks to the experts who've guided me, making sure I know how the police would proceed, and for understanding when I've twisted their advice for the purposes of drama. Colin Liversage is brilliant, inventive and patient. He should take credit for some of my better ideas. Kate Bendelow is the go-to expert on forensics and endlessly generous with her time. Graham Bartlett is always my fallback, because if he doesn't know, he knows a person who does.

Thanks to the wonderful team at Bookouture for launching me on the next stage of my crime-writing journey. And extra special thanks to my editor, Ruth Tross, for her smart and incisive editing and her encyclopaedic knowledge of crime fiction.

As ever I am lucky enough to have a back-up crew of fellow crime writers who are always generous with advice, support and encouragement. So thanks to the usual suspects, you know who you are. And loads of love and hugs to my friends and family for putting up with the grumps that accompany the writing life. Last but never least, my two first readers: Jenny Kenyon and Sue Kenyon.

Made in United States
Orlando, FL
03 July 2022

19387522R00214